About the Author

Born in Birmingham, I attended Sheldon Heath Comprehensive school where it was obvious my talents lay more with a football at my feet than in the classroom. I captained the Birmingham County side at U/18 level and was for a time, a member of the youth team at Wolverhampton Wanders but a career in football wasn't to be.

I entered the workforce in the roofing trade and have successfully spent a lifetime in that trade.

I hit gold when I met my wife, Yvonne and together, we raised an extended family and have children and grandchildren in both England and Australia.

We now live in tropical North Queensland along with our little dog, Alfie.

Balancing the Scales

Richard Cridland

Balancing the Scales

Olympia Publishers
London

www.olympiapublishers.com
OLYMPIA PAPERBACK EDITION

A CIP catalogue record for this title is
available from the British Library.

ISBN: 978-1-78830-219-7

This is a work of fiction.
Names, characters, places and incidents originate from the writer's
imagination. Any resemblance to actual persons, living or dead, is
purely coincidental.

First Published in 2019

Olympia Publishers
60 Cannon Street
London
EC4N 6NP
Printed in Great Britain

Dedication

To my wife Yvonne.

Acknowledgements

Memories and imagination, internet research and my wife's story.

Colin Butt, a successful author who found the time to talk with me about my book. He offered this advice whilst we enjoyed a cool beer at his beachside bar in Playa d'en Bossa, on the importance of this fact when writing a book, "It's not what you put in the story, it's what you leave out. Make the reader want to find out more." Thanks Colin and vale to a good man.

All at Olympia Publishing for their guidance and assistance through the entire process.

The loving family into which I was born, my parents, Emily and Bill, and my two brothers and three sisters; golden memories of a happy childhood filled with singing and laughter.

And to my own extended family thanks to you all for your love and support.

Author's Note

During the nineteen seventies the IRA disrupted life for millions of innocent people in England by planting bombs to kill and maim. These attacks on soft targets struck fear and terror in the minds of a nation. The objective of course was to force the British Government out of Northern Ireland.

One of the worst atrocities took place in nineteen seventy-four when two bombs were planted in city centre pubs in Birmingham, one at The Tavern in the Town and the other at the nearby Mulberry Bush. The bombs killed twenty-one innocent victims and one hundred and eighty-two were injured.

My wife's recollections of that night when she was enjoying a quiet drink with friends inside The Tavern in the Town when the bomb exploded were confronting. Unbelievably only her position behind a concrete pillar saved her life and she was able to scramble out bedraggled, in shock and uninjured.

Her story became the motivation; inspiring me to write a fictional story developed around that central factual theme.

The authorities believed they had caught the perpetrators, but later it was clear the investigation was flawed and thus to this day the true murderers have never been brought to book.

Whoever did carry out that cold blooded act had evil in his heart and brought our home city to its knees robbing so many families of their loved ones.

IRELAND 1998

They had been close companions a long, long time ago. It had been more than twenty-five years since he had last held her and her touch and feel reminded him of how comfortable they had been together. They were as cold and unemotional as one another.

Back then they had been an unstoppable force responsible for callously despatching countless victims. Most had meant nothing to them but this final kill was different. This was personal. And it would put an end to his nightmare.

He pulled her in to his shoulder as he had so many times before, the familiarity helping him to regain his composure.

Inhaling deeply to calm himself and to steady his index finger, he slowly let out his breath, gently caressing her trigger….

CHAPTER ONE

It was Friday, heralding the end of the week. It was also payday so it would be a heavy drinking session for the feckless bully, Bob Freeman.

After he had finished his shift that afternoon the need to slake his thirst was overwhelming, having spent the day sweating in the oven-like temperatures at the foundry. He picked up his wage packet and made his way to his local pub, The Grapes. He never moved from his position at the bar and stood there all evening, downing pint after pint until closing time.

He was sick of the job and sick of his situation. It was a struggle to keep himself going and the thought of what was waiting back home made him want to run. The beer would give him the courage to tell her tonight.

He staggered out into the darkness to make his way home. He was very drunk and although his vision was blurred, he managed to find the way to his back door. The door was unlocked and he barged his way in, slamming it so violently behind him that the loose glass rattled in the frame. It was an audible warning to all who lived there that he was back and he would brook no nonsense.

Reeling from his over-indulgence, he stumbled through the kitchen to the bottom of the bare wooden stairs where he paused for a few seconds, rubbing the stubble on his chin. He looked up to survey the climb that lay ahead of him. It appeared a daunting task in his present state. His foot found the first step. He swallowed hard, snorted then suddenly, with a final burst of energy, he scurried upwards bouncing off the walls as he made his way to the bedroom.

The tension was palpable as the children lay paralysed in their beds, frightened that he would take his belt to them or inflict another beating on their mother. The boys all hoped he had supped too much ale so that in his drunkenness he would be incapable of harming anyone.

They heard him mumble and stumble as he flung off his trousers then threw himself onto the bed, where he immediately fell into a deep sleep. They knew then they were safe, they had witnessed it so many times before. He would be comatose for the rest of the night; the only sound they would hear would be the roaring, deafening din of his snoring interspersed with periods of silence. Sometimes, those silent periods lasted for so long they hoped he had died, only for their dreams to be dashed when they heard him suck in a breath to prolong their torture.

These opportunities were perfect for his wily wife to go through his pockets, creeping quietly around to his side of the bed to extract any notes and coins from his discarded trousers. She would add them to the few pounds she earned by working as a core maker. To make ends meet she also had a part-time job, three mornings a week where she cleaned two offices in Ladywood, which meant an early start at five o'clock. Fortunately she wasn't afraid of hard work.

Sheila Freeman was a thin and wiry little woman with prematurely grey hair, which she scraped back and hid beneath a tied and knotted head scarf. Although small in stature, she was a strong and determined woman and her children were the centre of her life. Whatever it took to protect, love and nurture them she would do. It was a challenge for her to keep her family together and although there was a lack of money, they muddled through. They had little but they had each other.

At home after work and at weekends with chores to do, she dressed in a pink floral pinafore worn over her everyday clothes, and from early morning until late at night she toiled selflessly for the good of her children. She worked hard to keep them all above the starvation line despite the efforts of her good-for-nothing husband to do the opposite.

When the drunken bully hauled himself out of bed the following morning, he made his way downstairs to the kitchen and quenched his thirst directly from the tap, gulping at the cool water. He wiped his mouth on the back of his shirt sleeve.

He was too drunk to tell her last night so he would do it now. Without looking at his wife who was busily sweeping the floor, he made his way to the back door. He grabbed the handle, turned to his wife and said, 'I'm off to find better paid work. I'll send money back,' and with that he left the house with his few belongings packed in a small holdall.

Selfishly, he walked out on his family to escape the wretched poverty in which they all lived. He had abandoned them all and left his wife to suffer the strife of bringing up the bunch of ragamuffins in their back-to-back hovel in Birmingham. It would be left to Sheila to provide for the family. She knew her hopeless husband would be off to Liverpool and the docks, and the first available ship leaving port. It wasn't the first time he had done it. This time though, she hoped he would never return.

The truth was that the remainder of the Freeman family breathed a sigh of relief when they heard the news, and hoped that this time he had gone for good.

The family continued their struggle in their dingy home in Cuthbertson Street, only a hundred yards from Winson Green Prison's high walls, the proximity of which was used as a threat by Sheila to keep her kids in line. Often she would shout in her frustration, 'Any more bad behaviour and you will end up living next door.' This ploy only worked while the boys were young. As they grew up, the threat of the 'Winson Green experience' was a hollow warning. The older ones ignored it but the youngest of the six Freeman boys, Lenny, couldn't understand in his innocence why his mother would try to scare them by sending them all to live next door with the Irish family; he actually quite liked them.

The brothers all slept in the small back bedroom, which like the rest of the house had no wallpaper, the cracked plaster walls bursting to reveal its innards where insects had set up home. Two single beds were pushed together to accommodate them all, three in each with a thin blanket supplemented with old overcoats to provide more warmth. Tightly packed together like sardines in a tin, their guts growling and complaining from the lack of a good meal, they wondered if 'next door' the inmates actually received three meals a day. If so they would all gladly have suffered the incarceration in exchange for a full stomach.

Poverty was commonplace around the streets where they lived, and the Freeman boys began their early morning search for breakfast. Stale bread wiped around the frying pan again.

It was the same meagre rations for everyone in their street. When the boys asked the Irish immigrants next door what they had for breakfast, the answer made them laugh.

'We have two things for breakfast,' they would joke. 'A glass of water and a shit.'

It was an unequal struggle for Sheila Freeman and since her husband's sudden departure, she had found it increasingly hard to pay the weekly rent of five shillings and sixpence.

She had missed a couple of weeks and knew the day of reckoning was fast approaching; the rap on the front door that morning rattled both it and her.

She gasped and quickly ushered the children into the back kitchen, putting her finger to her lips signalling them to keep quiet as they all huddled together in silence, crouching beneath the kitchen table. They sat silently listening to the determined and incessant knocking at the front door.

The rent man was not put off by the lack of a response and continued to rap on the door with his famed sergeant major's pacing stick, a relic from his service for his country in the Great War.

The tension proved too much for Sheila so she deployed young Lenny to answer the door. She whispered her instructions to him and off he went up the hallway. Standing on his tiptoes he managed to open the front door and with his best angelic face on, he gazed up at the rent man. He then repeated the sentence word for word, much to the mirth of his older brothers who managed to stifle their laughter as they listened from the kitchen.

'My mum told me to tell you she's gone shopping.'

'Did she now?' the rubicund rent man replied, apoplectic with rage. 'Well, young man, you can tell her she had better find three weeks' rent next week or you're all out,' he barked angrily.

Annoyed and in a fit of temper he quickly spun round, causing his leather money bag to part circumnavigate his huge stomach due to the centrifugal force he had generated. In a military fashion, he then executed the remainder of the 'about-turn' procedure, stamping his feet and marching off, stuffing the pacing stick under his right armpit.

When Lenny returned to the kitchen he looked at his mum and saw the relief, but he could also see the sadness and fear. It was plain to see in her frightened eyes that every day was becoming a battle that was gradually wearing her down. He knew they were all dependent on their mother; after all she was the anchor to which they were all tethered and, secure in that love, they were a happy band of brothers.

The young boy lowered himself down next to his mum and cuddled her, nestling into the warmth of his mother's comforting arms, dreaming that he would find a way to make all their lives better.

In his young mind, Lenny had already decided that the answer to his family's woes would be money, lots of it, and once he had got it he would make it right for his mum and his brothers.

After all, he was the brightest of the bunch and knew it.

He had learned to read at an early age and to satisfy his thirst for knowledge, had joined the local library, becoming an avid reader enjoying both factual and fictional books. He enjoyed the escape that books offered.

On one of his trips to the library, whilst browsing through a magazine, he read an article about Charles Henry Harrod. He was fascinated to learn about the young man who started off with a small grocer's shop in Stepney, which he later expanded to upmarket Knightsbridge where his business became the store for the rich and famous with a reputation for high class goods. He contented himself with the idea that a poor boy like him could also achieve that success, and began to dream a young boy's dream of wealth and fortune.

As convincingly as he could manage, he looked into his mother's sad face and said, 'Don't worry, Mum, I'll make it all right. Just you wait and see.'

She heaved an emotional sigh and pulled him close as the tears flowed easily from her eyes.

'I hope so, Son, I really do.'

CHAPTER TWO

Running with his older brothers, Lenny became 'streetwise' at an early age and what he may have lacked in physical size was more than made up for with his ideas and plans, his contribution being more cerebral.

Saturday mornings started early for the boys with a long walk into Birmingham city centre as they didn't have the money to pay for a bus ride. They arrived tired after their trek. They would hang around the Bull Ring market area, sometimes making a few pennies helping the stall-holders by sweeping up and collecting boxes. In their hunger, any discarded good bits of old fruit they found would get eaten before they chucked the remainder into the rubbish bins. Importantly, they always managed to slip a few vegetables into their pockets to take home for Mum to put in a stew.

The tedium of their deprived lives was made a little more exciting when war was declared. The family gathered around the radio to listen to the broadcast and hear Neville Chamberlain, the Prime Minister, tell everyone that the country was at war with Germany. The boys were quite excited at the prospect and wanted to teach that bully Hitler a lesson he would never forget. The older generation were more anxious as they thought that they had already fought the war to end all wars.

Germany's plan to bomb Britain's major industrial cities in an effort to destroy factories which manufactured armaments for the troops, meant Birmingham suffered many a night raid, becoming a major target and a dangerous place to live.

At night, when the sirens wailed out the warning that the bombardments were about to start, the family would dash down to their cellar and huddle together until the all-clear was sounded.

Sheila didn't have the heart to send her boys away as evacuees and left the older ones to look after the younger ones. They found plenty of adventure locally investigating any new bomb sites, picking through the ruins. During the day, they would 'fight' the Germans in their own war games using sticks as rifles, and at day's end were happy to have forced a retreat from 'the invaders', pushing them back across the English Channel.

When the war was over, the whole country heaved a mass sigh of relief and celebrated the victory. The next battle everyone had to face would be the austere times ahead.

The city had suffered massive devastation from the bombing raids as homes, businesses and lives had been crushed. Money was hard to come by, and any job or scheme which enabled someone to earn a few pounds was a golden opportunity to provide for themselves and their family.

Lenny now a teenager, but due to a poor diet and inheriting his mother's slight stature, still looked like a young boy; indeed, in a set of Russian dolls he was the smallest duplicate of his brothers with their matching pallid skin and straw-coloured hair. Unlike his brothers though, he had an inventive mind and by chance came up with an idea for making a little money.

The gang still scavenged around the Bull Ring market and it was there that he discovered the art of acting, not in the true sense of the term as he had no ambition to 'tread the boards', but he was proficient enough to keep a small crowd of people entertained and preoccupied.

The discovery was made when he accidentally stepped on a fruit box, the thin tacks scratching his leg and piercing his foot. In his shock and pain, he screamed and hollered and danced around on one leg, doing a pretty good impression of a Red Indian war dance.

A small crowd gathered round; some tried to assist, others just watching as the injured boy performed. His older brother, Tony, rushed to his aid and Lenny whispered in his ear.

'Take the chance, Tone, while I keep 'em occupied. Get round the back of 'em and lift what you can.'

Some in the gathering were distracted enough not to notice the brothers lurking behind them and were relieved of two purses from their open shopping bags, plus a wallet which was 'lifted' from a well-dressed gentleman's back pocket.

They had discovered the classic diversion crime and later when they met up and counted their ill-gotten gains, they were all pretty pleased with themselves. They put away two half-crowns and a sixpence to give to their mother to cover the rent, spending the rest on a big bag of chips which they hungrily shared. They had just enough money left over to catch a bus ride home for once.

The gang developed their scam and worked a couple of other places around the market, but instead of spending all of the money Lenny began to save some. They all trusted him to be their banker, not really knowing what they should do with their ill-gotten gains. There were many suggestions from his brothers, but he remembered reading somewhere that 'money makes money' so that's what he would do; he would hang on to it, not waste it. In time he would decide what to invest in.

Lenny developed his act to Shakespearian proportions, adding a little more creativity, as he considered treading on a tack every time was taking the love for his 'art' a bit too far. His performance now was very dramatic, incorporating an epileptic fit, frothing at the mouth and shaking uncontrollably whilst writhing on the ground. They did good business at the 'box office' and its success enabled the boys to add more to their stash of cash.

However, one thing the brothers didn't take into consideration was keeping a lookout for the local market policeman. Numerous complaints had been lodged regarding pick-pocketing by a young gang and he was intent on catching the little blighters.

One Saturday afternoon, another young lad was watching Lenny's matinee performance from the steps in the corner of the market. From his vantage point he could see the copper approaching stealthily through the crowd. The boy could see the steely resolve and the fierce determination on the police officer's face. He was moving swiftly through the crowd of shoppers, hoping to catch the gang who had started their own mini crime wave.

The boy acted quickly and gave a shrill whistle to alert the brothers. They heeded the warning whistle and his shout of, 'Coppers!' The boy with red hair was pointing towards the imminent arrival of the local law enforcement officer. They all scarpered, scattering in different directions.

Their new-found lookout had made the dash with them. When they found a safe place behind St. Martin's church, they stopped to rest. They sat down in a line with their backs leaning up against the wall of the church while they caught their breath.

The boy introduced himself.

'My name's Teddy Criglan, sometimes known as Teddy the Hook.'

He laughed as he swung his right arm up to reveal a hook in place of a hand. The other boys' eyes were wide with wonder as they all gasped and gawped and tentatively touched the awe-inspiring hook. At that moment they would all have given their right arm to have a hook just like that; indeed that's what it would have cost them, but they all silently accepted the raw truth, that it was best to have two hands to get on in this life. That day Teddy the Hook was invited by Lenny to become a member of their gang.

Teddy had been born into similar poverty to the Freeman boys, living in a two up, two down, terraced house in Sparkhill. He was the youngest child, having two older brothers; their father had been killed not long after Teddy's birth in an accident at the foundry where he had worked.

Without a father and being born without a right hand were distinct disadvantages for young Teddy, but there were no allowances made by his family. No sentiment was offered or sought. He was expected to just get on with it and he did.

The harshness of his upbringing meant that the teasing, name calling and bullying started at home before he even joined his peers at school, so that when the spiteful remarks came his way in the school playground he was well prepared. He dealt with the problem by facing up to his tormentors. Brandishing his hook he would growl, 'Come on then, who wants to be first on the end of me hook?'

Some did entertain a fight with Teddy, but he had already honed his fighting skills against his older and stronger brothers and no one ever got the better of him in the playground or any other place. He was mean and vicious when roused.

His childhood may have been tough, but he had accepted his disability, never showing any outward sign that it was a weakness. He never suffered from self-pity, coming to the conclusion early on that instead of it being a negative, his hook could possibly be the one thing that got him on in life.

Every weekend, Teddy would meet up with the brothers and after their recent close call with the market policeman, there was much discussion as to what they would do in the future. They were all in agreement that the distraction scam was over and done with.

'How about we just corner some trader and beat him up and pinch his takings?' Lenny smiled, Teddy's idea was ridiculous but he didn't embarrass him by saying so because he knew in Teddy's world violence was his answer to solving difficult situations.

That next move, though, had been on Lenny's agenda for some time. He had realised long before the others that a change of direction was required. He had already decided that the next one would be a more legitimate business enterprise. He called the gang together for a meeting.

'Look, if these guys are making money at this market game so can we. My plan is we buy the fruit and veg. cheap off the market boys. The stuff they are ready to chuck out but that still looks okay. They will be happy to get a few bob for it and we can take it back to Winson Green and sell it round our local streets, a bit cheaper than the local greengrocer. To see if it works, we will invest part of our stash. We buy as much produce as we can, use our old trolley to deliver it and see if we can double our money. What d'yer say?'

They could see the logic and its sound economic sense, and all nodded in agreement with Tony, adding, 'You had better be right, Lenny, 'cos if we lose our money I will give you a beating you won't forget.'

Lenny was undaunted and continued, 'Lads, if this works, we can do it with anything. Let's face it, in business you buy cheap, sell high but keep your running costs low,' he intoned, just like he had read about in those articles about successful business moguls. His remark was aimed particularly at his oldest brother, and sailed over his and the heads of his other brothers.

The boys pounded their local streets at weekends, working hard. Before long, their little venture started to flourish, not by much but they managed to double their initial investment.

Lenny could see their money growing so he called another meeting one Sunday afternoon, held in the empty bandstand at Summerfield Park. The gang looked expectantly at Lenny as he put forward the idea that they needed to make themselves a little more professional. He revealed his new business plan.

'Stan Jones, from down the market, has an old barrow in his storeroom. It's stuck right at the back, I've seen it, and it's old and needs attention and repair. We will clean it up and give it a coat of paint. Green and gold are famous colours you know. It will be ideal for our business and an extra copper or two on our prices will soon pay it off, any opinions?'

As ever, they hadn't got anything to say and went ahead with Lenny's plan.

They renovated the old hand cart. They began to establish a solid base of customers which gave them all a small wage but most importantly, provided the rent money every week.

Ambitiously, Lenny began to invest in better quality and fresher produce from his contacts at the market, bold enough now to barter to secure a better deal. He also offered specials which enticed his customers to buy his latest low-priced items, which were all delivered to their doors on the barrow which now proudly displayed the name, 'Freeman Bros.'

When he told his mum she could give up her cleaning job, she burst into tears and hugged him tightly. He had a tear in his eye too and was full of emotion, but held himself together. Businessmen didn't cry.

He was pleased to have achieved the first part of his plan, but began to realise the next part, to make himself rich and successful, was going to be a massive challenge.

Limited by their stock and the prices they charged, the returns were small. He needed a bigger market and higher turnover. However, he was totally convinced that there were even better times ahead for him and his family. He was sure of himself and confident that it was just a matter of time.

He was delighted to see their family name on that barrow and, before long, business was so busy he had to expand his fleet of delivery vehicles to include two bigger trolleys. They now had more coverage of the streets in surrounding areas and they had to work six days a week, but took Sundays off for a welcome lie-in.

With all successful businesses, there is always a competitor who gets jealous and it wasn't long before the proprietor of the greengrocer's shop round the corner on Dudley Road began to get agitated as his takings were taking a hit.

Late one Saturday night after another dismal day in his shop, he decided it was time to call round and have it out with the young Freeman boy, who, word said, seemed to run this growing enterprise. Tony answered the knock at the front door.

'Hello, Mr Forbes, what can we do for you?' he asked.

'I'm here to see young Lenny,' he replied.

He entered the narrow hallway of the Freeman's house and found Lenny sitting on the settee in the cramped front room, calmly surveying the visitor as he was shown in. Lenny stood up and shook hands respectfully with his guest, noting his facial expressions and general demeanour as he did so.

Mr Colin Forbes, the owner of Forbes Greengrocer's, was a short, thin man wearing his well-worn, blue pin-striped suit and matching waistcoat, white shirt and a blue and white striped tie. When he had returned from the Great War, he had taken over the business from his father and the greengrocer's shop was his life. He was a confirmed bachelor, in his late sixties, but with the stress and strain of his faltering business, appeared ten years older.

He began by explaining that he was upset that his business was suffering as Lenny and his team seemed to be swamping the area with cheap offers. Lenny wasn't one to over-react or lose his temper as he had learned in his short business career that you listen carefully to what people say and even more importantly, listen to the silence too. He adopted this approach with his late-night visitor and was convinced Colin had no desire for an all-out war; he wasn't that type of man. Indeed, he perceived that Colin was extremely nervous and wanted peace and harmony.

Lenny could see it was all too much trouble for Colin to put up a fight and the visit appeared more a plea for help.

Lenny showed no emotion as he weighed up the situation, sensing an opportunity. If he could pull off the deal that was going through his mind he could satisfy that desire for a bigger stage. He stared into the face of the old man and the plan was born.

He didn't immediately reply to Colin's little speech, enjoying the silence and identifying from the silence that the old man was ready to crack. He looked straight into his eyes and with an unwavering piercing stare, went in for the kill.

For a young man, he had already got the 'front' of a businessman twice his age and began to suck his teeth before delivering his considered opinion, a habit which he would have for the rest of his life.

'Colin,' he addressed the older man on equal and Christian name terms, 'what you need is help and I am here to offer my company's services to you. I have a proposition. We will become partners in your business, we will increase your trade and we will split the profits. With the assistance of my team we will first repaint your shop green and gold, very famous colours they are. Next, we will change the name to Freeman and Forbes. Sounds better already, doesn't it? Then we will have a grand re-opening with lots of bunting and flags. My boys will ensure that the crowd you get that day will make you as much money as you would in a week,' he paused a while for effect.

'We will also be offering a home delivery service, new for you but a very successful part of our growing business, so that our customers will have their groceries dropped at their door. We will buy a couple of delivery bikes with baskets on the front. Paint those up with our company colours and establish ourselves as a business that puts customers first, with good prices, quality produce and prompt delivery. To start off our partnership, we will both need to put in a hundred and fifty pounds, giving us the buying power to secure the best deals available. Now this isn't an offer I make lightly.'

Lenny continued with his uncompromising business plan, adopting a serious look on his face as he concluded his proposal.

'We both have businesses to run and are busy people. Time is money, a commodity we both pursue to prove we are successful businessmen, therefore you have precisely two minutes to make up your mind. If the answer is no then we continue growing our business and eventually you will go broke, or we can become partners and be very successful together. In the post-war business world you need young, thrusting, energetic, ambitious people running things and I can assure you that our partnership will be,' he paused and smiled at the pun, 'fruitful.'

With that, he stopped talking and he let the tension build. The silence grew and if a silence can build to a crescendo, that's what happened in those two minutes. Like two gunslingers the pair eyed each other. Who would speak first? It wouldn't be Lenny. 'He who speaks first loses,' Lenny had read somewhere. He could sense the climax was near. Colin suddenly stuck out his hand and with a look of resignation, said, 'Okay,' and shook on the deal.

After Colin had gone the brothers were slapping Lenny on the back and congratulating him on the deal.

'But what gets me,' said Tony, 'is we haven't got a hundred and fifty quid to put in.'

'Well,' said Lenny, pausing and sucking his teeth, 'that's what's called front. Some of us have it and others don't. Either way, he has now committed himself to the venture. He don't know I ain't got the cash and I certainly won't be telling him. It's a done deal. The future of this family is secure and I intend to make this business all ours one day. Then watch me fly. I've got big plans so trust in me, because the scenery only changes for the lead dog and I know exactly where we're heading.'

They all smiled at his little speech, admiring the ambition of their young brother. That day, Lenny won Tony over for good. Although there may have been reservations from the brothers in the beginning, it was obvious to them all now that he had been born with an innate business talent. He would be the leader and brains in their small but expanding empire.

CHAPTER THREE

At the end of hostilities with Germany, many people from around Europe and the Commonwealth, and especially Ireland, chose the city of Birmingham to build a new life.

So it was that, early one autumn morning on the opposite side of the Bull Ring Market to where the Freeman boys used to work their scams, a young girl was just arriving in the city. Like all the other immigrants, she was determined to find happiness and a new beginning.

She arrived on that cold October morning full of trepidation and anxiety after her long journey by ferry and train. She sat on a bench beneath a threatening gunmetal grey sky, which matched her deepening mood of nervousness. Feeling that her emotional reservoir was running low, she might have given into thoughts of happiness and home. She could easily have decided right there and then to run straight back to the train station to make an immediate return, but she knew happiness and home didn't exist in the same sentence anymore.

She was wrapped up against the cold, wearing an old threadbare brown tweed overcoat her mother had given to her on the day Father O'Brien had come to take her away. She hadn't wanted to accept it, it was after all the only coat her mother possessed, but she had insisted. It was two sizes too big and swamped her slight frame but, with it buttoned up to the neck and its matching belt gathered tightly at her waist, it had proved to be an invaluable aid against the bitterly cold weather she had experienced on the journey.

She stood up and watched her warm breath stream out, each blast ballooning, similar to a smoker exhaling from a cigarette. She turned up her collar to provide even more protection and began stamping her feet in an effort to get her blood circulating to help warm her frozen body. After a few moments of pounding her feet against the paving stones, she re-tied her black woollen scarf and shoved her hands deep into her pockets to thaw her frozen fingers. She waited patiently but with every passing minute, the cold was beginning to make her shiver even more.

She sat down again on the wooden bench opposite the nearby church, whose clock up on high reminded her it was nearly nine o'clock. That was the time her aunt was due to meet her. Her small, battered brown suitcase lay next to her, packed with little more than a young girl's dreams, but she was determined she would do everything in her power to make those dreams come true.

Colleen Mary O'Malley was just sixteen years old, petite and slim, and stood about five feet six inches tall, possessing striking looks described on a pretty heart-shaped face. There was a hint of blush around her high cheek bones. Her full lips, emerald eyes and thick, beautifully arched, eyebrows made her a stunning beauty.

In Irish history, there were many tales of Spanish galleons which were shipwrecked off the coast centuries before. It was said that some of the survivors had settled there a while, enchanting the local girls, their unions producing these rare, raven-haired beauties. If these stories were true, she was definitely a descendant, having a mass of black curly hair which, when loose, tumbled down to her shoulders.

She was daydreaming and watching yet another bus dawdling up the hill from Digbeth, its engine exhausted and under pressure from the climb, issuing a fatigued protest by coughing out a charcoaled blast of black fumes.

Then, as if slowly awakening from a dream, her senses absorbing the gathering sounds of reality, she heard a woman's voice shouting from a distance and getting louder as she neared. It was undeniably the voice of her only aunt, Bridie Maria O'Sullivan.

'Colleen, Colleen,' she shouted again. 'It's you isn't it?'

It was a rhetorical question and the young girl replied by standing up, smiling and nervously holding out her arms for an embrace, all of which Bridie ignored and bluntly continued her welcoming salvo.

'Ah, Colleen, I know it's you. Jesus, you have the looks of your mother about ye. Sorry I'm a little late. It's good to see you looking so well after everything.'

She half-heartedly surrendered to a minor embrace, as if to be involved in a full public display of affection might be embarrassing in such a crowded place.

Bridie took a step back, unbuttoning her black knee-length overcoat and flapping it to and fro to let in some cool air as she had worked up quite a sweat on her rush across town. Then, satisfied that she had cooled herself enough, she blithely continued.

'Anyway, I'm here now, so let's get going.'

Colleen was sad she hadn't received any real hug or kiss. Her aunt appeared to lack any emotional attachment to a niece she was meeting for the very first time. Colleen could have done with a cuddle and a little bit of fuss. She had travelled hundreds of miles to a city she didn't know, and a few moments of bonding was the least she expected but her aunt had just charged off. She grabbed her case and followed.

The sights and sounds of this new city were overpowering enough, sucking away what little confidence she had left so at that moment she felt alone, longing for her mummy and the safety of home.

Colleen had grown up in rural Ireland and was the only child of Caitlin and Thomas O'Malley. Her mother had suffered complications after giving birth and could have no more children, so the baby was very special. Her parents both doted on their only child.

She was a most beautiful black-haired baby with a happy disposition, who could be quiet and calm at one time and then full of energy and lively the next.

Her parents toiled hard to scratch a living from their small-holding to secure their survival. The threat of destitution lay around the next corner for many families. It was a mammoth task for some due to the size of their families, with eight or nine children to feed.

As the only son, Thomas had inherited the land when his own father had passed away and he laboured hard for the meagre return he got from his vegetables and the few fruit trees he possessed, but they managed on a day to day basis. There was often bread or a cake baking in the range, eggs from their hens and occasionally a cheap joint of meat they had bartered for with nearby farmers, offering fruit and vegetables in exchange. The joint would be put in the pot to make a stew which would have to last the week.

The daily grind for Caitlin of doing the washing, ironing and cooking plus cleaning in the small dark, two-roomed cottage, added to the back-breaking stints in the fields alongside her husband, meant her life was an exhausting drudge. In the evenings there was no respite. She did sewing and knitting and took in other people's washing. Sometimes she would also clean at the houses of the better off local women which brought in a few more pennies.

Colleen was a bright child and attended her local school, for which her parents had to find the money to buy books, paper and pens. The nuns and the local parish priest ran the school along very strict religious lines, which discriminated against the poor and girls in equal measure. Girls were not expected to be educated as their lot was to become mothers, and devote their lives to keeping house and looking after their husbands and children. Indeed, the whole country suffered as the church and state were so closely connected, and little was done to encourage change to these archaic principles. Girls got married young and had many babies and so the cycle continued; some, however, were glad to emigrate and escape the oppression, allowing them a life with more choice and better prospects.

However, it became obvious to the nuns that the girl had potential, enough to stay on over the age of fourteen; unusual for a girl but a scholarship system did exist, awarded from local rates to cover the costs.

Colleen was awarded the scholarship and stayed on despite the bullying she was subjected to because of her looks and intelligence. She enjoyed her lessons and soaked up knowledge like a sponge. She also had strong self-belief and determination and although dwarfed in size by the bullies, she never let them get away with their intimidation. She fought back, both physically and verbally, ensuring they all knew she was no one's fool.

Colleen would help her mother with the sewing in the candlelight at night, sitting together by the range, making or repairing clothes, chatting away to one another. Her dreams and ambitions began to take shape, mainly involving getting out of the village and making something of her life, all fired by the stories her mother told her about Bridie.

Colleen listened intently as her mother told her the story of her older sister, Bridie. How many years ago, she had escaped the village and had set off for Birmingham in England. She had dreams to train to become a nurse. It had stunned their parents but Bridie was a headstrong, ambitious young woman and wanted a better life. Caitlin had been proud to tell everyone in the village that her sister was doing very well and basked a little in the glory.

As Colleen listened to the story, the idea of emulating her aunt's escape began to develop.

Hard times kept the dream alive and when she was alone in the cottage she would walk up to the small postcard-size mirror which hung on the wall near the front door, and remove it from its hook. Tucked behind the frame was a small folded piece of note paper on which she had written herself a reminder.

When life got tough she would remove the mirror, unfold the note and read those words. As she whispered the words the challenge became real. With her eyes blazing with passion, her jaw set firmly, she would repeat the promise.

'Colleen, you must fight for your future, chase those dreams and find happiness.'

At those moments, she felt she could take on the world and make a success of her life if she could just escape the poverty and isolation of her dreary life.

She wanted to experience the travelling and the discovery of new places and people, just like Aunt Bridie had. She had numbered her simple goals in that note and they read: 'One – escape. Two – find work. Three – find love. Four – have a family.'

Today, the pioneer and heroine of the young girl's dreams was some distance ahead in her race across this new city. Colleen had seen a black and white photograph of her mum and a young Bridie, posing by the back door of a ramshackle cottage. It must have been taken when she was quite young as she looked a lot leaner then than she did now. Today, in her mid-thirties, it was obvious that over the years Bridie had put on weight, possibly comfort eating because of her emotional issues. Or was it that now, having the opportunity to eat whatever she pleased, she had overindulged and was carrying the consequences? The only positive point about her size was that it seemed totally appropriate for the times that a nurse should be a very solid-looking woman with a matronly bust and a somewhat oversized rear end; she certainly fitted that image.

Earlier that cold morning Bridie had woken and quickly dressed. Ignoring any fashion guidelines and flouting any idea that she should dress to attract the attention of the opposite sex, her vanity having fled some years previously, she threw on what she felt comfortable wearing. She looked in the mirror and was reasonably pleased with the image that she saw there.

Her hair was newly permed after yesterday's visit to her local hairdresser and had been coloured a deep chestnut brown.

Perched on top was a small, black, brimless pillbox hat which looked a little ridiculous, given the scale of her physical features. Her sagging jowls hung at the jawline of her plump face. Lacking finesse, she had applied her make-up like an angry child let loose with a box of coloured crayons, scribbling in her red lips and pencilling in two big black swathes for her eyebrows. Both of her efforts were displayed on the canvas that was her over-powdered face.

Bridie O'Sullivan felt comfortable when hidden behind the camouflage of the 'clown's mask'.

She had decided on a floral-patterned dress with a wide black elasticated belt fastened at her waist, which only succeeded in accentuating her lack of a waist line and rather emphasised the fact that she was the same width from her shoulders down to her backside.

Her legs were like two vast cake decorator's piping bags, which tapered down from her thighs to her feet, where they poured themselves into a pair of white patent leather-look shoes. She finished the whole look off with short white cotton gloves and a shiny black handbag. Her saving grace was that she had those same beautiful emerald eyes as her sister, Caitlin, and her niece, Colleen.

She did a final check in the mirror, sighed and repositioned her hat slightly, grabbed her coat and rushed out of her house to catch the next tram into town.

CHAPTER FOUR

Bridie O'Sullivan had 'escaped' to England when she was fifteen. Her dream from childhood had always been to become a nurse.

Growing up in southern Ireland had been hard, but it was the accepted norm as poverty was rife, money was short and working the land was the only avenue open to rural folk.

In her teens she struggled to accept the concept of religion, the belief that she should be grateful to Him for the gift of this life angered her. She wanted to shout out at the nuns at school and into the screwed-up, angry red face of the local priest that she didn't accept this gift and wanted to demand a refund.

The shackles of the church and all its doctrine, and its low expectations for women, incensed her. She hated the repression of it all. Following blindly and obediently all that was fed to them from birth to the grave with no promise of a better life, was impossible to accept. She would make her own plans for a better future.

She only talked of this with her young sister, Caitlin, confiding in her that when she was old enough, she would wait until her father was in the fields, pack her few belongings and head for England. She was adamant that there was a better life waiting for her there, and vowed to find temporary work until she could realise her dream and start training in her chosen profession.

When the time came, she boldly walked out of her home and towards a rather uncertain future but she knew with each step she took, each hour that passed, she would be nearer to her dream.

On her arrival in Birmingham she found a rooming house to live in and managed to secure a job as a junior in Lewis's Department Store, earning just enough to pay for her bedsit, paltry food rations and her bus fares. It was a struggle but she felt that living in England, even in the straitened circumstances she was in, was better than a life back in Ireland. Here she felt she had opportunities.

She struggled for a few years to establish herself and eventually she was able to enrol for the nursing course she had dreamed of for so long. She was so proud of her achievements and wrote regularly to her sister, telling her all about life in a big city. She knew her younger sister would find the seemingly boring minutiae of her work and everyday life fascinating, and imagined her reading those letters by candlelight back in Ireland.

After exchanging their missives for a number of years, Caitlin, who was now fifteen, wrote back saying she was ready to 'make a run for it' herself. Then in her next letter some months later, she wrote to say that she had met a handsome young man named Thomas who had inherited his father's smallholding in the village, and that he had proposed to her. She had accepted and added that she would be getting married in the spring.

'Jesus,' Bridie said out loud as she read the news, 'the young girl will never be free now, God help her.'

It wasn't long before her sister wrote to tell her all about the wedding and the celebrations in the village. That letter was followed by another only three months later revealing she was pregnant.

'Oh, Caitlin,' Bridie sighed, 'the start of a brood and every year there will be another,' she said sadly as she wiped the tears from her eyes. She imagined her poor sister chained to the house and motherhood with no respite, ending up being spat out at the end of it all, a dried and empty shell.

However, sad news came in her next letter when she informed her sister that after delivering a beautiful black-haired baby they had named Colleen, there had been problems with 'lots of bleeding', but by the grace of God she had survived. There would be no more babies.

'That's a blessing,' thought Bridie.

Bridie lived alone in a little terraced house only a short walk to the hospital and had managed to make it a homely place to live her lonely and solitary life.

Often in the evenings she would suffer bouts of depression. When her spirits were low and despair closed in she would climb the stairs to seek the escape that sleep offered. Before she changed for bed she would stop a while in front of the full-length mirror in her bedroom, standing motionless, staring at her reflection. She became lost in memories of happier times, she would smile for a while only for a sudden bleakness to surround her.

Standing there with her shoulders slumped forward and her arms hanging limply by her sides, her face devoid of expression, her tears would begin to gently snake slowly over her cheeks before falling to the floor. She turned away to quietly make her way to bed and the refuge it afforded.

Bravely, she didn't let the sadness envelop her totally because she had her job. Thankfully, it provided her with an escape from her despair and when on the familiar ground of the hospital wards, a whole different person was on show. Exhibiting vitality and a caring nature which radiated from her in the safety and comfort of her workplace, she totally immersed herself in her busy and fulfilling career as a nurse. Busy at work, there was little time to consider her sad personal life.

She had been very much in love with Frank, 'my Frank' as she had liked to call him back then. Frank was a porter at the hospital. A slim youth with ginger hair which he greased back. He possessed a large domed forehead, piercing blue eyes and a freckled face on which a permanent smile was displayed. His nose was large and he had a receding chin which gave him a look rather like that of the reflection when looking into the back of a spoon. His small frame belied his all-action character as he zipped here and there. He was forever rushing around the wards and corridors, carrying out his duties with a cheery word for all he came into contact with. He was known as 'Frank the Ferret' because he was always darting about and, of course, he was small and ginger, just like a ferret.

They had first met when he was wheeling a bed through the corridor, carrying out his duties. He had nearly collided with Bridie as she left a side ward; he was very apologetic and with an easy charm, smiled and joked, 'Oh, so sorry, nurse, I nearly had you on the bed there, didn't I?'

Bridie blushed and hurried off to the sound of Frank calling out, 'I hope we bump into each other again.'

Frank made sure he bumped into her again and when he did, he managed to persuade her to go on their first date. He took her to his local pub, the Gun Barrels, which was situated on the Bristol Road near the university and not far from the hospital.

He immediately put her at ease and she warmed to his vitality and extrovert personality, which was the opposite of her own. She enjoyed just sitting back in the pub and watching him interact with others in his busy way, becoming very animated in conversation. He never seemed to pause for breath, arms and hands waving in a series of semaphore-like signals to emphasise his opinion on the topic under discussion. As the exchanges developed and emotions ran high, his forehead would furrow and then smooth just like a concertina as he disagreed or connected with a different viewpoint. He always had the last word, adding his own opinions of which he had a great many, on all subjects.

Together they looked incongruous. They were one of those couples who appeared oddly matched. An improbable-looking pair as she dwarfed him in size, being at least a foot taller and twice as wide, but they had found solace in each other's company. They were both basically solitary people who realised the odd truth of how lonely you can actually be in a big city.

She had never thought that she would find love. She didn't consider herself nice-looking in any way and was constantly aware of her size. Her love for Frank was founded much on the fact that none of her unattractive physical features seemed to matter to him as he appeared to love her for what she was. She was grateful for that.

Their attraction to one another developed into a loving but chaste relationship, although chastity wasn't something Frank appreciated and it wasn't for the want of trying that Birdie's virtue remained intact.

In their first year together, she ensured that Frank understood, much to his growing frustration, that as a good

Catholic girl, there was no way there would be any 'funny business' until they were married.

Their relationship settled into a routine; a happy companionship which suited them both and included the occasional night at the pictures. Mostly it was an evening at the pub, after which they would usually stop at the 'chippy' and buy a fish and chip supper. Strolling along eating their chips straight from the steaming, hot newspaper wrappings, neither could have been happier. However dark days were ahead.

The onset of war with Germany was on everyone's mind, and conversation tended to revolve around how long the war would last and what impact it would have on England. Many believed that it would be over very quickly and took to lampooning the little German leader with the bad temper and ridiculous moustache. Others thought it may threaten to disrupt the whole of Europe and eventually involve direct attacks on England itself. Many brave young men had already joined the forces, prepared to lay down their lives for their country, and Frank prattled on about becoming a soldier of the King.

One night at the pub, Bridie was concerned to overhear Frank talking at the bar as he waited to get the drinks in.

'Well, my money is on us giving Mr Hitler a severe battering and it will all be over by Christmas. We have beaten the Hun once and we will do it again, that's why tomorrow Francis John Smith will be signing up to serve in the Royal Warwickshire Fusiliers,' he announced to all gathered at the bar.

It wasn't his intention, but his announcement got him free beer for the rest of the night and he would later leave the pub alone, much the worse for wear. Bridie had realised what was happening and stood at the open door of the pub that night having decided to slip quietly away, leaving Frank with his well-wishers, knowing that he was lost for the night but hoped not for the rest of her life. Looking back at him from the doorway, surrounded by his new friends, understanding that like a lot of young men, he was determined to do his bit for king and country, she knew she wouldn't be able to dissuade him. He had already discussed the subject with her, but she had chosen to ignore the possibility until his little speech at the bar that night had confirmed her worst fears. As she closed the door to the pub that night, the last words she heard him say were, 'Tomorrow I'm off into the town to sign up. I've had enough of this sitting around while all the other young fellows are going off to war. I ain't hanging around to get the white feather from some evil old woman. I want to do my bit.'

So it was no surprise when Bridie asked the head porter a few days later of Frank's whereabouts, only to be told that there had been a message phoned through.

'Tell everyone I'm off to fight the Hun.'

She nodded sadly, turned and walked away, dabbing at her tears with her handkerchief and sighed, 'Short and sweet, that's my Frank.'

It was the last she saw of him. She later learned that he had been killed when a shell hit the truck he was travelling in on a road somewhere in France. She had loved him deeply and spent those intervening years waiting for him to return and romantically sweep her off her feet just like in the movies, but it wasn't to be.

The news of his death left her heartbroken and in grief for a dream she would never realise. She had waited for him in vain, the experience leaving her with an air of melancholy. She became introverted, slightly morose and somewhat bitter. Feeling cheated, she had settled for a spinster's life, throwing herself into her work to help her forget. She formed a hard protective shell around herself, letting no one in.

CHAPTER FIVE

Colleen trotted along, following the vapour trail of lavender water her aunt left in her wake. Bridie bundled her way through the crowds of people milling around the market area.

'Come on, let's hurry so we can catch the next tram and we can get you settled in,' Bridie called over her shoulder.

They made their way up the hill past the big church she had been studying earlier on, and noticed it had a sign attached to the railings which read, 'St Martin's in the Bull Ring.' The church stood at the bottom of a slight slope, next to the Bull Ring Market, a big open-air market place, consisting of rows and rows of canopied stalls, selling all manner of fruit and vegetables, clothes, shoes, household goods, fabrics, materials and more and was in full flow, busy with shoppers, buyers and browsers.

The sounds and smells attacked her senses as she pushed her way through the market, taking in the lively, vibrant scene. She was amazed at the skills of the barrow boys hurtling past her, trying manfully to control their carts as they steered them at high speed through the crowds. In an effort to bring the carts to a stop, their feet skidded on the cobblestones. A background, a cacophony of the traders, shouting and bawling, pitching their prices with colourful language and good humour, filled the air.

It was so different to Cork which she had visited a few times. Birmingham had no docks or harbour. No big river dominating the city. Cork was Ireland's second city and she knew

Birmingham was England's second city. She had swapped one for the other and dauntingly accepted that this was now her city, her home and her future.

They made their way further into the Bull Ring Market area where the sign over the F W Woolworth's building stood out boldly with its gold lettering on a red background. The store was under siege from the crowds of people pushing in and out of the swing doors to take advantage of 'Woolies' well known cheap prices and bargains.

She noticed more buses pulling in and regurgitating even more people to swell the numbers already pushing and jostling around the stalls, or just hurrying through on their way further into the city centre shops.

Bridie set a fair pace as they turned onto New Street. Managing to avoid the buses, cars and vans, they made their way up towards Navigation Street to catch the number sixty-nine tram to Selly Oak.

Colleen was falling behind in the route march across the city. Although trying hard to increase her pace, she was failing miserably but was comforted by the thought that it was nearly impossible to lose contact with her aunt as long as she could smell the perfume trail in the air.

Colleen paused as they passed Lyons Corner Tea Rooms and stopped for a short breather. Resting her suitcase on the ground for a while, she peeked through the window, admiring the smartly dressed staff in their black uniforms and white aprons.

The famed 'nippies' as the waitresses used to be called, were now history as the company now operated a cafeteria type service, meaning some of the pre-war old-world elegance was gone. Times had changed and waiting on tables was now a thing of the past, but the reputation lived on and the famous tea rooms were very busy.

She stood back from the window and caught sight of a white card with neat black print placed in the corner of the window, it read, 'Kitchen Staff Required. Apply within.'

'Will you quicken up a bit, Colleen, or we'll miss the tram,' Bridie called out.

They reached the tram stop and Colleen could see her aunt was breathing hard, with perspiration dotting her top lip and forehead.

'Jesus, Colleen, I think I need to lose a little weight, that walk has puffed me out,' she gasped.

They weren't waiting long before the tram squealed in with its peculiar screeching sound of metal wheels on metal tracks. They climbed aboard for the journey to Selly Oak.

The tram trundled away with the conductor shouting, 'Hold very tight, please,' as the pair swayed down the aisle to some free seats where they wearily slumped down, both exhausted from their sprint across the town centre.

The trip along the Bristol Road was exhilarating for the girl from the country and she took in the sights, noticing the big cinema, the university and all the shops and parks. Big houses, little terraced houses and all manner of people, even some foreign-looking ones. One other thing that struck her was the absence of horses and carts.

The city and its suburbs seemed to go on forever, but it wasn't long before they reached their stop and then made the short walk to Bridie's house.

It stood in a long road of exactly similar terraced properties, which stretched away to infinity. It had a little front stone wall about three feet high, directly behind which was a small, neatly trimmed privet hedge and a rectangle of lawn with a few plants and flowers scattered around the border, and a geranium bush at its centre.

The black wrought-iron gate squeaked as she pulled it to after letting Colleen through. Bridie then juggled with her keys, searching for the right one before opening the front door. They burst in and headed down the long hallway, Bridie pointing to the room on the left as she went past, issuing rule number one.

'Front room, only used for special occasions,' she stated.

The kitchen was sparsely decorated with cream-painted woodchip-papered walls. Two armchairs stood in the corner, separated by a small square coffee table. A drop leaf kitchen table with two chairs stood at its centre and marbled patterned linoleum covered the floor. By the window to the back yard was an upright storage unit with a pull-down shelf, then the sink and a stove completing the furnishings. Oddly, a framed painting of the Madonna hung on the wall, an unusual room decoration considering her condemnation of the church in her teenage years.

'Thank goodness we're back. Let's boil the kettle and have a nice cup of tea and a chat.' Bridie threw her coat onto one of the armchairs, followed by her gloves and handbag. She lit the gas and filled the kettle at the sink.

After a few minutes' silence in which she had made two cups of tea, she carefully carried them across to the table with a nervous rattle of cup on saucer.

'Well, you'll know that your mother has written to me.'

Bridie stared into Colleen's blushing face as she sat down opposite her niece, squashing her coat, gloves and handbag beneath her ample backside. In the process of leaning forward to extract the offending articles, she spilled her tea into her saucer. She then had to scrape the bottom of her cup on the edge of the saucer and empty the contents of the saucer back into her cup. Now at last comfortably settled, she continued, 'Father O'Brien has been a great help to your mother through it all.'

The subject matter and the subterfuge embarrassed Colleen. She became short of breath and stuttered, 'I'm really grateful, Aunt Bridie, for all the help you've offered me.'

Bridie, having never married and having no children of her own plus the 'Frank affair', meant she lacked a little subtlety when it came to discussing feelings and emotions. She continued in that same monotone voice, pushing Colleen's interest to its limits. Her escape was to stare at the picture of the Madonna on the wall. Focussing on those benign and forgiving features, Colleen was embarrassed at the thought of Her listening in and wondered if She knew her secret. She was brought back to the present with a jolt as Bridie shouted, 'Colleen, Colleen! Are you listening to me?'

Bridie was now standing in front of her, looking down into her face.

'So what are you going to do with your life now?'

Colleen was stung by the question and her eyes blazed as she returned from her reverie and, in her annoyance, stood up, hands on her hips, returning the stare.

'Shall I tell you what I'm going to do with my life, eh? Well, don't worry because I had a lot of time to think on the journey here and I decided on two things, no, three things actually. The first thing I am going to do is call myself Mary from now on. It's my middle name and no one here will know any different. The second thing I will do is early tomorrow, I will catch the tram into town and get myself a job. The third thing may take a little longer, but I intend to find me a good man and get married and have a family. I am going to have a life and a good life. That, Bridie, is what Colleen Mary O'Malley, sorry,' she corrected herself, 'Mary O'Malley is going to do. Now where's the bathroom because I need to take a bath and get a good night's sleep before I get all that accomplished, don't I?'

Bridie's mouth fell open in shock. She was taken by surprise by this newly confident, self-assured and assertive young lady smiling back at her, feet apart with the look of a professional pugilist prepared to pummel any opposition.

'Well, if you think so,' stuttered Bridie, 'that sounds great, erm, Mary.'

'Right, Bridie, show me where my bedroom is and then I'll take a bath and get some rest. It's been a long day.'

After that exchange, she never called Bridie 'Aunt' again, and from that moment on Bridie would always call her niece Mary.

Later, whilst lying in the bath washing the day off her, she concluded that to make all this work, she must try to be an adult and act responsibly, an attitude of mind she realised she would need to adopt to make this change in her life successful. She had heard her aunt was a troubled soul; she knew the story of Frank; her mum had told her.

She realised that her aunt carried a lot of sorrow. She too had her own dark past so they had that much in common at least. They were a pair of damaged women who would either drag each other down or help each other escape the web of grief that ensnared them both, letting in some happiness.

For her part, Mary was determined to make a success of this opportunity, accepting that her future may be full of hard work, but hoped that would lead her on a journey of adventure towards contentment. She was young and excited at the prospect of a new life. She was determined to pull her aunt along with her.

She smiled to herself as she soaped her arms and legs, loving the idea of being called Mary.

'Colleen, that poor victim, no longer exists,' she thought to herself. 'She's dead and buried along with all her bad memories.'

CHAPTER SIX

Each word was slowly enunciated in a broad, deep and rich, Brummie accent as she called out through the open office door.

'Miss Mary O'Malley, please come in.'

A nervous Mary was sitting bolt upright on her high-backed chair in the narrow corridor. She had called in a few days earlier and had been told to return today for her interview. She had got herself in a bit of a state worrying about this moment, and slowly rose from her chair and entered the office of Miss Thelma Stapleton, the manageress of Lyons Tea Rooms.

Always immaculately dressed, Miss Stapleton wore a grey jacket and skirt, a white blouse, her brown hair scraped back in a tight bun. She projected an air of calm control and unflappability. Her face was pale and lined and was dominated by her long thin nose, in the shadow of which sat an ugly red gash for a mouth, giving her an unforgiving expression. On the end of her nose was perched a pair of tortoiseshell round spectacles; her pewter-coloured eyes busily studied the applicant standing before her.

Mary was a little daunted by Miss Stapleton, but the tone in her deep voice was surprisingly warm and friendly as she peered over her glasses and pointed to a chair.

'Sit down, please,' and began reading through the few notes her senior assistant had made at the initial interview.

'Now I can see that you are recently over from Ireland and haven't worked before so I will tell you from the beginning that

I admire hard workers, good timekeepers, honesty and tidiness. We are all responsible as members of a team here to provide the citizens of this city with quality fare as befits our reputation. My standards are high and if for any reason you cannot fulfil these most important qualities you may walk out now.'

Mary looked straight into her eyes and replied confidently.

'I was brought up by a mother who taught me right from wrong and regarded cleanliness as being next to Godliness. I can assure you, Miss Stapleton, that if you give me the chance I will not let her or you down.'

Immediately impressed with this confident, attractive young girl, she thought for one so young she showed spirit and with the right training could become an asset to her business. A few seconds of silence passed as Miss Stapleton considered her reply.

'Miss O'Malley, I was actually looking for someone with experience and I usually take a little time to consider my decisions,' she smiled, displaying a perfect set of teeth, 'but in your case I am going to take a chance on you. You appear confident, enthusiastic and presentable. I would like to put you on two weeks' trial and, provided my senior assistant thinks you're worthy of a full time position after those two weeks, you will be taken on as junior kitchen hand. You will start at the bottom of the ladder and learn all aspects of food preparation before you are allowed upstairs to serve our customers. Do you understand?'

Mary suddenly recalled the last time she had worked in food preparation and that memory sent a shiver through her body, remembering that dark, scary place. A slight panic held her paralysed for a short period of time.

'Miss O'Malley, are you listening to me, do you understand?'

'Yes, yes, thank you, Miss Stapleton. I won't let you down. When would you like me to start?' she replied.

'You will report at six thirty tomorrow morning when my senior assistant Edith will meet you, sort out your work uniforms and put you to work. Miss O'Malley, please do not under any circumstances let me down. I will see you tomorrow at some point. Goodbye for now.'

As Miss Stapleton stood up, dwarfing Mary, she extended a long bony hand, nodding courteously. Mary quickly shook her hand and hurriedly left the tea rooms.

She rushed up New Street. As quickly as she could she found a side street, stopped and heaving for breath, leant against a wall. She had put on quite a confident front and it had been exhausting. She breathed hard and deep, trying to get herself sorted out.

'Foolish girl,' she thought to herself, 'that was nothing. I can do this. I am strong; no one can knock me down. This ticks off another one on my list. Maybe the final one won't be so easy but this is a good start. So far so good then, Mary O'Malley,' she smiled to herself as she said it.

A new identity. A new job. A new start.

CHAPTER SEVEN

Mary made good progress in the kitchens which wasn't exacting work, but presented with crocks to wash, vegetables to peel and cleaning up to do, she hoped her time in the kitchen would be short.

She was relieved when Miss Stapleton kept her promise and under the tutelage of Edith, she was allowed out front and began her duties. She was elated and wore her uniform with pride. She loved the interaction with the customers. Always polite, happy, efficient and well-presented, she became a welcome new member to the team.

There were a number of young girls on the staff and she made friends quickly, especially with Julie, who was one of her co-workers. Julie was short in stature and had eyes that sparkled in her podgy round face just like two shiny currants in a bun; she was rotund with short sturdy legs and a full bosom. Her uniform seemed a little too tight and the stitching appeared stretched to bursting point at the seams. She always appeared flustered as she carried out her duties, her face flushed and shiny.

Julie's twentieth birthday was coming up and she asked Mary if she would like to join her and a few of the girls on Friday night to go dancing at the West End Ballroom.

'Oh, that would be wonderful and thanks for asking me,' Mary replied.

She now had the problem of finding something to wear; she would need to have a word with Bridie as she only had the few clothes she had brought with her from Ireland. She would be embarrassed at the thought of her friends seeing her in any of those.

They both decided after a good rummage through Bridie's wardrobe, that there was nothing fashionable with the potential to be altered.

'My Lord,' remarked Bridie, 'There's enough material in one of my dresses to make a barrage balloon.'

Mary giggled out loud, Bridie couldn't stop herself joining in and they both collapsed in hysterical laughter, falling back on to the bed.

So having given up on that idea, they decided it was best that Mary should borrow a few pounds from Bridie and visit one of the big stores after work on Thursday and get herself something a little more stylish.

A visit to the ladies' section at Lewis' Department Store on Corporation Street ended up with Mary buying a bargain in the winter sale, an emerald green calf-length cocktail dress, fitted at the waist. When she got home she tried it on to show Bridie. She looked very stylish in it and finished it off with Bridie's pearl necklace.

Bridie had a tear in her eye.

'Mary, you look so beautiful, your mother would be proud.'

Friday night arrived and Mary was full of excitement. Although she was the youngest of the group, she had applied her make-up very professionally, which she hoped would make her look a few years older and would easily get past the door staff.

She met the girls outside the ballroom and on entering, eagerly pushed through the doors and was immediately awestruck as she had never seen anything quite like this before. She took in the surroundings, amazed at the draped ceilings with huge chandeliers which changed colour as the music played. She stood, mouth agape, gazing for a while, taking it all in.

The band was playing a version of Perry Como's latest hit song, 'Prisoner of Love', and the vocalist's velvety voice filled the room. Mary sat quietly with her hands clasped in her lap, slightly anxious and over-awed.

'Sometimes you don't get asked for a dance until it's nearly time to go home because, by then, the men have had a skinful. But you never know,' said Julie.

However, it wasn't long before one young fellow decided he would try his luck.

'Excuse me, miss, I wonder if I might have the next dance with you?' he said softly.

Mary controlled her nerves and managed to nod her agreement. Feeling self-conscious, she couldn't speak and silently rose to her feet, taking the chap's hand as he led her to the dance floor.

He was also very nervous but after a few faltering steps he took control and guided his partner masterfully around the floor. Neither spoke or even looked at the other. The singer finished his version of a Sinatra classic and the fellow showed Mary back to her seat.

As she sat down he asked, 'May I have another dance with you later?'

'Oh yes, certainly,' replied Mary.

'May I ask your name?' he ventured.

'Mary, my name is Mary.'

'And my name is William,' he replied, 'and I look forward to seeing you later for that dance, Mary.'

She had a couple more dances with two other young men, but it was getting late and she told the girls that she would need to be leaving pretty soon as Bridie would be waiting up for her. She bent down to pick up her handbag and as she turned round, she heard a familiar voice.

'Mary, I hope you're not going yet, you still owe me that dance.'

Smiling at the cheeky comment, she was happy to see William standing before her. He was about six feet tall and slim. He had jet-black hair and a friendly, honest-looking face. He wore a grey double-breasted suit with an open-necked white shirt and black shoes, which she noticed were well polished. He looked clean and tidy and comfortable with himself. A man who takes care of his appearance, she thought.

Not bad looking, well mannered, smartly dressed, olive complexion, brown eyes and nice teeth. He looked a few years older than her. So much information gathered in such a short time.

They had three more dances and this time they even spoke to one another and as the last dance ended, William took Mary back over to her friends.

'Thank you for a wonderful night and if it's still okay, I will pop into Lyons tomorrow and hopefully we could have tea together.'

'That would be nice, William, see you tomorrow.'

The rest of the girls excitedly gathered round Mary after he had left. They were full of giggles and questions, teasing her about her new boyfriend.

'Look, he's not my boyfriend – yet,' she chuckled with an infectious laugh.

The next day William had arranged his trip to the tea rooms so that he arrived half an hour before it was due to close, allowing him the opportunity to ask for another date, straight after work if she agreed.

When he arrived she busied round him and settled him at a table, but she couldn't steal a few minutes to sit with him as Miss Stapleton was keeping a beady eye on things. She served him a pot of tea and a buttered crumpet, and he managed to ask her discreetly if she would like to go to the Gaumont cinema after work.

'Ooh yes,' said Mary, 'I've heard 'It's a Wonderful Life' is showing and the story sounds great and most importantly, it has a happy ending and I love happy endings. I'll see you outside in half an hour when I get off,' she whispered as she left his table.

They both thoroughly enjoyed the film and each other's company and as they waited for Mary's bus, he stole a kiss. He was totally besotted with her.

'Tomorrow is Sunday, how about we meet up again. How about Cannon Hill Park? We could have a stroll, an ice-cream and get to know each other a bit better. Let's meet at the main gate opposite the cricket ground, say two o'clock,' he said.

She nodded her agreement and they kissed again as she climbed onto the tram.

On the ride home she thought about William and tonight's date, and how wonderful it had been. Suddenly, she realised that she had no idea where that damned cricket ground was. She hoped Bridie would know.

They had such a pleasant time that afternoon and discussed their young lives up to this point. Mary learned that William had been born in Birmingham and that his parents were originally from Northern Ireland, and that he worked at the Austin car factory at Longbridge. He had returned to his job after his army service, which he told her had taken him to the deserts of North Africa and on into Italy before a final push had them in Germany to celebrate victory.

Mary skirted around any embarrassing questions about her life by giving an abridged version. But he didn't seem to be listening; he just stared into those beautiful green eyes and drank in her beauty. She was in mid-sentence when he simply kissed her, long and passionately.

'I'm never letting you go, Mary O'Malley,' he said as he gripped both her hands tightly in his.

William proved to be as good as his word and the following June the pair were married at Birmingham Register Office on Broad Street. Her Aunt Bridie and her friend Julie from work attended, as did William's young sister, Kathleen, and his parents.

Mary was dressed in a two-piece black tailored suit with a fitted jacket and a long narrow pencil skirt, which were all the rage at the time and which was a present from Bridie. The style enhanced her figure and she finished off her look with that very stylish black pillbox hat borrowed from Bridie, plus the pearl necklace. She had 'borrowed' that permanently.

William looked smart too, wearing his one and only suit. Fittingly enough, he had been wearing the same suit when they first met. As usual, his shoes had been polished to a high sheen.

After the ceremony, during which Bridie had cried for most of the time, the whole group posed for photographs over the road in the Gardens of Remembrance.

Miss Stapleton had arranged tea and sandwiches back at the Tea Rooms for the small group after the ceremony. She had also personally made a beautifully decorated single-tier wedding cake as her special present to the happy couple. Julie and Bridie fussed round and took more photographs, and generally tried to make it a special day for Mary.

After a few days' honeymoon in a bed and breakfast in Weston-Super-Mare the couple started their married life off at William's parents' home in Northfield. However, Mary was determined they would get a place of their own. She had seen from the top deck of the bus on her way into work the ideal house in Selly Oak. Her natural drive was to push forward and she had kept her eye on that little terraced house which was up for sale. She decided to approach the agents to request details of the price.

They had saved a little and William's parents had given them a wedding present in the form of a cheque for five hundred pounds, which was a major help and with them both in gainful employment, the small mortgage was well within their means.

When they moved into their new home, Mary was the happiest she had ever been. She loved that house. It had a front garden with a lilac tree at its centre and a back garden where they could grow vegetables. The contrast of its dark grey slated roof and its cream-painted pebbledash render gave it a tidy and attractive appearance. It also provided enough rooms for a family to fill it with happiness.

Their children came along quickly, just as Mary had planned. First, two boys, William who they called Billy, then Ryan and finally a beautiful baby girl they named Maria, after whose birth Mary told William, 'Three's plenty to deal with and our daughter now completes the Casey Family of Selly Oak.'

CHAPTER EIGHT

The corner shop of Freeman and Forbes had never been so busy with the carts and bikes out making deliveries; business was good, just as Lenny had predicted. However, he found that some of his delivery boys were coming back to him with tales of customers who hadn't enough money to settle up. Lenny wasn't having any of that so he decided it was time to unveil his secret weapon and unleash it on the unsuspecting debtors.

The not-so-secret weapon was Teddy the Hook. Lenny had struggled to find him a position within his business as working in the shop was a little difficult with a hook and one good hand, making it nearly impossible to weigh and bag the goods. So with the hook being the question, Lenny decided he would turn the problem on its head and make the hook the answer. He realised a feisty, aggressive debt collector with a hook was a pretty frightening prospect for bad payers, so Teddy was installed as 'debt collector'.

Never was a man more suited to his work and his brief was simple. Lenny impressed upon him, 'Come back with money, even a little. If they genuinely haven't got it, bring back something out of the house that's worth a few bob. Never – and I repeat, never – come back empty-handed.' He paused for a moment then added, 'Or in your case, empty hooked.' He laughed loudly at his own joke.

It wasn't long before Lenny realised another thing. All the gear Teddy was seizing from the defaulting customers which he brought back on the big barrow, had to be stored before he could sell it and turn it into cash. Fortunately, the shop next door, a ladies' fashion shop, had gone out of business and Lenny managed to secure a short term rental on it, giving him the perfect opportunity to display the goods in this new showroom.

Then the final part of Lenny's rise and rise hit him straight between the eyes.

'What these people haven't got is money, so I'll sell them money – well loan it to them –at excessive interest, and who better to scare the shit out of the fuckers if they don't pay up but my man Teddy.'

The money lending was a big earner and not just to his household clients who needed to borrow little sums, but a few local small business men who needed immediate cash to help them through a cash flow crisis. His underworld connections, from time to time, needed to avail themselves of Lenny's services too.

It was a big day for Lenny when he removed the name of Forbes from the sign above the shop. Colin had decided that he was too old to carry on and with a golden handshake from Lenny, he tootled off to spend his retirement with a cousin in Bournemouth.

At the age of twenty-one, the young Lenny became the main man and decided a change of personal style was necessary if he was to project the image of an up-and-coming successful businessman in the city.

After a visit to Burtons, the tailors in the city, he now cut a smart figure with his double-breasted suits, white shirts and tie, which he always tied in a tight half Windsor style. He now felt more comfortable and confident in his appearance. His thinning fair hair was parted down the middle, swept back with the aid of Brylcreem, just like the pictures of Dennis Compton, the famous cricketer and footballer on the advertising hoardings. He had also cultivated a small moustache so although he possessed youthful features, he hoped this new style would make him look a little more mature.

The times presented their own set of problems for businesses but with the success of his first shop and having established himself with the wholesalers at the market plus a strong network of contacts, he decided the time was right to expand.

Flourishing in his role as an entrepreneur, he bankrolled an expansion to two more shops, firstly a small one in Summer Hill and then another larger one in Ladywood. His brothers ran the shops while he and Teddy involved themselves with more questionable interests related to money lending and fencing stolen goods. The interaction with the criminal element allowed him to hear the whispers about what was cracking off around the city.

Ever open to new ideas, Lenny was ready to change direction if there was money to be made and one day whilst checking the frontage of the shop deciding it could do with a lick of paint, he was surprised to see an old face from his past. This meeting would reveal a scam that would provide the vehicle to drive him to the pinnacle of his ambition.

'I heard you was a big noise in the green grocery trade, Lenny, my old mate, how are ye?'

'Bugger me!' exclaimed Lenny, 'Richie Thompson, where ye bin?'

After explaining he had just got out from having done time at her Majesty's pleasure in Winson Green for burglary, they retired to The Grapes down the road.

After sinking his first pint on the outside for over twelve months, Richie wiped away his beer moustache with the back of his hand.

'Lenny, you've been good to me in the past, helped me out of a few sticky situations and when I needed some muscle you got Teddy to sort things out. How is Teddy, by the way?'

'You know Teddy, as long as he's punching he's happy.'

Richie laughed and continued, 'So what's your next move then, Len? I can't see you as a greengrocer for the rest of your natural.'

'I've got plans, you know me. I don't like to let the grass grow. Clubs, that's where there's plenty of cash but I need a fair wedge to get me started.'

'Well let me tell you what I heard inside about a way to make big money without rough house. This is where the money is now; running around with shooters or climbing through windows like I do is old hat. It's harder to catch the boys who do this scam successfully and let's face it, after all the bird I've done up here and down the smoke, I can tell you that this is loads safer and more profitable.'

'What d'yer mean, Richie?' Lenny enquired.

'Well it's like this my old mate. I'm in the same flowery dell as this guy who's doin' bird for armed robbery. We get on well and although in there you don't open your mouth about too much he told me about the latest scam down the smoke,' he paused for another mouthful of his pint.

'Long firm fraud, it's called, Lenny, and they are pulling in thousands doing it down there and you don't get your hands dirty or need to be armed to do it. Just have the brains to plan it all, a good professional back-up team and plenty of front. Lenny, this one is made for you.'

Lenny listened carefully as Richie told him as much as he knew and was given the name of a face in London who might help him a bit more. With fifty quid to help him on his way, Richie left his old mate with plenty to think about.

The whole idea got him thinking. If he could pull it off, his next move in the business world appeared to be within reach. He knew the local club and pub bosses and had seen them strutting about the town. They were in for a bit of competition because Birmingham's clubland was about to welcome a young man with big plans.

He would arrange a meet with the man in London.

CHAPTER NINE

Lenny and Teddy made the trip down to London and entered the busy, noisy, loud and smoke-filled Blue Lantern club. They stood at the bar and ordered a couple of drinks. Before the barman walked off to serve another customer, Lenny asked if Mr McClean was about; his answer was a casual nod towards the restaurant where a lone figure sat at a table in the corner.

'I wonder if you could let him know that Lenny Freeman is here.'

The barman headed over to where his boss was seated and after a short, whispered conversation, he returned and informed him that he could join Mr McClean at his table. 'Mr McClean asked that your guard dog should remain at the bar,' the barman informed Lenny.

Lenny didn't appreciate his mate being insulted but nodded and said, 'Best to stay here for a bit, Ted, but keep your eyes peeled.'

He approached the table and gingerly offered his hand, which was ignored and met with a steely gaze and a motion for him to sit down. Conversation didn't start as Lenny thought it might and the air was icy for a while. A busty waitress brought over two prawn cocktail starters. With his mouth full of his seafood starter, Joey garbled, 'If ye doon here thinkin' ta open a club, dinnae bother yersel; it's like the wild west doon here and yer'l be a dead mon. That's a friendly warnin' from me as I consider myself well mannered,' he growled. 'Sum a tha rest will nae chat so long, they'll just stick a shooter up yer arse and pull the trigger.'

Joseph McClean was a hard man; a no-nonsense Glaswegian. A big solid Scotsman standing about six foot six tall with wide shoulders tapering to a slim waist and a face that carried the scars of many a street fight back in his home city. He had a broken nose which was par for the course, but a fearful wound that ran from the corner of his right eye down to his chin was a reminder that no one should try to take any liberties. Indeed, Richie had warned Lenny to 'tread careful' as Joey was famous for sudden outbursts of aggression, smashing everything and everyone around him in his madness.

Lenny realised that Richie had revealed Lenny's future plans but that was okay. He let the silence continue awhile as there was nothing much he could say after his host's opening salvo, deciding it would be best to sit quietly for a while and project an image of calm.

He didn't touch his prawn cocktail, he wasn't keen on prawns. Joey noticed it lay untouched and snatched it from him and snaffled that one as well.

After demolishing a T-bone steak which was so big it hung over the edge of the plate, Joey seemed a bit calmer and began to talk without the threatening Glaswegian hard man act and accent. Lenny was relieved that he wouldn't need a translator as 'the Jock' could speak the Queen's English quite clearly, he now realised.

'Mr McClean, I'm not about to open up a club down here. What I'm after is some information. I was told by a mutual acquaintance that you would be the man to approach to get the word on this long firm fraud caper and hoped you might point me in the right direction.'

73

Lenny opened his jacket to reveal a thick brown envelope. That action certainly melted the ice and although initially taciturn, Joey now revelled in his role of lecturer. After a question and answer session which lasted a good hour, Lenny fully understood the scam.

Joey revealed a few names of useful contacts, forgers, bent accountants and inside men at banks who would help him to set it all up, all for a fee of course.

Lenny knew the ropes and when their discussion was over, he pushed the plain brown envelope across the dining table, stood up, didn't offer his hand a second time, nodded his thanks and left.

CHAPTER TEN

The Caseys scraped along like most families in the fifties. Both parents worked hard and with Mary's careful management of the budget, she was able to ensure her family always had food in the larder and the bills paid.

They lived in a community where everyone tried to be helpful and neighbourly. They were looked upon as a friendly, hardworking and happy family. Many times Mary would lend the neighbours that half a bag of sugar or a little cash to pay the tally man when they were short. William even gave his old Gillette razor blades to one of their neighbours who was out of work and couldn't even afford to buy one. The man's appearance and dignity were improved by having a regular shave and he never missed an opportunity to wave to the family whenever he walked past their house.

William had turned the bottom half of their back garden into an allotment, and grew potatoes and carrots and constructed a frame from bamboo canes to grow his peas and runner beans. The garden was big enough to leave an area of lawn for the kids to play on except when the washing line was full. The children knew better than to mess up Mum's washing.

The youngsters flourished in the loving atmosphere at home and attended the local schools. Mary encouraged them to go to church, although she was secretly ambivalent about the whole

'Catholic thing' and only kept the faith for her children's benefit, ensuring the family were always at early Mass on Sundays.

Mary made Sundays an important day, with Mass and then dinner being the highlights of the day. Sunday would also mean the two young boys would get their comics: the *Tiger*, the *Lion* and the *Eagle*. They both avidly read about the latest escapades of Dan Dare but especially their favourite character, Roy of the Rovers and his goal scoring exploits for Melchester Rovers.

The joint would be in the oven at about midday and all the vegetables peeled and ready, sitting in the saucepans on the stove. When a leg of lamb was on the menu Mary would shout, 'Ryan, away down the garden and pick me some mint.'

He would then help his mum by chopping it up and adding the sugar and vinegar, and pouring it into the little glass bowl, setting it on the table along with a silver spoon.

When she had the whole family gathered at the dining table, Mary had a warm feeling of contentment. Her family meant everything to her and as unimportant as it may have been to them, a little thing like watching them all sitting down, interacting, laughing as they ate their dinner were golden moments for her. She remembered her own harsh childhood and would never take this gift for granted; she felt so lucky.

They always had the radio on as they ate their dinner and although under pressure from the new form of family entertainment, the TV, it was still very popular with the family. They all enjoyed listening to one of England's favourite comedy programmes, 'Round the Horn', the youngsters ended up in fits of laughter at the funny voices and hilarious characters, in the popular radio comedy show.

Then in the afternoon, William would open the doors to the cabinet which housed their little TV. They would all settle down to watch the black and white films of the day, maybe Old Mother Riley or George Formby. Will Hay was another favourite but their parents favoured the variety programmes later in the evening.

Sunday tea was served up around six o'clock, consisting of sandwiches and iced fairy cakes with red, green or yellow glace cherries on top. Ryan and Billy always fought over who would get the ones with the red cherries.

Of course, Bridie had an open invitation for Sunday dinner and Mary welcomed her presence at all family gatherings for birthdays, Easter and Christmas.

Mary ensured that Christmas was a very special, magical and happy time for the children, even though she had never experienced anything similar in her own childhood. Like a lot of parents, she tried to give her children all the things she had missed out on.

A real Christmas tree in the corner of the front room; Mary loved that pine aroma. Along with the children's excited assistance, she would decorate it with pretty lights and baubles and stack the presents neatly beneath it.

As the special day approached, there was always the obligatory trip into town to see Santa at Lewis'. Long queues of parents and children waited in line to see Father Christmas slowly entering the grotto which consisted of Christmas characters in a series of side booths. Billy and Ryan were more impressed with Uncle Holly: an extremely tall man dressed in a green suit with a big green top hat and a snowy white face, but when they eventually met the awe-inspiring figure of Santa, they made their solemn admission to him that they had been good and whispered in his ear what they would like for Christmas.

William helped to embrace the family spectacular and added to the occasion by donning a Father Christmas outfit and creeping around the house late on Christmas Eve giving the little sleepy ones a fleeting glimpse.

Christmas Day was a lot of hard work including the preparation of the turkey and vegetables plus a home-made Christmas pudding, which was all a labour of love for Mary. She laid the dining table with green and red serviettes, placing Christmas crackers next to the cutlery. The children pulled their crackers and extracted their little gifts and party hats which they wore as they sat down to eat.

Mary had that familiar warm feeling again. The happiness radiated through her as the excitement level rose and she couldn't help but be amused at the speed they ate as she always made them wait until dinner was over before they could open their presents. The squeals and screams and excited laughter as their presents were ripped open were a delight and reward enough for Mary.

The year William bought a cream-coloured Ford Consul with a red roof was a memorable day. Few families in their street owned a car and Mary sat in the passenger seat so proudly, feeling quite regal. The children would pile into the back seat and the family took many a Sunday afternoon outing to the nearby countryside. Usually they would call in at a country pub, where the kids would have pop and crisps and play in the gardens whilst William and Mary had a drink inside.

It also meant they were able to go on their first holiday as a family, staying in a caravan on a big site near Poole in Dorset. The holiday camp had its own food market, restaurant and social club offering evening entertainment for all the family. The kids thought it was heaven and on day trips to Bournemouth they splashed and played in the sea. The two boys learned how to swim with encouragement from their dad, who taught them the basics of the breast stroke and crawl. As the sun went down, the day was completed with a kick about on the beach.

The summer school holidays always seemed endless to the children, stretching away towards an infinite happy sunny horizon. Mary put Billy in charge at home while she was out at work. If they weren't playing football or playing in the park, he would keep them occupied with their favourite board game, Monopoly. He also introduced his brother and sister to a special treat which he called 'the Outer Circle Holiday Tour', 'A favourite of all Brummies,' he had lied to them.

The number eleven bus was a double decker as were most city Corporation buses, and its route followed the boundary of the city and its outskirts, hence it was called the 'outer circle'. Its route covered more than twenty-six miles with buses running both clockwise and anti-clockwise, and the trip could last nearly three hours if the traffic was bad.

Billy knew the trip would take most of the day and would make two lots of sandwiches: corned beef and pickle, and cheese and tomato, filling up old pop bottles with water to quench their thirst.

They would catch the bus in Selly Oak, go upstairs and ignoring the cigarette smoke, sit at the front to get the best views. The trips would involve hopping off for a toilet visit at Lightwoods Park, right on the border of Birmingham and Smethwick, where they would sit by the paddling pool and eat their sandwiches. If their mum had given Billy enough coppers, he would buy them all an ice cream cornet from the kiosk there.

Further adventures at various points included Swanshurst Park for a little play and to stretch their legs, or a swim at Stechford Swimming Baths and even a visit to the Tivoli Picture House at Yardley to watch the latest kids' movie. The two younger ones loved the 'Outer Circle Holiday Tour' and Billy made sure it was always a day out to remember.

William enjoyed his work on the line at the car factory and brought in a steady, regular wage, and Mary still worked at Lyons, her ambition driving her onto the position of assistant manageress. In the evenings, just like when she was a child in Ireland, she did a lot of sewing, making and repairing clothes. Her mother had taught her well. Old habits die hard.

Mary was the driving force and liked the fact that her husband was prepared to leave her in control. She was the one who pushed the children to achieve their goals and encouraged them to be the best they could be. She would remind them that she never had the opportunities that were available to them and they should not waste them.

She had a lot to thank Bridie for and would never forget those early days in the city when her aunt had provided her with a home. She also ensured that the children learned to love and respect their great aunt and regaled them with tales of Bridie's pioneering journey as a young penniless girl to this city, a trip without which none of them would be there today.

William supported the Blues and went to most home games at St Andrew's, the home ground of Birmingham City Football Club. When he felt the boys were old enough, he sneaked the pair into the ground, lifting them over the turnstiles to give them their first view of professional football.

He told the boys early on, 'The Blues may not win the cup or league but as this city has given us all a chance, it seems right to support the team who proudly carry the name of the city and not, definitely not,' he emphasised, 'not that other team from the other side of town which only represents a suburb called Aston.'

He had set in motion a love for the team that the two boys would have for life.

As the boys got older and entered their teens, it was all about football. They played along with their mates, morning, noon and night, practising and dreaming of one day pulling on that blue and white jersey of the Blues.

Billy devised competitions to improve their skills, with special tests for how many 'keepy-uppies' you could do with a tennis ball and another for the number of headers between two players. At the local park with the rest of the local lads, it was jumpers for goal posts, playing with plastic footballs which they loved, striking with the inside or outside of their foot and bending it just like the Brazilians they read about in Charles Buchan's *Football Monthly* magazine. Later, when it was getting too dark, they would practise under the street lamps until it was time to go in.

William and Mary had joined the local social club and would go to the Saturday night dances and enjoy a few drinks. The club operated a number of football teams and William encouraged Billy to join the youth team. His skills were such that at fifteen, he was invited to play in the open age league against grown men, who didn't take too kindly to the young upstart making them look fools on the pitch. Many a Sunday afternoon was spent nursing sore shins from the battering the youngster took from the older, but less talented, defenders he came up against.

He began to build a reputation in Sunday morning football in the area and became well known by the other teams, and especially referees, as a bit of a character. Ryan sometimes played alongside his brother if they were short of a player but even when he didn't play, he always turned up to watch the entertainment provided by his brother, who never shut up when he was playing.

Billy's problem was that he wanted to be in charge and would give the referee lots of helpful hints and advice as to their supervision and control of the game, and the application of the Rules of Association Football. Much to the ref's annoyance, Billy was persistently talking and shouting, congratulating the ref on good decisions but berating him for bad ones, which usually led to the ref blowing the whistle. In his frustration the ref would call Billy over and advise,

'Button it, there's only one person in charge and that's me.'

He was sent off a number of times for arguing with referees.

On one particularly occasion on a cold Sunday afternoon in December at Billesley Common, a council sports ground which stretched as far as the eyes could see like a green desert of football pitches, his team were unlucky enough to be playing on a pitch somewhere on the horizon. It involved a ten minute trek to the pitch at the farthest end, carrying the nets which had to be put up when they eventually got there. That was a game in itself, with a couple of the bigger lads having to lift a smaller one on their shoulders so that they could hook the nets in position.

As the game progressed, the referee was getting fed up with Billy trying to run the match and finally in exasperation called him over to book him.

'Okay, I've had enough of you and your mouth, what's your name?'

Billy didn't reply and stared in amazement at the ref.

The reason for Billy's reticence in identifying himself was based on the fact that they knew each other very well indeed. The ref, Fred Jenkins, lived next door to the Caseys. Often they would chat about football over the back garden fence or if they bumped into each other in the street. Therefore it was with much frustration that Billy replied, 'Are you joking, Fred? You know my name, I live next door to you for fuck sake.'

The ref persisted with his line of questioning.

'I know that, Billy, but you must tell me your name.'

'Oh, fuckin' 'ell, Fred, this is ridiculous.'

Embarrassed, Fred became even angrier.

'Don't be a smart arse, Billy. Give me your name now.'

Billy quipped, 'Father Christmas?'

'Right,' said Fred, 'You're off.'

'Yeah, and you ain't gettin' any Christmas presents, Fred,' Billy retorted.

'Just fuck off, Billy,' replied Fred, his frustration boiling over. Once more, Billy made the lonely trek back to the changing rooms.

CHAPTER ELEVEN

A few roads away and not far from where the Caseys lived stood Woodside, a children's home, and in the complete antithesis of the loving family home in which the Casey children were flourishing, a desperately angry young man had lived his formative years in that lonely, loveless place.

The boy was now a few days away from his fifteenth birthday and it was time for him to leave the home. He had been called to Mother Superior's office. She sat behind a large desk with a sister standing on either side of her. He hoped this meeting would provide some answers about his parents. 'The bastards who gave me away,' was how he referred to them.

'The Good Lord knows we have tried to give love and direction to your life and teach you the importance of His words. We hope that you will appreciate later in your life that we did the best we could in your time here,' said the Mother softly.

'It is time for you to leave us now and you have expressed the wish to know a little bit about any relatives you may have. I can only tell you that when you came to us as a baby you were brought to us by a dear friend, the Mother Superior from our friends at the Sisters of Mercy in Harborne. She is aware of all the salient facts appertaining to your birth. Which parts she is prepared to release to you will be her decision and hers alone. I have already contacted her so she is obviously expecting you to visit her when you leave us today. We wish you well in the rest of your life.'

As he walked out of the main entrance and left Woodside for the final time, the sun disappeared behind the gathering grey clouds, heralding an imminent storm. He didn't look back as he walked off down the road with his duffel bag slung over his shoulder and fifteen pounds in his pocket. A number eleven bus would get him to Harborne and some answers.

His meeting, though, was short and only revealed his mother's name at the time of his birth and where she had lived. Two pieces of information, that was all he was told. The news made him angry again and once more the rage was intense. He would find his parents and make them pay for a childhood full of misery.

CHAPTER TWELVE

He was so tired now; hungry too. Other than some stale sandwiches and an apple he had slipped into his duffel bag the previous morning before he had left Woodside, he hadn't eaten for ages. He was beginning to feel nauseous. He had slept fitfully and had spent most of the journey on the overnight ferry to Dublin feeling light-headed and sick. He had thrown up numerous times as they crossed the Irish Sea. If this trip was meant to be one of discovery, the first thing he had learned was that he would never join the navy.

After disembarking, he asked for directions. Eventually making some sense of what a local man had told him, in a peculiar accent he found difficult to understand, he made his way to the bus station and bought a ticket for the journey further south.

He sat at the back of the bus next to the window. He gazed out at the green and lush countryside which seemed never-ending, with fields stretching out into the distance, little villages and farms dotting the landscape. Hills and mountains filled the horizon. He had never seen much countryside in Birmingham other than a day out that the nuns organised wandering around the Lickey Hills, so when the bus made the transition from country to city, he began to feel a little more comfortable with the surroundings.

He arrived in the city of Cork in the early afternoon and by now was desperately hungry.

He noticed a sign announcing, 'the English Market' and decided this may be a good place to start. He walked briskly off in the general direction to find a café. He was ravenous.

He turned off Princess Street and became aware that a couple of young guys were following him. He had a feeling that they had been tailing him all the way from the bus station but he didn't panic as he needed time to weigh up the situation. He quickly ducked into a shop doorway. He was on the main street, the Grand Parade, which was fairly busy and as pretence to act as naturally as possible, he studied the display of a giant watch in a shop window, which showed the internal mechanism of how a wristwatch worked. The shop was a watchmaker's with a German name, Wolfgang Gabe, or something. However, his purpose was to check out what was happening behind him by looking at the images reflected in the plate glass shop window. Just like looking in a mirror he could see the reflection as his stalkers moved in on him.

'Give us ye bag and we won't hurt ye,' shouted the bigger of the two as they approached menacingly. He waited until the last second and swivelled round. He kicked hard and fast at the big fella, catching him just where he wanted, right between the legs. He went down, howling. The other one came in from his right. He grabbed the lad's shirt and pulled him towards him and head butted him, smashing his nose with a sickening crunch and splatter of blood. He left them both on the ground moaning and calmly walked away, making good distance from the scene of the incident without looking back. He felt good. He always did when he hurt someone. He felt powerful and strong and the release of some of his pent-up anger had a calming effect on him in the aftermath.

He hadn't noticed the man who had watched the events unfold from across the street and who had then trailed him to the English Market.

The boy found a small café inside and was studying the menu, wishing he had more money, when the man pulled out a chair and sat down.

'Well, young fella, you can certainly handle yourself.'

The boy grabbed his bag and was about to make a quick exit when the man pushed him back into his chair.

'Don't run away from me, son, I'm not the police. I just want to talk to you. Now order yourself whatever you want. I'll pay and maybe we can chat afterwards. You look as though you need a good meal.'

He was happy to take up the offer and ordered bacon, sausage, tomatoes, eggs, toast and a mug of tea and wolfed it down. When he had finished he looked across at his benefactor.

'Thanks, mate, but if you're expecting any favours you can get fucked!'

'You're a lively little bastard and a cheeky one at that. Look, I watched what you did to those two lads and I liked your style. What's your story?'

The boy felt a bit tentative and nervous. Who was this guy anyway and why the big interest? He decided to grudgingly impart a little information, enough to keep him satisfied.

'To be honest, I've only just arrived on a little bit of business, from England.'

'A little bit of business, is it?' the man teased. 'Well when you've finished your little bit of business, I might have something for you.'

He searched inside his pocket and pulled out a little note book, scribbling down his phone number.

'Look, if things don't turn out like you thought, ring me and I might be able to help you out. My name's Mick, by the way.'

The boy didn't offer his name in return and snatched at the note in a hurry to get away, adding, 'Well, thanks for the food, anyway. I must get off.'

He walked off in the direction of the bus station, not having much of a plan other than to get out to Ballystiven, where he had been told that his maternal relatives had lived.

'If this business takes a bit longer to sort out, then maybe I'll have to get some casual work,' he thought to himself. 'Maybe I'll phone that Mick.' It was a back-up plan of sorts. He was big and strong and possibly a labouring job of some kind would suffice for a while, but what he really hoped was that this visit might reveal something about those people who were responsible for ruining his life. When he reminded himself of the reason for this journey, revenge still burned deep within him.

CHAPTER THIRTEEN

He arrived in the village and jumped down from the old bus. He was taking in his surroundings, feeling like he had made a journey back in time. He was standing outside an old village shop which appeared to double as the petrol station with one solitary, ancient pump. The far end of the building appeared to be a pub.

There were rows of terraced houses standing either side of the shop. It seemed that the village consisted of just this one street, with other houses and cottages stretching away in the distance. Some looked like they needed wholesale renovation and repair; others, set well back from the road, had plots of land with vegetables and fruit trees growing. He looked to his left and saw a village school, a small church. That was it.

He stood a while, noticing there were very few cars about and just to prove the point at that very moment, a horse and cart trotted out of one of the garden tracks. It was driven by a man wearing a flat cap, his children sitting on the back of the cart. He marvelled at the use of this old form of transport, only ever having seen one before back in Birmingham, and that was driven around by the rag and bone man.

He pushed open the door of the shop and was immediately assailed by the musty, damp odour and an eerie sensation in the dark and deserted shop. As if from nowhere, he heard a voice croak, 'How are ye, young man, what is it I can get ye?'

He looked around in his search to locate the voice and advanced a couple of steps on the creaky wooden floorboards. He discovered as he peered over the display of canned goods stacked on top of the counter, the top of an old lady's head. He was relieved to find, on further investigation, that she was not a frighteningly scary dwarf, or a terrifying fairy tale character but a very old, wizened, grey-haired woman, wearing a black headscarf. She was sitting on a chair, busily knitting.

After a little moment of hesitation, he politely replied.

'Hello, missus, I'm over from England and I am looking for someone, name of O'Malley, I was told that they came from this village.'

The old lady sighed as she placed her knitting under the counter and slowly got to her feet. Standing up and with the aid of a walking stick, she limped along to a clear section between the towers of cans before continuing the conversation.

The lenses in her black spectacles were so thick they magnified her eyes to twice their normal size, and the effect of her thick black caterpillar-like eyebrows ensured she held the boy's undivided attention.

'There's no one left, sure there's not,' she continued. 'It was a tragedy. Bad luck dogged them. First the O'Sullivans who had two daughters: the oldest, Bridie, runs off to England when she was fifteen; and then the youngest, Caitlin, who was a pretty thing, sure she was, gets married to Thomas O'Malley. Only ever produced one child they named Colleen. Thomas worked night and day on his land and that killed him, sure it did. He died just after Colleen left home. It's said that she left the village in Father O'Brien's car early one morning and we never saw her again. Became a lay-sister, Father O'Brien said. All of that broke her mother's heart and God rest her soul, she died about three years ago. The O'Sullivans emigrated to America to live with an uncle, that would be just after the war, the same year Thomas O'Malley died.

'So there's no one left here then?'

'No one at all, I'm afraid.'

'Any ideas where Bridie O'Sullivan went to live in England?'

'Well, she used to send letters to Caitlin, who enjoyed telling everyone in the village how well her sister was doing in her new life in Birmingham. She was really proud of her. She might still be there, I suppose. Sorry I can't help you more. What relation are you anyway?' she asked.

'What makes you say that?'

'Well, you've got the eyes,' she replied.

He was taken aback by her remark and feeling embarrassed, blurted out, 'Look, I appreciate your help and thanks, missus.'

Without further conversation, he quickly exited the strange world of the Ballystiven village shop.

CHAPTER FOURTEEN

On the way back to Cork, as the bus rumbled through the countryside, he thought about what he had learned from his conversation with the old lady, which didn't seem to add up to a lot. A couple of names. Colleen O'Malley he already knew but now Bridie O'Sullivan too. So it appeared if he wanted to get more answers, he would need to go back to Birmingham.

When the bus pulled in he found the nearest phone box and dialled the number on the little piece of paper he had kept. It was getting late and with little money left, he needed a bed for the night. The phone rang three times before it was answered.

He was relieved to hear the man's voice.

'Hello, Mick. I wondered if your offer was still open. Only my little bit of business was over and done with pretty quickly. I'm back in Cork and I intend to stay around for a while, make a few quid and then get back to Birmingham.'

'Right, okay,' said Mick, remembering the young lad he had met earlier. He continued, 'Look, I'll meet you outside the entrance to the English Market in half an hour,' Mick replied.

He was a little concerned that he was putting a lot of faith in this man who he had only recently met and hardly knew. But it was late and he was getting nervous. He didn't have much option really; the fact was it might help him get a bed for the night, at least.

He was leaning against a wall, looking down the road, when suddenly Mick was there by his side. He was unnerved and surprised at how silently Mick had approached him without him being aware. He realised he would need to be alert wherever this man was concerned. He couldn't really remember Mick's face so he studied his features as he shook him by the hand, receiving a fierce, strong, bone-crunching grip in return. He had sandy-coloured hair and bushy eyebrows, a flat broken nose and a mean-looking thin-lipped mouth. He was sturdily built and stood well over a foot taller than the boy. He looked to be in his mid-thirties. He felt intimidated and imagined that Mick, too, could look after himself if need be.

He stared at the boy for a while.

'Okay, so it might be an idea to tell me what your name is before we go any further.'

'I'm Connor Flynn.'

'Okay, Connor, nice Irish name so it is. You sound like a Brummie with that accent. Answer me this, are you Irish or English?'

'I was born here so that would make me Irish by birth.'

'You know, from the moment I saw you operate, I hoped you would give me that answer. So let me offer you a job with me which gives you free board and lodging. Now, in return, I will expect loyalty and hard work. What I say is the law and you don't question my decisions, ever. I've seen your work; well, dealing with those two lads was enough to convince me that you have something that I can work with. Potential. What do you say?'

'What will I be doing?'

'I have a few business interests, but mainly a building company, and garage and workshop. I run it all from my farm out in the country. You will be learning a hell of a lot as long as you listen to what you're told.'

Connor didn't have to think about the offer for long. What had he got at the moment? He had been in care all his life. He hated the people who put him there and in his fevered mind his life up to now had been a hopeless punishment. It was little wonder that the whole experience had twisted his young mind and defensively had turned him into a selfish, boorish, cold and unemotional bully boy. He was totally unaware of his problems and in his ignorance, didn't realise that his future prospects were grim. However, when it came to self-preservation he was quick to spot an opportunity and this was it. Casually he replied, 'Fair enough, then. Thanks for giving me a go, Mick.'

They walked to where Mick had parked and climbed into his battered white Commer van.

They drove north in silence. Connor was beginning to fathom just how lucky this break was. He had hoped to track down his family and get revenge, but he hadn't thought the whole thing through and without the offer from this bloke, he could have been sleeping rough with the bleakest of prospects. He was quietly grateful.

The farm was down a lane and after leaving the main road, they travelled through a wood for what seemed like ages, down a single bumpy and potholed track before they finally pulled up outside a very old and dilapidated farmhouse and outbuildings.

'I've lived here all my life,' said Mick as they got out of the van. 'It was my mum and dad's place and my brother and I grew up here.'

It was obvious to Connor when he went inside, that there was no woman of the house. The kitchen was untidy with crocks and pots and pans on all the work benches.

'There's a bedroom for you upstairs, second on the right. Drop your bag up there and come back down and I'll show you round.'

Connor climbed the creaking staircase, entering the darkness at the top of the stairs, felt for the light switch and flicked it on. He walked along the landing and found the bedroom, pushing open the door. He switched on the light. There was a single light bulb hanging from the centre of the ceiling without a shade. It didn't give much light but allowed him to see the dingy bedroom. Dust seemed to cover every surface. He pulled back the curtains, which were really nothing more than rags, and opened the window to let in some fresh air. The bed was a single with one pillow and a sheet, both items must have originally been white but were now yellowing from lack of a good wash; a brown coarse blanket was folded up at the foot of the bed. A mahogany wardrobe with ornate carvings around its top and golden-ringed handles, stood next to a matching chest of drawers of the same design.

He dropped his duffel-bag on the bed and began to unpack his few things. One pair of trousers, two shirts, three pairs of pants and four pairs of socks and then, at the bottom of his bag, he noticed an envelope with his name written in tidy script on the front. He opened it and pulled out a black and white photograph of him and her. They were sitting next to each other on a wooden bench in the garden smiling nervously at the camera, frozen in time. He turned it over and on the back she had written, 'You will never forget me – C.'

He fell back on the bed and staring at the ceiling, his mind began to wander back to those days at the home.

CHAPTER FIFTEEN

It was inevitable, given the gene pool from which he was descended, that Billy Casey would grow into a handsome young man with his jet-black hair and brown eyes. He was athletically built with an olive complexion inherited from his dad, married to the self-belief and outgoing personality inherited from his mum. He was a battler, a confident young man who was certain he would become a success.

After leaving school, he secured himself a job down at the Bull Ring Market where he put to use his 'gift of the gab' and his undoubted good looks to charm his customers, especially the ladies. The older ones loved his charismatic banter. Besides being a charmer, he had a way with people and his openness and confident smile meant he was well liked. He sold fruit and veg on the stall of an old schoolmate, Roger.

He chatted away easily, never forgetting a name or a face, which impressed his customers. His friendly and outgoing personality encouraged the shoppers to visit 'that nice young man on the fruit and veg stall'. He hooked them further by offering them a 'Billy bonus' as he termed it, consisting of an extra apple, orange or banana in the bags of his regular customers, especially the older ones.

'Don't look inside that bag 'til you get it home, my darlin,' he would tell them, 'and you will have a nice little surprise for after your tea tonight. It's a Billy bonus, only for my very special customers though.'

They would come back. He had just made a contract with them, formed a bond with that simple action topped off with that winning smile, and the job was done.

His constant chatter and sales pitch was a feature for any passer-by to stop and watch, outshouting the other stall holders and getting good crowds round him. Roger loved having Billy working for him as he brought in plenty of trade, moving the produce quickly, and that meant more money in his pocket. He appreciated Billy's efforts over his first couple of years and in return for his hard work, he lent him the deposit to buy a second-hand Mini. They were a very popular, cheap to run and nippy little car which saved him getting up so early, allowing him an extra half hour in bed.

Billy became a well-known face around the market, well-liked by the other traders who would often pop over to his stall for a chat and a cup of tea with him during their break, to swap stories or more usually, talk football.

The market was full of characters but one in particular, regularly seen around the market selling from a suitcase, was a fellow by the name of Teddy 'the Hook' Criglan. Teddy enjoyed selling dodgy gear during the day and spending his nights doing whatever was required by his boss. For many years Teddy had been in the employ of Lenny Freeman.

His two favourite cons at the market involved selling cheap fake perfume and ladies' stockings: the former being bottles with 'authentic' stickers filled with a substance knocked up in his kitchen at home; and the latter, stockings that had no feet in them; funnily enough, with his reputation and his hook, he never suffered from customers coming back to complain about the faulty goods he had sold them.

Teddy didn't fear anyone and never had to do much more than give a look or a wave of his hook to anyone who thought they might want to take a liberty. However, to those who knew him well, he was a big friendly bear of a man. To those who upset his boss, he became their worst nightmare.

He looked every bit the enforcer, having quite a large head with long beer-jug handle ears, thin orange eyebrows over azure blue eyes, all topped off with red hair styled in a crew cut. His nose, because of his profession, had been redesigned on a number of occasions. The majority of it was flattened but the tip still stood up proudly. He permanently had a cigarette dangling from the corner of his mouth and most of his conversations took place through the haze it created. If there was ever a stereotype of the local 'heavy' Teddy was it, down to the sheepskin overcoat.

Stories of Teddy's fighting prowess were legend and he had been responsible for causing some horrific injuries, usually on behalf of 'the gaffer', settling some dispute or other. At his worst he was a cold-hearted, violent man and other villains feared and respected the man. His brutality, however, kept some sort of order in the city's underworld, of which Lenny believed he was king.

A few young bucks had chanced their arm against Teddy in an effort to steal his crown, but always with an unsatisfactory outcome. One of the guys at the market had recently told Billy the story of an incident involving Teddy which had taken place in a pub in Digbeth the previous week.

Apparently, a local young pretender, full of drink, made some silly and regrettably stupid comments loud enough for

Teddy to hear. Teddy tried to ignore the lad but as he left the gents' toilet at the rear of the pub, the pissed-up young hard man was waiting for him and continued his tirade of abuse.

Teddy had only wanted a quiet drink with a few friends and didn't particularly want any trouble that night but now he had had enough.

'Look, you drunken little bastard, I'll give you five seconds and if your ugly dial is still in front of me I will seriously rearrange it.'

'Fuck off, you old bastard,' screamed the youngster, who took a swing at Teddy.

That was his first and sadly last mistake. Teddy was an old hand at street fighting and he saw it coming, ducked and swayed and slid around the side of the lad whose momentum took him past Teddy, who then swung his hook and buried it in the right arse-cheek of the unfortunate youth. The guy, who squealed like a pig, was lifted on to his tiptoes as Teddy jerked up his hook. Now facing the wall and his hands reaching up to support himself, he squeaked, 'Ooh, my arse! Teddy, I'm sorry, please.'

'Repeat after me,' grunted Teddy as he pushed hard with his hook, 'I am very sorry for interrupting your evening, Mr Criglan, and I promise not to fuck with you ever again.'

The lad repeated the sentence and as Teddy pushed him off his hook the lad fainted and immediately fell to the floor.

Apparently, after the lad regained consciousness he got a taxi to the hospital and when asked what had happened, explained that he had fallen off a step ladder onto a spike, on top of some metal railings, while cleaning the front windows at home. At least he had the common sense not to mention Teddy's name.

Funnily enough, the lad's name was Roger Cox, so his initials were RC and from then on everyone called him 'Arsey', in a double reference to the part of his anatomy in which Teddy's hook had been inserted and his own initials.

Billy's approach had always been not to judge anyone until they gave a good reason why you should take a dislike to them. Teddy warranted respect, that was a fact, especially with his connections, but he had been civil and friendly towards Billy on the few occasions their paths had crossed.

Today he would get to know him a little better.

Teddy always had a watcher whilst dealing from his suitcase. A quick shrill whistle from his lookout would alert him to shut up shop and scarper, as the police were nearby. He had set up near Billy's stall when he heard the warning whistle and in his haste and with his cumbersome hook, he fumbled his suitcase and tripped over the open lid, sprawling on the ground. He was lying prostrate, looking up, when Billy swiftly leaped over the side of his stall and bundled both Teddy and his suitcase under his stall and out of sight.

A policeman rushed round the adjoining stall and gasping for breath, shouted, 'Okay, where's he gone?'

'Who?' replied Billy.

'Teddy the hook,' said the policeman.

'Oh, he disappeared off down towards St Martins,' Billy lied.

Off the officer ran and up popped Teddy from under the stall.

'Billy boy, I owe you one.'

Billy stuck out his right hand to shake hands, only for Teddy to proffer his hook. They both burst into laughter as they looked down at the absurdity of the situation.

CHAPTER SIXTEEN

Upstairs in the farmhouse, he had fallen asleep and woke to the sound of Mick shouting up to him from the kitchen, 'Breakfast's ready.'

He slowly opened his eyes and looked around the room and realised he had slept the whole night through. He was still clutching the photograph to his chest. He jumped out of bed, put the photograph back in his bag and made his way downstairs to the kitchen where Mick was serving up a monster fry-up.

As they both tucked in Mick said, 'After breakfast I'll show you round the place so that you get your bearings.'

'Fine, Mick,' Connor replied as he wiped his toast round the plate to soak up the sauce.

They left the dirty plates next to the sink and walked out into a cool morning. Mick motioned Connor to follow with a nod of his head and they made their way across to some barns. He pulled open the big wooden doors to reveal the garage workshop with various cars and vans in different stages of repair. A drop side tipper wagon, used for delivering building materials for his building jobs, was parked at the back near piles of bricks and timber, a cement mixer, odd pieces of scaffolding and other equipment.

He began to swing the doors closed and said, 'That's about all I can show you, laddie. Tomorrow you get yourself up and be on time; wait outside the doors here at seven and Shane will set you to work. By the way, there are acres of woodland to walk round and explore if you like. I've got an area down there where you can practise some shooting. I'll show you that at the weekend when I've got time to teach you how to use a rifle. And see that old car over there?' he pointed to an old battered Ford Anglia. 'Get in that when you want and teach yourself how to drive.'

They settled down back in the kitchen and they finished off their mugs of tea. Mick revealed that he used to run the businesses with his brother who had died some years ago, and then bizarrely switched subjects to make it plain that women were good for one thing only, adding, 'and after that you have to get rid because they talk too much and talking in my line of business is dangerous.'

Connor wasn't upset by his remarks as women had ruled and ruined his own life, so as odd as the change of subject may have been, he was happy to feel in good company.

He had a couple of weeks working in the garage with Shane, Mick's mechanic, and then did a couple of weeks out on the building site. He decided he preferred working outside; more freedom and the open air suited him better, finding that he liked the physical nature of the work.

The brickies Mick had working for him laid the bricks pretty quickly and kept the youngster busy with their constant need for mortar, leaving the lad worn out at the end of each day. He wasn't fazed by the hard work and gained their respect for his strength and determination.

After a couple of months, the foreman bricklayer allowed him to lay some bricks and taught him the rudiments of bricklaying which he picked up quickly, listening and learning just like Mick had wanted.

Connor was happy in his own way for probably the first time in his young life and the pair settled down to a comfortable relationship working and living together.

But Mick had bigger plans for Connor. Part of his plan would ensure that the young lad learned the skills that each trade brought to site by putting him with all the different trades: the ground workers who dug the foundations; the concreters; the bricklayers; carpenters; roofers; plumbers and electricians, so that his knowledge of each process was thorough and comprehensive. He also learned how to read and understand building plans, how to scale off measurements from drawings. Mick introduced him to his suppliers and discussed how to contain costs and negotiate deals.

'If you are going to be a builder you need to know what these lads do on site. What constitutes good workmanship, but especially what is poor and below standards because you will find if they can get away with delivering unacceptable quality, they are making you look stupid. I never like them to believe they can get away with that.'

Connor developed into a reliable second-in-command and as time went on, Mick found he could confidently rely on the young man who had become a tough and threatening character, mimicking his boss. He was a good organiser and when Mick was away he would take over and Mick seemed to be away a lot.

His confidence grew and he became a harsh task master. The men on site came to both fear and respect this young man, who allowed no slacking and had a hair-trigger temper if anyone upset him.

They remembered the day he had stopped them all working on site and had called them together. He was taking a tip from

Mick and aimed to make sure these lads didn't take him for a mug. He walked over to a garden wall the brickies had just finished building, and began ranting.

'If you think this is good enough for me, you're dreaming,' he shouted as he pointed to the brickwork. 'Whoever laid these bricks has lost the perpendicular joints and made a very fuckin' shoddy job. I didn't know we had Ray Charles laying bricks for us. This is not good enough and—' he pushed with all his might, causing the wall to fall over, 'you will clean up the bricks and rebuild it. Do you understand me?' he glared at the cowering group.

He was confident they wouldn't chance an argument with him and as he stared them down, one by one they shuffled over to the pile of bricks and started the process of cleaning them up and rebuilding the wall. He had laid down his marker and established his position with the men. He knew they would take no more liberties. He had that rush again, not as good as sex or a fight, but he felt good about himself.

At nineteen, he was responsible enough to take on the challenge of managing a building site from the start of the build, dealing with materials, men and the scheduling. The first part of Mick's plan had been a success and he was proud to see Connor adopt a similar style to his own.

So the second and most important part of Mick's plan was about to be unveiled.

After work, they usually sat in the kitchen relaxing, talking about what had gone on that day. Mick decided that tonight would be different. He wanted to educate Connor on the history of Ireland. He felt it was important that the lad knew why he, and many like him, hated the English and hoped it would spark something in the boy and align him to the cause.

'What do you know about Ireland and its history, laddie?' Mick asked.

'Nothing,' came the reply.

'Well let me tell you what the British did to the people here when they used to govern it. Way back in time in the seventeenth century, when they had managed to quell what they termed 'the belligerent native Irish people', they rewarded those who helped them in the battle by giving them vast tracts of land. Those Irish, Scottish and English Protestants who had aided William of Orange in his victory over James the Second were encouraged to settle here. Mainly in the north, these people established the Protestant religion. Down here, we were always proudly Catholic.'

Mick warmed to his subject. 'We had some very rich aristocratic English families owning thousands of acres of our land and the Irish families who worked the land made very little money for their hard labour in the fields. They were saddled with having to pay their rent even when their crops were ruined by bad weather. A deep hatred grew in the hearts of the people, who couldn't fight back against the tyrannical rule of their landlords. Any tenant who didn't pay up was summarily evicted with the aid of the local police, who often knocked down walls and took off roofs of the cottages to ensure the tenants didn't return.'

Mick stood up and became a little more animated as he clenched his fists and continued. 'They devastated whole communities and were harsh and heartless. We were not meant to be ruled by them and our people were badly treated. They were vicious in their treatment of us but they couldn't break us. Many starved and many died but we are a strong and proud people. Was it our religion that carried us through the struggles? I don't know but they were Protestant and we were Catholic and that became the barrier that could never be breached. From the beginning, it was a religious fight between Protestants and Catholics, Britain and Ireland. So money from Britain improved life in the north, whilst in the south we were still classed as farmers and labourers and had little. But the belief remained that the north was ours and any rule that kept the two separate was unacceptable. No true Irishmen worth his salt could accept that the English had claimed a part of Ireland; it was an insult and so the War of Independence began, a battle which the Irish Republican Army would commit to until Ireland was reunified and the British were kicked out. The battles fought against the British were organised from Dublin but in many people's eyes, especially round here, Cork was the real capital of Ireland, not Dublin,' he said.

'Cork,' he added, 'was very active in the fight and was termed Rebel Country and we are proud of it!'

He told of the Easter Uprising and how the British had sent in thousands of troops, and how they had killed many civilians. Mick sneered, 'Later, they even sent in the evil Black and Tans, all ex-soldiers from the First World War, to help keep control. They were violent and vicious bastards. In December 1920, the story goes that the local IRA boys managed to shoot dead a soldier just north of here. The retaliation from the British Army was severe and brutal and they burnt Cork to the ground. They set fires in major buildings in the city and burnt down about five acres of the city centre. That night – and this is where the whole thing gets personal – they also killed two IRA men.'

Mick coughed to clear his throat as the emotion of what he was about to say overcame him.

'One of those men was my father. I was only two and my brother was a babe in arms at the time but my mother told me that they were lying in bed that night, when soldiers burst through the doors around midnight. They pulled them both out of bed and shot my father dead in front of her. She grabbed me and my brother and hid in the woods. She had to move in with friends as she was too frightened to return to the farm although a couple of years later, just after home rule had been established, she felt it was safe to return home. When I was old enough I joined the local brigade with my brother and we made a promise that one day we would get revenge. My mother died when I was a young man. She never got over what happened to my daddy and hated the idea of us being volunteers, and worried that we would follow him to the graveyard. I'm afraid she beat us to it.'

Silence followed as Mick sat staring out of the window distraught at the memories, his distant look faded.

'I think that's enough history for tonight. I need a drink and a little space if you don't mind. There's more to tell you but we'll leave it 'til another time.'

He filled his whisky glass and went out on the veranda.

The next morning being a Saturday, Mick had cooked breakfast which they both devoured ravenously, after which Connor sloped off down the fields. Mick left it a while and then decided it might be an ideal time to check out something that had recently been on his mind.

He knew that Connor had been spending a lot of time down the fields, practising shooting. He was very keen to find out more about Connor's ability with a rifle as he knew the young man had enjoyed his introduction to firearms. Mick had encouraged him to practise and set up some targets to aim at.

The lad had recently been telling Mick that he was getting better, bringing back some of the targets that were riddled with bullet holes. Now was the time for Mick to see for himself.

He found Connor in the bottom field. He had brought along his powerful binoculars and sat on a fallen log.

'Okay, laddie, let's set up and you can show me what you can do. Fire away.'

From the distance of about fifty metres the lad hit every target, even scoring some bulls' eyes. Mick lowered the binoculars and said, 'Not bad, laddie, not bad at all. Now let's move onto the next line of targets. Now they would be about a hundred metres away so it will take a little more concentration and a steady aim.'

The lad's unerring accuracy astonished Mick as he looked through the binoculars.

He lowered them once more and raised his eyebrows.

'Connor, that is some shooting. You have an obvious skill with that rifle and I'm amazed at your accuracy. I think you have a God-given talent and it's given me some ideas. Set up some two and three hundred metre targets, then four and five hundred and keep practising.'

He said no more and began walking back to the farmhouse, deep in thought.

Connor had grown to respect Mick and they had built a strong relationship, for which he was grateful. No one had really bothered much with him and the feeling of contentment with his lot in Cork since he had met Mick made him feel confident and self-assured. He would never have had the chance to learn the building trade, learn to drive, shoot rifles and guns or enjoy the freedom that he had here.

The negative and angry feelings which had been so raw and dominated his life had been quelled, for a while. He had also found Mick's story regarding his father and the reasons for joining the IRA very revealing. It had shown something deep inside the man: a steely resolve and a cast iron mind-set which gave him a fierce belief that what he was doing was right. He understood how Mick felt. It was a deep, dark anger, a hatred even; an emotion that was a serious motivational driving force. A force that drove them both.

That evening after dinner, Mick concluded his story. They sat across from one another at the kitchen table and Mick began.

'So, Connor, let's finish off your history lesson and maybe at the end you will understand a lot more about what makes us feel the way we do about our country and what's been perpetrated on us by the British.

'When the Government of Ireland Act was passed, dividing Ireland into two self-governing entities, of course the Protestants up north accepted it readily but so did we. We at last had our own country, the Irish Free State with De Valera as our first leader. So the division was made but we hated them for stealing the north and many of us would never forgive them. Over the following decades, the IRA continued the fight and I was part of it, along with my brother, causing a little havoc. As time went on though, a feeling of anger and discontentment grew because a lot of us in the movement felt that we were ineffective and disorganised. The old ways weren't working. We needed new direction. Arguments over differences in ideology became fierce. Many of us felt guilty of never offering enough protection and support to our Catholic brothers in Belfast, and the violence from Protestant paramilitary groups up there was increasing. They were getting stronger and more organised, and were launching attacks against our people indiscriminately. We were ill prepared. Most of our arms were what was left over after the Border Campaign and they were old and out of date. If we were seriously going to take the fight to them, we needed the arms of modern warfare. We needed to re-organise ourselves, establish a fighting army of volunteers with a proper structure, well-armed and prepared for the battle. So we reorganised and from the ashes of the IRA, the Provisionals were born. It's our duty, Connor, as good Cork men, to continue the fight for all those who have given their lives for the cause.'

There were a few moments of silence before Connor said, 'Wow, Mick that's some story.'

'It's no story, laddie, it's the truth and I hope you took in everything. It's important you understand the history of your country because in the future you might need to make some decisions based on the Irish truth not the British lies, and why we must never surrender.'

The history lessons had been an insight into what drove the man. The murder of his father was something Mick would never forgive and revenge burned in his soul. These people would never give up their fight.

So Connor's lessons were complete and with it came the realisation that he would have to play a part in this war, if for no other reason than out of respect for the man. But Mick already knew that.

CHAPTER SEVENTEEN

Billy Casey had started a relationship with a girl named Rita Moss, whom he had known since they were kids at school. She had the look of a 'sixties pop star with her beehive hairstyle and choice of make-up. She was tall and slim with a bright personality and sparkling hazel eyes.

They were both at one of the Friday night dances at the social club and got talking, finding they got on well. So it wasn't long before they started dating regularly. A lot of girls chased Billy, so Rita felt quite proud that he had chosen her, but his attraction to her was not just based on the physical looks. He liked her common sense and her work ethic which matched his own. He got up at five every morning to get into town to set up the stall in the market and Rita also started early, helping her father at the bakery. So they had a lot in common.

Rita also had a calm and caring nature and that seemed a good thing as he was like his mum, a voluble character. They dovetailed nicely. She had captured him by just being herself and being 'normal'.

Rita's father, Harry, was delighted when she brought Billy home to meet him and his wife Gloria. Harry could see Billy was confident and had a 'can do' attitude. He had big ideas and plans and an engaging personality. Mr and Mrs Moss believed that Billy would certainly amount to something in the future, so they encouraged the relationship. They also knew William and Mary as good people in the local community and that counted for a lot too. Both sets of parents were happy with the match.

While they were courting, Sunday afternoons and evenings were usually spent at the Moss' house. It caused a slight upset to Mary as she too enjoyed the ritual of Sunday dinner with her family, but she accepted it all with good grace because she could see her son was happy.

After dinner, Harry and Billy would often go out into the back garden to sit and chat while the washing up got finished inside. They talked of many things and one warm September afternoon, while enjoying a glass of beer, Harry turned to Billy.

'Did you know that Fred Steele, who runs the café two shops up from us, was considering selling up and moving on? He's got a bit worried now the battery factory has closed down and he thinks it will hit him hard, so he wants out.'

'Oh, does he?' replied Billy, whilst he watched a busy bee collecting pollen from one of Harry's foxgloves in the well-kept beds of flowers. He turned to look back at Harry and said, 'and what does that mean to me?'

'Well, I think with a new team taking over and sprucing the place up and breathing a bit of life into it, it could still make someone a very good business.'

'Are you thinking of expanding then, Mr Moss?'

'Look, Billy, it's about time you started calling me Harry, especially if my plans come together. So the answer to your question is no, I'm not thinking of expanding but I do know a young couple who would be the ideal new owners.'

Harry Moss waited for his moment and a few months later, when the young couple were celebrating their engagement, exactly two years from the day they first met, he took them aside.

'You two are made for one another and this business will be the making of you. So here's a present that will give you an opportunity to build something together and fulfil some of your dreams. I'm sure you will make a success of it.'

Harry presented them with the deeds to the café.

The pair didn't take long over being engaged, getting married in June just six months after their engagement party.

Their white wedding at St Edwards Church was a great Casey family celebration. The mother of the groom could hardly contain her pride at seeing her oldest son getting married, her youngest son as best man and her beautiful daughter as bridesmaid.

The weather had been kind to them, having started off with a huge thunderstorm in the morning only for it all to blow over to leave a bright, sunny afternoon for the service.

After the ceremony, in a quiet moment as the photographs were being taken, Mary slipped back into the church. She crossed herself automatically as she walked to the front pew, where she sat down and offered her thanks to God for the happiness she had been given. But Mary asked one more favour before she left.

'Please keep my children safe from harm.'

She crossed herself again and made her way towards the blazing sunlight which filled the doorway, regarding the brilliant light as a sign of His agreement to her request. She walked happily into the bright light.

The reception was held in the private room upstairs at the social club and after a sit-down meal and the speeches, the evening was spent dancing to a popular local band, drinking and enjoying the occasion.

As the evening was drawing to a close Billy climbed upon the stage and took the microphone, calling for hush.

'Just for a minute, please,' he shouted above the din, 'if I can just say a few words.'

As everyone quietened down, he continued.

'This has been a wonderful day which, without our parents' input, would never have happened.'

The remark got some jeers and cheers but Billy continued.

'No, I didn't mean like that, you dirty lot, I mean Harry and Gloria and my mum and dad, Mary and William. Both sets of parents have been brilliant to us and we want to thank them for their love and support. Family is important to both our parents; I know my mum has made it her life's work to ensure our family was safe and secure, loved and cared for. Her early life wasn't easy, coming over from Ireland as a young girl with nothing, but she made a future for herself and as we grew up, we had what she and dad could afford. They showed us that hard work and determination will provide its own reward but more importantly, they gave us something that didn't cost a cent – love. When you have grown up with that solid foundation, you look for a partner who has those same points of reference and luckily I found Rita, and I love her and thank Harry and Gloria for producing such an amazing woman.'

His audience were emotional, with tears and cheers and sobs, especially from his mum and Bridie who were holding each other's hands and weeping together.

'I'll tell you all something else my mum told me. In life, we all have one love and we are just plain lucky if we find that special one. You know when you have found it and your heart sings. Mum found it and I have too. But enough of all that. I know you have all been waiting for this moment,' he paused. 'I will now sing a classic Elvis song which sums up marriage and is entitled—Jailhouse Rock. No, no, not really,' he laughed. 'That was a joke; this song says it all, Reet.'

He turned to his bride and looked lovingly into her eyes. He had captivated his audience with his touching speech and as a hush descended on the noisy gathering, he took Rita's hand and began to sing their favourite Elvis classic, 'Can't help falling in love'.

At the end of his performance there was a rousing ovation and as he passed Ryan on his way down from the stage, he pulled him towards him and hugged him tight.

'There you go, brother. as I always say. Leave 'em wanting more.'

There was no time for a honeymoon as the newlyweds had decided that the next two months would give them just enough time to complete the renovations and fit out their café. They both wanted to get the business up and running as soon as they were officially Mr and Mrs Casey, and set themselves a deadline. After painting and decorating, cleaning and getting some new appliances fitted, installing a new counter, cash register and new tables and chairs, they were more or less ready to go.

Harry Moss knew a thing or two about business and helped the young couple to set up, advised on a business plan and gave them the working capital to get going. He, of course, benefited from the new owners buying all their bread, cakes and pies from him. Harry was indeed a smart business man.

Mary and William were delighted to see their oldest son's life develop so well and his marriage to Rita was a happy event. Mary was especially happy, relishing the idea of her children blossoming and growing, forming happy and solid relationships and settling down.

Billy getting married and opening the café, young Ryan being made an area manager with his company and Maria starting work, were all great achievements for Mary's parenting. She realised that she had to accept the fact that as they got older, the children would need her less, leaving home and pushing on with their own lives. One by one, she knew they would flee the nest of comfort and love she had built for them all and she feared that prospect, knowing it would hit her hard.

CHAPTER EIGHTEEN

One night, as he was on his way back from the toilet, Mick passed Connor's bedroom door and could hear the lad was restless and mumbling in his sleep. He thought he heard him say a girl's name.

The next morning, Mick cooked them up a breakfast and as they sat eating at the kitchen table, he asked Connor if he had had a bad dream or nightmare as he heard him calling out a girl's name.

'My past, Mick,' he said, only revealing part of the story.

'Well, young fella, I think the sap must be rising. You need a woman and I think it's high time we went into town and had ourselves a night out. A belly full of beer and a couple of whores would sort us both out, what de ye say?'

Connor felt a familiar feeling stirring in him.

'I'd like that just fine, Mick.'

Later that night they found themselves in a rough pub down by the docks and Mick was well on his way to getting drunk, lurching up from his bar stool, throwing his arm around Connor and pulling him towards him, slurring his words.

'Come on, young fella, let's find ourselves a couple of women.'

A little drunk himself, Connor was excited at the prospect of having some sex again. It had been a long time.

It didn't take long for them to get propositioned as they walked down the dark alleyways. Two women appeared from the shadows. Mick pulled one aside, having made his choice. She looked like an old boiler. He pushed her up against a wall and was demanding she gave him a blow job.

'Not for a fiver, ye tight bastard,' she screamed.

Mick slapped her hard across the face and forced her onto her knees as he opened his trousers. He began to force himself on her and threatened her with another beating unless she performed right there and then.

Connor was calmly taking stock of what he had got: the overall look suited him fine, a busty woman with peroxide blonde hair and black roots, heavily mascaraed eyes, ruby red lips and a skirt short enough to urge him into immediate action.

He thrust his hand between her legs. She pushed his hand away coolly.

'Steady down, cowboy, let's discuss prices first. A hand job'll be a fiver and full sex twenty.'

'I need a good fuck,' he replied.

As a clap of thunder exploded over head he pushed her under the eaves of an overhanging warehouse roof. He spun her round and pulled up her skirt, pushing her head forward so that she was bent over, leaning against the wall. He was ready for action, unzipping himself and with a grunt he pushed hard and entered her, rhythmically plunging in and out. Holding her hips tight he increased the speed.

Suddenly he thought of her. Would he always see her when he was having sex? It didn't matter: it wasn't such a bad image to have in his mind at this moment.

As the rain cascaded down and soaked the cobblestones, the street shimmered under the low light giving the appearance of an ice-skating rink. In a distorted and grotesque parody of an Olympic Pairs performance, the conjoined couple danced to their finale.

CHAPTER NINETEEN

The notice boards at Ryan's secondary school were full of news of trials or practice sessions for various sports to encourage the new intake to have a go. He possessed excellent hand-eye coordination and was confident in his ability to excel at most of them.

Whatever he tried, he didn't take long to become more than proficient.

He joined the table tennis club, enjoying for the first time in his life being able to play on a full-size table and not on the small dining table back at home. Basketball, cricket, rugby, tennis, badminton, athletics; he was more than capable at them all but some would need to be given a miss. He needed to make choices.

Rugby was a 'no-no' as it coincided season-wise with football, and the racquet games seemed a bit middle class to him. Cricket in the summer and football in the winter were his major decisions, plus he managed to fit in basketball and table tennis.

His football skills were way ahead of the other kids, having played with his older brother and their friends. He was stronger and physically more able to match the skills and strengths of older boys, being invited to play in school age teams two years older than him. He was aided by physical education teachers who imparted their knowledge to develop his talents, ending up captaining the football, basketball and cricket teams.

He was proud to represent the city at all of those sports but one of his highlights had been leading out his school eleven at the Nursery Ground, which was right next to Warwickshire Cricket Club in Edgbaston. It was the final of the Docker Shield.

His team won that day, with Ryan hitting the final runs needed by smacking a six over the high fence surrounding the ground, the ball sailing over Edgbaston Road and directly into Cannon Hill Park.

Ryan's young life was totally entwined with Billy's and when he was old enough, he was proud to be on the same football pitch, happy to play second fiddle. He just enjoyed being part of it all.

When he was a youngster, he was always tagging along with Billy and the bigger lads, joining them at St Andrew's to cheer on the Blues. He loved the passion and fervour created by the crowd during the matches and the raw emotion experienced in those ninety minutes. He was as hooked on the drug that was Birmingham City as his brother was.

He was a diligent and steady worker at school rather than a standout but still managed to get six O levels, staying on at school to study for his A levels. He managed to get a pass in English literature but really the main objective was to play sport and delay the passage to adulthood, responsibility and work.

Eventually, he couldn't put off the next phase of his life and having searched the local newspaper, he found an advertisement for a job that seemed interesting and challenging. He applied and after attending the formal interview, was employed as a trainee contracts representative for a national roofing company.

He learned estimating, product knowledge, ordering, labour control and management skills from his boss, Les, and the other senior reps who took the young fellow under their wings.

As far as his love life was concerned, Ryan had chased a few girls but hadn't met anyone he could get serious about until he met the love of his life.

He met Jennifer when she had arrived at his Aunty Kathleen's house as an au-pair girl, helping round the house and looking after her two young children. The placement was organised by William as a favour for an old friend, who had moved 'down under' to retire and wanted his granddaughter to have a taste of life in England.

The news of the arrival of this strikingly attractive young girl from Australia captured his imagination and he couldn't resist visiting the big Tudor-style house in Harborne to see what all the fuss was about.

He would never forget the first time he saw her. She was standing with her back to him doing some washing up at the sink. Quietly, he stood in the doorway and gave himself the opportunity to run his eyes over her from top to toe and drink in the stunning figure, the legs, the pert backside, the dark brown hair. When she turned round with those big brown eyes, those sexy full lips, the sculptured high cheek bones, the special curve of her eyebrows, she was stunning. He was speechless for a while.

The moment when she turned round seemed to be burnt into his memory, caught in slow motion; forever on replay when he needed to be reminded of what they were about. He would never forget it. Some people say you can't fall in love at first sight but the proof was, it happened for him that evening.

'Hello, I'm Ryan, Kathleen's nephew,' he said as she slowly turned round.

'Ooh and nice to meet you, Ryan. I'm Jenny, and how long have you been standing there?'

'Not long enough,' he cheekily replied.

She took the compliment in good humour.

'Would you like a cup of tea?' she offered, trying to hide her embarrassment.

'I reckon that would be a good idea,' he replied and stretched out his hand which she held and gently shook to greet this handsome fellow. She definitely liked the look of him.

He sat at the kitchen table and she brought back two cups of tea.

'Have you been out much and had a look round Brum since you arrived?'

'No, not yet, I was just waiting for the right person to come along to be my tour guide.'

'Well, luckily for you, I happen to be a fully-fledged Brummie. Born within the roar of the crowd at St Andrew's; the Blues by the way are the only team to support in this city. I am available for unpaid tours of the city's fleshpots and drinking dens, and know the city like the back of my hand.'

Jenny laughed and the ice was broken. They sat and chatted about their young lives, discovering that they had a lot in common. They were both born in the 'fifties, with their teenage years straddling the 'swinging 'sixties' which brought with it a revolution in popular music, fashion, art and culture which enthralled a generation. They both loved Tamla Motown and the Beatles, enjoyed sport and treasured their respective families. A couple of hours passed without them realising it. Jenny suddenly stood up.

'Oh, look at the time, I need to get the kids organised for bed.'

'Look, Jen, if you're free Friday evening we could go out for a drink and maybe take in a club too, if you like?'

'I would love that, Ryan, pick me up at eight.'

As they moved to the front door they both leant in at the same time and kissed each other gently on the lips. They had immediate and perfect synchronicity so soon in their budding relationship.

CHAPTER TWENTY

Jenny was only in England for a year. She had promised her parents she would fly back to Australia and continue her education, take up the offer of a place at university and gain the degree she had set her heart on. She realised the attraction she had for Ryan was serious and that was a concern. She wanted to stay in England and be with him but that was the easy thing to do and her conscience wouldn't let her. The thought of what the wrong decision would do to her parents was unthinkable, so it was an option she knew she wouldn't take. So, without saying it out loud, the pair made an unspoken and tacit agreement that they would enjoy these twelve months together and see what happened after that.

She had grown up listening to stories of Birmingham from her granddad and it had always been her dream as a young girl to eventually go there and experience it all. The lifestyle would be so different to her beach-style life. She wanted to visit the places she had heard of and read about in London, which in the 'sixties seemed to be the centre of a world explosion in modern cultural terms.

Australia had its own music scene but it always appeared second best, with the artists wearing the latest British fashions and singing with American accents. No, she longed to be where it was all happening and that was England.

She worshipped the Beatles and was one of thousands who welcomed the Fab Four to Australia, paying homage to her heroes on Pitt Street in Sydney. She screamed and shouted as her teenage emotions overflowed at seeing them in person, especially Paul McCartney who she dreamed of meeting and marrying. With millions of others she was captivated by their clever lyrics, beautiful harmonies and their cheeky nature. The rain that day didn't dampen her feelings.

Soul music from the 'Motor City' of Detroit where Motown had a conveyor belt of talent, as their black artists seemed to have discovered the rhythm and heartbeat of a generation. That music became her favourite to dance to.

She loved her beach side lifestyle and had grown up at Avoca on the Central Coast of New South Wales, attending the local primary school, and then went on to high school where she excelled at sport and music. She was a 'little nipper', as they termed the youngsters who took part in the life saving training and competitions, loving the ocean and the surf club. Most of all, she loved the endless golden beaches at Avoca where the ocean waves crashed in hard and strong.

At sixteen, her parents gave her a little more freedom and after the Surf Club dances, she would sleep at her friend, Sharron's, house in nearby Terrigal.

In 1967, the Beatles had changed it all again as 'Sgt Pepper's' was released and at Sharron's house, they played it non-stop. 'She's leaving home', was Jenny's particular favourite.

'You really are gonna go to England, aren't you, Jen? I've seen the way you sing those words, it's as if they were written just for you but you won't just run off, will you, and meet a man from the motor trade?'

They both laughed at Sharron's pun on the lyrics in the song.

'No, of course not. I wouldn't do that to my parents or you. We've had a long chat about it and they have agreed that when I've finished Year 12, I can go over to England for a year as long as I promise on Pop's life to come back and do my uni course. I still want to become a doctor and have my own practice out in the bush, you know.'

'Yeh, you've always had that dream. Jennifer Dianne Morrison, the country doctor, still sounds good, doesn't it? But you'll be off to London and I've heard that place can turn a girl's head.'

'Well, not me. I'll be too busy doing a bit of au pair work for one of Pop's old mates. Two kids to look after in a big house in Birmingham, not London, so don't worry. Dad says they are good people and they will keep an eye on me. Knowing Dad, I'll probably have an escort wherever I go but what the hell, I'm going and I can't wait. Anyway, I'm prepared to accept anything they say if it means I get one chance to visit England before I settle down and start uni.'

'You're very brave, you know,' said Sharron, 'but you've always had this thing about travelling and adventuring. Even when we were kids, do you remember those hikes you used to take us on? Remember the time we camped for the night at Kincumber Mountain? That was real fun and scary too, wasn't it? A camp fire to cook on and a night-time worrying about snakes crawling into the tent, it was really scary but fun.'

'Yes we've had some great times but you know, Sharron, I feel like this trip to England will be life-changing. Who knows, I might meet a real nice guy and settle down,' she teased.

CHAPTER TWNETY-ONE

Ryan became Jenny's personal chauffeur, taking her to country pubs and the odd restaurant on the outskirts of Birmingham.

One day trip to Stratford on Avon, they found their favourite type of food was lasagne and salad, which they enjoyed in an Italian restaurant in a quiet back lane. Afterwards, Ryan displayed his complete lack of skill with rowing boats. They both laughed so much at his ham-fisted efforts at rowing that in the end, Jenny had to take over the oars and row them back to the boatyard.

'It's a good job I was brought up by the ocean and passed all my life saving badges,' she joked, 'otherwise we would still be out there.'

They sat together on a bench by the Avon, eating an ice cream and reliving their 'lost at sea' moment, both giggling at the memory.

On the walk back to the car, arms linked, he asked her if she would like a weekend in London; he didn't expect such a reaction.

'Oh my God, Ryan, I would love that,' she screamed. 'I've dreamed of going to London since I was a little girl. Can we do all the things I want in one weekend? Oh, this is such a dream come true for me,' she squealed excitedly. 'I'm going to London; I'm going to London,' she repeated over and over.

'We'll do whatever you want. We can make a list,' he said as he pulled a notebook and biro from his jacket pocket. 'Right, what's first on your list?'

'Well, there are all the historic places first. Buckingham Palace, Tower of London, St Paul's, Westminster Abbey, Houses of Parliament, Big Ben. That'll do as a start. Then Oxford Street, Carnaby Street, Harrods, Hyde Park, and the Ritz and—'

'Whoa,' Ryan butted in. 'We've only got two days not two weeks you know.'

'Oh, Ryan, this is so exciting, I'm so happy,' and with that she threw her arms around him and kissed him long and passionately.

They planned their weekend away to tie in with Aunty Kathleen and her husband having no special engagements coming up. Jenny was so excited that for days before, she spoke of little else.

They set off on Friday evening and pulled up to their hotel in a road just off Kensington High Street just after ten at night. They were both worn out after the drive through London's nightmare traffic, so they decided that they would have an early night.

This would be the first time they had slept together, and they both self-consciously got undressed and slid into bed.

Ryan found her warm lips and gently kissed them as he lightly caressed her face. The passion rose in them both and hungrily their bodies writhed in their love for one another, with each taking their turn to dominate from on top until they reached their climax, leaving them both gasping for breath.

The next morning Jenny had risen early and showered, her spirit for adventure naturally waking her, excited at what the day ahead held for her. She had already walked around the streets of Kensington while Ryan slept. When he opened his eyes, he saw her sitting on a chair by the window just taking in the scenery, watching life go by in the 'big smoke.'

'Sorry, Jen, have you been up long?' Ryan said sleepily.

He jumped out of bed and rushed into the shower.

'I've been up since six,' she shouted so he could hear her from the shower. 'I've had a walk up to Kensington Palace and round Kensington Gardens and checked out where we catch the tube. I've mapped out a route for the day from the brochure I picked up in reception. So come on, let's get going,' she giggled.

He got dressed quickly and was ready to go.

They managed to tick quite a few off the list. Together they marvelled at the architecture of Westminster Abbey and the Houses of Parliament and admired Buckingham Palace, where Ryan took a photograph of Jenny posing next to one of the Queen's Guards standing in front of his sentry box.

Then, barrelling down Oxford Street with what seemed to be a million other shoppers checking out the shops and stores. Then there were further stops at Carnaby Street and Trafalgar Square which had Jenny squealing excitedly, 'My friend, Sharron, will never believe this.'

They were walking along Oxford Street, when Ryan suddenly stopped and waved down a black cab and stuck his head through the window to talk with the driver. When he had finished he bundled Jenny inside.

'Ryan, what are you doing?' she asked as they settled into the back of the cab.

'I've got another treat for you,' he smiled.

The journey didn't take long and as they pulled up in a nondescript North London street, Jenny was still oblivious as to where they were and looked across at Ryan for a clue. He said nothing and jumped out of the taxi. He held out his hand to coax her out. He held her hand near the busy road and then taking her by the shoulders, he turned her round.

'Now,' he said, 'have you ever seen that anywhere before?'

It took only a second before it registered.

'Oh my God, Ryan, this is so surreal. We are actually here where they had that photograph taken.'

Tears welled up in her eyes and she kissed Ryan warmly on the lips.

'Go on then.'

'What,' she replied?

'Get on that zebra crossing and I will take a photograph of you.'

Proudly, she walked on to the crossing bare-footed, just like Paul, while Ryan took one more photograph that Sharron wouldn't believe.

On the way back to the hotel, they stopped off in Knightsbridge to visit Harrods, a visit which left Jenny amazed at the size and extravagance of the store and its expensive, luxury goods.

Sunday was spent visiting sites of culture which surprised Ryan, as he thought it might be a bit boring, but he enjoyed studying the paintings at the National Gallery. After the V & A they had lunch in a pub just off Kensington High Street; all brass and Victoriana.

They had already loaded their bags into the car before setting out that morning so they were ready to make the trek back to Birmingham in the late afternoon.

Ryan had really enjoyed the weekend and was grateful to Jenny for organising such an interesting and fascinating tour. It made him realise what a highly intellectual young woman she was and that her thirst for knowledge outstripped his own meagre needs.

On the drive home she slipped her hand into his.

'Ryan, I've loved every minute of our weekend, thank you so much and I want you to know how much I love you.'

He was surprised at her admission as it was the first time she had said those words. He had hoped he would hear them before she returned to Australia and now seemed a good time to tell her how he felt too.

Quickly diverting his eyes from the road, he gave her the little present he had bought for her. He leant across and kissed her warmly on the lips.

'I love you too, Jenn, and,' he paused, 'I bought you this to keep you safe wherever your adventures take you.'

She opened the little blue box and inside there was a gold St Christopher and chain.

'I know you are going back to Australia and I've a feeling you will keep on with your adventuring for some time yet,' he smiled, 'but 'til you come back to me, I want you to be protected. Remember that while you're wearing it, you are carrying my love with you.'

'Oh, thank you, Ryan, I will wear it forever.'

He spent the rest of the trip home deep in his own thoughts, accepting the undeniable fact that he had fallen madly in love with her. He had never met anyone like her. She was vivacious, exciting, full of life and she had captured his heart.

Their time together became more precious as the date for her to leave approached. They crammed in as much time together as they could, with many a night spent at city centre night clubs.

Their particular favourite was the Rum Runner with its small dance floor, seating in side booths fashioned to look like big barrels, and a big bar which was always four deep of punters waiting to get served. Positioned down a cobble stoned laneway off Broad Street, the pair spent many a night enjoying the music and atmosphere there. Usually, they left feeling hot and sweaty, calling at the Tow Rope, the all-night café opposite the club, to get a hamburger and coffee in the early morning.

However, the time was fast approaching for her return to Australia and she would keep her promise to her parents.

Love would have to wait for them both. Neither would have guessed how long that wait would be.

CHAPTER TWENTY-TWO

Their business was a reflection of the two hard-working, caring and resourceful characters who owned it. The caff was a traditional English affair, ideally positioned on the Bristol Road, drawing its fair share of the stragglers but also pulling in others from the building trade, office workers, business men, hospital workers and students.

The doors were always open at six in the morning, by which time the oven and tea urn had been warming for half an hour and it wasn't long before the first customers of the day came pushing through the door. Mugs of hot tea and 'a full English' were the top sellers.

The café stood in a terrace of similar sized businesses with a pub on the corner, a newsagent, supermarket, chemist, a second-hand furniture shop and ladies' hairdresser's, all side by side. Then a small side alley separated those from the three, the café, the bicycle shop and then Moss' bakery.

The café was a warm and welcoming place with the alluring smell of a fry-up enticing the customers through the door, especially in the winter months with the weather outside icy cold and its windows all steamed up.

The walls, or what parts you could see of them between the photographs of Birmingham City stars past and present, were yellowed from the smoke and grease. The cheap, but serviceable, tables and chairs were arranged either side of a central aisle which led up to the counter, behind which stood the ovens and grills positioned against the rear wall. The big tea urn stood on the other side of the till, steaming away.

Billy felt that the mark of a good boozer, or café for that matter, was what it represents to local people, how it fits into the local community, how hard the people who run it are prepared to work to ensure that they provide a warm, friendly and welcoming atmosphere.

The Greasy Spoon, a name Billy chose for its irony, was a place where all and sundry could pop in to have a mug of tea, or even as the students and old folks did, get their one hot meal for the day.

They also had to listen to his incessant chat. His time working the market stalls was now put to good use, in his new role as top of the bill at his 'personal entertainment venue'. He viewed it as his special way of bonding with his customers, entertaining everyone with his wit and humour. His delivery was more old style music hall which the old folks loved and the students viewed with quiet amusement. He was very inclusive though as he liked to involve everyone.

He espoused most subjects: the government; the council; football (mostly concerning his beloved Birmingham City); the weather; his customers; life in general. Somewhat like a master of ceremonies, with his audience, captive, seated, tucking into their fry-ups, he would recount some tale or other.

He also felt it was important to develop links between his regulars and local businessmen, announcing to all as soon as any of them entered his café. It was as if they were the next act on the bill and were making their entrance from stage right. He believed that the introduction of the local tradesmen encouraged trade and bolstered relationships within the community.

'Hello, everyone,' Billy announced, 'we now have Michael, your local milkman, here with us today,' as he backed through the door carrying a crate of milk. He would have his usual mug of tea and a bacon sandwich.

John Cripps sat at the table by the door, demolishing a full breakfast with double everything; he had a big appetite. Back in the day, he had played centre half in the same Sunday football team and his uncompromising style afforded him a similar reputation to a mafia hit man. When he took to the football field, the opposition players were a little terrified.

Who could forget Crippsy? He stood six foot seven and if the height factor wasn't enough to scare the opposition his uncompromisingly aggressive style matched by his fearsome demeanour indeed was. The full force of a cricket ball in the mouth was responsible for him losing those front teeth so when he removed the plate to which they were attached it gave him an unforgiving, scary and fearsome look.

They remembered the one legendary match when having scythed down the opposing centre forward, there was a bit of a tussle in which Crippsy had managed to nut the centre forward. The dazed player got up quickly to continue the tussle, only to end up flat on his back after a right cross connected with his jaw. Then two more tiresome players who wanted a piece of him, followed their teammate to the ground with a perfect one-two. Most hilarious of all was the picture they still had in their minds of the vertically challenged referee slowly backing away to a safe distance from the brawling madman, with total fear in his voice, repeatedly squeaking, 'You're off, you're off.'

The pitch was like a battle field with bodies everywhere. Everyone had a good laugh about it at the social club after that game.

He had his special intro from Billy, 'And at the table with the spectacular view of the Bristol Road, we have 'No drips with Mr Cripps', your local plumber, John Cripps!'

Billy regarded everyone as his bread and butter, so to speak, and his plan was always that they came back often, that's how he liked it. It was his simplicity that won the day; a little humour, an interest in the people and their problems, some social work to new and old customers alike.

A wide network grew around him: friends, businessmen, and he was a great believer in keeping the local constabulary on side too. In fact, his dad's old mate, ex-Sergeant Beefy Jones of the Birmingham Police had a son, David, who was now a detective sergeant and a regular caller who kept Billy up to speed with the dark deeds going on in the city.

In some ways, Billy and Rita were both stuck in the 'fifties of Elvis Presley, Cliff Richard, 'winklepickers' and teddy boys.

Billy still used Brylcreem on his hair just like most kids of his generation had back in the day, with a style that swept it all back and 'quiffed' it at the front, just like Elvis. And in a final tribute to the King, he turned up the collar on the white overall he wore for work.

His wife was his foil. If they had been a comedy double act, she would have been the straight man. She kept the meals rolling while Billy held court. She cleared the plates and wiped the blue marble patterned Formica tables and blue plastic chairs while Billy served up with panache in more ways than one.

Still a chick of the 'fifties with her panstick make-up, heavy with mascara and back-combed beehive hairstyle, Rita was a sort of Dusty Springfield lookalike.

She knew all their regulars by name and revelled in the social life the café allowed her. She chatted away comfortably with all the customers, especially the old dears who would confide most of their problems in her, from ill-health to the next door neighbour's yapping dog. She listened intently and took an interest in their lives, dramas and dilemmas.

They both loved their café life.

CHAPTER TWENTY-THREE

He had come to accept the fact that it rained a lot in Ireland as, once again, it was a very wet Sunday evening. Earlier that afternoon, gathering clouds had signalled that the rain was in 'til the following morning.

He had been shooting rabbits down in the woods. He always had a peculiar feeling when he was in those woods, as if there was an evil force present. He was thinking about what made him feel that way when he saw the headlights of a vehicle enter the property. He walked on in his rain-sodden coat, splashing through the puddles in his wellington boots and as the van drew level with him, he could see it was Mick.

'So I'm back for your birthday, young fella. Let's have a celebratory drink, eh? Jump in and I'll give you a lift back to the house.'

Mick always liked to take a drink in the evening after dinner. Sitting out on the covered veranda, relaxing in a battered but much loved old sofa, gazing out over his acreage and on to the woods in the distance. Tonight would be no different, other than inviting Connor to sit with him because he had a birthday present for the lad.

As they sat on the old sofa together, Mick passed the package across to him. It was impossible to disguise the item although it was rolled up in an old blanket in an effort to provide some surprise.

Connor unfurled the blanket.

'Shit, Mick, what a beauty.'

Mick poured a whisky for them both and eyed the rifle.

'It's known as 'the Widow-maker' as it's been responsible for many a man not returning home to his missus. It's the sniper's rifle of choice. An Armalite AR-18. What do you think?'

Connor closely examined the rifle. Touching it gently, he ran his fingers lightly over it. He embraced it and held it to his shoulder, looking through the sight, wrapping his finger around the trigger, holding it at arm's length, feeling its weight and examining the special folding stock. Folding and unfolding it, admiring his gift.

'Do you like it?'

'It's a fuckin' beauty, Mick,' Connor replied, glassy-eyed.

Mick held up his tumbler of whisky.

'Here's to you, Connor. Happy birthday.'

Connor picked up his own glass and tapped it against Mick's.

'Thanks, Mick.'

They both threw back their heads and swallowed their drinks in one gulp. There followed a few moments of silence.

'Look, Connor, you're a bright lad and you know how involved I am with my work for the Provos. We are stepping things up. Things are going to get more serious and since the split in the organisation, my OC has been heavily involved with the new executive council and the intention is to hit them hard up north. We need to give our people some support up there. The UDR and UDF need a lesson or two and we need to teach them that we are a force to be feared.'

Mick looked straight into the eyes of the young man.

'If you are willing, I think it's time you got a bit more involved in things. You have done me a magnificent job of running the building side of things and if you agree to join me in the fight, we can put young Liam in charge of the building business, if you're up for it? You know something, with your skill with a rifle I think you will make an excellent sniper.'

Connor was proud that Mick had complimented him on his skills, so his decision was easy. He nodded his head and shook hands. Since they had first met, it had always been Mick's plan to train the lad for this day. He was content that his long term strategy had come to fruition.

By way of introduction, Mick decided to take Connor with him on a trip up north to give him some insight into what the troubles looked like at close quarters. He made arrangements, ensuring their trip up north would be safe from intrusion by troops at border control points. This would involve them diverting along tracks and through fields close to the border before meeting with friends from the north who would provide transport.

When Mick drove him around the safer areas of Belfast, Connor was surprised by the amount of graffiti painted on the walls of the houses on the estates. He was awe-struck at the colourful murals painted on the gable walls by both Catholic and Protestant groups alike. The murals gave a sense of belonging and identifying with their area but also sounded a warning to opposition factions to stay clear. Some displayed poignant messages to dead heroes lost in the conflict, others a political statement, but all were a testimony to the violent history of the place.

The one that stuck in Connor's mind was of an IRA sniper holding his AR-18 rifle high, dressed in black and wearing a black balaclava. That mural had become an emotive symbol of the campaign for all IRA followers.

Mick drove him along the Shankhill Road, a strong Loyalist area and then they neared the Falls Road, a staunch Catholic stronghold.

'You see how close these two areas are to each other and how they are separated. It's all nice and quiet today but anything can set it off and within minutes the crowds are out, closely followed by the troops and RUC. One of the worst things the Catholics in the north have to deal with is the marching season. You get parades by the Protestant Orange Orders marching right near Catholic homes, displaying their colours with brashness and bravado, knowing they are legally allowed to march, taunting the locals. They are protected by the RUC and goad the Catholics with it. You can imagine the anger and the response. There are tit for tat reprisal attacks by both sides which continually disrupt life here. You live with the threat of death every day.'

The trip to Belfast really opened Connor's eyes to the hatred that existed between the two factions there and what was happening in the city. It was totally different to life in Cork. His initial view was that it looked like a battle zone, the city divided on sectarian grounds with very obvious boundaries separating the warring factions. Extremely dangerous if you were to stray into opposition territory.

Connor was deep in thought, looking out of the car window later that day as they made their way back south. Mick was wondering what effect the trip had had on Connor and asked him what he had thought of the day in Belfast.

'To be honest with you, Mick, I wouldn't like to live in that hell hole. The stress of living every day knowing a sworn enemy could murder you, doesn't suit me. I like the whole thing we have going on down south; I don't think I could operate up there on a daily basis.'

Mick smiled. He had lived through the chaos, the bloodshed, the danger, the hatred and the killings on many a mission in the north. He had seen men killed in front of him, seen enemies blown to pieces and heard the screams of the injured in the aftermath. He was battle-hardened.

'I know how you feel. You weren't brought up with the killing and the madness. More to the point, I know where your skills lie and if we can use your talent at a distance where you feel safe and in control, I believe we can cause a few problems, don't you?'

Connor felt more comfortable with Mick's suggestion and nodded in agreement.

Mick knew he had him now. He had watched many of his practice sessions down in the woods and accepted that his skill with the rifle was remarkable. The lad was special and from what he had seen of his reaction to the trip north, he was relieved that Connor wasn't fazed by the experience. Throughout the visit to Belfast there was no panic or fear in the young man. He was one cool cookie.

Mick reported back to his OC of the South Armagh Brigade. The decision was made. The pair would form a sniping team, allowed to choose their own targets as long as the OC was kept informed.

The brigade operated more independently from the organization and sided with the Provos. Mick enjoyed the freedom afforded him due to his family's long association with the Armagh Brigade. They appreciated his commitment to the cause and his efforts during the Border Campaign. He had never let them down.

CHAPTER TWENTY-FOUR

Mick received information from local boys on the ground about a prison officer from the Maze who travelled down from Belfast to Crossmaglen to visit his old mum every other weekend.

Mick was informed that the guy liked to take a drink or two at the local pub on a Saturday night. He was known to drink too much and frequently left the pub blotto. Apparently, he never drove his car to the pub as it would be an easy target for a car-bomb. He walked there but took a tortuous route, aware of putting himself on show. His journey to and from the pub however was always the same.

He was known to slip out of the back door of the pub at about eleven and take his usual shortcut down a side alley, which ran behind the pub and came out in a cul-de-sac. He believed he was keeping a low profile and drawing less attention. He was wrong. People had noticed.

Mick had a call early one Saturday morning, informing him that the guy had arrived at his mother's house and would be there for the weekend. The hit was on.

The pair travelled up later that afternoon, waiting until darkness fell to slip over the border and reconnoitre the area. The village lay just over the border in South Armagh and the local boys had left them a van at a disused and derelict farmhouse.

In the evening, darkness had fallen early. They dropped their gear in the barn and drove through the village, identified the pub and checked out the rear exit.

Further checks on the alleyway, a meeting up point, and a safe escape route were carried out. Connor's experienced eye established that there was an unbroken line of sight from the village church. Even more, he could see that from high up on the roof, he would have an open and clear view down to the cul-de-sac, at the end of which stood the exit from the alleyway. Connor would leave nothing to chance. He needed to be sure of the ideal position to deliver his shot.

They drove round once more, and Connor slipped out of the van. Mick would give him ten minutes then return to pick him up. He noted a low-level porch roof over the main entrance from which he could get access up to the main roof of the nave. Up there he could see a parapet wall. He was satisfied that would be the perfect position from which to deliver another man to meet his maker. He slipped away to meet Mick.

Later, at their laying up point, as they relaxed in the old disused farm building, they settled down for a few hours to wait until ten o'clock. The weather was turning from misty light rainfall to a deluge. In the silence and cold of the empty barn, the two sat quietly alone with their own thoughts.

Connor sat with his back to the wall, stripping down the rifle and cleaning each part with intense concentration. The two never wasted words when they were on duty.

He broke the silence and said, 'Mick, it might be a bit slippery getting up to that roof with all this rain, but once I am up there it will be business as usual, no problem.'

'Good lad, Connor. You're happy then?'

'No problems, Mick. Let's get it done and get out of here.'

He carried on reassembling his rifle.

The pair had carried out many missions together but tonight would be their last together. Mick looked across at the young man whose life was about to change.

They had enjoyed a good run over the years since Connor's sniper baptism where he shot dead a British soldier in Lower Falls.

Mick remembered that night very well. It was manic to be in Belfast for them both but it was a mission they needed to execute perfectly to prove to the men at the top that they could be relied upon.

He had studied the young fellow as they drove back south and there was no sign of any emotion. No anxious reaction. Nothing. Cold blood ran through those veins. It was as though he had just shot a rabbit. He remembered nudging his sleepy partner awake as they drove back home and congratulated him.

'You did the business tonight. One question for you, though, Connor,' he added, 'do you know the difference between a shooter and a sniper?'

'What's that then, Mick?'

'A pulse, Connor. A sniper doesn't have one.'

The lad smiled. Those words resonated with him when he thought about it; summed up his existence really. No pulse, emotion or heart. A cold-blooded killer. He liked the thought. He knew he was selfish and cold. He never considered anyone's feelings but his own. He had never had to. He liked this job and he was chillingly efficient at it.

After that first mission, the pair developed into a very well organised and effective team. Targeting British troops, the pair carried out missions successfully in Ardoyne, Andersonstown and Ballymurphy, extinguishing the lives of those enemy soldiers with that special birthday present from Mick.

They trusted each other to carry out their respective responsibilities. Mick's job was to ensure everything was organised to safeguard his sniper and himself. The operations were well prepared.

He was always aware of the possibility of being followed, and would get a bit neurotic and pull over and wait for an hour to ensure that no one was following them. That would make the journey north very time consuming but much safer for them both. He would remind the lad, 'It never does any harm to be careful. One slip up and we end up dead or in the Maze and we don't want either of those.'

The bombs would be laid by others now and if Mick was honest, he was much happier with this arrangement. He often thought about his brother and was determined that the bombs would not claim him too. The only thing Mick would miss was the screams of the dying, knowing that another had died to avenge his father. No matter; his greed for vengeance was now being played out vicariously.

Connor's job, on the other hand, was simple. Sniping appealed to Connor's emotionless and cold nature, he enjoyed the loneliness. He had learned over the years to like his own company. The waiting never bothered him; he became robotic in some respects but none the less effective, getting off his one shot. That's all it ever took.

Mick had drummed it into him. He'd told him that within the organisation it was termed, 'One shot, one kill'. Connor had always kept to that maxim.

In the barn that dark night as time ticked slowly by, Mick chose to reveal the story of how he had lost his brother.

'You know I've mentioned my brother to you before. Well, let me tell you about the night he died.'

Connor looked up in surprise. He had never thought Mick would tell him this story but he was anxious to hear the details.

'Me and my brother were both involved in the Border Campaign; he was one of the main bomb makers in our brigade and I was a planter. We were hiding out at a safe house in a little country village. He was making up the bombs which we used to disrupt the local police forces and troops by cratering the roads and blowing up bridges.

I had left the house for an hour to recce the next target we intended to hit. When I got back, the house was in flames. Some locals had tried to break in to save him but the blaze was so fierce, due to the amount of explosives we had there. I suppose he must have made some mistake. The locals said the noise of the explosion, when it all went up, was ear-splitting. Hopefully, he wouldn't have known much about it.'

He continued, 'So that was another member of my family lost to the cause. It made me question my commitment for a long while but I never lost focus of why I had to keep fighting. In fact, it made me more certain that I was doing the right thing and that my father and brother would have expected nothing less. I do it all for them. I don't feel sorry for myself but I miss my brother badly. I accepted early on that with the struggle, there would be casualties and I have lost my daddy and brother so it's in my blood, and revenge consumes me. I will never give up the fight.'

Mick gazed into the distance and Connor stood up, patted him consolingly on the shoulder and left him alone with his thoughts.

Just after ten that night, the pair pulled up in the church car park. Connor jumped out carrying his holdall and Mick moved the van to the agreed meeting up point in a road a short distance away.

Connor slipped into the dark night. He stood for a short while, just listening. It was still raining but only lightly now and as he stood in the shadows of the church walls, he heard nothing other than the general noises of the night; a distant thump of music, a woman screeching at her kids to get to sleep; and a baby crying somewhere. With his back up against the church wall, he moved noiselessly around to the front to scale the porch, knowing once he had hauled himself up to his sniper's nest, the rest would be simple.

Standing on the wall of the porch, he reached up and felt for a good hand-hold and heaved himself up onto the small gabled roof, his holdall secured over his shoulder. He then carefully walked up the slated roof from where he could scale the outer wall stonework, which had plenty of hand and foot-holds. But as he made his way up the slope of the roof, a slate broke beneath his foot and the broken half of it skidded down and caught in the gutter. He lost his balance for a second and grabbed at the stone wall to steady himself. He waited a while, his heart thumping at the close call. He got both hands on the parapet ledge and pulled himself up and over. He sat down in the box gutter and breathed deeply to calm himself after the exertion.

He was now hidden behind a three-foot high dwarf wall and safely inside a deep, wide lead box gutter from where the slated roof stretched up at an angle behind him. No one would be able to see him from the ground.

Having got himself into position, he unzipped his holdall and took out his binoculars. He was about three hundred yards from the alleyway exit, which he could make out clearly from the ambient light of a lamppost. He had chosen the perfect spot, which provided him with unbroken vision along a short straight road terminating in the cul-de-sac and the exit from the alleyway.

He ran through his routine, assembling his rifle and then carried out another visual, this time through the telescopic sights. He set them for clarity and focus. He checked the force of the wind, very little that night. He would make allowance as his shot was from a higher elevation down to his target at ground level. He would add any speed of movement of the target and factor in the distance and possible bullet drop.

He had practised so often down in the woods, firing off hundreds of rounds, and had noticed the need to make allowances to his aim to take into account different weather conditions. This procedure had become an automatic process, mystical in some ways, as though he was at one with his rifle. He settled the stock of the rifle comfortably into his shoulder, knelt on one knee and steadied his elbow on the top of the wall, resting his finger lightly on the trigger, remembering Mick's words as he got out of the van.

'This bastard gives the lads a hard time inside and he deserves to go. No hesitation, just do it. Hesitate and you are finished.'

He checked his watch. Ten thirty-five. He felt calm. It was well after eleven when the target eventually appeared in the alleyway, his face red and sweaty from too much ale. The easiest shot was always the body, a bigger target but as the man neared the end of the alley and strode into the arc of light from the adjacent lamppost, Connor had the man's head centred in his cross hairs. He breathed in. As he exhaled he smoothly squeezed the trigger. The sound filled the night for a split second then the high velocity bullet smashed into the man's head, which exploded like a smashed melon. He coolly folded away his rifle, picked up his binoculars and packed them away in his holdall. He descended silently to the ground and keeping to the shadows, moved swiftly to the pick-up point. His final mission was complete.

***

The next morning as the pair sat in front of the fire back at the farm, sipping mugs of tea, Mick looked over at Connor.

'Last night was our last operation together, mate. The Brits have started to put the pressure on. The troops raided our boys' homes in Belfast a few days ago, smashing down doors in early morning raids. They arrested hundreds of what they termed 'suspected terrorists' and carted them off to prison. They are upping the pressure so we are going to do the same. The fight is going to continue and our brigades in England are on alert. We plan to cause more disruption than they have seen before. We have active cells in most major cities. There can be four, sometimes up to eight men in the unit and most have a specialist bomb maker. You are probably wondering why I am telling you all this and, well,' he paused, 'it's been decided. You have built up a reputation in the organisation and they are well aware of your talent with a rifle. They have plans for you. Who knows, they might even get you to bump off a member of the government or even a Royal. Anyway, you will be heading back to Birmingham, laddie, and as you came from there originally your return shouldn't ring any alarm bells. You will start off as a sleeper in the Birmingham Brigade, on call when they need you,' Mick paused, noticing the lad was already thinking about what this could mean to him.

'There's another important part though. We want you to establish your own building company and go about your business. There will be money spent on setting you up as we believe that using the front of a building company would be great cover for us, enabling you to establish bank accounts with local branches of the Irish banks. We can then get dirty money in and clean it up, plus the profits you will be making can all be used to finance our operations all over the country. So it's important to get that business up and running as quickly as possible. We have sympathisers who donate money to the cause from all over the world but the executive feel it's high time we made our own money from businesses run by our own. You're young and you're smart and I have told them they will have no worries with Connor Flynn.'

Connor was taken by surprise. He was quite content with the status quo and hadn't bothered to consider his future but he knew better than to argue with Mick. He knew that would be a mistake and he also knew the shadowy figures behind Mick were a murderous bunch and once you were in, you were expected to dedicate your life to the cause. He didn't have a choice. He didn't like being forced into it but he thought it may provide him with the opportunity to finish off some old business.

'What do you think, laddie?'

'Well, that's a bit of a surprise, Mick. I'm pretty happy here. But I suppose the time has come for me to move on. The building company idea is great and I think with what I've learned from you over the years I can get by, and of course a return to Birmingham will give me another chance to do that bit of business that's been on my mind for years.'

'When I first met you,' Mick laughed, 'you said you had a bit of business to do and now it's come up again. All I can say is I hope you get it done this time.'

'Yes, I hope so too,' replied Connor. 'I really hope I do.'

The following day Connor didn't go out to work as it was his last day on the farm. He would be sorry to leave this place and Mick. Living alone wouldn't cause too much hardship either. In his mind he was always in a cold lonely place.

He packed his bags ready for his departure later and while Mick was out organising the lads on site, he had a final walk around the farm and woods.

In the afternoon as the sun began to sink in the west, it cast long shadows. On the veranda, Mick was sitting on the old sofa, relaxing with a glass of whisky, looking out into the distance when Connor returned from his walk carrying a shovel over his shoulder.

'Have you been doing a little bit of gardening before you leave, laddie?' Mick asked.

'Just had to take care of a little bit of business, Mick,' Connor replied. They both laughed.

CHAPTER TWENTY-FIVE

When Jenny returned to Australia, Ryan chased a lot of girls to help him forget but none compared to her: it was just sex in loveless relationships.

Billy had a feeling about his brother and Jenny. He decided he would need to have a chat with his brother with regards to his future.

The brothers sat face to face in the booth at the café when Billy started in.

'I know your problem, Ryan, and it won't be cured by moping around. You can't fool me. This is all about Jenny and I want you to listen carefully to what I'm going to say. When she comes back, and I've no doubt she will, you will need to have yourself sorted out. Start your own roofing business, Ryan,' he advised, 'and within five years you will have established something of which you can be proud. I believe in you, brother. And the best part is,' Billy smiled, 'you could make a lot of money, but you must do it for yourself. Running your own business certainly concentrates the mind and that will take it off other things, and when you're successful you will be a happy man.'

'I don't know, Bill, it's a big step to go from the comfort of wages every month to borrowing money, paying interest, getting enough work, establishing accounts. No, it's too big a risk. I won't be able to do it.'

'Okay,' Billy said thoughtfully, 'so you know all the problems you are going to face and that's half the battle. Do me some projections, you know, simple stuff like a chart with each month of the year and how many sales you expect to do then beneath that your costs, labour and materials, and then running costs. Once you have that plan, we will discuss the next step.'

'Okay, okay,' Ryan repeated. 'I'll try and get it done tonight,' he added, slightly bemused.

He rose to his feet and in the few steps he took towards the door, he brightened and turning back full of confidence, he said, 'You might be right, I can do this. Thanks, Bill.'

His years spent learning the trade, gaining the knowledge required in the roofing game and encouraged by a renewed self-belief and his brother's support, he took that massive step. He borrowed the money from his brother, got an office sorted and employed a good team of quality roofers, having managed to entice them away from his former employers.

He started small and began to establish a good reputation around Birmingham for dealing straight with people and cutting no corners on workmanship.

'Good reputation means repeat business. Deal with people like you would want to be dealt with yourself; look after your clients and your staff and you won't go far wrong,' his brother counselled.

Ryan would keep to that mantra and work long hours to make it a success. It took him a couple of years to get over the losses he made early on but after that he had built a business that was going well. He was on first name terms with the men who counted, the buyers responsible for placing the orders for roofing contracts. Mainly dealing with local builders and homeowners, the fledgling business was now something of which he was justifiably proud.

He also found that he could afford the time to indulge his new favourite pastime of golf, a game which he had taken up after having done irreparable damage to his anterior cruciate ligaments whilst playing football.

Once, football had been the only sport he was interested in but after a knock about with a few mates at the municipal golf course at the Lickey Hills, he found that he had a talent, enjoying the challenge so much that he played at least twice a week to improve his handicap.

Golf would end up becoming a major part of his social life. Even more so when he realised how many of his important clients played the game and how much business was done on the course. To that end, he became a member at Edgbaston Golf Club.

He was grateful to his brother for pointing out the shortcomings of his life and the bits that he needed to work on, without which he wouldn't be where he was today. He enjoyed being his own boss with no one telling him what to do, the freedom to make decisions that were best for his company without consultation elsewhere. He was extremely proud at seeing his name, out and about on the vans, the signage on his new warehouse unit, but especially up high on the scaffolding which announced, 'Another Roof by Casey Roofing.'

However successful he had become, he still carried the emotional damage of having lost Jenny and her return to Australia had hurt him deeply. Although they had spoken by phone a few times and exchanged letters, the news that she was following her dream of becoming a doctor which would take at least five years before she qualified, was a shock to him. He believed he would never see her again.

So life went on for the Caseys.

Billy and Ryan still steadfastly followed the Blues and amazingly, a bright light began to twinkle in the eyes of the city supporters. They had managed to unearth a supreme starlet in the form of a young lad named Trevor Francis. 'Superboy' as the Blues fans had named him, made the first team at just sixteen years of age and his performances were breath-taking to watch.

He had skill and pace and was unstoppable. The coaches hadn't got to him yet so he didn't conform to the safe notion of keeping possession, and would continually try to take on and commit defenders with his turn of speed. He presented something unpredictable to defenders and sorely tested any of them who were slow off the mark.

He scored some memorable goals and the Casey brothers along with the rest of the City faithful, watched in amazement as they admired this raw talent. Billy reckoned he had never seen a better sixteen-year-old, although their dad reminded them that a certain local lad named Duncan Edwards was bigger, stronger and better.

Still, it made for great entertainment and successes against many of the bigger clubs which, including some stunning cup runs and brilliant performances from Superboy, had the Casey boys enthralled to the point of considering that they might win something. Success would be hard to find and that dream wouldn't happen while Trevor wore the blue and white.

CHAPTER TWENTY-SIX

James McAndrew was a member of the Birmingham Brigade and he was detailed to pick up Connor from Birmingham's Elmdon Airport. James, who by day was a bricklayer and foreman for one of the biggest builders in the city, was waiting outside the arrivals area smoking a cigarette. On seeing Connor emerge from the arrivals lounge, he stubbed out his cigarette and walked towards the car park. Connor followed the man in the black leather jacket who he was told would be outside the arrivals lounge. No words were spoken.

They loaded the case into the boot. The pair got into the car and at last spoke.

'It's good to meet you—' Connor paused, allowing time for the man to fill in the blank.

'James,' the man replied. 'James McAndrew.'

'Well, thanks for arranging things here for me, James. What's the craic now?' Connor said with a slight trace of an Irish lilt in his Brummie accent, unavoidable after all the years of living in Cork.

As they made their way across Birmingham from the airport, James answered Connor's question.

'Well, first I will be taking you to your house in Edgbaston. It's got an office on the back to help you organise your building business. Tomorrow I will take you to meet Daniel Murphy, our friendly solicitor. He will run through items such as personal bank accounts, business accounts, registration of business and all of the stuff you need to arrange before you can get going; all above board and legal. Remember, you are a clean skin, you've never been in trouble with police and as far as we know you don't appear on the radar of British Government terrorist lists. You have been hidden away from the UK for a long time so that makes you the invisible man. All you need to do is blend in and create the image of the local friendly builder.'

As they drove through the city many memories flooded back. The city centre seemed to have changed a fair bit since he had left. The Bull Ring and the major roads around it had been redesigned to give the area a new look. Pretty soulless, Connor thought.

They arrived in a nice, quiet tree-lined road of detached houses and as James pulled the car into the drive, he added finally, 'As far as other matters are concerned, you will be contacted and we will let you know how you can help the cause here. We will talk later but 'til then, have a look round your house and relax. I've left a note pad by your phone in the hall with Daniel's address and he is expecting you at ten tomorrow morning. There is some grub in the fridge, milk, bread and butter, and tea. Here's some cash to keep you going for a few days. We will be in touch.'

He handed over the house keys, an envelope and shook hands.

Connor unlocked the front door of his new home and dropped his suitcase in the hallway, deciding to familiarise himself with the layout.

Off the entrance hall, he walked into a lounge with windows overlooking the front garden and driveway. The room was furnished with a sofa, two armchairs, a coffee table, wall units and a television unit, complete with TV.

The dining room was through a double pair of doors and led into the kitchen, which looked really impressive with long expanses of work top, pine units, cooker and fridge. A staircase led to the first floor where there were three bedrooms and a white-tiled bathroom. After living with Mick in those medieval conditions, this was all a bit of a culture shock for him and peculiarly, for a moment, he felt lonely and isolated in this tidy house.

Back downstairs, he found that a door led from the kitchen out to the back garden which was neat and tidy, with the lawns trimmed, and all the plants and shrubs looked well cared for.

He walked out in the darkness and carefully followed a narrow path which led to the back of the garage at the side of the house, attached to which there was a separate flat-roofed building with a couple of windows and a green door. A sign was attached; it read, 'Office' just in case he was in any doubt as to its use.

He opened the garage door, flicked on the light and sitting there was a white transit van. Obviously, they had thought of everything. He realised that they had set him up very comfortably and he knew they would want their money's worth. He wasn't going to let anyone down. He would ensure he played his part, even if it meant building extensions or doing repairs to start off with, it didn't matter, he just needed to get the show on the road as soon as possible.

The next morning after meeting Daniel and getting the paperwork for the business organised, Connor set about getting his company, Flynn Developments, advertised in the local paper and a couple of local trades magazines.

It didn't take him long before he started to pick up small extension jobs and then whilst driving to work one day, he noticed a 'for sale' board advertising a building plot in Harborne which was coming up for auction.

When he got home that afternoon, he contacted Daniel to let him know he wanted to buy it and that he would need some finance to pay for it. He regarded the building plot as his chance to establish himself, leaving Daniel in no doubt that he should secure the plot on his behalf. The next thing he did was to sketch up some rough plans for a four-bed detached house.

A few days later, with more detailed scaled plans in front of him on his dining room table, he began to organise his programme of works, materials list, trades required, a timetable and a costings schedule which highlighted what he planned to make as a profit.

His self-belief and ego had always dictated that he never doubted he would be successful in anything he did. It was the same with this project. He was sure the plot would be secured and considered the work he had already put in would give him a head start once he started the build.

The next day at Daniel's office, his solicitor looked up from studying the projections of costs and profits. 'A very thorough plan and presentation; showing these sorts of margins and you will be proving your worth to the boys at the top.'

Connor nodded and replied, 'In which case, you had better make sure you get me that plot.'

A couple of days passed and when the phone rang at home that evening, Connor was sure the call would be good news. He had already had his company advertising board made up, which was sitting in the back of the van. At the end of the call, he got into his van and drove to the building plot.

Although it was late at night and he could hardly see what he was doing, he opened the back door to the van and took out a spade. He dug a hole and secured the sign board displaying his company name. He proudly stood back to admire his work and nodded his head, realising this was an important moment. Smiling as he leant on his spade, he said to himself, 'Give me time and Flynn Developments will be all over this city.'

Construction went to plan as he drove his sub-contractors hard to get the house finished in quick time. It didn't need to go on sale as a local businessman negotiated a deal to buy the house before it was finished. That first contract doubled the company's bank balance.

It was the start of Connor's rise. He had gathered a good team around him and by keeping a tight rein on his costs, the cash began to flow in as he built house after house. It was in his nature to screw the best deals he could from both his suppliers and his subbies. He had had a good teacher. The benefits were beginning to show in the bank and in his safe back at the house.

It was nearly twelve months before he was summoned to meet Thomas, the OC of the Birmingham Brigade. Having been given directions, he arrived outside a very run-down terraced house in Sparkbrook and parked up.

He was even more surprised when an old man dressed in jeans and tattered old cardigan with a gaunt-looking grey face, answered the door. With the steely-eyed stare of an assassin, he studied Connor then said in a deep Irish brogue, 'Good to meet you, Connor. I'm Thomas. Come on in.'

Connor entered a room at the back of the house where six other men were sitting chatting, but when the old man followed Connor into the room, they all went quiet. As he looked around the room he realised that if he had met any of them in the street, he would never have guessed that these ordinary, non-descript men were part of an IRA cell intent on causing death and destruction.

The silence was broken as Thomas addressed the new arrival.

'Young fella, you've come with a reputation that we in the movement are very proud to hear. We appreciate the funds you are raising through your business and one day you may be called on to use your other skills, but at the present time, we will continue the strategy that is tried and trusted. You concentrate on your business because that's more use to us as the more cash you can get us, the more arms we can buy. Maybe we can get some of this new explosive called Semtex that's coming in from Libya. But for now, we have some serious business to discuss, so you are excused. The boys here are all glad to see you on board. We will be in touch when we need you.'

Connor was happy to push on with the building business which suited him fine, knowing that if he was ever called upon by Thomas, he would have no option.

Actually, business was good for Connor but socially he needed something with which to occupy himself. The lonely evenings spent at home encouraged some deep introspection. He thought back to his time at the home and her, remembering their assignations, which triggered memories of the things they did together. He had a stirring which didn't last long as his thoughts were mixed with anger at those responsible for him ending up in that place. He hadn't got any further with his investigations regarding his parents, but the time would come when he would track them down and make them suffer.

He realised that he needed to find something to occupy his mind and he found two perfect outlets which were right on his doorstep. The first was golf and the second was just a short drive away, Gillott Road, a prostitute's haven.

He decided he would sign up with the golf professional for some lessons, see how that went and then consider joining and playing regularly. That would fill one void and he might even socialise; only a little though, he wasn't that keen on people. That was something he had always found difficult: mixing with people; having to make small talk was anathema to him; he was much happier with his own company.

He practised hard at golf and over the next few months, became a steady player with a determination to improve on his twenty-four handicap. Those lonely summer nights were now occupied with a resolve to get that handicap down to a figure which his ego would find acceptable.

In the dark of night, he occupied himself with his other interest, satisfying his lust with the whores on Gillott Road whenever he felt the stirrings. Unfortunately, he found the process unfulfilling. He needed a little more comfort than struggling around in the back of his van.

He decided to arrange a home visit from a more high class agency; this would give him the opportunity to relax and enjoy his guilty pleasures in the comfort of his own home.

He sampled a few girls, but hadn't found what he was looking for until a woman in her mid-thirties with a good figure, pretty face and thick black arched eyebrows turned up one night.

She had black hair, long legs and when dressed in the outfit he had bought specifically for these occasions, he was back in heaven.

He found the experience electrifying and totally sexually gratifying. She performed her duties in a very erotic and sexy manner, taking him back to those halcyon days of his youth. The cost of a hundred pounds a time was, he felt, money well spent.

Life was good for now.

CHAPTER TWENTY-SEVEN

To bolster relationships occasionally, Connor would meet with his tradesmen either in the city centre pubs or at a social club in Selly Oak, where some of the lads were members. He would buy everyone a drink or two. The boys partied and chatted up girls and enjoyed themselves. It wasn't his scene really.

However, on one occasion his brick supplier's rep turned up and they got chatting. He asked Connor if he had been to the casino before and when he said he hadn't, it wasn't long before they were both in the back of a taxi and on their way.

The Dragon Casino was situated in the more salubrious part of Edgbaston, on the other side of the Hagley Road to the prostitute haven of Gillot Road. Situated about ten minutes from the city centre, it attracted a clientele of well-heeled business men but, of course, wasn't limited to that crowd.

Its marble pillars and floors gave it a spectacular grand entrance which shouted a brassy, chintzy welcome. It had glitzy and glamorous decor with a wide sweeping staircase, at the top of which was the reception area. Then on through large double glass doors into the gambling and bar area, where the décor embraced all things Chinese, all reds, golds and dragons, with the croupiers dressed in their overly fussy multi-coloured waistcoats and black trousers, standing by their tables.

The restaurant to the far side of the gaming floor was always full, with happy, smiling punters taking a break from the tables and enjoying the superb Chinese cuisine on offer.

The visual impact of the casino as Connor walked into the reception, stunned him for a while. He filled out the forms to become a member and felt hot, sweaty and uncomfortable in this new and unknown place; too many people.

But that night, he found another form of escapism which delivered a further exciting, exhilarating and pleasurable experience. He felt the buzz of excitement, tangible as the croupiers called out, 'Place your bets,' and then a few seconds later, 'No more bets.' The ping of the roulette ball bouncing and jumping in the spinning wheel and the expectant look on the faces of the punters surrounding the tables as the croupier called out the winning number and colour. Two and three deep, the punters were full of anticipation, jostled for position, some studious with an obvious strategy, others confident in their hope that their favourite number might come in next time. The whole atmosphere was highly charged, which wasn't lost on Connor who was being drawn further into this new world. As his initial nervousness evaporated, he found he was getting quite a buzz from playing roulette.

On that first visit, he was unbelievably lucky and at the end of the night he walked out with a wad of notes.

A few days later, after concluding another land purchase and discussing how he was settling in, he mentioned his visit to the casino to Daniel. He was surprised to find that Daniel wasn't upset with his new-found hobby, but added that he must remember never to gamble with any of 'the boys' money, but as a way of laundering dirty money it was superb.

'But just be careful, Connor, and remember we have invested money in you so don't do anything which you might regret, as punishment would be swift and painful,' he added finally.

The next time he visited the casino, the manager, Alan, and his staff remembered the big fellow who had such luck on his first visit and he was offered free drinks all night.

Connor was content with this new life. The building business was very profitable and the profits in the books looked acceptable. The cash deals were mounting to many thousands and needed to be 'cleaned up', so his visits to the casino dealt with that small problem. He took to his task with gusto.

Soon, though, the tranquillity of his life was to be disturbed as there would be a need for him to become involved in something he had always found messy and a little terrifying.

CHAPTER TWENTY-EIGHT

It was mid-November and as daylight broke, Connor drew back his curtains to reveal a thick frost on the ground. 'It looks mighty cold out there,' he thought to himself.

After a quick cup of tea, he left the house dressed in two jumpers, a thick jacket, a pair of well-worn blue jeans and his working boots. He unlocked the van and climbed in; starting the engine to get the heater working to remove the thin layer of ice from the windscreen.

He switched on the radio while he waited for the heater to do its work. The news came on and he was stunned to hear the headline news report of a suspected IRA terrorist who had blown himself up whilst planting a bomb in Coventry. It struck him as a stark reminder of the dangers involved in bomb planting and was relieved to think he never had to get that close to the action.

He sat for a while in the van thinking what the repercussions of this would be and wondered which of the 'ordinary blokes' he had met at Thomas's house might have been involved. As he sat there deep in thought, James pulled up.

'Connor, we need to talk,' James whispered through the open van window.

'Okay, let's go round the back to my office,' he replied.

Connor unlocked his office door and nodded towards a chair which James pulled towards the desk and sat down.

James explained what had happened in Coventry and told him that Dublin, and especially Thomas with the dead eyes, were both angry at what the incident would look like to their enemies.

'Thick Paddies blowing themselves up,' were the words Thomas had used.

'There will be a serious response to this. The body goes back to Ireland next week and Thomas wants to make a big statement. He knows the police will be on high alert and will be trying to ensure the safety of the public. The press will be watching every move so he knows whatever he does will get massive coverage for the movement and send a message to the government that we will never surrender. I think he wants to hit a night club, football ground or pub. But we are one man down now and we will need you to step up. The boss wants you at his house next Thursday, five o'clock sharp and he will run through the plans because it will all be kicking off that night.'

After James had left, Connor sat for a while considering his options but realised there weren't any. He knew he had no choice.

CHAPTER TWENTY-NINE

The attractive girl on the edge of the group stood out from the rest of the crowd. Her raven-coloured long curly hair and good looks had caught the attention of a young man watching from across the room. He had briefly talked with her last week and was intent on getting to know her better.

She was excited to see that he had come to the social club again. When she had chatted to him the previous weekend, she had felt flushed and slightly embarrassed. Tonight his friends were their usual boisterous selves, making her wonder if he was just out for a good time too. She wasn't that shallow and wanted something a bit deeper.

The pair couldn't seem to get enough time to chat properly with all the banter going on but he did manage to whisper in her ear, 'Look, I was going to ask you out on a date but it's a bit embarrassing with my mates about and now I feel stupid.'

'No, don't feel embarrassed. If you don't ask me now I will be insulted.'

'How about we meet up without all this lot and have a drink and get to know each other a bit better?'

'That would be nice,' she replied. 'When?'

'How about Thursday night? We could meet in town for a drink, the Tavern or somewhere, eh?'

'Okay, that sounds good.'

The group of lads returned and started to tease their mate and tried to pull him along with them but he managed to break away from the group and went back to talk with her.

'Look, don't worry about that lot,' he said, nodding to his mates, by way of apology. 'I'm already looking forward to Thursday and just wanted to make sure it's all okay with you and to make sure this leery lot haven't put you off.'

'Oh, no, it's all fine. So what time shall we meet?'

The lads were all ready to go and pulled him away but he managed to shout back, 'Tavern in the Town, downstairs by the juke box around eight.'

'Great, see you then,' she called out.

She hoped she didn't appear too desperate but inside, her stomach was churning with the excitement of her first real date and she couldn't wait.

CHAPTER THIRTY

In the bleak and fairly squalid terraced home that Thomas haunted, a disparate group of men were sitting in his front room listening to their instructions.

'We are planting three tonight,' said Thomas. 'The boys doing the pubs, make yourselves blend in, don't draw attention to yourselves, act naturally, have one drink and leave the package. Cool is the word.'

Thomas named the teams of 'planters' and Connor looked across at the guy called Martin who would be his partner. He looked twice at the man. Last week after a business meeting in the city centre, Connor was walking down New Street and passing Piccadilly Arcade. It stuck in his mind because the corner office had a peculiar curved glass window. He noticed it was a staff agency office. The man whom he had first met at Thomas's house some months previously, the very same man who was to be his partner tonight, was sitting behind a desk. It was obviously his place of work. Connor was surprised that such an ordinary office worker in the heart of the city was involved and fully prepared to put his life on the line for the cause.

He looked over at that same man sitting on the settee. He was wearing a grey suit with an open-necked shirt, his beer belly spilling over his waistband. His blue overcoat was laid across the arm of the chair and beads of sweat glistened on his forehead.

Connor hoped that he wasn't prone to nerves, not tonight. Connor under pressure would be ice-cool.

A couple of the men looked strained, a few tried to appear unruffled with the prospect of their task. Connor only had one thing to do and carrying the duffel bag didn't seem such a difficult job. He didn't want to think about what was inside though and what would happen if it went off early, like last week in Coventry. However, he was composed and listened to Thomas run through the plans once again.

Connor was relieved to hear his exit plan. After dropping the duffel bag in the pub, he and Martin would split up and make their escape. He would cut through past New Street Station, head down the Ringway and Daniel would be waiting near the Albany Hotel to pick him up. Quickly back home, showered and changed. A solid alibi, an evening at home with Daniel, his solicitor, discussing business before a night at the casino, seemed plausible enough.

Although Thomas talked with quiet confidence about their mission and all its implications for the movement, Connor was unmoved by the patriotic fervour. He had always been ambivalent. He had never really felt the same passion as they did. One thing he did feel, however, was the need for self-preservation. He remembered from his past that being too close to the action was something he hated.

CHAPTER THIRTY-ONE

The Greasy Spoon was indeed the making of Billy and Rita. They were able to put a good deposit down on their own little semi-detached house around the corner from his mum's home. And in May, after a visit to the doctor's, they had the confirmation that Rita was pregnant, the baby to be born mid-November.

The two families were delighted. The thought of being a grandmother brought Mary to tears. As the matriarch and driving force of the family, she was happy to see the success her children had made of their lives.

She remembered her own tentative beginnings when she had arrived in the city without a penny in her pocket. Now she could revel in the knowledge that she had made all of this possible, plus William of course.

'Yes,' Mary thought, 'November will be an exciting month for us all.'

CHAPTER THIRTY-TWO

She was the baby of the family and very special to them all. Mary's own experiences as a young girl had made her that bit more watchful of her beautiful daughter and the rest of the family picked up on their mother's feelings being very protective of her. Billy always took his brotherly duties very seriously.

Maria's childhood was happy and without major mishap, unless you counted her First Holy Communion when she was eight years old. Mary, who was usually good with a needle and thread, had made the communion dress much too long, so long in fact that Ryan had to trail behind his little sister, lifting the train to prevent her from tripping over the excess material. So as she walked down the aisle like a bride, Ryan was her oversized pageboy. The family smiled happily.

Maria had worked hard at secondary school and later attended Bourneville College to train as a secretary, recently securing herself a really good job at a big insurance company in Moseley. She was happy and content with her life and was looking forward to enjoying herself a little more now she had a bit more cash left over, after giving her mum her house-keeping money.

The growing sense of freedom she felt at this time in her life was exciting and her expectations of this first real date were making her stomach churn. She had managed to keep it quiet from the family but she had a feeling her big brother knew she was up to something. She didn't care. Billy had seen her the previous Sunday lunchtime at the social club with some of her friends and a group of guys. He had given her one of his looks. He had warned her about men and what they were after.

She took her time applying her make-up and curling her hair, and began thinking about what tonight might hold and her pulse began to race as she stood up to study herself in the mirror.

Unlike her mother, she was tall and possessed a fuller figure.

'You've got a wonderful figure, Maria,' her mum would remind her, aware of how young girls needed continual positive reassurance about themselves.

She teased out some curls and applied her mascara, liking what she saw. Her emerald eyes sparkled and her raven-coloured, newly curled hair fell to her shoulders. Her full lips shone with the new lipstick she had bought from Boots the Chemist's on her way home after work. Make-up complete, she went downstairs.

Her mother and father were in the front room watching TV as she opened the door to say goodbye.

'Jesus, Maria, you look a picture,' her dad said from his armchair in the corner of the room.

'Now don't be out too late,' her mother added. 'Don't forget its Thursday and there's still work tomorrow.'

'Don't worry, Mom, I'll be back by ten. I'm meeting Shirley and Gwen and we're only having a few drinks in town to celebrate Gwen's birthday, so I won't be late,' she lied.

'Which pub you going to then?' asked Billy, 'Just so I know,' he added.

'Oh, we'll probably start off at The Tavern in the Town, Mr Nosey,' she joked and poked out her tongue at him. Then she closed the door, sighed for telling lies to her parents and hurried down to the bus stop to catch the next one into town.

'Aagh, the Catholics always beating themselves up over some lie they've told. Anyway, it's no time to be bothering yourself with that, Maria Casey, just get out and enjoy the evening,' she thought.

She was so excited as she boarded the bus into the city, settling down next to an old lady who smiled at her.

'You look lovely, dear, have you got a date?'

She giggled, 'Yes, I have and I'm really looking forward to it. I'm meeting him in town.'

'Well, you enjoy yourself, dear," adding, 'You know, I can't believe it's only just six weeks to Christmas and I reckon if the cold weather carries on like this, we could have snow by then. I hate these dark evenings,' she complained. Maria wasn't listening, she was too busy contemplating what tonight had in store for her. The bus droned along, pitching everyone's head forward and then back as the driver changed gears or hit his brakes.

***

As Maria's bus made its way towards the city, two men were making their way along New Street towards the Tavern in the Town; one wearing a blue overcoat and the other in a donkey jacket, with a duffel bag slung over his shoulder. Not two minutes away, another two men were already in position and ordering their drinks at the bar of the Mulberry Bush. A third group were approaching a bank in Edgbaston.

***

After Maria had gone, the family sat in silence and an air of anxiety surrounded them all for a while. Billy, who had only popped in to see his parents after work, turned to his mum and said, 'Look, I've got some business to sort out tonight in town, so I'll go round home and see if Rita wants to pop into town for a drink. Maybe we can keep an eye on Maria while we're at it. I can see you're a bit concerned about your little girl, especially with what's been going on but don't worry, she'll be okay. I'll make sure.'

'Ah you're a good lad, Billy, but don't be forcing Rita to be charging round the town in her state, it could be any time, remember!'

'Don't worry yourself about Rita, Mum. She will let me know if it's all too much.' He kissed his mother goodbye and waved to his dad as he left the room. He walked quickly from their house to his own, to get the car and Rita.

***

Steam was exploding from the radiator of the young man's Ford Escort. He had pulled into a side road off Broad Street and lifted the bonnet. This was going to ruin his night. Even if he could get it fixed quickly, he knew he would be very late. This could take hours to sort out. He had been really looking forward to this date and hated the idea of letting Maria down.

***

Maria felt a nudge from the old lady, 'Got to get off at the next stop, love.'

As the old lady squeezed past, their faces met and she whispered, 'Just be careful, dear, with the bombs and that. My son's a policeman and the word is that we should all be careful after that one blew himself up in Coventry last week.'

Maria nodded but her thoughts were miles away with the anticipation of her date. The bus pulled up in the middle of the city and she checked her watch; she was well ahead of time to meet him, 'downstairs near the juke box'.

The Tavern in the Town was in the basement of a row of shops on New Street so Maria had to descend a flight of stairs to get to the bar and lounge area. The juke box was belting out a recent hit song from ELO called 'Can't get it out of my head', as she pushed through the doors; she agreed with the lyrics as she couldn't get him out of her head either.

The atmosphere was lively but not raucous and cigarette smoke clouded the air. She walked over to the bar and noted that two men were sitting at the table next to the juke box. One of them seemed to be looking straight into her eyes.

A couple of young girls pushed their way past her to check out which song they would put on next. She ordered herself a coke and carried it over to the empty table as the two men had now gone. They had forgotten their duffel bag, which was left on the floor against the side of the juke box. She would sort that out in a minute after she had nipped to the ladies' and had a little tidy up.

***

Billy and Rita made good time into the city and parked up. As they headed down New Street towards the pub, they heard a commotion and sirens in the distance. They looked at one another. Billy felt his heart thumping in his chest. He looked at Rita in alarm.

'What do you think that's all about?'

As he finished his question, he saw a couple of lads he knew from the market trotting up towards him.

'Jimmy, what the hell is happening?'

'Bill, there's big trouble. A bomb just went off at the bottom of the Rotunda and its blown the Mulberry Bush Pub to pieces. They reckon there could be more; God knows how many are dead or injured.'

'Oh no,' he blurted out, 'I think my sister's at the Tavern in the Town.'

***

Maria checked her watch and noticed it was just after eight twenty-five. He was a bit late but she was excited to think he would be here any minute. She looked at herself and applied a little more lipstick and smiled at herself in the mirror, running her hands through her curls. She checked herself once more and was happy with what she saw and opened the door to leave.

As she took her first step through the door, there was an enormous, thunderous boom as the explosion ripped the pub apart. An intense orange flash lit the whole pub for a second and the room seemed to crumble around her as timber and glass flew through the air. Then a couple of seconds of silence in the blackness. Then the screams and plaintive cries of the injured filled the air. Alarms were blaring. The devastation and wreckage of mangled chairs and tables was strewn everywhere. Sparks and small bursts of flame momentarily lit the darkness.

Pieces of glass and splinters of wood had embedded themselves in her body in the blast. She didn't move. The force of the blast in such a confined space had blown her off her feet. Her mutilated body lay still, the only noises she made were pitiful attempts to pull in her last rasping, coarse, gurgling breaths as she fought for her life. Around her in the blackness, there was chaos and pandemonium. Shouting, screaming, sirens and mayhem. Smoke and dust hung heavy in the air. In the dark tomb that only seconds earlier had been bright, vibrant and full of life, the dead and injured bodies lay strewn in the devastation.

***

Billy was running towards the pub when the bomb exploded, rocking the buildings around him. He felt the ground vibrate beneath his feet. He stood motionless as he saw the flash of light and heard the enormous explosion. His heart was pounding. He felt sick. His mind was racing with all sorts of images of what had happened. His legs felt weak and he nearly fell to his knees in the horror of what was going through his mind.

'Maria, my sister. Oh, God, please let her be okay.'

He rushed towards the pub but the frontage was a wreck and there was no way in. A policeman was already there and was taking charge of the situation. His uniform already covered in the dust that was settling around him. Billy tried to push his way through.

'My sister's in there. Please, please let me through.'

'Look, mate,' the officer replied, 'we don't know who's in there, nor if there's another bomb ready to go off. Please get back.'

Billy cried the frustrated tears of fear and desperation. He seemed to be short of air, he was gulping in deep breaths to try and calm himself. The waves of shock began hitting him. What would he tell his mother and father? Tears filled his eyes as the night became manic with a cacophony of blaring sirens and blue and red flashing lights. It seemed every fire engine, police car and ambulance was racing into the city centre, some already skidding to a halt outside what was left of the bombed-out entrance.

The main entrance to the pub was nearly impossible to get through and fire crews were extracting many, as quickly as they could, from the side alley and bringing them up on to the street. Billy watched as the walking wounded assisted by ambulance crews, fire fighters and police, were brought out from the alleyway through a gaping hole in the side wall of the pub that had been caused by the ferocity of the bomb blast.

'Keep moving, please, there might be another bomb,' Billy heard another policeman shout.

He was manically checking each person as they were brought out, to see if she was still alive but it was difficult to see. They all seemed as though they had been covered in a coating of soot, their hair bedraggled and clothes ripped and torn; some were helped to the hotel opposite the pub to wait in safety while they tried to recover from the shock of their horrific experience. The chaos across the road continued.

Many emergency vehicles were now being held up in the congestion in the city and the few that got through, were struggling with the scale of the emergency.

As he watched the growing numbers of injured standing or lying in the street, the first of the black cabs started to arrive. Then another and another until there were so many he couldn't count. The news had spread quickly and, unconcerned as to the danger or their own safety and regardless of what else might happen that night, the courageous and brave beating big heart of his city was there for everyone to see. The unending line of taxis helped to ferry the victims to the nearest hospitals.

Billy waited, searching the blackened and bloody faces of the walking wounded, some wrapped in red blankets, moving in slow motion, limping, some being carried out on stretchers, others on table tops. Members of the public joined in to assist the firemen who were struggling while they awaited further fire crews to arrive.

But there was still no sign of his sister. He must have missed her being brought out. Or maybe she wasn't in there at all. He pushed his way through the people milling about and started to run. In his fevered mind, at first he didn't know where to. Suddenly, as his lungs were bursting from the effort, he realised that he had been on automatic pilot and was heading up Corporation Street towards Steelhouse Lane and the General Hospital.

Out of breath and feeling nauseous, he made it to the hospital but it was chaos. It resembled a scene from a war film, with ambulances and taxis disgorging one after another injured person. The reception was full of people milling around, police, nurses and doctors. The police were trying to get some semblance of order but it was difficult with so many people crushing into such a small area. Stretchers and gurneys seemed to be everywhere. Some of the injured were crying in pain, others in shock, just staring into the distance, barely registering what had happened to them and oblivious to the scene around them.

'Billy, over here.'

Rita was in the crowd of people standing near the entrance to the emergency treatment cubicles. He pushed his way over to where she stood.

'Oh my god, Reet, what's happened? Have you seen her come in, where is she? Please let her be all right.'

'I've reported to reception and asked if she is here. I've given them a description and that receptionist lady reckons she might have been one of the early injured admitted.'

Billy pushed his way over to the lady but was told to try and keep calm, telling him to sit and wait. They sat and waited. Holding hands. Silent in their own thoughts.

'Anyway, I thought I'd told you to go home.'

'I couldn't just leave you with all this going on, so I got Jimmy to drop me here. Don't worry, I feel okay but I want to be sure Maria's safe before I go anywhere.'

***

William and Mary were at home watching TV when the programme was interrupted by a newsflash. The newsreader looked solemnly at the camera.

'There are unconfirmed reports that two bombs have exploded in the city centre of Birmingham. The explosions, which happened at around eight thirty tonight, are believed to have taken place at two separate city centre pubs, both packed with drinkers enjoying a Thursday night out. Police and emergency services are attending and as yet there are no confirmed reports of how many may have been injured but as soon as we have further information, we will bring you more details and a full report later in the main news at ten.'

The news hit Mary like a shock wave.

'Oh, sweet Mother of Jesus!'

She jumped up out of her chair.

'The kids are there. Oh my God, oh my God,' she repeated, 'please let them be okay. Please, please!'

The tears cascaded from her eyes as she held her head in her hands and then covered her eyes as if she was trying to shut out the horror of what was happening. She wiped away her tears and then slowly started to shake. First her hands and then it spread to her whole body. She was in severe shock and William held her trembling body gently to him. He stroked her hair, trying to comfort her.

'Mary, come on, don't worry now. They will all be fine. Billy's there, he'll keep them all safe.'

'And what if he hasn't, what if he couldn't, what if they're all lying there dead? Oh my God, please let them be safe.'

William was trying to remain calm but his stomach was churning. He was trying to remain composed for Mary but inside he was falling apart. A mother's intuition is an extraordinary thing. William felt her body go rigid. At that moment, she felt an ice-cold hand rip its way into her chest and wrench out her heart. She knew immediately that she had lost someone very special.

***

It was some time before the receptionist approached. 'Mrs Casey, please come with me,' she said.

'This is my husband, Billy, he's Maria's brother,' Rita replied.

'Oh, right. Okay, both follow me, please.'

They walked through the swing doors and were led along an aisle with a series of treatment cubicles on either side, nurses busily tending the wounded. As the nurse pushed through some more swing doors on to a ward, she stopped outside some curtains drawn around a bed. With as much compassion as she could raise, she said softly, 'We have just brought your sister down from theatre where she had emergency surgery. She's very, very poorly.'

She drew back the curtains and there lay Maria. Her eyes were closed as if in a deep sleep. She didn't look in pain. There were numerous tubes and machines bleeping intermittently.

'The doctor will be in in a minute and he will explain Maria's situation. Excuse me for a while, please. I'm sure you understand I must help out elsewhere.'

They stood either side of the bed, looking down at her bandaged face and head. Both started to cry quietly. Billy took his sister's hand which was cold and clammy and then the doctor appeared. Noticing Rita's huge baby bulge, he beckoned to Billy.

'Can I just have a word with you out here?' he said. 'Mr Casey, you are Maria's brother?'

Billy nodded and the doctor continued, 'The stress of all this is not good for your wife and sometimes the shock of bad news can badly affect pregnant mothers so please keep that in mind. We have carried out emergency surgery on your sister but she has suffered massive internal pulmonary contusions, lost a lot of blood due to the blast and flying debris, which has caused severe injury. There isn't much more we can do other than to make her as comfortable as possible. She's a damned good fighter and we are amazed she has held on for so long but—' his voice trailed off.

He waited a few moments to let the gravity of what he had said sink in without uttering the specific words. He looked at Billy for some recognition that he understood fully what he was being told.

'So, Doc, you mean—' He paused for a while to compose himself. 'How long has she got left?' he asked.

'Look, it's difficult to say,' he replied. 'We thought we had lost her on the operating table but managed to resuscitate her. She's a brave girl. Maybe she has hung on to wait for you but she hasn't got long. I'm so very sorry. She has fought so hard. Have the last moments with her and be strong for your wife.'

The doctor excused himself and Billy returned and took Rita in his arms, hugging her tight. Looking over her shoulder at his sister, he whispered, 'Reet, we're going to lose her. The doctor told me to break it easy to you but there's no way of saying it nicely. Her injuries are so bad they can't do anything for her. She'll be so scared, Rita. I don't know what to do,' he wept as he held his wife close to him.

'Let's try and make these last moments with her as special as we can,' Rita said as the tears streamed down her face. 'Take her hand and tell her how much you love her.'

Billy took his sister's hand.

'Maria, I know you can't see me but I hope you can hear me, it's me, Billy. I want to tell you how much I love you. Don't be scared. I'm here and—' As Billy said those last few heart-breaking words, the machine next to the bed let out a continuous long beep and Billy knew she was gone. He stroked his sister's hair and sobbed uncontrollably. His whole body heaved and shook as he cried in sorrow and despair at losing his beloved little sister. Now he would have to make that phone call to his mum. He dreaded the thought.

***

When William, Mary and Ryan burst through the doors on to the ward, the look on Billy's face told them it was too late.

CHAPTER THIRTY-THREE

Ryan sat in his flat, alone and forlorn. The sadness he felt over the loss of his sister was breaking his heart and he hid away from everyone and everything. His curtains remained closed although he knew it was morning and the sunlight was breaking through the chinks in his badly drawn curtains.

He lit another cigarette. He'd not long conquered his need for nicotine and was going well but this was all too much. He was back on them with a vengeance.

The phone rang but he ignored it as he had for the last couple of days, preferring to be alone with his thoughts. It rang again and then a third time and he picked it up saying nothing.

'Ryan?'

It took him a couple of seconds to realise who it was.

'Ryan,' she repeated.

'Jen?'

'Yes, Ryan, it's me. I have heard the terrible news about Maria and I'm coming back to help you through it.'

For once, his head ruled his heart and he calmly explained his feelings.

'Jenny, listen to me. My heart is broken but you would know that. My baby sister is dead and I will never see her again, and the last thing I need is you coming back for a visit and then just leaving me again. No, when you come back it will be when you are back to stay. Not because of sympathy but for love. I appreciate the call, but leave me alone for now.'

She swallowed hard and squeezed out a last few words. 'Ryan, I understand, just know I'm thinking of you at this very sad time. Goodbye.'

***

It was left to Billy to have the emotional strength to pull his family through, he was the backbone through those miserable and darkly wretched days, making all the arrangements for his sister's funeral.

The rain fell lightly on a grey and gloomy day as the funeral cortege slowly came to a halt outside his parents' home. He ushered his mother and father from the house and into the first car along with Ryan, his great-aunt, Bridie, and his now heavily pregnant wife.

He followed them, stopping for a moment to lay his hand flat on the side window of the hearse to hopelessly caress the floral tribute that sat inside the glass and spelled out his sister's name.

Mary had cried her tears already and sat, stoic and broken hearted, staring out of the window. Bridie, however, was inconsolable and hadn't stopped crying from the time she got up that morning. In the car, she continued all the way to church. Mary had tried to console her but that just brought on more tears.

'Oh, Mary, she was such a beautiful girl. It was such a short life.'

There was more weeping and sobbing during the service and when Billy read a touching eulogy dedicated to his beloved sister, the words reduced everyone in the church to tears.

He had already decided that the wake back at his parents' house would be a celebration of Maria's life and had arranged for pictures and photographs to be on display in every room. He encouraged everyone to recall happy times with Maria but it was too much for some and a few disappeared into the back garden to have a few moments alone with their thoughts.

He wandered into the garden, exhausted and emotionally drained by it. He lowered himself down slowly to sit on the garden bench next to Gwen, one of Maria's childhood friends.

'Oh, Billy, I miss her so much. It's all so sad.'

'Those evil bastards murdered a lot of innocent people that night. You were lucky you didn't get to the pub early or we would be mourning you and Shirley too.'

Gwen's face reddened and she began to sob.

'Billy, we were never going with Maria that night. She had made up that story to cover up the fact that she had a date which she didn't want any of you to know about. I think she was embarrassed.'

Billy turned to Gwen and with massive self-control, managed to growl, 'What do you mean, Gwen?'

'She had a date that night and we were sworn to secrecy. We didn't think it mattered much and went along with it. She wouldn't even tell us who she was meeting.'

'You must have some idea who it was, for God's sake, you were her best friend. Had she been seeing anyone or met someone at the club maybe? Think, Gwen,' he pleaded.

'No one in particular, no. There were a group of lads in on Sunday who we were all talking to, I suppose it was one of them but I don't know for sure.'

'I know, I saw them. Who were they? Have you seen them before?'

'Builders or something I think, just out for a good time.'

Billy was silent for a very long time as he slumped back down on the bench. Staring into the distance, he managed to compose himself. His mind was racing. He steadied himself, took a deep breath and thought that this was not the time or place, not with his mother and father inside in the state they were in already.

Something was nagging him though, something at the back of his mind. A shiver ran through him as he cast his mind back to that Sunday at the social club. He now remembered the face and the name. He hadn't seen that face for a long time. He had heard rumours around the town that he was back and was doing nicely, running a building company. But, so what? It was believed he had been in Ireland for a number of years. But, so what? His mind was racing, trying to disseminate the thoughts going through his mind. He thought back to all those years ago.

It was a big cup match in local schools' football, a semi-final and a place in the final at stake. Billy was younger than the others playing that day and was confident but naïve. The opposing centre-half was a brute of a boy and a few years older, big and uncompromising. Billy had 'nut-megged' him early on, curled the ball into the corner of the net to put his team one up. Later in the game he tried the same move again. This time he was pulled down with a rugby tackle. As the two boys writhed on the floor, the older boy got Billy by the throat, squeezing hard, madness on his face.

'You try that on me again and I will kill you and your perfect family. I know where you live.'

Billy was dumbstruck. He had bantered with opposition players before but this was just pure evil. He was really frightened and in his inexperience of such tactics, he 'disappeared' for the rest of the game and his team lost.

Later, he heard stories about the boy with the vicious temper and avoided crossing paths with him, keeping away from the area near the children's home where the boy lived.

He knew the face in the club that Sunday was unmistakably that of the man that Connor Flynn had now become, but that was pure coincidence, surely? It was madness to link him with his sister's death, though the thought invaded his mind. Tomorrow, the first item on his agenda would be a call to his old mate, Detective Sergeant Dave Jones.

In their phone conversation the next day, Dave had revealed that they were certain they had the right men but Billy had told him he should check out Connor Flynn, just on a hunch.

Dave listened and then dismissively said, 'Look, Billy, so you've got a gut feeling about Flynn. You heard a whisper that he had spent some of his life in Ireland, saw him at the club the Sunday before the bombings, and he was in a group with your sister and others. You had a fall-out with him when you were kids. Not much for me to convince my super that we have another suspect but as a favour to you, I will do a little digging.'

A few days later Billy had his reply. Dave's phone call made it pretty clear.

'It's all too circumstantial, Billy, and we have no real evidence to confront him with, and cannot place him near the pub or connect him with the local brigade. The men we have in custody are, we believe, the men responsible. So as hard as this is to tell you, accept it and try and help your family through it.'

For a short time at least, Billy did manage to put the loss of Maria to the back of his mind, as early the next morning Rita went into labour and the despair in his heart turned to happiness as he held his new born son in his arms.

'One out, one in,' he said sadly to himself. 'Sean,' he said to his baby son, 'I am so happy you have come into our lives; Maria would have loved you so much.' He held his son up high to show him to Maria, knowing she was looking down on them both.

***

The big news on TV and headlines in the newspapers declared that the police were holding six men. They were arrested just as they were about to board the Heysham to Belfast ferry on the night of the bombings. They had made their way north from Birmingham that evening and, furthermore, had connections to the IRA. Indeed, it appeared that most of the men were travelling to attend the funeral of the IRA man who had blown himself up in Coventry. That was enough for police to hold the men for questioning.

In Birmingham, the aftermath of the bombings hit the city very hard. The anti-Irish feeling brought out an outrage against the Irish community that shook the city to its foundations. Workers from factories around the city marched in protest and the local papers were full of stories of fights and bashings of innocent Irish people. Many honest, hardworking Irish families suffered the backlash due to the actions of the bombers.

The IRA did not officially take responsibility for the bombings. Many believed the public's reaction had made them ashamed to be associated with this outrage.

The people of Birmingham, in particular, and the country as a whole, both English and Irish alike, had had enough. By the force and physicality of their protests, it was believed to have convinced the IRA leaders that the killing of innocent civilians in such a vile fashion was never going to advance their cause. Later, it was said that the outrage influenced the IRA to place Birmingham 'off limits'.

The alleged bombers came to trial, which took place away from Birmingham as the overwhelming public hostility against the accused would make it hard for police to contain the emotions of the people in the city.

The trial of the six men was held in Lancaster and the prosecution's case was supported by forensic evidence which alleged that traces of explosives were found on some of the men's hands. At the trials end, the verdict was universally accepted and the six men were sentenced to life imprisonment. The Caseys had to accept that although the punishment handed out was some justice, it would never bring Maria back.

***

The brothers had arranged a little rota so that one of them would call round in the evenings to sit with their parents and talk. But their father was becoming more introverted. He preferred to sit in his back garden, alone with his thoughts. Since Maria's death, William was a shadow of the man he used to be. He had now withdrawn into a silent, self-imposed solitude that not even his wife could break into.

Billy and Ryan tried to keep their mother occupied. She still managed to hold down her job at Lyons Tea Rooms, which was more for the escape than love for the job, but going back to an empty house brought her down most. Maria was never coming home, she would never see her, never hear her voice, never hold her again, she was gone but she was everywhere in that house.

On one of Billy's evening visits, he was sitting with his mum at the kitchen table, chatting about the old days. Reminiscing about the good times, tucking into the Sunday roast, arguing about everything and nothing. Who had finished the last of the mint sauce? Whose dinner was biggest? His mum's eyes lit up as she remembered those days with her young family. All safe and happy, never contemplating the sadness that would befall her cherished family and the horrific events that they would all be involved in.

'Happy days, Billy, happy days,' his mum said softly, 'and it all changed in a split second at the hands of evil people,' she sighed.

'Since Maria's death, it's as if your father has left me. I know that sounds stupid but it's as though the man I knew so well and loved so much has gone, walked out. All that's left is this zombie who goes through the motions. He's dead behind his eyes, Billy, and I can't seem to bring him back.'

'I know, Mum, me and Ryan have seen what's happening and we've been thinking of how we might bring him out of his despair and we thought, how about a holiday? That might do it. All of us together might snap him out of it. A change of scenery, a different beat of the drum; leave that with me for a while and I'll see what Ryan reckons. We can both shut up shop and enjoy the break too. I'm not having the old fella drive himself insane.'

'Thank you, son, let's see what can be done. It's hit us all hard but your dad's sinking, there's no fight in him and I'm buggered if I'm losing him as well.'

After consultation with his brother, they decided it would be easier if he and Rita, and little Sean, should accompany his parents on this break. For once, the Greasy Spoon's doors would be closed.

So Billy set to work on finding a holiday. He was down at the meat market buying his bacon and sausage from his mate Terry. Billy told him how his father was so down after everything and that they needed to get him away for a while. Terry knew Spain pretty well and had visited the Balearics too, and he recommended Ibiza.

Billy's initial reaction was, 'You've got to be kidding,' but he was swung by what he heard next.

'Bill, they can run Ibiza down as much as they like but the reputation for it being a party island doesn't do it justice because away from the madness of San Antonio and Bossa, there is some beautiful scenery. You can find some quaint villages and towns, visited by older people and families, which would suit you fine. Last year, I stayed in Santa Eulalia, a small town on the east coast, nice hotel, views of the ocean, nice safe beach and not a lager lout in sight.'

What Terry told him next had Billy thinking.

He continued, 'But here's the thing, in the sixties the hippies chose Ibiza as their home and that was for a reason. They believed it was a special place because it has an energy, a white light which repairs the soul, a healing quality that you have to experience. In fact, you must all visit a little beach at Cala d'Hort where you will see a massive rock called Es Vedra that rises from the sea; it sits in the bay and towers over the surrounding land. The hippies reckon it has special magnetic powers, who knows?

But a swim in the sea there might make your dad feel a lot better. It's worth a try.'

That was good enough for Billy. Anything that might help his father was fine by him.

The holiday was a tonic and the two weeks they spent at the Hotel Tres Torres did enliven his dad. He and Billy took walks around the port and sank a few ice-cold beers as they relaxed and gazed out at the ocean. The girls soaked up the sun, with little Sean safely protected from the sun in his push-chair under the parasol. After lunch and a siesta, they wandered around the local shops looking for bargains. William even took to the dance floor in the evening entertainment around the pool, leading Mary around just like in the old days when they first met.

They hired a car and drove out to Cala d'Hort, parking up on a sand covered, rough, uneven road near to the beach. They made their way down to the beautiful crescent-shaped bay where they stood in awe as they looked up at the mini mountain that rose from the sea. They gazed in wonderment at its visual impact.

They found a spot on the beach and sunbathed for a while; Billy was even able to coax his dad into the sea, hoping that those special magnetic powers might magically mend his broken spirit.

After their swim they sat at the bar overlooking the beach, under a parasol for shade, and the father and son enjoyed a beer. A slight sea breeze drifted in to cool their sweating bodies and William explained as clearly as he could how he felt, tears brimming in his eyes.

'Billy, I know I'm an old fool but to bury one of your kids before you go yourself, isn't right. To lose someone as beautiful as my Maria is a blow I just can't seem to get over; it's there when I go to bed and there when I wake up, it's even in my dreams. It's never out of my thoughts. I put it like this to you, son: God forbid, but what would you feel like if you lost your Sean, eh? I know how much you love him. They're irreplaceable. You feel like your heart has been ripped out and that you would rather die yourself than carry on without them in your life.'

Billy understood how he felt and tried to convince his father that he mustn't give up the fight. He explained how much he meant to them all, especially his mum and that they all just wanted their old dad back. But in tears, William cried once more, 'I don't think I can come back, son, it's all too hard but I'll try.'

The holiday had been a good escape and they all returned a little more relaxed. There was an improvement in William and they all hoped he could regain his love of life.

***

The pub bombings were never far from the news and every related news item in the intervening years, made it difficult for the family to move on with their lives. There was to be no long term escape from the tragedy which still captured the headlines as an appeal by the six men was launched, heard and dismissed. But dragging it all up again didn't help the family who were still struggling.

Then, some years later, a number of articles started to appear in the newspapers regarding the behaviour of the West Midlands Serious Crime Squad in quite a number of investigations and convictions in the past. It was alleged that their actions in the process of gathering defendants' statements was unlawful, casting reasonable doubt on verdicts given by the courts. The methods they employed to gain information and subsequent signed statements, including those of the Birmingham Six, were questioned.

It all culminated when a Granada TV programme entitled 'Who Bombed Birmingham?' was broadcast. It asked just exactly who did plant those bombs and examined some of the forensic evidence. In the search for the truth of what really happened that night, the Caseys and relatives of the others killed and injured were forced to go through the pain and horror once more.

This time, however, it was all too much for William who suffered a huge heart attack while sitting on his bench, alone in his back garden. Mary had told her sons, 'The doctors can call it what they like but it wasn't a heart attack that killed your father, it was a broken heart.'

Their father was buried in a grave next to his beloved daughter.

The news the next day revealed that on further appeal, the 'guilty' verdict had been overturned as being unsafe and unsatisfactory, and the six men were to be released from prison. The torture for the family continued. They tried to put on a brave face but they had lost a daughter and sister, and now had buried a loving husband and father too. Nothing would bring either of them back.

CHAPTER THIRTY-FOUR

Billy kept up his visits to see his mum and noticed the change in her since his dad had died. Sitting at the kitchen table together, he could see how tense she was.

'Billy,' she said, 'I've had so much time on my hands to think, that sometimes I feel I am going mad. In my search for peace of mind, I have never gone back to the church to find the answers. They promise that He is the way but in my opinion, He has let me down. After all my struggles and battles over the years, from the age of fifteen to the present day, surely He would allow me to have my daughter live a full and happy life. I know other people have a harder time than me but I was a believer, deep in my soul. I never expected life to be easy and accepted that life threw up challenges which had to be met. The rubbish clichés I have been fed of, 'He never gives you more than you can cope with', or that, 'It's all part of His wonderful plan', are just paying lip service to a doctrine that squeezes you tight, holds you breathless, constricts you and forces you, by fear, to follow it, to gain that everlasting salvation.'

She got up from the kitchen table and started to fill the kettle and continued.

'On the day you got married, I went back into the church and I asked Him for just one thing, and that was to protect my most valuable possessions, my children.'

She laughed at the irony and continued, 'and look how He has let me down. No, there will be no more church for me; there's no God. If there was, he wouldn't allow these sorts of things to happen, would he? No, there are people who try to do good and people who do evil. The vast majority of us get on with our lives and live in peace, unless we are unlucky enough to cross paths with those evil people. It's just fate, luck or coincidence.'

She poured the boiling water into the tea pot and replaced the lid.

'There are evil people in the world, of that there is no doubt. Are they born that way or a product of their environment? Their childhood fashions them as adults. Some suppress their inner feelings and suppression is a bad thing. Eventually, it all boils over with horrifying consequences. I bet those who placed that bomb were of the same religion as me. Now that doesn't make sense does it? Catholics killing Catholics? I have decided that Catholicism, the whole thing, is a sham; religion is for the weak and those who can't think for themselves. I think it's all a magnificent lie and has been a way of controlling millions of people by fear and ritual for a thousand years. It worked when people were uneducated and could be controlled with the threat of eternal damnation. Even in my day, I experienced the harsh and strict nuns at school, planting the seeds of religious control. They were backed up by a roaring red-faced priest, screaming from the pulpit about the fires of hell which they threaten will engulf us all if we waver. Repressing us. Frightening us. No, it's all over for me. I have become a non-believer.'

Billy was shocked to hear his mother's vitriolic tirade against her religion, and added sadly, 'In the end, Mum, we are all flawed, some more than others. We can only hope that the amount of good we load on to our side of the scales balances the evil the few try to heap on the other side.' They sat in silence at the kitchen table.

CHAPTER THIRTY-FIVE

Mary doted on her grandson, Sean, which offered some relief and escape from thoughts of her daughter and husband. She focussed her attention on the young boy, watching him play football with that odd pigeon-toed gait of his as he ran around the pitch. She helped him with school work and sometimes gave him his tea after school. It all helped to delay the inevitable because at the end of each day, her loneliness and grief would chase her to bed where her thoughts would tumble around in her head before, eventually exhausted, she would fall into a fitful sleep.

She was delighted to watch him grow into a strapping young man who had now got himself his first job working for Sidney Jacobs, the owner of the bicycle shop. He was learning the trade from top to bottom, spending most of his time in the rear workshop under Sidney's instruction, mending and repairing bicycles.

The added bonus for Sean was that Sidney had a very attractive daughter, whose name was Suzanne. She had long, silky brown hair which hung to her waist and had a special way of walking where she seemed to flick her hips from side to side as though she was a model on a fashion runway. The movement hypnotised him when she sashayed around the shop.

Whenever she called into the shop, the visit would leave him embarrassed, flustered and tongue-tied. It took all his courage just to say hello. He hated himself for his stuttering attempts at conversation with her, always feeling like an awkward teenager in the presence of a woman.

One day, Sid had gone to the wholesalers and had left Sean in sole control but he was struggling with a difficult customer who was complaining about a puncture repair, when thankfully Suzanne glided in. She took control of the situation, gracefully slipping behind the counter and asking, 'How much did the repair cost you, sir?'

'It's not about the money, love,' he moaned, 'I just wanted a proper repair done.'

'Very well,' she replied, 'leave your bike here for fifteen minutes and we will fit a new inner tube, and there will be no extra charge.'

'Oh, well, that would be great, thank you very much,' he said as he went outside to bring his bike in.

He parked up his bike and said, 'See you both,' pulling the door to as he left.

After he had gone, Suzanne said, 'Okay, Sean, where's my dad?'

'He's gone to the wholesalers,' he stuttered.

'Right, let's get the bike in the back and fit that new inner tube,' and with that, she locked the front door and put up the 'back in fifteen minutes' sign.

Sean's heart was beating out of his chest at the prospect of being alone with her. She approached him, pinned him against the work bench and whispered seductively in his ear.

'If we are quick, we can get the inner tube done after we've finished,' and kissed him passionately. In shock, he responded by burying his tongue in her mouth and their lips hungrily sought pleasure from each other.

In complete control of the situation, she unzipped his jeans and began rhythmically to pull energetically at his throbbing manhood. He was so excited and it wasn't long before he lost control.

He stood breathless and wondering what had just happened. He zipped himself back up. He wasn't sure if that was love but there was time to work on that later, he thought. After such a promising start to their relationship, he could only dream of what it would be like in the future.

'Right,' she said, 'we go no further than that 'til we're engaged. You change the inner tube and I'll go and open up the shop before Dad gets back.'

When she returned, she looked straight into his eyes.

'Now, Sean Casey, has that loosened your tongue?'

'That's not all it's loosened,' he quipped.

'I hope you don't think I go about doing that sort of thing with just anyone but I read this book once where this shy young boy had a terrible stutter which he was cured of once he had sex, so I thought that might work with you, too. Let's face it, if we are going to have a relationship, I don't want everyone to think you are some stuttering half-wit, so I decided that that was the way to find out if the theory worked. So what do you think, did it work or not?'

'Well, SSSUEzanne Iyyy mm nnnot ssssure,' he playfully stuttered. 'Iy ththink Iyy neeneed www one mmmore ttttreatment,' he teased.

'You cheeky bugger,' she said as they embraced and kissed once more.

'Can I ask if that means we are going out with one another?' he asked as he held her in his arms and looked into her eyes.

'Yes, Sean, we bloody well are,' she sighed.

'Oh brilliant,' he said, 'my own personal therapist, on hand, to give emergency treatment any time I start to stutter.' She playfully punched his arm and they embraced and laughed, and from then on they were inseparable.

***

Mary loved having Sean and Suzanne visit her, enjoying their energy and vitality, and zest for life. She liked listening to their stories of their nights out together, the descriptions of their friends and the problems they encountered in their young lives. Mary liked Suzanne, she reminded her of herself when she was younger, confident, driven and ambitious. 'This girl knows where she's going in life,' she thought, 'and Sean is in for an exciting journey.'

Mary dispensed her wisdom and entertained the two with her stories of the old days back in Ireland; the nuns and priests, rural life and the challenges she faced when she first came to Birmingham after the war, recounting the trials and tribulations of her life over the years. The youngsters listened intently to Mary's tales and a strong bond was formed between the three of them, one of love and respect and friendship which bridged the generation gap.

CHAPTER THIRTY-SIX

Ryan was now the owner of a roofing company that was turning over a million pounds a year and with cute buying and labour cost control, he could be heading for a bumper year. So, in the midst of peace and acceptance of what he and the family had endured, an unexpected phone call threw him into a panic.

'Ryan?' a woman's voice asked.

'Yes, this is Ryan,' he replied, holding the phone in the crook of his neck so that both hands were free to use his scale rule whilst carefully measuring a set of building plans on his desk. Suddenly, he recognised whose voice was on the other end of the phone; his heart was beating a busy drum roll.

'Jen, is that you?'

'Yes, it's me,' she said rather seriously.

Ryan picked up on the sombre tone.

'Is everything okay? What's the matter, what's happened?'

'Well,' she paused, 'I've done something silly.'

'What have you done?' he asked, fearing she had found someone else.

'I've taken a big chance.'

'What, what do you mean?'

'Well, me and Christopher are here,' she said. Ryan thought the worst and his heart sank, and he felt sick. 'She's brought him with her, what's going on?' he wondered.

'We've never been apart since the day I left and he's brought me back to you safely.'

Ryan needed time to think and in a few seconds he unravelled the puzzle then laughed out loud in relief.

'That would be a certain St Christopher, would it? You had me worried there for a second. Where are you?'

'I'm not far away, actually; I'm sitting in a very swanky booth at a small café called the Greasy Spoon.'

'Whoooh,' he whooped, 'I'll be there in ten seconds.'

She was waiting in the booth at the café and as it was near to closing time, the place was empty of customers. He walked through the door and then rushed towards her. He picked her up in his arms and held her tight. Billy and Rita quietly slipped out of the back door to give the pair some time alone.

'Well, that's some welcome back. I'm thinking I made the right decision, then?'

She looked deep into his eyes, searching for any reluctance or hesitation; there wasn't any, for which she was grateful and slightly ashamed, knowing that to have made any man wait so long was insane. But she knew Ryan was no average man. He was special and that's why she had come back to him, and would dedicate the rest of her life to him.

'I've missed you so much. I thought you would never come back to me. Can I ask you, why now?'

She realised that they hadn't kissed each other yet. Something so intimate and easy in the past, was at this moment crucial to her. But she understood that before he would entertain that next important step, he was due an answer to his question.

'To start with, Ryan, when I went back I was full of ambition and decided after talking it over with my parents, that I should commit to my uni course at least, then I would have a degree. I would have the opportunity to make a career choice in the UK or at home. It had always been my ambition to become a doctor which I knew would be a long process, realising the longer I left coming back to you the harder it would be. I never looked at another man although I had plenty of offers, some tempting too. No, no; nothing like that ever happened, Ryan, because I knew if I strayed, that would signal the end of us. So I studied hard and dedicated myself to the profession, and qualified. Eventually, my wanderlust took me out into the bush and a job with an elderly doctor who was looking to do less and retire but he was quite adamant that the person coming in should be dedicated to his beloved practice. He wanted to give his patients the continuity he felt they deserved. So as time went on and he retired, I took on the practice and settled into the country life. Months turned into years and I can't say I didn't enjoy it all but then, as happens in these situations, something silly set me off and all the plans and sensible decisions I had been making as an adult, were suddenly lost in a moment of madness, or was it clarity?'

'Okay, let's hope it was clarity,' he said.

'So there I am, watching a country wedding taking place at our local church, sitting in my car at the side of the road watching the bride and groom walk out of that church. Suddenly a song came on the car radio which reduced me to tears. That was when I decided to take the chance. I wasn't getting any younger and that happy bride set me wondering. What did I want the most? And the answer to that was you. I realised, at that moment, that I needed you more than anything else in the world. It wasn't simple to get out of the practice but it was worth all the hassle to be free of it and once I had made that decision, I felt a relief and a massive rush of excitement.'

'You mean, you came all the way back here on a chance that I hadn't met someone else? That's hard to believe.'

'Well, to be honest, Ryan, I had someone on the inside who kept me up to date with what was going on, so I knew I could chance it and hope you would have me back.'

'Don't tell me, Billy?'

'Yes, I would occasionally phone and get him at the café in the early morning for an update.'

'So the crafty bugger has known all along, has he?'

'I'm afraid so. I hope you don't think it was duplicitous of him but he always had your best interest at heart.'

Ryan sat looking at her for a long time while he let everything sink in.

'Okay,' he eventually said. 'One last question. What was the song you were listening to that made you so emotional that you gave everything up?'

'Now here's the funny thing, Ryan. You remember how often we talked about our love of music when we first met and how the Beatles had made such an impression on us both? Then in that third year when I was back at uni, you were still keeping in touch and you sent me Wings' latest song, with Paul's sweet voice singing 'My Love'? When I played it I was in floods of tears. The opening bars with that continuous note before the guitar kicks in, sent shivers down my spine and the lyrics upset me so much I had to hide it away from view. I put it in the back of a cupboard and vowed never to listen to it again, or I knew I would be on the next plane over and I still had so much to achieve. Well, that day there it was, playing on the radio and there

I am watching the happy couple, and it was all too much. I sat there in my car, bawling my eyes out and as the song played, I made the decision there and then that my life was worth nothing without you in it. I realised that as Paul succinctly put it, you have the other key to me, so here I am. Well?'

His eyes gave her the answer she wanted and this time he held her gently, kissing her long and lovingly, accepting her back without reservation.

She had walked straight back into his life and it was as if they had never been apart. It had been a long, long time but the magical thing was that he felt exactly the same about her now as he had back then. He held no anger towards her for leaving him for so long. He accepted that if she ever came back to him, it could only ever be her decision, he couldn't force her. It had to be after she had purged herself of her wanderlust. And now that moment had arrived, a moment he thought would never happen. He remembered some years ago when Billy had given him that talking-to about sorting himself out, that he had promised him that she would come back one day. And he was right, again.

Ryan decided quickly that she would not escape a second time and within three months they had named the day.

Unlike Billy and Rita, the pair opted for a quiet family wedding at the Register Office in Birmingham. Only Ryan's family and special close friends were invited. It still added up to a fair crowd, which included Mary, Billy and Rita, Sean and Suzanne, Great Aunt Bridie, Harry and Gloria, Sid Jacobs and his wife, Rachel, Margaret from work, and Aunty Kathleen and her husband, Ray, who had first employed Jenny all those years ago.

Her family back in Australia couldn't make it to the wedding and she sadly accepted that fact but she was happy to at last become Mrs Casey. She hoped that one day she would be able to coax Ryan to make that trip and meet his in-laws.

Mary had a few moments of sadness after the ceremony as she remembered her own wedding at the same venue, over forty years ago. The sepia-coloured memories came flooding back as she pictured her handsome husband in his best suit and her in that pencil skirt, wearing Bridie's pillbox hat and pearl necklace. Her friend, Julie, her wonderful Aunt Bridie, William's little sister, Kathleen, and his parents were all there that day.

She replayed it all in seconds, a short black and white movie, the story of her life over the last four and a half decades, gone in the blink of an eye. Sadly, William and Maria were now both gone and she sighed, a big emotional sigh, and dabbed at her eyes with a tissue.

The reception back at the golf club in a small private room was a low key affair which wouldn't have been complete without his big brother making a speech.

He rose to his feet to mild applause and nodded his thanks to everyone.

'Ryan,' he began, 'at last you have married the woman of your dreams. It took a long time to catch her as she bounced around Australia like one of those kangaroos but I promised you that she would come back eventually and she did. It was always pretty clear to me that you would end up together. I'm just happy that you are now man and wife. Since Jenny left us all those years ago, we have endured some very sad events in our family but I speak for us all when I say that I hope this is now the start of happier times. Little brother, you have been a steadfast and reliable friend and confidante to me, helping to get me through some of the darkest moments in our lives and you have always been there when I needed you. I want to thank you for that. I'm not sure if we will hear the patter of tiny feet any time soon but I'm sure Jenny, as a doctor, knows that pregnancy in more mature women is on the increase. Let's face it, a further addition to the Casey family would be most welcome to prolong this family's name. So see what you can do, remember the biological clock is ticking, so you'll have to be quick,' he joked.

'Jenny, I never lost faith that you would come back, although the time it took was pushing it a bit. But from the first time I saw how much you two loved and cared for one another, the fun you had and the love that sparkled in your eyes, it was enough proof for me that this day would come, eventually. I am very proud to welcome you into the Casey family, our first professional, too, I might add. Finally,' he concluded, 'if you would all like to raise your glasses in a toast to the bride and groom, Jenny and Ryan.'

The happy couple got to their feet and basked in the love of their family and friends. Ryan nodded to the barman, who flicked a switch and from the speakers came that long, stretched chord before Paul sang their song. The loving couple exchanged a knowing smile, looked deep into each-other's eyes and kissed.

They settled into married life very easily; they were of a similar temperament and besides loving one another, more importantly they enjoyed each other's company. Ryan's apartment in Edgbaston had suited him fine for all the years he had spent as a single man and he was by habit a tidy person. However the clothes and possessions a woman carries with her began to spread into every room and he could see they would need somewhere bigger, a house maybe, with more rooms and a garden too, perhaps.

There were only two bedrooms in his flat and he had always kept the second bedroom as a store for a few boxes of bits and pieces that he had gathered through his life. Now, with Jenny's recently arrived shipment of her possessions, the second bedroom was packed solid, leaving just enough space to open the door and squeeze into the room.

The next morning as they ate breakfast, Ryan asked his wife's opinion on the subject of living surrounded by boxes.

'You know, Ryan, one thing we haven't discussed is money; I haven't come back here to sponge off you and I have already looked into helping out as a locum until something more long term comes up. And,' she added, 'I have the money I got for my share of the practice and my savings, too, which over the years, being a frugal wench, have built up nicely. So what I am saying is, yes, let's get ourselves a house. I can throw my money in and we should be able to get ourselves somewhere new to start our married life together.'

'Right, this weekend we start to look. You make a few enquiries from the local agents and also decide whether we live city or country or somewhere in between. As long as I'm not far from the office I don't mind,' Ryan added.

He had got to the point in his business life where he could afford a fair deposit and a hefty mortgage without the need to sell the apartment, which he had already decided they would rent out. The weekend would be the start of the search for a house that would become their home.

CHAPTER THIRTY-SEVEN

If it was possible, the bond between the brothers grew even stronger following Ryan's marriage to Jenny; they could now enjoy each other's company with the added bonus that their respective wives got on like sisters.

Saturday evenings were set aside, and the two couples enjoyed nothing more than getting together for what Rita called her Saturday night take-away. A night away from cooking, which consisted of a take-away and a few glasses of wine and a beer or two.

The boys would go off to get the take-away and while it was being cooked, they would take the opportunity to have a crafty one at The Black Horse. While they were away, the girls took the opportunity to catch up on things. As they stood in the kitchen waiting for the plates to warm in the oven, Rita continued their conversation.

'So how late are you?'

'Well, I missed last month and I was due this week. I know it sounds a little ridiculous, me being a doctor and all, but I'm just so scared to do the test. I'm no spring chicken anymore and the whole idea of becoming a mother at my age seems a little bizarre but—'

'Look,' Rita interrupted, 'don't deny yourselves the happiness that is coming your way. Do the test tomorrow and tell Ryan straight away. Believe me, if he's anything like his brother, he will be over the moon. Ooh, I'm so excited. Don't worry, I won't say anything but now you've told me, I won't settle until I know the results. Phone me tomorrow, yeah?'

'Okay, Rita, but to tell you the truth I'm still in shock. All I could think about since the whole thing hit me, was your Billy's speech at the wedding and his comments about older mothers and the pitter-patter of tiny feet; it's as if he knew it would happen.'

'Well, you know him, always reckons he's got all the answers. Probably tell you he saw it in the tea leaves in the bottom of your teacup. Anyway, I think I can hear the car pulling in, so let me know, okay?'

'I will. I've got a pregnancy test at home but I haven't been able to bring myself to do it. I will tomorrow, though, I promise.'

The front door opened and the boys bundled in with the beer, wine and take-away.

'I was just asking Ryan,' began Billy as they set the food down on the table, 'why is it that when I order a portion of chips off the old fella at the Chinese, he always asks if there's something wrong with my finger?'

'What do you mean?' asked Rita.

'Well, before he wraps up the chips he always says 'sore finger'.' He let the joke sink in and then unnecessarily explained, 'but he's really asking if I want salt and vinegar, see? Sore finger, get it?'

'You bloody fool, Billy, shut up, sit down and serve up,' admonished his wife.

After finishing their meal they retired to the lounge and discussed house hunting. Jenny laughed as she told them of their day viewing some houses.

'There were some hellish properties but also the dream ones which captured our imagination, especially a big detached house in Barnt Green with massive gardens, a private driveway with its own gate and a detached double garage. Not too far for Ryan to get to work but far enough away from the city and situated in a rural enclave of pricey, classy properties.'

They told them about a few others which were either too small or over-priced and vowed to continue the search the following weekend. As the conversation dipped for a moment, Rita looked at Jenny who was deep in thought and probably on the point of giving the game away. She nudged Billy into action.

'Erm, oh, so tell us a bit more about life back in Aussie then, Jen,' he blurted out.

She was relieved to get her mind off the subject occupying her every thought and perked up. She began to tell them about her years spent in rural Australia.

Jenny was a good raconteur and gave an entertaining account of her life out in the bush, describing the landscape, the town, the weather and the local people.

She tried to convey to them the vastness of the country and relate the size compared to England.

'Some of the farms are so big, the farmers use planes and helicopters to get around them. Some still use horses just like American cowboys but the use of motorbikes and quad bikes is more common. Farms range in size from five thousand acres, big ones can stretch from fifty to a hundred thousand acres, and there are a number of million-acre farms. I know it's hard to imagine the vastness, when here in England if you travel for four hours you would be in another country, whereas in Australia you could drive for days and still be in the same state.'

'Imagine an area as big as France,' she continued, 'and then consider that when the floods come, all of that area is under water and that's just in New South Wales. Do you know the UK would fit into New South Wales three times and over thirty times into Australia, with room to spare?'

Her audience were amazed and sat wide-eyed; she could see them trying to comprehend what she had told them.

'The country people are a bit different to the city folks; they talk a little slower and are a lot more laid-back. Sometimes, you might believe you are in the Wild West, seeing them in their jeans, checked shirts, cowboy boots and hats. It's an accepted fact that the bigger the brim on the cowboy hat, the more money the farmer wearing it has. They also love country and western music and the Friday night dances are always a bit lively. You can imagine that after a hard week working all-out on their farms they're up for a party, so the pubs are full of boisterous, boozy girls and fellas out for a good time.'

She knew that any second she would be asked about spiders and snakes, the favourite questions from Poms.

'Did you have to treat anyone who had been bitten by a snake or spider?' ventured Rita at last.

'It happens less than you would imagine, especially when you consider that Australia is said to have many of the world's deadliest spiders and snakes. The incidence of any fatalities from bites or stings is quite small. I have only treated a few as most victims call emergency services or rush themselves to hospital as quickly as possible. However, the advice to snake bite victims is very clear: keep still, as the less you move about, the less the venom spreads around the body and the more chance you have of surviving. Place a pressure bandage on the site of the bite to help slow its spread, and get hospital treatment immediately, where they will have the anti-venom which will save your life.'

'Ooh,' said Rita, 'I think I'll stay in good old Blighty. I hate spiders and snakes.'

'I might add,' said Jenny, 'that snakes are part of Australia's finely balanced eco-system and are one of many protected species, so killing even venomous snakes is illegal.'

They looked at each other in disbelief and laughed.

'Just to put it all in context for you, the weird and wonderful world of snakes, spiders, kangaroos and koala bears apart, day-to-day medicine in my practice was much the same as anywhere else. Coughs and colds, aches and pains, heart attacks, cancer. The Aussies are no different, except maybe for skin cancer, which is on the increase,' she added finally.

It was another enjoyable evening for them all and as Ryan had an early tee time the next morning, they left for the drive home.

Sunday morning arrived, and Ryan had left early for his round of golf so Jenny took the opportunity to stay a little longer in bed to contemplate the tumult that had happened in her life since she had returned to England.

Marriage, house hunting and possibly a baby! Well she would find out now, it was no good putting it off any longer. What had she to fear anyway? The prospect of a baby at her age did concern her but as her father used to say in the accepted Aussie way of not worrying too much, 'She'll be right.'

She hurried to the bathroom and did the test, flushed the toilet and washed her hands. She headed towards the lounge, not daring to look at the stick yet. She sat down on the edge of the sofa and waited for a couple of minutes, relaxing with her head back and eyes closed.

Then she decided it was time. She opened her eyes and raised the stick to eye level. She checked it once and then again and couldn't believe it; her head fell back on the sofa and she began to cry.

'I'm forty-two soon and for this to happen so late in my life is unbelievable. I'm pregnant! Oh my God, I'm having a baby,' and cried more tears of joy.

She knew Ryan would be finishing his round at about midday. They had arranged to have a spot of lunch in Rackham's top floor restaurant and take the opportunity to do some shopping, too. She made herself look beautiful, ignoring the lines on her face which seemed to be multiplying at an alarming rate. Looking in the mirror, she applied her make-up and smiled at her reflection and said happily, 'Hello, Mum.'

Ryan wouldn't be late, he never was, he didn't like being late and felt uncomfortable if ever he was. She nervously checked her watch again then looked up; there he was. He looked very tanned and handsome after his round of golf. He kissed her gently on the lips.

'Hello, darling, you look gorgeous today,' and looking into her eyes, he sensed something.

'Go on,' he started. 'What is it?'

She nervously played with her St Christopher and then reached across the table, taking both of his hands in hers.

She took a deep breath.

'Ryan, you're going to be a dad!'

'No, you're joking,' he said, falling back in his chair.

'No, I'm serious, we are having a baby!'

'That is so fantastic, how brilliant, you are brilliant, you wonderful woman.'

'Well, you played your part too, you know,' she giggled.

'When did you find out?'

'This morning, for certain. I did the test and it was positive and after getting over the shock of it all, I have been all over the place since.'

'Right, this calls for a celebration, let's have some champagne. Wait 'til Mum hears about this and Billy and Rita, Great Aunt Bridie – well, everybody. I can't believe it, when's it due?'

'Well, first thing is forget the champagne, it's just orange juice for me from now on and secondly, I've worked it out to be around mid-March next year, a month after I reach the grand old age of forty-two.'

'Don't you worry about that, you look radiant and could easily knock ten years off that.'

They had a light lunch and ignored the shopping, spending the rest of the afternoon calling round to see the family and letting them all know the news. Mary was of course first on the list and burst into tears as soon as she was told. A visit to Rita and Billy had his brother overjoyed, with much hugging and back slapping. Rita was more controlled as she had taken a phone call from Jenny that morning, as promised. Great Aunt Bridie, of course, was thrilled and wished the pair well.

The rest of Sunday was full of love and happiness, chatting and making plans for the future.

CHAPTER THIRTY-EIGHT

It was Monday morning and Ryan Casey pulled into the yard of his roofing business, parking his Range Rover beneath the sign that read, 'Casey Roofing.'

Margaret, his secretary, bookkeeper and general factotum, was at the office window watching his arrival. She began to organise Ryan's first coffee of the day, as she always did at seven every morning. She was as reliable as clockwork. She never let him down, did a brilliant job with the books – especially the VAT returns – and never, ever, questioned Ryan's creative use of the petty cash tin, nor made mention of the cash jobs. She was another reason that Ryan had to thank his brother.

Billy had known Margaret was a very capable woman as she had done his books on a part-time basis when he started running the café. When her husband had died suddenly, some years previously, it was obvious she needed something more to keep her mind occupied. He recommended that Ryan should employ her full time; he remembered the conversation they had at the café that day.

'Look, it's about time you got over the idea that you need a dolly bird with big tits. You've never been able to keep your mind on the job when you've had one of those working for you. The important thing is making sure your business is running well and making money. No, what you need is a mature, plain, efficient, no frills, safe and sure lady who will care about you and your business. Remember, you've had too many of the other sort and where are they today? Gone, that's where they are, leaving you in the shit and the books in a mess. I know you had to fill your boots when Jenny went back to Oz but now's the time to concentrate on the fucking business and not the business of fucking.'

That memorable speech of Billy's seemed a lifetime away now and two very strong women were responsible for bringing calm from the chaos. Margaret had been the safe and reassuring presence that Ryan had indeed needed in his business. She had brought order and composure and over the last seventeen years had proved to be irreplaceable.

Jenny, on the other hand, had come back into his life and filled it with love and joy, friendship and companionship, and now a baby, too.

Rattling the spoon in the instant coffee jar to ensure she scooped out the final residue, Margaret turned to greet Ryan.

'Good morning, Ryan.'

'Morning, Margaret,' he replied. 'I won't start the day with my usual question.' He then mimicked himself, 'Is everyone in today, no phone calls from George or Chris with some excuse as to why they're not in? You know those two jokers have worked for me for the last twenty years, yada, yada, yada.' He laughed at his characterisation of himself then told her his news. 'No, Margaret, not today because I don't care as I have some brilliant news for you. Me and Jenny are having a baby,' and with that he lifted her up in his arms and swung her round. 'Isn't it great?'

'Oh, Ryan, that's brilliant news. I'm so happy for you both,' she then had to steady herself, leaning against her desk as her head was still spinning a little from Ryan's celebratory hug.

He laughed happily as he strode down the corridor to his office to open the post.

CHAPTER THIRTY-NINE

Pregnancy wasn't easy for Jenny; her age played its part as she continually felt tired and bloated. Her ankles always seemed to be swollen and she was forever going to the toilet, all common symptoms she was very much aware of as a GP.

Karma crossed her mind as she remembered the little speech she so often made to her expectant mothers without thinking and in a slightly off-hand manner, 'What did you expect?' She would react a little differently now she had experienced the discomfort associated with the whole process.

She attended all her pre-natal classes and was under a super specialist at the Queen Elizabeth Maternity Hospital. Obviously aware that Jenny herself was a doctor, he was able to discuss the details of her pregnancy in detail.

Towards the thirty-eighth week and due to her high blood pressure, he advised plenty of rest but Ryan began to worry when, in the following week, she had a number of painful twinges. After hearing her complain once more that day, he decided to take no chances either and against her advice, drove her to the maternity hospital to get things checked over.

Fortunately, her specialist happened to be on duty and he decided to take no chances, sending her straight to a ward so that he could run some tests. Having monitored the baby's heartbeat and checked Mum's blood pressure too, he and the midwife discussed the results from the printout. It revealed signs of distress in the baby's heartbeat and there were worries that the umbilical cord may be wrapped around the baby's neck. Without further ado she was off to theatre for a Caesarean delivery.

Ryan was in a state of shock and worriedly paced up and down outside the delivery room doors, nearly wearing away a trench in the floor while he anxiously waited for news. He wasn't allowed into the operating theatre and his nerves were flayed. After what seemed an interminable wait, the doors swung open and the midwife appeared with a little bundle wrapped tightly in towels. She carefully passed the baby to Ryan.

'Mother is well, but tired, and will be out of theatre soon and you, Mr Casey, are the proud father of a little boy. You can have a few minutes with him and then I will take him back in, but everything is fine.'

He carefully cradled the baby, the emotion of it all proving too much. He gently kissed his newly-born son as his tears dropped softly, falling onto his son's face.

They named the baby Donovan and the birth of the little boy brought so much happiness to the family, who were all gathered at the flat for the return of mother and baby. Everyone got to hold him. Mary didn't want to hand him back but he was due for a sleep and Jenny managed to wrestle him away to settle him into his new crib.

The chaos such a small being can cause in such cramped conditions was unbelievable and Ryan hoped the plan he had put in operation the previous week would have a happy outcome.

At nine the next morning, he received a phone call at his office, at the end of which he smiled, nodded and said, 'Thank you so much.'

He tapped in a number to make an important phone call and when that familiar voice answered the phone, he said, 'I've got some more good news for you. Start packing, darling. We are now the proud owners of a five-bedroomed home in Barnt Green. Our offer has been accepted and we move in thirty days.'

Jenny couldn't contain her happiness and screamed, 'Oh, Ryan, how wonderful. I love you. You made it all happen. How exciting! Another adventure but this time with the two men I love so much. Donovan will love that house as he grows up. I can't wait to move. Let's talk tonight and sort it all out. Love you,' she said as she put down the phone.

Ryan and Jenny accepted that the chances of more babies at her age were limited and were thankful for this late opportunity to be parents, concentrating all their love and affection on their son. Without knowing it, he gave them so much in return.

He developed into a happy child, playing in his garden or kicking a football with his dad. He was forever laughing and talkative and contented except when it was time for bed, when he would have to be coaxed to give in to sleep.

Mary embraced her role as grandmother for the second time and was always available for baby-sitting duties, enjoying getting involved in Donovan's early education. She helped him to learn through play and as he got older, encouraged his first efforts at reading and writing. When he started kindergarten he proved to be a bright and intelligent little boy.

CHAPTER FORTY

One other thing Harry Moss was good at besides baking, was business, so when he had concluded the deal on the café all those years ago, he had studied the contract and attached plans very closely. He realised early on that if ever there was a wholesale redevelopment of the old battery factory, there might be a need to buy up the café and possibly the adjoining shop premises.

The area of land the old battery factory stood on covered nearly ten acres of prime industrial land and the faceless conglomerates would salivate at the thought of developing the site, especially with the evolution of the huge shopping park developments. Harry knew that this was the beginning of the end for many small shops like his own as they could never compete against these behemoths of the retail world. So with the closure of the battery factory, he had recently approached his solicitor who confirmed that what Harry understood, was indeed correct. The present owners of the café held what might be termed as a 'ransom strip'.

Harry informed his son-in-law that they may be sitting on a gold mine but not to be hasty in making any decisions. He revealed that he had already received a letter from an agent acting for a very cute developer who had identified the potential of the site and wished to make an appointment to discuss, as they put it, the way forward.

Billy too had received a similar letter. His, however, was followed up by a visit.

A busy morning in the café was suddenly disturbed by a visit from someone Billy didn't expect to meet that day and he was definitely caught off-guard.

'A mug of tea, and a bacon and egg sandwich, please, Mr Casey.'

'Now what the fuck do you want?' Billy said, finding it hard to hide his loathing of the man. He stared into that emotionless void which was Connor Flynn's face.

The visitor was annoyed at the welcome and replied in a similar vein.

'That's what you do here, isn't it, sell sandwiches and tea to the down and outs. Well, I've just lifted the status of your clientele in this crumby establishment by dropping in for a chat. We need to discuss some stuff and if you just hear me out, I think we can come to a happy conclusion for us both.'

He coolly continued, 'Don't let personal differences ruin what could set you up for life.'

Billy could hardly contain his anger. 'You think you can stroll in here and everybody's gonna roll over so that the big 'I am' can get what he wants. You might think you have this town all tied up but not here, buddy. You can go fuck yourself 'cos I ain't playing your game. I'd rather give this joint away than sell it to you.'

'You may regret that, Billy, and it could be that in the end you will have to give it away.' Connor's eyes narrowed and he grinned, 'We'll see. I've got plenty of time. I'll be seeing you soon, Billy,' he spat the words as he turned and left the café.

Billy was seething but kept control. 'Don't get mad, get even,' he said to himself and began to relax, remembering what his old man had told him when he was playing football. He intended to take this guy down a peg or two and give him a kick up the arse.

Later in the day and a few miles away from the café, Connor Flynn had returned to his office, happy with his morning's work. He knew he had got under Billy Casey's skin and regarded their argument as a win on points. He would now play a patient game and wait for the right moment.

It was the first time they had come face to face since they were young schoolboy football players and his threats to his opponent on that day had the desired effect. There would be no quarter given in this battle either, he always came out on top.

His life now was a world away from that of the boy he was back in the children's home. He was now running a successful building company with sites all over the city, with big plush offices in Edgbaston. He had proudly steered his small one-man band from nothing to a multi-million pound building and development company and this little matter with Billy Casey was just a hiccough which he would overcome, whatever it took.

Over the years, he had become a driven and formidable businessman, who was both respected and feared, and had friends in powerful positions in local planning departments and on councils. His brashness upset a few people along the way but in his experience, there were always casualties in a battle and his plans never included being one himself.

His reputation for playing hard ball in business with the backing of his millions, enabled him to manipulate most situations to his own benefit, closing many a deal on land no one else believed would ever get planning permission. He intended to get this project over the line too, as this deal would be worth many millions. No, he needed to be patient. Anything could happen to that café in the meantime; an unexpected fire would be pretty damaging and possibly mean the closure of the little business for ever. He smiled at the thought.

Then a window of opportunity presented itself. His company was building a small site of executive houses in Solihull. Connor's brain had ticked over since the meeting with Billy Casey and he remembered that Billy's brother was a roofing contractor. He had met him and played golf with him as they were both members at Edgbaston.

'I'll use one brother to draw in the other,' he thought. He buzzed his secretary and asked her to get Ryan Casey of Casey Roofing on the phone.

'Now, Ryan, it's good to talk with you. I know we haven't done any business as yet but reports are that your company is professional and does a good job. I have a little site in Solihull coming up, all handmade clay plain tiles and I need a top class job. I need a price from you as we start roofing very soon.'

He paused for a moment then added, 'It is your brother runs that little café in Selly Oak, isn't it?

'Yes, why?'

Connor smiled, 'Just business, Ryan.'

He liked the idea of the leverage any dealings with Ryan might afford him in his negotiations with Billy. He knew that Ryan would report back to his brother. He knew that would wind him up even more. He also knew that people did silly things when their minds were unbalanced, and he would coolly sit back and wait for the fallout.

He ended their conversation with, 'Okay then, Ryan, I'll get my surveyor to send over the drawings. Make sure your price is competitive. Maybe I'll see you tomorrow for a hit round Edgbaston.'

CHAPTER FORTY-ONE

Ryan first became aware of Connor's company in the mid-seventies as a growing and expanding business but he had kept away, having heard the stories from other roofers and subbies who had worked for Flynn. Stories of stand-up arguments on site due to what Flynn reckoned was poor workmanship and tales of delayed or, worse still, no payments.

It had annoyed Ryan no end when he first noticed Flynn at the golf club and it was near impossible to avoid bumping into one another. Indeed, they had played in Saturday medals together and had formed a relationship via the golf but never discussed work.

Recently, Billy had become obsessed with Connor Flynn after the set-to in the café, so his own reluctance to do business with Flynn was taking a back seat to his brother's need for revenge. Under instruction from Billy, he was told that it was imperative to establish not only a working relationship but a social one of sorts too; he had his own agenda, it seemed.

So, the phone call from Connor Flynn the previous day had been what he thought was the opening gambit between the two. Ryan had hardly said a word and Flynn had seemed quite amiable for a change, which was odd. Ryan knew he was now in the middle of what could be an all-out war.

Later that night, he and Jenny arrived at Billy and Rita's house for dinner. Grandma Mary was babysitting little Donovan and Ryan knew that besides excited debate regarding the local derby with the Villa this coming Tuesday, there would undoubtedly be discussion of Connor Flynn. He was hoping for more of the former and less of the latter.

After the meal, Billy and Ryan retired to the lounge while Rita and Jenny cleared the table and attacked the washing up.

Billy returned to the subject which was dominating his thoughts.

'He walked in the café as bold as brass and acted as though the deal was done. I told him there was no way I would do business with him but it was his attitude, Ryan, he's such a smarmy bastard. He needs taking down a peg or two and I've got an idea to solve that one.'

Ryan had heard this story a number of times already but there was no changing the subject and he was ready for a one-sided discussion.

'But that's short-term business,' Billy continued. 'You know I've always had a feeling about him. I just know there's something but I haven't got there yet. We need to gather a bit more information on him, dig round a bit, so keep your ears and eyes open. We all remember the part in 'The Godfather' where he says, 'Keep your friends close and your enemies even closer'; well, that's what we need you to continue doing. That's your job.'

'Yeah,' Ryan replied, 'not by choice though. Whatever your magnificent plan is, I feel like a pawn in it all. It's all very stressful, you know.'

'Look, Ryan, I understand that but you are the important link in all this.'

'All this,' Ryan repeated. 'Exactly what is all this?'

'You might stumble on something, who knows?'

'I hope we find something quick because I hate having to get involved with him. He's trouble and I can never relax around him.'

'I know, but we have to look at the bigger picture and play the game our way and not his. The end result will be worth it, don't worry. Now how's your quote going on that job for him in Solihull?'

'Well, as I knew I was coming here tonight and that I would get fifty questions if I hadn't, I phoned him this afternoon and promised to send the quote to him by tomorrow.'

'Good work, Ryan, so now let's see what we can learn about our man, shall we? I know how his mind works and I've no doubt that he will give you the order because he knows you're my brother. He knew you would tell me about his phone call to you. He will enjoy the power he believes that will give him and how he can use that to get what he wants, which is my café. We just need an angle, Ryan, anything we can use to bring him down.'

'Cash might be an angle, Bill.'

'What do you mean?'

'Well, he always puts plenty on the tables at the casino; always has plenty of cash. I know he's a wealthy guy but I think he has access to cash from somewhere else.'

'No, Ryan, that would be too hard to prove. We will never know whether it's business cash or dirty cash. How will we prove that?'

'I don't know, but we might get a break somewhere. He likes me to go with him to the casino during the week after our game, which is a pain, but it's given me the chance to get to know Alan, the manager, pretty well. I even put him a new roof on his house in Harborne a couple of months ago. Did him a real good deal and he paid me in readies, and he's invited me to their golf day which is coming up at Edgbaston in a few weeks' time. Then to top off all that, I've got an invite to their private box down the Blues to watch the derby game next week.'

'Interesting.' Billy was deep in thought. 'See, the time you are spending with him gets us more information. Who knows what that character is into? But I'm sure we will find something to help us. Now, is he going to the match?'

'Alan says Flynny is presenting the match ball.'

'Presenting the match ball, eh? Very interesting.' Billy was silent for some time, lost in thoughts and plans. He stood up and massaged his temples. 'You know, after Jenny told us that Australia has all those killer snakes, well, I reckon I have discovered another venomous snake, living right here in Birmingham. Goes by the name of Connor Flynn,' he said seriously, 'and we need to cut off the head of the vile serpent. Let's have another beer to round off the night.'

'Not for me,' replied Ryan. 'It's time I hit the road.' As they reached the front door, Billy told Ryan that he would speak with him tomorrow and told him not to worry. He added that all-encompassing gesture where someone taps their nose, meaning, 'It's all under control.'

'Anyway, brother, keep your wits about you and see what you can pick up. You have the match with the Villa to look forward to and I know that is going to be one hell of a night, in fact I guarantee it,' he smiled.

CHAPTER FORTY-TWO

Ryan was sitting in his office chair, rocking backwards and forwards, sipping his early morning coffee and thinking about the upcoming match.

Margaret shouted through, 'Oh, Ryan, there were no phone calls from the roofing teams but there was one from Connor Flynn, asking if you had his prices yet for the Solihull job. He also thanked you for the donation you made to his holiday fund after the golf last Saturday. He said he looks forward to taking a little more cash from you next time.'

'Doesn't that bloke ever sleep? Shit, it's only just gone seven and he's chasing business. And, oh yeah, nice one about the golf. That bastard did me over again. Billy is getting me more and more involved with that man but he reckons he has a plan.'

Ryan stood up, still sipping the steaming coffee from one of Margaret's new office purchases, china mugs. With her cultured accent, her school-mistressy character and her professional manner, she had brought a bit of class to his company.

'Connor Flynn. I ask you, Margaret, what's the story, eh? There's always something nagging Billy when that name comes up and they had a little face-off last week in the café so I think things are reaching a crescendo. You know something, Margaret, they are so alike in so many ways, both very stubborn and always scheming.'

'Ryan, you know your brother and his ways by now and if he has some grievance with Connor Flynn, you can be assured that there will be good reason.'

He shrugged his shoulders and started to open the post. The big envelopes were always enquiries but he liked the smaller ones better as they were usually cheques or orders.

'There's a few more enquiries for those council re-roofing jobs in Handsworth as well, Margaret, plus a couple of cheques for you to pay in. I'll have a look at the enquiries later. I just need to get to work on this one for Solihull.'

Without waiting for a reply he smiled to himself.

'Happy days and tomorrow we shit on the Villa! Yeah.'

CHAPTER FORTY-THREE

Monday was a busy day at the café and Billy was all done and dusted early, giving him just enough time to get through the afternoon traffic and park up in the city. This afternoon, he would visit one of his mates in the Bull Ring Market who ran a stall selling party gear, masks, outfits and fancy dress.

It was an important trip into the city as the local derby with the Villa was going to be a big night tomorrow and his purchases would ensure it was going to be unforgettable. He found just what he was looking for at Tommy's stall and headed home. He immediately phoned Ryan and left a message.

When Ryan got home, he pressed the red flashing message bank button on his phone which stood on a little black table in the hallway. He heard his brother's happy voice message.

'This one will be a lot of fun, brother. The big arsehole will have a bit more to think about come tomorrow night. Now don't be late, whatever you do, you must be in position early. It's going to be one hell of a pre-match presentation. It will be very entertaining.'

Billy's voice was loaded with excitement and anticipation. He really did look forward to these 'derby games' against the Villa. Ryan imagined that he would fall asleep that night dreaming of a Blues victory and the pleasure that it would bring to him and to the Blue half of the city. Everything seemed wonderful in the world to Blues fans with a win over the old enemy and if Ryan understood correctly from his brother's message, it would be a day to remember for more than just that.

'What has he got planned?' he wondered as he switched the machine off.

***

The visit of the Villa to St Andrew's was building to the usual crescendo and was the major topic of conversation in many pubs, clubs and workplaces. The banter between the opposing fans, many of whom worked alongside each other, ran the whole gamut from sarcastic and funny to outright offensive and aggressive. Both sets of followers swapped insults but both too dreamed of being the top dogs in the city so that they could enjoy the bragging rights, 'til next time.

Tuesday evening arrived and the atmosphere in and around the St Andrew's stadium was electric, and Ryan could feel the tension as soon as he got out of his taxi. He joined the crowds of supporters making their way up the hill past the old Kingston cinema.

Looking into the distance, he could see the floodlights illuminating the stadium, lighting the stage on which the actors would perform. The noise grew louder as he neared the ground. There were tens of thousands of excited fans who filled the night with their singing, chanting, cheering, shouting and yelling. Everyone seemed boisterous and lively. A high-pitched squeal of police sirens filled the air, drowning for a moment the raucous crowd and the shouts from the programme sellers and merchandise vendors. The familiar smells also attacked his senses: hot dogs, hamburgers and chips, beery breath, cigarette smoke and the malodourous stink of the police horse droppings on the road.

Many of the supporters proudly sported their colours and wore their replica shirts with pride as they crowded the streets and made their way towards the turnstiles. The more outrageous followers decked out in crazy outfits hired for the day to celebrate party time on the terraces. Fancy dress outfits were common on these occasions. He noticed the Marx Brothers, three fellows in Elvis white jump suits, along with the sunglasses, Superman, Batman, all manner of superheroes and famous faces.

There was the inevitable crush of bodies as they funnelled into the turnstiles, all hoping with every stride towards their place in the stadium that tonight was going to be their night.

The excitement was palpable: the first view of the pitch as they entered the stadium, big and green and virgin, newly mowed and marked out. Twenty-odd thousand voices belting out the Blues anthem, 'Keep Right On to the End of the Road.'

Ryan smiled and thought to himself, 'It's all set up. The theatre is full and the audience want a top class performance. Pure magic and, fingers crossed, it could be a big night; well, Billy promised me it would be.'

Ryan made his way to the private boxes and showed his ticket to the reception team at the main entrance where a security officer pointed along the corridor and cheerfully said, 'Third room on the right, sir, the door with the dragon motif on it.'

When he entered the room, he found the usual suspects were already there, tucking into the free booze and food: Big John; Jimmy Wong; Raj and Sanjay, the Indian brothers; along with Alan and his co-manager, Barry. Lisa was also there to operate the bar and keep everyone's glass full.

'Ryan, glad you could make it, have a drink and watch Connor, he should be out on the pitch soon to present the match ball. Have you brought your camera?'

'No camera, but I've bought a bazooka to blow his stupid big head off,' Ryan whispered in an aside to Lisa who quietly giggled at his joke.

The last thing he wanted to see was old big head on the pitch, acting all smug and pleased with himself but as he looked out towards the pitch, there he was, strolling out onto the field. The cheeky git was even waving to the crowd, who responded with some applause but thankfully plenty of jeering, especially from the Villa fans.

The announcer blared out over the public address system, 'Ladies, gentlemen and children, we are proud to welcome a new sponsor tonight, Mr Connor Flynn of Flynn Developments, who will present today's match ball along with our commercial director, Bob Jones. We, at Birmingham City, thank Connor and his group of companies for their support.'

Connor shook hands and posed for the photographers, holding the ball in one hand and shaking hands with the other, smiling and enjoying the moment.

Then, unexpectedly, from the corner of the Tilton Road end, a chant started up.

'De de de de de de de de, De de de de de de, Batman.' Then, again, the same refrain of the famous Batman tune. Suddenly, there, clambering onto the pitch, came the Caped Crusader himself, making his entrance near the corner flag at the Tilton Road end. He began to run across the pitch, his cape flying out behind him, he was heading straight for the presentation area in front of the main stand. The stewards hadn't noticed and were slow off the mark and no one moved to intercept him. He was too quick for them.

Connor and the commercial director were oblivious to what was unfolding behind them as they posed for the media's photographers.

Batman made swift progress across the pitch, swooping upon his unsuspecting target and with a single motion, delivered the kick up the arse he had been promised. Sprinting off, he made his way diagonally across the pitch where he executed a perfect swallow dive into the crowd near the Spion Kop, making good his escape.

Later that night, back at Billy's house, the brothers sat in the kitchen, drinking a cup of tea.

'You know our dad always said when we played football, get your retaliation in first. Well, we did tonight. A bit of a pre-emptive strike, or should I say, kick. The 'coupe de grace' delivered by a comic book character in front of twenty-odd thousand people, none of whom would be able to identify the perpetrator and each one of them enjoying seeing a bit of good old fashioned British slapstick. Not only that, but the photographs the 'Evening Mail' took will be priceless. I hope they got the one of Flynny clutching his backside as though a firework had just exploded in his pants, looking shocked, bewildered and totally embarrassed. It's pure comedic gold.'

'From where I was sitting in the private box the whole thing was surreal. Everyone in that box stood there open-mouthed at what unfurled on the pitch. And, I might add, most everyone was laughing like dogs as he copped his just desserts; I loved it all,' added Ryan.

Billy leaned back and laughed out loud. He loved a plan to come together.

***

The next day, the 'Evening Mail' printed those pictures including one of the Caped Crusader, along with a banner headline which asked the question everyone wanted the answer to: 'Who is The Caped Crusader?'

As Ryan read the story of the events from the night before, he had his own idea of the identity of the person. He remembered he had seen that odd pigeon-toed running style before.

CHAPTER FORTY-FOUR

Alan Goldman smiled and moved on to mingle with the other guests he had invited to the Dragon Casino Golf Day. He was the supreme host and a very amiable and engaging character, surrounded by all the melodrama and excitement of the casino of which he was the managing director. There were rumours that some shadowy Jewish family, who no one ever saw, owned the casino and that Alan was somehow related to them. What was true was that they couldn't have chosen a better man to schmooze the high-rollers.

A John Denver look-alike with a mop of floppy straight fair hair and gold-rimmed spectacles, Alan was always immaculately dressed. His designer suits were hand made of cashmere and silk, with silk shirts and ties. Tall and willowy, he was the face everyone knew at the casino. Everyone liked Alan, especially the Chinese and Asian punters who always shook his hand warmly and said hello to Mr Alan, as they called him.

Ryan had often seen him pull out rolls of cash from his pocket, wads of fifties, 'Enough to choke a donkey', Ryan reckoned. The money was ostensibly to entertain his special punters, picking up the tab to ensure a great time was had by all before they ended up back at the casino.

The golf day was one among a number of some very special events he organised for those classed as high-rollers, treating them to lots of freebies. These included Royal Ascot,

Wimbledon, boxing and football matches, cricket, golf and 'the biggy', which was a week's break in Vegas. His golfing guests that day were expected back for the dinner and presentations which, of course, would all be free and gratis.

Connor was a definite high-roller. Ryan considered himself more of a 'low roller' who was more than happy to fulfil this role, establishing himself within the group as a friendly and sociable small businessman. More importantly, on behalf of his brother, he was using his position to gain a little more insight into the man Billy despised so much.

Fortunately, Alan had chosen a clear and sunny day to hold 'The Dragon Casino Golf Day' at the beautiful parkland course designed by H S Colt located in one of Birmingham's top suburbs. Set in over a hundred and forty acres with an ornamental lake and woodland including gardens designed by Capability Brown, it was a top class venue for the event.

Ryan had been a member there for many years and played at least twice a week, grudgingly accepting the fact that his brother's arch nemesis was a member too.

He was very apprehensive about today's round of golf with Connor after recent events at St Andrew's plus the contretemps with his brother, believing it all might prove to be too much. He knew he would suffer if the surly, bad-tempered side of the man's character surfaced. He was also acutely aware that his roofers had finished the tiling work at the Solihull site and the invoice was due for payment. He was worried that it was an ideal situation for Connor to mess him about for the money.

Ryan felt like he was some sort of conduit between Connor and his brother; caught in the middle of the two, he didn't much care for the position. It was hard work to keep Connor as a pseudo friend. His brother's long-term strategy was to keep him close but he worried that Billy too was developing a dark side in his quest to best his foe.

Those thoughts were on his mind as he parked next to Connor's black BMW. He walked around to the rear of the clubhouse to find the booking-in table out on the terrace which overlooked the course. The invited participants were greeted there by Lisa who was sitting behind the welcome desk, organising things.

'Hi, Ryan, here's your score card and a welcome gift. Please help yourself to a cold drink to take with you on your round today. If you go straight through to the dining room, you'll find Alan in there and there's a lunch buffet set up for the players today.'

Ryan could hear that voice even before he went through the double doors into the dining room. Connor looked up and called over, 'Oh, good, my playing partner has arrived. Here, sit with us, I want to sort out these handicaps and our bets for the day.' Connor always liked a bet on the outcome and would coerce Ryan into chancing his skill and nerve when money was at stake.

Connor, surprisingly enough, had fostered the social side of their relationship recently and they had spent many an hour at the course and later at Dragon's gaming tables. There were times he thought, very worryingly, that Connor actually liked him and wasn't sure why that would be.

From the beginning, they were always amiable to one another and agreed to play together when they were both free in the week, but certainly every Saturday morning. This agreement had developed into an encounter between two very competitive men, neither one giving ground, both battling hard to win the game. Generally, it turned out that they shared the winner's mantle equally. Ryan had the better handicap playing off ten but the handicap system allowed for some close encounters.

Last week's game had ended up all square but all wet too, as the heavens had opened halfway round and they had both got soaked to the skin.

Today's game would be a competitive and gruelling game but it was a further step along the road to knowing their prey a little better. 'Softly, softly, catchee monkey,' Billy reckoned. Ryan wasn't so sure.

'Understand your foe,' Billy had said.

The pair strolled across to the first tee and Connor teed up. Ryan stood back, taking a good look at the guy; it wasn't that he'd never looked at him before but while he had the chance, he studied him a little more closely. Billy's thought bounced around in his head.

'Okay, so,' Ryan thought, 'here goes. Connor Flynn is a big man, solidly built with wide shoulders, tree trunk legs and a barrel chest. Weather-beaten skin, probably the result of many years of outdoor hard labour also witnessed by a deep chestnut tan, inevitable when working outside. Mean, thin lips below those heavily lidded eyes, giving him the look of a gunslinger from the westerns. Not hard to imagine him back in the old days with a pick or shovel in his huge hands, sweating away, working as hard as anyone on site and getting great enjoyment from it. He was big and ungainly so sport would be hard work for him. No finesse.'

Ryan confidently knew, on the other hand, that he was a natural sportsman so he found it amusing to play against someone so uncoordinated but Flynn had a determination to compete which in some opponents became so strong, it overcame their obvious shortcomings. He was dangerous, was Ryan's final conclusion.

The round developed into a battle as usual and when they arrived at the eighteenth, Ryan had his nose in front, one up and one to play.

The par four eighteenth was stroke index eight, meaning Connor had the last of his shots in hand, giving him an advantage of sorts.

'Right, this is the last hole and I get my final shot,' he reminded Ryan as if he didn't already know. Ryan could only imagine winning from the position he was in now and, for once, he would be able to have a bit of a go at the casino later on without too many worries about doing all his cash. He'd be doing Connor's instead.

Ryan knew this last hole very well: the fairway lined with trees both sides and a slope from high on the right down to the left. He readied himself and fired his tee shot off to the right with a little draw to allow the ball to run back left and finish in the middle of the fairway. The plan worked beautifully; the ball flew all of two hundred and twenty yards and then ran on for another twenty. His Titleist ball, with his initials and smiley face drawn on in marker pen, sat right in the middle of the fairway. He would now be left with a not unreasonable chance to hit a slightly downhill six or seven iron to the green. A birdie opportunity if ever he had seen one and a great chance to stuff it up his playing partner for once.

Connor gave a half smile and breathed, 'Mm, not bad,' as he approached the tee. He steadied himself as he addressed the ball then suddenly stopped himself on his backswing as Ryan said, 'Just to make it interesting, how about double or quits?'

His opponent was a gambler and his massive ego wouldn't allow him to resist a bet or a challenge. Ryan had seen him in action on numerous occasions and like a lot of successful businessmen, he loved to unwind at the casino. He enjoyed a game of poker or blackjack. But roulette was his great love; if he was really going for it, he would sometimes build a big tower of ponies on his favourite number, thirty-five; a pony or two on thirty-two. Then twenty and fourteen, with a couple of pink hundred-pound chips as back-up bets. He wouldn't turn a bet down.

Connor was already looking at losing five hundred pounds today, so double or quits wouldn't be too big a stretch and could make Ryan a grand if he could pull this off, but he was taken by surprise when Connor stepped back from his ball and casually nodded and said, 'Right.'

Ryan began to panic inside. Connor continued, 'I tell you what, let's make it even more interesting and see if your arsehole twitches. You know those roofs you've just done for me in Solihull, how much do I owe you for that?'

Ryan swallowed hard and knew the ante was about to go higher than he could afford.

'Hold on, Connor, there's no way I can afford to put that on the line, that's twenty-five grand.'

'Oh, you big pussy, too scared and frightened to take me on. Let's face it, without your big brother behind you, that's what you are, a big pussy. Look, you started it, now we play this one hole; forget what's happened in the rest of the round, this is a one hole, winner takes all bet. If you win it, I pay you in full for the job as I should plus twenty-five grand on top. If you lose, I get that job for free. So, there you go. If it's a bit much for you and you haven't got the bottle, don't worry. I know one thing, your brother wouldn't back down, no. He's got big bollocks, that man.'

Ryan was stung and couldn't believe the words as they came out of his mouth.

'Right, you're on,' he brashly replied, immediately regretting it.

Then the whole tone of the game seemed to change. Ryan knew Connor had a nasty, vindictive side to him, especially if things didn't go his way. A raw nerve had been touched somewhere. War was about to break out. Who would be cool under pressure? One of them was confident. He'd operated under immense pressure back in Ireland and had never cracked. There would be only one person who would collapse under pressure and that wasn't going to be Connor Flynn.

He took up his stance again and looked down at his ball, then up the fairway as he struck his ball fiercely and sliced his drive well into the trees on the right.

Ryan was relieved. Connor would have no shot from where his ball had finished. As he saw the situation now there would be a chip out, making two, and then possibly lay up short of the green for three, and chip on for four. A good putt would give him a five, but more possibly he would end up with a six less his shot, so a net five.

Ryan confidently strolled down the middle of the fairway to where his ball was lying, not even bothering to help Connor look for his ball. 'Stuff him,' he thought, 'I need to concentrate on my next shot to the green; there's too much riding on this.'

After searching a while in the line of trees stretching along the fairway, he shouted over for Ryan to carry on and play his second shot while he continued to look for his ball.

'Don't let the pressure get to you, there's a lot of money riding on your next shot,' he called across.

Ryan tried to ignore the comment as he stood over his ball. He kept running through his set-up, saying to himself, 'Practise swing, no, not so fast. Back, take it back more slowly, turn the hips, head steady, nice rhythm, just scrape the turf, no big divot, gently—' Before he was settled, he had excitedly hit through the ball just bringing his right hand over a little. He caught it cleanly but pulled it to the left. The pressure had got to him. His shot sailed high and though it was the right distance, it bounced left and down into the valley to the left of the green.

He turned to slam the guilty seven iron into his bag. Then, to make matters even worse, Connor seemed to have found his ball, well over to the right of the line of trees separating the eighteenth and tenth fairways.

'Must have bounced off a tree and rebounded out here,' he shouted across. If he managed to hit it well he could now play back over the trees and hit the green.

Ryan was sure he must have 'improved' his lie; he didn't see him kick his ball and could never accuse another player of such behaviour. He had been told when he first started playing golf that if you cheat at golf, you cheat in life. His opponent however was unprincipled and would do whatever it took to come out on top, in golf and in life.

Connor settled over his ball and hit a mercurial shot over the trees, just like a professional, landing five feet from the pin. His grinning face was beaming as he pulled his trolley to the edge of the green.

This was now serious. Ryan had to find his ball. They both searched a general area where they thought it had landed. The clock was ticking. Suddenly Connor scooped up a ball.

'What ball are you playing?'

'My usual Titleist two with a smiley face drawn on it,' Ryan replied.

'Oh, bad luck,' Connor smirked as he pocketed the ball. 'This one's an Ultra.'

It couldn't possibly get much worse now because a lost ball would mean having to go back and play another from where he had hit his last shot and suffer a penalty stroke. Time was running out. 'We can't look any longer; we'll be late up the club and its seven o'clock already. I'm afraid it looks like you will have to go back and drop another ball and take that penalty stroke,' Connor said.

Ryan's concentration was broken. He hit a poor iron shot, this time overcompensating and flying off to the right, a fluffed chip shot. A thinned contact. A missed putt. Missed again going back.

As he had said before, a dangerous opponent.

***

In the changing rooms, Ryan had taken a shower and was getting dressed, his head still spinning at what he had just done. He was livid at being drawn into such a ridiculously big bet and fuming with himself at how Connor had so easily wound him up.

Connor was looking in the mirror and carefully shaving whilst talking with Raj and Sanjay; they were whispering, and Ryan thought he heard the word 'cocaine'. Was this that bit of information they had been waiting for? He needed to find out more but they had broken off their conversation while he was about.

He gathered his wet towel and packed away his golfing clothes in his bag.

'You might as well leave your car here and I'll give you a lift in, Ryan,' said Connor. 'You can pick your car up tomorrow. I'll be out in a minute.'

'Okay, I'll just drop my clubs in my car and I'll see you out there,' replied Ryan.

Connor returned to his conversation with the brothers.

He closed the changing room door behind him then a burst of adrenalin exploded in his stomach. He knew something was going on but how could he get to listen in? Then he remembered that immediately around the corner from the changing rooms was the boiler room where many of the members left their waterproof suits to dry out. The two rooms were separated by a thin wall with vents along the top.

He quickly put his bag in the back of his car and hurried back in through the pro's shop. He looked around. No one was about so he opened the boiler room door as quietly as possible and slipped inside. The air inside was dry and stale but as he looked up he noticed he was right about the vents. If he could get close enough he might be able to get to listen to what was being said on the other side.

He put the chair against the wall and stood on it. He was now high enough to put his ear to the vent.

'Look, Connor,' he heard one of the brothers say, he couldn't tell which one but that didn't matter, 'Yes, you can buy twenty-five Ks' worth and once it's cut, you could be looking at multiplying your investment by four.'

'I know you boys have been in this game a long time and so have I. When you punted the idea to me it was natural to do some homework. The checks on your background have already been carried out. We know where you live, the names of your wives and children, which schools they go to and where your wives like to shop,' Connor added threateningly. 'So I take it the quality will be excellent and—' His voice trailed off as someone entered the changing room to pick up their bag. The person left and closed the door behind them and the conversation restarted.

'If the returns are so good, I might raise the ante a bit, say you get me two hundred and fifty thousand pounds' worth, then if I multiply that up I can be looking at over a million return. Now, that's more interesting.'

'That's typical,' Ryan thought, 'Greedy bastard.'

It seemed an age before one of the brothers answered.

'That's a big order, Connor,' one of them said.

'Look, if you can't cope, I can go elsewhere.'

'No, no we can do it, no problem. As usual, we are talking cash, high denominations, used, and let's keep to the original plan and do the exchange when we go to Ascot. Our contact will be there anyway as he likes a punt from his private box. He's a big player and wouldn't like any mistakes.'

'Good,' replied Connor, 'He can depend on me, just make sure I can depend on you.'

Ryan had heard enough, he put the chair back in the corner and quietly opened the door. He was creeping out with his waterproof suit in his hand and bumped right into Connor who was just leaving the changing room. Connor gave him a quizzical look. Ryan shot back with a confident smile and said, 'Just getting my waterproofs, I left them in the boiler room after our game last week, still a bit wet but—are you ready to go now?'

Connor didn't question Ryan's story and heading for the car park, he smiled. 'Okay, let's get going. I want to spend some of that twenty-five grand I've just won.'

That brought Ryan back to earth with a bang.

'Well,' said Connor as he gunned his car through the leafy streets of Edgbaston, 'pressure gets to some people. That lost ball and thinned chip shot cost you big time and then three putts and it was all over. But the biggest mistake you made was thinking you could take me on, trying to psych me out. Maybe I taught you a lesson. Spread the word, don't ever try taking me on, not ever.'

'Sanctimonious bastard,' Ryan thought, noticing Connor's face developing that quirky, evil smile—

After the exchange in Connor's car, there was an uneasy silence which continued at the dining table at the casino's restaurant. As dessert was being served, Alan got to his feet and made a short speech thanking all who had attended the Golf Day. He presented some small prizes to the winners after which Connor and Ryan made their way onto the gaming floor.

Unfortunately, the tables were unkind to Ryan. He asked, 'Do you want another drink, Connor?' as he placed his last pink hundred-pound chip on his favourite number. High stakes for him but he thought if it came in, he could possibly end this disastrous day on some sort of high. He didn't receive a reply and said, 'Watch my bet while I'm at the bar,' as he squeezed past him.

Despondently, he chatted with Lisa as she poured him a drink and he recounted the day's events.

'Well, one thing's for sure,' she said, 'You never get one over on Connor Flynn. Everyone in this town certainly knows that, Ryan, and so should you. He's not one to cross. Be careful around him.'

'Here,' she said, 'Cheer yourself up and have one of our complimentary cigarette lighters. Alan's just ordered a few in, for special clients only, of course.'

'Thanks for that, but ooh, I was so close today. Until my ball mysteriously disappeared, that is,' he said wearily.

Ryan stood at the bar examining his new silver lighter with the red dragon motif and thinking of what might have been. Suddenly there was a great cheer from the casino floor. Ryan could hear Connor's voice above the excited squeals, cheering and laughter. Someone's number must have come in big time.

He hoped it was his. His mouth was suddenly dry, and he could feel the excitement rise as the adrenalin pulsed through his body. He pushed his way to the front through the masses of punters now gathered around the table.

He gasped a little for breath, throat dry, and heart beating fast and as he approached the table he could see Connor's laughing face.

'Has my number come in?' Ryan blurted out as he arrived at Connor's shoulder.

'Oh yes,' said Connor. 'Your ball's in seventeen.'

Ryan looked over and there as the wheel slowly spun round to a halt, he could see the ball was indeed sitting, imperiously, joyously, happily in his favourite number, seventeen black.

He grimaced. It wasn't the little roulette ball though and as the roulette wheel came slowly to a halt, there was Ryan's Titleist golf ball with his initials and smiley face drawn on it in marker pen.

Ryan was fuming; he scowled at Connor and stormed off. He had been swindled twice now. That was the last straw. Until this moment, he hadn't bought into his brother's hatred of Connor but today he had seen that side of the character that Billy had told him about. That man would stop at nothing to get his own way. The only good part of today, he thought, was the overheard conversation and what his brother might do with that information.

He decided to have to lick his wounds and take a nightcap. He sat forlorn at the bar gazing into his gin and tonic as Lisa returned after delivering some drinks.

'Your mate, Connor, is having a night to remember. Apparently he's twenty grand up already and flying.'

As Ryan looked over to the table where Connor was gambling, he could see his hands moving as fast as lightning, placing his chips on his favourite numbers, as the croupier called out, 'No more bets.'

'That's my lot tonight,' he told the crowd gathered around the table watching in awe as he went for it big time. The roulette wheel spun and the ball bounced and jumped and eventually as the wheel began to slow, he heard Connor bellow, 'If thirty-five comes in, that'll be the cream on the cake.'

The next words Ryan heard made his day even more unbearable.

'Thirty-five black,' announced the croupier.

Connor clapped his big old clown hands together and roared with laughter.

Everyone congratulated him as he raked together his chips and with pockets bulging, he trundled over to the cashier to weigh in.

Ryan had already left.

CHAPTER FORTY-FIVE

It was later next morning when Ryan got to the café and began to reveal to his brother the events of the previous day.

'Bill, I'm telling you. I had him. One up and one to play. Stupidly, I tried to up the ante with a double or quits which I thought was a safe bet but he turned the tables on me. Called my bluff, was I man enough to take him on. Said I was nothing without my big brother. Somehow he got me to bet the cost of that job in Solihull. Twenty-five grand, Bill. I can't afford to lose that money for those roofs. That bastard Flynn, he had me over. Lost my ball on the eighteenth. You'll never guess where my ball turned up.'

'Go on.'

'In the fucking roulette wheel later that evening.'

'What do you mean?'

'That bastard Flynn must have found it on the last hole when I hit a wayward shot into the rough. He must have pocketed it, then later, at the tables, just to give everyone a laugh at my expense, put it in the roulette wheel. In my favourite number too.'

Billy was not amused and that old feeling of burning hatred showed on his face.

'The devious bastard. He'd do anything to come out on top. I suppose he laughed like a dog. Well he's not getting away with this, Ryan. I bet the place was in uproar.'

'Yeah, I felt a right prick. They must have all been in on it, Alan, the croups. I really thought my number had come in. I wish I'd never got involved with the bloke. When he pulled that final bet on me, my ring piece was going from plug hole to manhole. I tell you, Bill, he knows how to pressurise a situation but the annoying thing is, he always seems to come out on top. I was up half the night thinking how I could get him back. Bill, what really pisses me off is I've done this for you for so long, I don't know how much longer I can deal with this shit. It's totally out of order. But there's something I overheard which may be the break we've been waiting for.'

He then filled Billy in with what he overheard in the changing rooms whilst precariously perched on the chair in the boiler room.

Billy was staring out of the café window, collecting his thoughts and deliberating on what he had just been told. He was weighing up the possibilities of what this information could mean. He looked over at Ryan.

'Now calm down and have a cup of tea while I do you a nice full breakfast. Reet,' he called across, 'do Ryan a full breakfast.' Like all good bosses, Billy knew how to delegate. He turned to the big urn full of boiling water, dropped a tea bag in a mug and began to fill it up.

'You know, I think I've got something brewing,' they both laughed at his bad joke but Ryan was still fretting about how yesterday had gone.

'Look, Ryan, don't worry too much because I have had my fill of the guy and I intend to sort him out. Oh, one last thing,' Billy asked as his brother tucked into his breakfast, 'you did say that Ascot trip is in June, didn't you?'

Ryan nodded.

'So I need to know as much detail about this trip as possible. Get me the whole schedule of events, times, route, coach operator and numbers attending. You've got enough time to get me the stuff I need to know, eh?'

'Easy, I need to phone Alan anyway to firm up what's happening on the day so I'll let you know this evening. Flynn obviously deals in drugs so that makes him an even bigger shit than we first thought. Not only could we shop him to the police, we could finish him in this city for good.'

'Yes, maybe we will,' Billy replied, 'but let's take one step at a time and the first item on the agenda is getting your money back. Call me later with the details I need, yeah? Now finish your breakfast, I've got some thinking to do.'

That afternoon, Ryan made a few site visits to check on his men and as Jenny was working late as a locum at a nearby practice, he decided to drop in at the Dragon and check out the details of the Ascot trip. He called Billy from the phone in the reception and filled him in.

It wasn't late when he got home, and Jenny was already asleep. He had the beginnings of a crushing headache and crept quietly into bed. He snuggled up to Jenny without waking her. After the exertions of the last few days, he fell asleep immediately.

He woke early next morning and freshened himself up with a shower. He got dressed, made himself and his wife a coffee, and went on the balcony adjoining their bedroom which overlooked the back garden. He lit a smoke while he waited for her to join him.

Jenny swept on the balcony dressed in a black silky negligee and gave Ryan that look that meant, 'You're not going to work yet, mister'. She settled down in the chair opposite him. As she drank her coffee she playfully opened her legs to reveal that she had no panties on and crossed her legs up to improve his view. He lost control. He rose from his chair, pulled her towards him and kissed her passionately. She giggled and pushed him back towards the bedroom. He unbuttoned his shirt and struggled out of his trousers. They fell on the bed. He rolled on top of her and with their lips fused with the heat of their passion, they made fierce and passionate love.

'You know, Jenny,' he gasped in the aftermath, 'you still turn me on like mad. You are one sexy woman.'

'Just shows how much we still love each other then and never forget it, Ryan Casey.'

'Look, I need to get to the yard or that other woman in my life will get upset if I'm late in.'

'Okay, darling, I know Margaret will have your morning coffee waiting. Get going, big boy,' she said as she playfully slapped his bare bottom. He slid out of bed and headed for his second shower that morning.

CHAPTER FORTY-SIX

The plan was sorted. Sitting in his booth, deep in thought, he remembered the conversation he had with his dad when they were on holiday in Ibiza. His father had confided in him how useless he felt and that he should never have allowed Maria to go out that night. Feeling guilty, he blamed himself and felt responsible for putting her in danger.

Now Billy thought, 'Here I am, not just putting my life in danger, but my brother and my son too.' He felt guilty and was on the verge of binning the whole thing but then the face of that man rushed through his mind and the hatred was so strong he felt sick. The need to take him down was all-consuming. This job would be a gamble. The spoils would be worth it but it was about more than that for himself.

'Fuck him,' Billy thought. 'He won't come out on top in this one. He's up against Billy Casey this time.'

The plan would require a few extra faces and some equipment to tackle the job he had in mind. He arranged a late night meeting of those involved at the café.

The clock on the wall, another piece of Birmingham City memorabilia, showed it was nearly eleven o'clock and the May night was still warm and close. A small lamp above the booth swung slowly to and fro with each gust of wind which blew through the high transom window over the entrance door.

He looked at the assembled faces gathered around the bank of seats, all mates he would trust with his life which, considering what they were all going to be involved in, was gratifying. Johnny Cripps, Winston Reid, Micky Styles, and Billy's son, Sean, made up the team, plus Ryan, of course.

'Right, lads, I want to run through the plan. There's one big bastard in this city and other than the fact he robbed my brother, the main part of my beef is to teach him that you don't fuck with my family. There's some other stuff which is a bit more personal but all the same, we need to sort him out good and proper. I have as fool-proof a plan as I can come up with, but very dangerous all the same.'

Each man picked up the sheet of paper in front of them and began to study the fact sheet.

Billy continued, 'As you can see, note one: the coach is on hire from Chesney's Coaches of Harborne. Fred Chesney is a big pal of mine and I've had the privilege of having a look round the actual coach myself on the pretext of hiring one for a family celebration later in the year. It's a big luxury job with tables, toilets and a flat screen TV on board. Note two: it can carry forty comfortably but Ryan has found out there are only about ten down to make the trip. As far as we are concerned, if one particular name drops out, the whole thing will be aborted. Note three: the coach is due to arrive outside the casino at eight thirty in the morning for the party to board and depart by nine. Note four: the route, I have been reliably informed, will take the coach down the Hagley Road; round the island at Five Ways; down onto Lee Bank Middleway to the traffic lights at the Bristol Cinema and left on to Bristol Street; down the underpass of Suffolk Queensway, and into the Queensway Tunnel. Eventually, on to the Aston Expressway, M6, M42 and on to

Ascot. As far as we are concerned, we are only interested in the part of the journey up to the entrance to the Queensway Tunnel. I have driven the route over the last three Saturdays. The average time is about twenty minutes from the casino to the entrance of the tunnel. So let me explain in more detail.'

Crippsy piped up, 'Bill, maybe you should tell us what's in it for us?'

'I'm sorry, John, in fact all of you, my apologies. You can imagine from my point of view, there is more at stake than pinching some money. It's going to be dangerous and if something goes wrong, we're all going to be eating porridge for a long time. The guy I'm after has form and a reputation of enjoying a good scrap so we will be using a shooter to ensure that everyone knows we're not fuckin' about and behaves themselves. You all know what armed robbery can get us. But in answer to John's question, everyone gets twenty-five grand.'

'Yeh, man,' laughed Winston. 'Twenty-five big ones will do for me, man.'

'I want you all to think about the consequences of what we will be involved in and after we go through the plan, anyone who wants out can leave with no recriminations,' said Billy. He hoped no one would take that option.

Billy stood up and pulled a white board on to an easel and began to reveal the plan. It was way past one o'clock by the time Billy had completed his presentation, and had fielded and answered all their questions.

'Look, lads, we will need to run through this a few more times before the day and ensure that each of us knows what their responsibilities are. No one can afford to cock-up, so if any of you is unsure about anything, check it out with me any time. On the day it must go like clockwork. Sean has got two of his mates to ride the motorbikes and as they are still serving Queen and country, they prefer to keep a low profile, but I am assured by

Sean that these two guys are smart and fit and a couple of grand in their hands for an hour's work will ensure their silence. Needless to say, we don't talk about this with anyone, wives, girlfriends, family, no one. Do you understand that? Many a good plan has been fucked up before it got off the ground by someone opening their mouth. Right, let's all go home to our beds and get some rest and remember, keep schtum. Oh, and as I said earlier, if anyone wants to withdraw they can do so now.'

Billy looked around the room. No takers. The boys were with him and inside he was grateful; he knew he was asking a lot.

Okay, then let's get home to our beds. Mickey, before you go I want a word.'

Billy then explained exactly what he wanted Mickey to do on the day.

When Mickey had gone, Billy sat for a long time considering what he was getting involved in. What they were all getting involved in. The way his mother had raised her children left no margin for getting involved with the seamier side of life. Ethically, he knew he was crossing that line but his hatred of this man left no room for further contemplation. He would do what was necessary. Revenge drove him. He wouldn't give in. Although he was still uncertain about Flynn's involvement on the night his sister had died, one thing he did know for certain was that he had ripped off his brother.

Thinking back, he didn't know how he had managed to keep his madness under control after Maria's death. The memory of that horrific night, and keeping a lid on his own feelings, had screwed him up. It had torn his parents apart and over the years, he knew it had taken its toll on himself and his brother.

Peculiarly, now he had made the decision to hit back hard, he felt a certain amount of relief. He desperately wanted to take this man down, hoping that in the process he would find some peace of mind.

CHAPTER FORTY-SEVEN

The area around St Phillip's Church behind Rackham's department store in the city centre, is one of the biggest parking areas for motorbikes for those commuters who prefer to make the journey in on two wheels.

Sean and Crippsy had decided that they would steal the two bikes they required from the varied pool on display. Over the previous few days, they had identified a Honda and a Suzuki which were ideal for their purpose. The bikes always seemed to be parked next to one another, which made it perfect.

The two men stood in the emergency exit side doorway of an office block, holding their crash helmets. Sean was checking around for any policemen or nosy parkers. Satisfied that the moment was right, he nodded and they both put on their helmets. They approached the bikes and quickly Sean produced a pair of bolt cutters from inside his jacket. He snapped the chains which were wrapped around the front wheels of both bikes. Crippsy got them started, Sean stuffed the bolt cutters back inside his jacket and they quickly mounted the bikes and roared off up Colmore Row in the direction of a disused warehouse down the back of the Jewellery Quarter.

The big roller shutter doors were already open and the white transit van they had stolen from outside a builder's yard in Nechells the night before, was parked inside. The two bikes roared in past Winston, who took a quick glance both ways up and down the street to be sure nobody was about before he wound down the doors. He trotted over to the boys and slapped them both on the back heartily as the guys pulled off their crash helmets.

Winston was excited and shouted, 'Well done, my men. Just what we needed, these are ideal machines, just like Billy arks.'

The three settled down next to one another on the old sofa in the corner and relaxed.

Crippsy appeared deep in thought and after a while turned to Winston.

'We've known each other a long time, Winston, and it's something I've always wanted to know the answer to. It makes me smile how some black people can't pronounce 'ask' properly, they say 'arks' exactly like you've just said it. I've seen loads of programmes on TV, interviews, news items and nearly every time they say 'arks' instead of 'ask' just like you did then. What's all that about?'

Winston thought for a while, giving the question his full consideration and then he delivered his answer, 'Don't arks me.' The three laughed.

The back of the van was open and Sean could see that Winston had fitted two car seats against the bulkhead, facing the back doors. He had also welded some angle iron to the roof, from which hung some nylon webbing.

'Nice job, Winston, and have you made the metal ramps too?'

'No problems at all with it, Sean, it fits as snug as a bug in a rug. I have tuned up the engine too and welded the bull bars to the front as well. The rear windows have been blacked out. New number plates have been put on and later I will check out the bikes, and put some new registration numbers on them too. All as Billy arksed.'

Sean took the opportunity, as they sat around, to run through the plan for the day as his father had reminded him that all of them needed to be 'word perfect' come the time. When they had finished, another run-through, Crippsy nodded and Winston said, 'No worries, man, I got it,' and smiled, showing his big white teeth.

Winston had been a big mate of Billy's from way back. He had played representative football at schoolboy level with Billy and over the years they had formed a close friendship. When he played, he was a no-nonsense defender and had a quick turn of pace which enabled him to cover any breakaways from the opposition forwards. Most notably of all, he always played with a big smile on his face.

He was big: not so tall, standing at just less than six feet, but with the size of his chest and arms, he appeared massive and could easily have been mistaken for a body builder. He kept himself fit at a local boxing gym and with his sparkling white teeth topped off with a shaven head, he looked amazing, even though he was in his early fifties. He exuded the air of a person not to cross, however, and his laid-back temperament rarely attracted aggression.

When he was a younger man, his happy and engaging personality attracted a large group of friends, especially at the nightclubs where he loved nothing more than dancing the night away. He loved his Ska and reggae music and the soul music of Otis Redding, and it was at the Rainbow Suite situated over the top of the Co-op in town that he met his wife-to-be, Joy. He fell deeply in love with this Caribbean lioness and five kids later, he still loved the bones of the woman.

When they left school, Billy had helped him to get an interview with one of his dad's mates from the club and become an apprentice garage mechanic. Winston loved his work and soon worked his way up to become senior mechanic at the garage. Later, Billy helped him with the cash to set up his own workshop in Selly Oak. There was nothing Winston didn't know about motors and nothing he wouldn't do for Billy.

He could also handle a car like an F1 driver which was another bonus, considering what was coming up.

CHAPTER FORTY-EIGHT

Billy's mind was busy. He needed to run some errands and closed up the café a little earlier than usual. Driving down to the Bull Ring Market, he looked up an old friend, which would be the second visit within a few months.

He strolled up to the market stall and shook his friend warmly by the hand.

'Well, if it ain't my old mate, Billy Casey,' said Tommy Butler. 'I don't see you for ages and then within a couple of months I get to see you twice. What's going on, you having dressing up sessions at home with the missus to liven things up a bit? Oh, I know, she obviously enjoyed Batman so much you've come back for another superhero. How about a Superman outfit this time, eh?'

'Well, if I'd wanted a cowboy outfit I'd just go and buy the Villa, wouldn't I?'

They both loved a dig at the Villa and had a good chuckle at that one.

Billy looked over Tommy's goods, especially the face masks.

'What else you got in the face mask department then, Tommy?'

'Depends on what you're after, Bill. Scary, comical, famous film stars, politicians, royalty. I've got the lot.'

Billy sorted through and after a few minutes made his selections.

'Okay, I'll take these three. No, wait a sec, I'll take that one over there, too,' he said, pointing to the mask of a well-known film star.

'Well, best of luck with all that. It all seems to be getting a bit scary so I'll ask no more questions. You just enjoy yourself, Bill.'

Tommy bagged the goods up and Billy handed over the cash. After a firm handshake, he moved on to the next item on his shopping list.

He made his way to a big sports shop just outside the market and purchased a set of Villa shirts. Whilst stood at the counter waiting to pay, he nearly laughed out loud when the assistant asked if he had supported the Villa for long.

'No, no, these are a surprise for someone I owe a little something to.'

CHAPTER FORTY-NINE

The Queensway Tunnel in Birmingham City Centre runs more or less north to south and vice versa beneath the city, helping to relieve the pressure of traffic on the congested roads above. Inside the tunnel there are two lanes on either side with a central dividing wall. When driving north, it leads out to the Aston Expressway and then accesses the motorways via the infamous Spaghetti Junction interchange, enabling drivers to head north or south on the M6 and link to the M42 and M1. Going south through the tunnel, drivers can access the Bristol Road to Selly Oak , Edgbaston and other adjoining southern suburbs.

***

It was a quarter to nine and the coach was waiting with its engine running outside the front doors to the casino, and Ryan could see the last stragglers coming out. He had taken his seat early so that he could sit behind the driver, a position from which he had a clear view, able to see everything that was going on, front and side.

He was relieved to hear some nameless newsreader over the radio, report that traffic that morning was running smoothly.

Connor Flynn was one of the last in the group, along with Raj and Sanjay. He was carrying a designer holdall as he climbed the stairs, nodding to Ryan.

'I bet you are looking forward to getting some money back today? I'll give you a few tips to help you out if you like. You must be short of readies after what's happened to you just lately.'

Ryan managed to squeeze out a weak smile. 'Cheeky bastard,' thought Ryan. 'After today, the tables might be reversed.'

He would have liked to have smacked him in his smart mouth but he controlled himself and said, 'No, you're okay, I already know my winners.'

Connor moved on past Ryan and took a seat at a table halfway back, placing his holdall on the seat opposite him.

***

Sean was sitting in the front double passenger seat of the Transit next to Crippsy. Winston was behind the wheel and Sean's two army mates in the back, along with the bikes.

Time seemed to pass slowly as they waited but Crippsy didn't mind, he was dozing as usual. Sean checked his watch for the umpteenth time. 'Right,' he said, 'we give them five minutes and then we start moving.'

Winston looked eager to get going. They were parked on a side road off Bath Row.

He had run through the plan many times and Sean knew the plan backwards.

He checked his watch for the final time and said, 'Right, Winston, the five minutes are up. Let's go.'

'It's show time, man,' Winston added as he elbowed Crippsy in the ribs to wake him up. He rubbed his eyes and stretched.

It was a June day and the sun was shining. Winston nudged the van into the line of vehicles which were stopped at a red light, all heading down Lee Bank Middleway.

After a slight delay at the traffic lights, they arrived at the main intersection with the Bristol Road and Winston turned left towards the city. He switched on his hazard warning lights, pulling in to the side of the road. He pulled the catch inside, allowing him to release the bonnet and quickly jumped out. He put the stays under the bonnet and jumped back in the van. It all looked good so far.

Sean checked his watch again. 'Approximately seven minutes before we should see the coach, guys.'

Winston did a cursory check of his side mirror and with panic in his voice, he said, 'Forget the coach, we've got the boys in blue pulling in behind us. Fuckin' 'ell, Seany, what do we do?'

'Right, let's not panic. Sit tight for a minute. Oy, you two in the back,' he said just above a whisper, 'Keep it quiet, there's a cop car behind us.'

Suddenly, the blue lights started flashing. The boys in the van thought the game was up and Winston punched the steering wheel in frustration. Then, just as suddenly as they arrived, the police car pulled out from behind the van and sped away to answer some emergency call elsewhere.

There was a cheer from the back of the van and the three in the front laughed out loudly and madly with relief.

Sean jumped out of the van for a breath of fresh air, stretching his arms and flexing his back. He looked back down the street and could see the Chesney's Coach at the traffic lights with its blinker on waiting to turn left. He ran to the front of the van, slammed the bonnet down and jumped in, shouting, 'Okay, lads its go, go, go. Winston, get ready to get in the traffic, they're on their way. Everybody, this is it. Winston, Crippsy, get your jackets off and masks on.'

The coach was now fifty yards behind as Winston clicked on his right indicator and nosed into the line of traffic, trying to get into position in the outside lane. A Ford Escort was in his way and Winston veered out to make him move but the driver wouldn't give way. Winston blasted his horn and shouted at the driver, 'Fuck off, blood clot, I'm comin' over there,' and added a hand gesture to emphasise his impatience. The car driver got the message and accelerated away from any confrontation with the mad man in the van.

Winston was now in the outside lane and about three cars behind the coach, which was in the middle lane. As the two vehicles approached the underpass for Suffolk Street Queensway, Sean shouted above the rattle and noise inside the van, 'Keep up with him, Winston, we need to be level just as we enter the tunnel.'

The van's engine screamed as Winston pushed it hard.

'No problem, we just need no silly fucker trying to push in between us,' he shouted.

***

On the coach, everyone was settled in for the trip, some playing cards, others drinking, others just sitting back and relaxing. Connor was sitting alone, swigging beer from a bottle and staring thoughtfully at Raj and Sanjay, who were sitting two seats nearer the front and across the aisle from him.

Ryan was a little tense as he knew that any minute they would be entering the tunnel and all hell would be let loose.

Both vehicles were now side by side as they entered the Queensway Tunnel and Winston accelerated as he fought hard to draw level with the coach. He was now alongside and blasted his horn, getting a look of confusion from the coach driver who was shocked to see Mr T staring across at him, with Prince Charles and the Queen shaking their fists.

Winston pulled down hard on the steering wheel and applied the handbrake, swerving in towards the coach. The coach driver jammed on his brakes to avoid a collision. It was just what Winston wanted.

The coach slammed to a halt as Winston's final position had the van's back end blocking off the outside lane. The two vehicles now completely blocked the northern lanes of the Queensway Tunnel.

Everyone on the coach was pitched forward except Ryan, who had braced himself against the driver's seat. Chaos and confusion reigned for a while as everyone thought they had collided with a van. They didn't realise what was happening.

Sean and Crippsy were out of the van as soon as it came to a halt. They looked a picture dressed in the outfits chosen by Billy. They presented an odd sight; Sean wasn't sure what his dad had been thinking with the masks. The two regal characters rushed to the coach and pulled open the doors to gain access.

Sean led the way, carrying the sawn-off shotgun, racing up the steps and putting the first round into the roof of the coach. There were shouts of panic at the blast. Sean took control.

'Everyone down on the floor now,' he barked in a quasi cut-glass royal accent.

'Charles,' he said, 'Go, go, go!'

'Yes, ma'am,' Crippsy replied, playing his part.

He moved carefully, but quickly down the aisle of the coach and stopped in front of Connor, who was lying on the floor in the aisle. The holdall was on the seat and as he went to grab it, Connor suddenly pulled at his legs, causing him to lose balance and fall forward onto the seat. Connor swiftly jumped to his feet and grabbed a beer bottle off the table, smashed it and held the jagged end up to Crippsy's throat.

'Right, you pair of gobshites, drop that fuckin' rifle or I slice his throat,' Connor yelled. Sean didn't drop it and kept it pointed at Connor, edging nearer.

'Fuck you,' Sean shouted nervously but regally.

He was playing for time and stared Connor down. His mind was racing with ideas and scenarios, and in those few seconds, all his ideas seemed to end up with Crippsy getting blown to bits by a bad shot or his throat cut by Flynn. Either way, there didn't seem much of a way out of the stalemate he was in.

The clock was ticking; Sean heard Winston roar away as per the plan and the bikes were revving up ready for the getaway.

Beads of sweat were now covering his face beneath the mask and his mouth was so dry his tongue was sticking to the roof of his mouth.

'Drop the sawn-off, you don't have a fuckin' hope, pal,' Connor growled as he pushed the jagged end of the bottle against Crippsy's neck, causing a dribble of blood to form.

Sean was in a state of flux. Panic had made him freeze and he couldn't think clearly of what he should do next in this stalemate.

Suddenly, the toilet door at the back of the coach burst open and approaching from the rear of the coach, was a man wearing an evening suit and a James Bond mask. He was holding a hand-gun which he quickly pressed firmly into the back of Connor's head and whispered in a very recognisable warm Scottish accent, 'Drop it or your brainsh will be all over the fucking ceiling.'

Connor grunted, realising he was outsmarted, dropping the bottle immediately, after which he was unceremoniously kneed in the back and shoved to the floor.

'Thank you, 007, as usual impeccable timing,' said 'the Queen', unable to hide the relief.

Crippsy grabbed the holdall and dashed to the front of the coach, and stood next to Sean.

'Right, stay down on the floor, all of you,' 007 shouted. Connor looked up at Bond, who delivered a kick with all his strength to his stomach. Years of anger and frustration began to flow freely as Bond delivered three more kicks to his victim.

'I said stay down,' he repeated as Flynn gasped for breath, now curled up in the foetal position.

Bond swiftly picked up the broken bottle and slipped it into his pocket... Then made his way to the front of the coach and said, 'One more into the shceiling if you would be so kind, ma'am,' in a plausible Conneryesque accent, 'just to make schure they keep their headsh down a little bit longer.'

Ryan hadn't moved since the pair had instructed them all to lie down the first time. His ears were still ringing from the opening shot in the enclosed space of the coach. The second only added to his pain.

He didn't look up until the three had made their escape but he did have a little smile to himself as looked down the aisle and watched Connor Flynn retching and breathing hard.

'Suffer, you bastard!' he thought.

The royal pair jumped down from the coach and 'the Queen' and 'Prince Charles' jumped on the backs of the two waiting motorbikes. 007 rushed across from the coach, having slammed the coach door behind him. He stood alone, looking helpless in the middle of the tunnel with no means of getting away.

Sean's mind was once more paralysed. Two bikes, five people, it was an impossible situation. The two boys on the bikes waited for the signal from Sean to get out of there but he was bricking it now. What could he do? He tapped on the helmet of his driver. 'Wait!' he shouted above the screaming motorbike engine and pointed back to the forlorn and lone figure standing in the middle of the road, and wondered what he could do to get Bond away.

People were beginning to get out of their cars to see what was going on and Sean could see movement on the coach too. The wail of a police siren filled the air and as he looked beyond the backed-up traffic, he could see the flashing blue light in the distance as the police motorbike weaved its way speedily through the stationary traffic.

'Fuck it!' Sean screamed, 'we've had it.'

The police bike passed the last few cars and approached with a roar of engine and a screech of tyres as it skidded to a halt in front of Bond.

It was the weirdest copper Sean had ever seen because he, too, was wearing a Villa shirt and a black crash helmet, although the Norton Commando police bike looked pretty authentic. Bond hopped on the back quickly and the three bikes sped away, out of the tunnel to safety.

CHAPTER FIFTY

There weren't any lights on and Billy had left the back door to the café unlocked. Sean let himself in, carrying the designer holdall which he hastily dropped on the floor before turning around and locking the door. The reflected lights from the street lamps and the car headlights bouncing off the rain-soaked road, helped to provide enough light for Sean to navigate safely to the corner booth where Billy was waiting.

He dropped the bag on the table in front of his father, who touched the end of his cigar to a small fat candle that sat in the middle of the table. The candle flickered to life.

'Well done, son, you handled yourself well in a much pressurised situation.'

'Thanks, Dad. Celebrating with a cigar, are we?' Sean chuckled. 'I tell you what though, that was the most exciting experience I've ever had. When you suddenly appeared behind him and stuck the gun in the back of his head. Brilliant. You should have seen his face. You always say have a back-up plan and I'm glad you did 'cos I thought it was all over. Don't ask me how we would have got out of it. It all happened so fast.'

He slipped in to sit opposite his father and continued, 'I was keeping watch on the boys on the coach just in case they tried anything, but with a sawn-off pointing at them no one had the bottle. Flynn was so quick, he had that broken bottle up to Crippsy's throat before I knew what was happening. I was shitting myself. He must have grabbed him as he reached over to get the bag but then you appeared and saved the day. I nearly laughed out loud. That was inspired. Then, relief, we were away but no, no-one to pick up James Bond. Christ, I almost cried. I thought it was all over then. The tension was killing me, the stress was massive and then the siren as the police motorbike got closer and closer, I'm thinking I'm too young to spend the rest of my life in jail. But shit, that was brilliant. You know I'd completely forgotten about Micky. Two back-up plans. Amazing. But why did you pick up the broken bottle?'

Billy looked worn out.

'John Cripps blood was all over it. We didn't want the coppers finding that did we? I knew Flynn would be trouble so I needed to come up with a special surprise,' Billy said, blowing out a wisp of blue smoke, 'But I tell you what: sitting in that toilet from seven in the morning was well stressful and very fuckin' hot. I was so worried, Seany, I can tell you. I couldn't take the risk of it all fouling up and us all doin' time so I had no option really. I kept that part quiet from you all so that you didn't rely on it. Still we pulled it off, so let's see what we've got then.'

Billy pulled the bag towards him. He didn't take any notice of the heavily monogrammed design by Louis Vuitton as he didn't care much for designer gear, other than to mutter, 'This is a bit poncie!'

He unzipped the bag and slowly looked across at Sean and smiled.

'Bingo, that's our Ryan's money back and pay day for all the lads,' as he pulled out rolls of fifty-pound notes and threw some on the table.

'You beauty,' he laughed as he and Sean celebrated with a sideswipe high five.

'Did you get rid of the Villa shirts, masks and gloves, and chuck the sawn-off?'

'Yes, Dad, all done as ordered. I'll tell you another highlight of the day.'

'What was it?' Billy asked

'Burning those fuckin' Villa shirts!'

They both chuckled and Billy sucked hard on his cigar.

'I've heard from Winston and he's confirmed that he has disposed of the three bikes and the van at Noel's scrapyard. They're probably an Oxo cube of crushed metal now.

Flynn will be fuckin' furious about this and I know who he will be sorting out first, the only other two people who knew what was in his holdall and that'll mean hard times ahead for Raj and Sanjay. That will give us some breathing space.'

Billy stood up and held out his arms and gave his son a bear hug.

'Right, Sean, off home with ya. You've done a top job today. Suzanne has your alibi all covered, at home having a late morning lie-in with all the extras, eh?'

Sean smiled and left by the back door.

Billy sat back and closed his eyes, letting the relief wash over him.

***

The national news led with the story of the Queensway Tunnel heist in Birmingham, with the newsreader telling the nation the details of a stunning and cheeky hold-up carried out by a gang dressed in party masks and football shirts. Police reported that the hold-up had netted the gang ten thousand pounds and were investigating links to a local football team as the robbers were sporting similar shirts. The news report ended with the usual statement that police were appealing for anyone with information to contact them.

CHAPTER FIFTY-ONE

He wasn't a man to be paranoid but after the incident at the football ground and now the loss of all that cash, he was thinking that someone had it in for him. It was ironic, he thought, as in his life he had always been the hunter and now someone had turned the tables on him. It appeared he was quarry. He was unsettled for once in his life.

What was worse were the phone calls from seriously important members of the Provos, warning him in no uncertain terms that he had better find their money quick, then find those responsible and deal severely with them. They made him aware that they were running out of patience and threatened him that they would be visiting him soon.

The loss of the cash had caused a mighty storm, the waves of which were still rippling to shore. Rumours were already circulating about gambling debts and he was uncomfortable with that, as it was far from the truth. He had never used their money for that. But the pressure on him was growing and he didn't like it.

Raj and Sanjay had already had a visit from a couple of 'the boys' but after suffering a severe beating and torture, had managed to convince their captors that they had nothing to do with the heist.

He believed that whoever had carried it out was a serious player and a smart operator, and may possibly move in the circle of local criminals. Therefore he needed to talk to the man he had been told moved in those circles, Birmingham's 'King of Clubs' and local underworld boss, Lenny Freeman. Connor would contact him and arrange a meeting.

He was told to meet Lenny at his less-than-salubrious club, Devines, situated at the Smethwick end of the Hagley Road. Connor pulled into the car park and walked to the front of the club where a neon blue rectangular sign hung over the entrance. It had similarly gaudy pink lettering announcing the club's name, the whole perimeter surrounded by small pink light bulbs which flashed intermittently.

It was very busy, noisy, dirty, dusty and cigarette smoke filled the air as hundreds of youngsters danced and partied the night away, spending their 'hard-earned'. Although Lenny could have operated from a more modern and comfortable office in any of his other clubs, his first 'baby', Devines, was where he liked to relax and do most of his business.

Devines had been the start of the big money for Lenny after he pulled off that major scam all those years back.

That scam all those years ago would have been impossible without two very important people who were integral to the scam: Jimmy Jeffries and Delores Jones. Jimmy was a scammer from the early days and had borrowed heavily from Lenny; Delores had been a bold and brazen brunette brass. When they first met, Jimmy had been a punter of hers but then they found that they liked and cared for one another. They decided to work with each other in Jimmy's cons, which meant Delores could earn her money in a more vertical position, luring many a 'mark' into their scams.

Lenny was 'old school' and in his circle of contacts there was still honour amongst thieves. He knew that they would play their part and a sizeable pay-off would keep their minds focussed.

The pair adopted the positions of the 'front men', the directors of the company with headquarters in a disused warehouse near Dudley. Lenny had managed to secure the unit on a no questions asked, cash up front basis.

The company was established, purporting to deal in furniture and kitchen sales. Lenny had spruced up the offices with cheap office furniture and hundreds of empty boxes were stacked in the warehouse, giving the business the appearance of a busy, thriving concern. The façade was further enhanced by the addition of a map of the UK hanging in the reception area, with lots of red stickers indicating the areas to which they delivered. The company paperwork, like bank accounts and registry of the company, was crucial and Lenny used one of Joey McLean's bent bank employees to sort that out.

Delores manned the 'switchboard', which looked real enough although there was only one line. Special connections were made from a back room enabling them to ring the phones in the offices to give the impression that they were busy, busy, busy.

Having made contact with the manufacturers and suppliers, Jimmy had presented himself well and they seemed impressed with his story of a growing successful business. He placed the first order and paid in cash. The suppliers would need to check out the company's credit before they would extend any lines of credit but the first order was paid up front in cash, which impressed the management. That first order was delivered promptly and stored in the warehouse, ready for delivery when the time was right.

Lenny had organised the big scam to coincide with the Christmas rush and the next order would be huge. The suppliers received the order and arranged for their national sales manager to call to see Jimmy and check out the set-up.

Mr Savage, the sales manager, was due to call at the offices to ensure his company were looking after this new client. Lenny knew he was really coming to snoop about.

It was critical that on the day Mr Savage was due to visit, the impression he took away was one of a thriving, busy but professional company. Lenny ensured there were enough bodies wandering about in the warehouse. Some dressed in overalls, carrying clipboards and looking really busy. Delivery trucks were being loaded with those empty boxes and the phones were made to ring on cue, completing a picture that Mr Savage couldn't help but be impressed by.

Jimmy had to rush out on a business call and assured Mr Savage, in their short conversation, that the way things were going they would be opening another depot in Evesham early next year.

He shook hands with Mr Savage in the reception area where Delores was answering the phone with a throaty, 'Hello, Furniture and Kitchens, how can I help?' He gave her a wink and said, 'Delores, please look after Mr Savage as I've got that important meeting in Evesham to sort out our new warehouse. Make sure he's happy with everything before he goes,' he said with a smile and left her to it.

He knew he could rely on Delores to take it on from here. Poor Mr Savage was unprepared for the full-on charm offensive he was about to face from Delores, who was more than ready to play this 'mark' with all she'd got.

All alone in the office with the middle-aged, balding Mr Savage, she set to work, fluttering her false eyelashes and heaving her huge breasts at him. She was flirting outrageously as she sat on her desk, flashing her stocking tops and suspenders as she crossed and uncrossed her legs provocatively.

She noticed it was having the right effect and watched with suppressed laughter as the man's eyes spun round like Catherine wheels at the expectation of what might be in store.

He was taken on a tour of the warehouse and sales office where the salesmen were all busy on the phones, but back in the reception it was obvious that he was more interested in what Delores might offer. When she asked if there was anything else he wanted to look at, he replied, 'Not really, Delores, I feel that we could work very well together.'

She moved over to where he sat and leaning forward to reveal her pendulous breasts to the google-eyed old chap, she ran her fingers up the front of his trousers, nearly causing him to embarrass himself in his pants. His excitement made him feel uncomfortable and with his briefcase in front of his trousers, he stood up and said, 'Many thanks, Delores. I will process your order as soon as I get back to the office,' adding, 'We must pop out for some lunch together next time.'

Delores knew exactly what that meant and as he walked out of the office she whispered in his ear, 'I know a little hotel where they ask no questions. We need our delivery pretty quickly as Christmas is coming and we need to get the stuff out to our retailers, so phone me to let me know when we can expect delivery. At the same time, you can let me know when you can spare me some time to thank you properly.'

Mr Savage left the offices with big expectations and an even bigger hard-on. He jumped into his car, not believing his luck. Delores' charm had worked and he felt that he was on a sure fire winner. He also took away an order for forty-eight thousand pounds' worth of goods.

The blag was on. Everyone was holding their breath in the days that followed. Would the wholesalers release the goods on credit? It was a risk, considering their invoice was not payable until the first of the month following.

They all waited to see if Delores had managed to pull it off.

On a dark afternoon in late December, the phone call came through. Delores smiled as she chatted away to Mr Savage, finishing her conversation with, 'No, don't worry, my husband will be away on business for a couple of days down south and I know a nice little hotel where we can spend an afternoon of passion.' She paused and then added, 'Yes of course I will be wearing my stockings, I always do. You're in for a very big surprise, don't you worry.'

After she put down the phone, she smiled at the expectant faces sitting around the office and said, 'Dirty old bastard.' She then paused to add a little drama, 'But who gives a fuck, deliveries will start to arrive first thing tomorrow,' she screamed.

Lenny said, 'Well done, Delores and everybody. Let's get ourselves organised for tomorrow, it's going to be a big day.'

The next morning, three big trucks arrived from the suppliers with the mighty order which was quickly unloaded. As soon as those trucks had driven off, Lenny's own fleet of smaller lorries drove in and loaded up. It was a quick turn around and they were soon driving back out again.

So, within four hours, the warehouse and offices were stripped bare. The cookers, fires, boilers, TVs, fridges, kitchen units and furniture were on their way out of the gates to other areas of the country to be sold off in one-day sales, where everything must go; cash only, of course!

The bills for the business would be unpaid, cheques would bounce and the irate wholesalers would harangue the police for answers. But the trail would be cold. Indeed, the only thing that would be left was the sign outside the premises which if anyone had bothered to notice, had been designed specially by Lenny.

The sign writer had done an impressive job with the company name and highlighted it just as Lenny had ordered. The first letter of each of the words was a capital letter picked out in bold black, inset inside a white square. It emphasised the company's initials. Lenny smiled as he and Teddy drove away behind the last of the fully-loaded trucks. Laughing out loud as he looked back, 'Yes,' he chuckled, 'you have been well and truly FUCKED!' The sign read, Furniture Units Contemporary Kitchens Evesham Dudley.

***

The scam all those years ago had given him the money to expand into the club business, just like he had wanted. It coincided nicely with the opportunity to purchase an abandoned old three-storey hotel operating from a huge detached Victorian house on the Hagley Road. It was in need of a bit of tender loving care. Indeed, a lot of tender loving care as the run down grotty building would need a lot of work before it could become what Lenny had in mind. He visualised what it could look like and that was enough for him to make his decision. Teddy, who was as usual by Lenny's side as the pair viewed the property, just thought it was a wreck. Lenny, however, could see pound signs, lots of them, and bought it for cash the very next day.

The renovation work was done in double quick time and the opening of his first club was a cause for celebration for the kid from the back streets of Winson Green who had achieved his goal. He was now a face about town.

The club was the first in his empire, although it was nothing special. In the coming years there was another in Hockley and then two in the city centre.

As clubs and pubs became his life, he became very wealthy and a big catch for the right woman. Dawn caught his eye when he noticed her working behind the bar in the early days at Devines. When Lenny became interested in her, he moved her into the reception and away from the drunken, leery clientele, and then eventually into his bed.

They married quickly as Dawn was pregnant and in a complete reversal of his own family, managed to father only girls, four of them.

Life and Birmingham had been good to Lenny and he had been accompanied on the journey by his brothers and his old pal, Teddy. When left to his own devices, Teddy still enjoyed doing a bit of market trading during the day, although Lenny insisted that his trusted lieutenant was by his side in the evenings at the club.

Teddy had also been instrumental in setting up the security business, initially organising the right type of guys on the doors at Lenny's clubs. They also hired out more men, where muscle and bouncers were provided to other publicans.

Freeman Security became a well-known name around the city and branched out into protection which was organised by Teddy's assistant, Vince.

Vince had a fool-proof method of pulling in more business. Basically, his plan consisted of calling to see the landlord of a busy and successful pub to discuss security, and get them to sign up there and then. Most didn't bother to argue. They were bright enough to realise that it was better to be a member of Lenny's 'organisation' and enjoy a trouble-free life. However, the few who ignored the initial offer soon signed up after a brawl and riot happened on their premises, organised by Vince. He was happy to take their call the following day as the events of the previous evening had encouraged them to change their minds. Vince firmly advised them not to refuse Mr Freeman's hospitable offers again. Freeman Security ran a tight band of bruisers who also became Lenny's eyes and ears out on the street, forming a tight network of informants who kept the boss abreast of criminal activity in the city, reporting back to the gaffer any gossip they picked up.

***

So it was that Connor arrived in the reception of Lenny's first love, Divines, hoping for some assistance in his search for his money and the culprits. He was directed by an extremely large muscle-bound bouncer towards a short staircase at the side of the reception desk, at the top of which was the door to Lenny's office.

Connor knocked and the door was opened by an oaf of a man with a shaven head and with what he thought looked remarkably like a hook for a hand.

Lenny was sitting behind his desk in the poorly lit room, a single lamp angled over his shoulder, shining in the face of his visitor. Thick plumes of cigar smoke hung heavily in the air at eye level, through the haze of which he directed Connor to sit on the bar stool in front of his desk. He took great pleasure in the discomfort people experienced when they were perched on that stool. No leaning back as it had no back-rest, no relaxing or slouching, no armrests to steady themselves; he liked people to be on edge and it appeared to be working a treat with this guy.

Lenny, with all his wealth, enjoyed the good things in life and his over-indulgence showed in his red bloated face and his ever-expanding waistline. He joked about it with Teddy saying it was, 'the excess of success', and in these later years he couldn't be bothered to change his drinking and eating habits for vanity's sake.

'How can I help you then, Mr Flynn?' he rasped, exhaling another cloud of smoke.

'I need some assistance, Mr Freeman,' Connor stated in a well-mannered opening. 'I'm sure you heard about the heist in the Queensway Tunnel in which I was relieved of a lot of cash, a lot more than the police believe. I had to tell them there was only ten grand in the bag, for obvious reasons, but there was considerably more than that involved.'

'More than ten, was it? Well, how much? Don't be shy.'

'The bag contained a quarter of a million in cash, which I was investing on behalf of a group I represent.'

Lenny leant forward and sucking his teeth said, 'That is indeed a serious amount of money and I too, would be distraught at such a loss. What might I ask were you investing that amount of money in and who are you representing?' he asked.

'Cocaine,' he replied.

'Now, don't be coy. If you want help, you need to tell me who you are representing. This is my manor and I don't like cowboys coming onto my patch without prior consultation. I run a tight ship in this city and commissions have to be paid, otherwise,' he nodded towards Teddy, 'retribution is swift and painful.' The final word an obvious signal to Teddy to lift his hook, which he waved on cue as always.

'The IRA,' replied Connor with an assuredness that the name might stop any further doubts as to the strength of the team he had backing him up.

'Okay, but you have some nasty boys on your team, why are you coming to me?'

'Mr Freeman, we have some powerful weapons in our armoury and we have made enquiries, so to speak, but we need someone who is in touch with the underbelly of this city, on a level where we don't operate. Someone who knows the little people that need turning over to get some information and I thought of you.'

Lenny wasn't sure if he had just been insulted or not, but pushed on regardless.

'So, what we find ourselves with here is a missed opportunity to pay proper respect to myself and without respect, we have anarchy. As you are aware, I run a closed shop here in Brummagem and I don't like anarchy because from anarchy comes chaos and in chaos we lose control. This city has been good to me and I don't like the equilibrium upset. The good people of this city know they have a top police force to protect them. Occasionally, the boys in blue don't see it for what it is, so there needs to be action taken by outside forces. I run a little security company and we often get called upon to sort out people's problems, which we undertake for a fee. If – and I repeat, if – I agree to help find the villains of the piece, I will need ten thousand pounds paid up front, with a final payment of a further fifteen once we get the cash back. That's if the bastards haven't spent it all but no matter, those are my terms. Ten per cent, take it or leave it.'

Connor knew before the visit that he would have to pay for any help he might get from Lenny. The money wasn't the important point of this exercise. He had lost face in a big way and wanted the names of the gang involved so that he could settle matters properly.

He had ten thousand in his inside pocket and he took it out and placed it on the desk. Lenny then asked for the full story as Connor saw it and any names he might put in the frame.

At the end of Connor's story, Lenny said, 'That was novel: royalty, party masks and Villa shirts. Mate, I promise you this, if the thieving little bastards are in this city, I will find them and get your money back. I will be in touch.' He leant back in his chair and released a further plume of smoke, smirking as Connor clumsily got down from the stool to make his exit.

When he had gone, Lenny waved Teddy over and said, 'Right, Ted, get to work, I want you to turn over every little villain in the city because someone, somewhere must know something, but here's the thing. Fuck him, 'cos if we find it, we are gonna keep it. Murdering IRA bastards, after what they did in this city, they can fuck off, the lot of 'em!'

There was no word on the street and as annoying and frustrating as Lenny found it, he had all but given up the chase, happy to have pocketed the ten grand. He believed that it must have been the work of some out of town team from the 'smoke'. Given what he was told about the IRA connection, he didn't feel inclined to put himself out too much anyway.

Teddy continued to dig about but came up with nothing, roughing up a few small-time hoods and dealers, asking his lads on the doors if they had heard anything, but gaining no leads. He too began to ease up, concentrating on other matters, namely doing his little bit of scamming down the market. Not from his suitcase anymore; Lenny had got him a bona fide stall and an assistant so that when he felt the urge to go back to his old stomping ground, he could spend a few hours down there.

Teddy loved the atmosphere down the market, walking around the other stalls and having a chat. It may have been a coincidence but as he turned a corner to go up another aisle, there it was: a stall selling party masks. It started his mind turning. He decided his idea was worth a punt; he would give it a try and see what sort of reaction he got. Over the years, an initial furious onslaught with plenty of aggression usually softened up his prey and they talked.

Teddy smashed his hook straight through the display on Tommy Butler's stall and left a hand-sized hole in the plywood stand.

'Whoa, Teddy, what's up, mate?' Tommy screamed.

'I know you know something and now I want to know, so you'd better be quick because the hook is hungry for information and sometimes I find it hard to control, it's like it's got a mind of its own,' Teddy madly bawled.

'What do you mean, Teddy?'

'Masks, Tommy, masks.'

'I'm not with you, Teddy, what do you mean?'

'Someone has upset Mr Freeman and carried out a heist without permission on his manor, and he is very unhappy. The gang wore masks. You sell 'em and I want to know who you sold 'em to.'

'It could have been anyone, you know that, it's not just me that sells them. There's hundreds, probably thousands out there,' Tommy replied, trying to hide his panic behind a cool front. Teddy's experience told him there was something he was hiding; he could smell the fear and subterfuge, and went in for the kill.

Teddy grabbed Tommy and with the hook firmly held to his throat, he whispered, 'Tommy, you're forgetting something here, I'm not the police who I know have already visited you and gone away with nothing. I know where you live and I wouldn't want to call round when you're not there and bump into your wife or kids. Because you know something, this hook is no respecter of age or gender, it just hurts people.' He pressed the hook into Tommy's neck. 'Tell me now and save your family the trouble of meeting me and this hook of mine,' he growled, pushing his hook a little harder.

'Okay, Teddy, okay. It was Billy.'

'Billy. Billy who?'

'Billy Casey!'

CHAPTER FIFTY-TWO

Billy was relaxing, taking five, reading the newspaper when he looked up to see Teddy come through the door of the café.

'Teddy, my mate, it's nice to see you, do you want a mug of tea and a breakfast?'

'That would be very kind, Billy,' he said as he sat down opposite him with a stern look on his face, giving off an aura which made Billy feel decidedly uncomfortable.

Billy ignored the look and the odd atmosphere, and called over to Rita to rustle up the breakfast while he organised two mugs of tea and brought them back to the table.

'Help yourself to sugar, Teddy. Now, to what do I owe this pleasure, you coming up to see me?'

'Well, let me tell you a little story,' Teddy started. 'Mr Freeman gets a visit from a guy who lost a lot of cash, says he was off to the races to meet a man to buy some Colombian marching powder. Little did he know, but a very clever plan had been put together to relieve him of the quarter of a million he was carrying. Unable to unravel the puzzle himself, he asks Lenny if he could help him find out who did it. Now, Lenny ain't too worried 'cos the finger in question happens to have connections to the IRA and he's got no time for them after what they did in this city and after your own loss, I'm sure you agree with those sentiments but—' he paused, 'and this is the funny thing, I know who did it,' looking Billy straight in the eyes, the two holding each other's gaze in a competition to see who would blink first.

Probably because he liked Billy, Teddy wasn't concerned as to who won the staring competition and he broke first, reaching across to the packets of sugar. He picked two up with his left hand, passed them over to Billy and looking down at his hook said, 'Bit of a problem opening them with this, you can do the honours if you would, Bill,' which broke the tension.

'Now, let me assure you of one thing, Billy. I'm no grass and I always remember favours done in the past and as I said at the time, I owe you one. Let me tell you, Lenny is not a happy man at present. Once I found out who it was, I told him. I've never kept anything from him. I explained to him how you helped me out all those years ago and that you're a good market man. So he calmed down a little but he put it to me like this.'

Billy leant back in his seat as Teddy continued.

'Lenny is a creature of habit, Bill. So I tell him the story and he does that sucking of the teeth thing, and then he gets up and walks round the desk. He puts his hands on my shoulders and says, 'Go and visit Billy and tell him this. He used to work on a fruit and veg stall, so tell him to imagine a set of scales and he's weighing out some fruit on his scales. What we have is a grape on one side of the scales representing how he helped you out all those years ago, and a massive bunch of bananas on the other side representing what we are now doing for him. That means there is an imbalance. Now, that's an analogy, Teddy. You, or rather we, are doing him a big favour keeping this quiet, which outweighs what he did for you all those years ago and he needs to balance those scales so he had better think of a way to pay me back, otherwise I'll come knocking.'

After relating the story Teddy looked at Billy, whose face had drained of all colour.

'Bill, maybe you know what anal—analogy is. Lenny lost me a bit there, I thought it was something to do with your arsehole.'

Billy visibly winced as though something had just been shoved up his, but followed Teddy's reasoning and nodded in agreement; managing a grimace, he added, 'No, that's okay. I get the message.'

'Have we got an understanding, Billy, because what you have here is a situation where not only could you have Lenny on your case, you could also get knocked off by the IRA. Serious stuff, mate, serious stuff,' he repeated for emphasis.

Billy stared into the distance and took a few minutes to gather his thoughts. Of course he was concerned that he had been found out but it wasn't that, it was something else that Teddy had said that was filling his mind.

After a long silence, Billy said, 'Okay, so Lenny's not gonna shop me to the IRA, as he would have done it by now and you wouldn't be sitting here giving me a chance. From what you have told me, Lenny is happy as long as I make amends. A good market trader always look after his regulars and if you give me time to organise myself, I will look after the pair of you.'

'Good lad, Billy, I'll square things with Mr Freeman, tell him what you've said. Believe it or not, he has got a heart and he felt bad for you when I told him how you lost your sister, and the other good thing is he hates that Connor Flynn. Thought he was a cheeky bastard, asking us to sort out his mess, and I tell you something else, even if he had found that money, he was going to keep it, fuck 'em, he said. So don't cross him.'

'Thanks, Teddy. Finish your breakfast and I will be in touch,' he said as he got up and slapped Teddy gently on the back. He told Rita that he had to go out for a while on a bit of business but he was heading home, to think.

When he got home he sat in his lounge and began to piece together everything from Maria's death up to the present, and began to draw some sickening conclusions.

The immediate problems with Lenny and Teddy could be sorted from what he had left in the bag from the heist, which was sitting in a safety deposit box at the bank, still about a hundred grand after he had paid off the lads. It was all meant to be his but he was prepared to give it up to protect the lives of those involved and especially his family. But the problem of Connor Flynn was another thing entirely. The thing that had nagged him since his sister's death was that somewhere along the line he had always thought that the bastard was somehow involved. Teddy had now confirmed that Connor was a member of the IRA and it was reason enough to hold him responsible for his sister's death.

His temples throbbed as his anger grew. The thought that that piece of shit was still walking this earth after what he had done to his family sickened him. He slumped back on the settee with his head back and his eyes closed, trying hard to contain his rage and calm himself. A few minutes passed as he sat still, paralysed with the dark thoughts running through his mind.

Suddenly he jumped to his feet, unable to cope with what was happening inside his head. He decided he would exact revenge right there and then. After all the years of trying to contain his emotions over the death of his sister, the floodgates opened and the tears ran down his face.

He pulled open the door to the cupboard under the stairs. From behind a loose board in the floor he lifted out the handgun which he had hidden there after the heist. He checked that it was loaded and slipped it into the pocket of his blue cashmere overcoat. He would do it now, no questions; he would confront him in his office and blow his brains out.

He opened the front door to leave and there stood his brother.

'Hey, Bill, this has got to be a one-off. You're never out of that café and when I drove past and noticed the car in the driveway I thought something must be up for you to be home, so what is it?'

Billy heaved a sigh and invited his brother in. They sat in the lounge and Billy shook his head.

'No, I couldn't have done it.'

'What?'

'I was just on my way to finish him for good. Look,' he said as he pulled the gun out to show Ryan.

'What the hell are you doing with that? You weren't serious, were you? No way, Bill, whatever he's done it's not worth a life behind bars.'

'You don't know the half of it, Ryan.'

He then told his brother about Teddy's visit and revealed the stunning news that Flynn was a member of the IRA, with all its implications.

Ryan was struck mute and got up and paced the room for a few minutes.

'That fucker, he blew up our sister and that killed our dad too. Bill what are we going to do?'

'Look, we've got Bridie's funeral coming up and we need to get Mum through that first but I swear to you, brother, one way or another he is going to die.'

CHAPTER FIFTY-THREE

Connor Flynn was one of those types who had never read a book and didn't bother much with newspapers either, so when he picked up the 'Birmingham Evening Mail' which was sitting on the coffee table in the reception area at his offices, it was a bit of a one off. The headline had caught his attention though. The story concerned the Good Friday Agreement.

He was astounded to read that the sworn enemies in Ireland had all sat round a table, Protestant and Catholic, Ulster Unionists and Sinn Fein, Orange and Green. They had all entered an agreement to share in democratic elections, prisoner release programmes, and try to live alongside one another in peace.

'That Mo Mowlam must be some woman,' he said to himself.

His mind wandered back to those days back in Ireland. They seemed such distant memories now, as if his own part in it all had been played by a young man he didn't know. The lives he had taken didn't seem real at the time and now all these years later, were even less important. He had done a job for Mick and although it felt callous, that's all it ever was to him, a job.

When he had moved back to Birmingham, he was still doing a job for Mick and all the money he had provided to the cause over the years was to repay him for providing a home, a trade and a future. Without any of which he wouldn't be in the position he was now. No, he appreciated what had been done for him and he had paid his dues, so his conscience was clear. But with the disappearance of all that cash, the pressure was growing. He could pay it back himself but that would still leave too many questions unanswered.

He began to thumb through the rest of the paper and when he got towards the back of the newspaper, his heart froze. There in the births, marriages and deaths columns was the name O'Sullivan. As he read the entry he gave a wry smile.

Over the last decade or so, the desire to find his mother and father had taken a back seat as he pushed on with building his business empire. Some of his anger had also dissipated as he had grown older but suddenly all those old feelings came flooding back as he read the notice.

'BRIDIE MARIA O'SULLIVAN' was the heading, 'LOVING AUNT AND GREAT AUNT. SADLY PASSED AWAY 10th APRIL 1998. SERVICE AND BURIAL AT LODGE HILL CEMETERY, WEDNESDAY 15th—'

'So after all these years, when I'm not looking, I find what I'm looking for!'

He picked up his phone and made a call. After a short introduction, he continued, 'And the funeral will be held at Lodge Hill Cemetery next Wednesday, so I need you to sniff around for me. I particularly want you to make note of any elderly women and men, close family relatives probably. I want addresses. Where they live.'

He replaced the handset without a goodbye.

***

It was nine-thirty, Thursday morning, the day after the funeral when he received the call he hoped would provide some interesting information. He made notes on a writing pad as he listened to the details.

CHAPTER FIFTY-FOUR

He had been given two addresses to check out: one in Selly Oak and the other in Yardley. On instinct, he chose Selly Oak to visit first and hoped his hunch would prove right.

He had sat and waited patiently for many hours in his younger years in his previous occupation. Patience had always come easy to him but for some reason as he sat in his car, a few houses away from the address he had been given, his patience was running short. The anxiety and anticipation was starting to give him a headache.

He checked his watch, it was gone nine. He glanced back at the house and could see an elderly lady opening the front door and placing two milk bottles on the step. His hands gripped the steering wheel like a vice as he stared, as though in a hypnotic trance, his eyes wide open and his mouth clamped tight. He let out an audible grunt. He whispered out loud, 'Christ, I think I've found her. That's her, I've found her!' he repeated.

He sat for a while, trying to remain calm before deciding what to do. He had waited all his life for this moment and had rehearsed what he would say over and over in his mind but suddenly he could wait no longer. He got out of his car and strode up her garden path and rang the doorbell.

The elderly lady opened the door and after a double take, looked at the man in shock.

She knew immediately without question who he was, a mother's intuition. And those O'Malley eyes. He pushed past her on his way into the house, paying no heed to her and stood in the hallway. He waited for her to shut the door. He was breathing heavily and beads of perspiration began to appear on his forehead.

She turned slowly and stared into those eyes.

'Jesus and Mary,' she exclaimed, 'It's you isn't it, my son? Thanks be to God. After all these years I can't believe it. We have found each other.'

'Well, I'm not up for calling you Mammy just yet,' he sneered. 'Sorry if it comes as a shock to you, but the pair of you made my childhood a living hell, full of pain and misery. Where is he? Is he here too?'

'What's your name, son?' Mary asked, ignoring his ill-mannered outburst as she motioned him into her small lounge and sat in an armchair.

'Connor Flynn,' he replied. He remained standing.

'Connor is a lovely name, just what I might have called you,' she said gently. 'This is a dream come true for me but I understand the emotions you must be feeling, the sense of abandonment you must have felt all your life, must have twisted your mind and made you resentful of everyone and everything. I imagine your life growing up was unhappy, I can see it in your face. There's an anger and rage bubbling beneath the surface.'

Mary spoke with a feeling and understanding of him that Connor found eerily profound, consequently making him forget his rehearsed speech. In one sentence, she had summed up his life and how he had felt about his miserable childhood. She had disarmed him totally and in place of hatred, he began to feel closeness; an invisible bond was forming between the mother and her long-lost son.

She continued, 'There was never a day I didn't think about you, where you were and what you were doing and especially what you looked like, but I had a life to lead and responsibilities as a wife and mother. I could never have found you. I didn't know where in this world they had taken you. As soon as you were born they took you away. I didn't even get the chance to hold you, kiss you or cuddle my baby. I cried for days but the nuns told me to buck up and that you were better off living with someone who could afford to look after you properly. Give you all the things I could never do. The church, Connor, was so strong and ruthless. I heard stories of babies being taken off to America, even Australia, and being adopted, so it seemed impossible to ever track you down.'

'But did you try, did you ever try to find me or didn't you care?'

She knew there was no answer to that question and continued.

'When I came to Birmingham, I believed that I would never see you ever in my life, but of course always hoped there would be some miracle and I would meet you before my life ended. But as time went on, I had accepted that we would never meet.'

'So that's all you can say, is it?'

'You don't know how it was for me, Connor. I didn't really have a chance back then. I was fifteen when I had you, only a child myself. When I came to live over here and met and married William, my life seemed to blossom. That is, until I lost my daughter.'

He sat with his arms folded, staring coldly, unconvinced so far but impressed by the honesty and love that emanated from this woman.

He started to look around the room. Framed pictures stood on the mantlepiece above the old fireplace and also adorned a nearby wall cabinet. She noticed him staring at the pictures as though transfixed. She got up from her chair and stood by the pictures displayed on top of the wall cabinet.

'This one is my son, Billy, this is my son, Ryan, and this one, God rest her soul, my daughter, Maria. She was killed in the Tavern in the Town pub bombings in nineteen seventy-four.'

Connor was struck dumb. His blood ran icy cold and he felt a stabbing pain in his chest. He couldn't move or speak. The paralysis seemed to last minutes but it was only seconds as his mind absorbed all she was telling him.

Mary suddenly felt the grief again as she held the photograph of her daughter tight to her chest and sobbed uncontrollably.

'Yes, Connor,' she continued, 'my baby was taken by evil men who blew her to pieces that night and I will never forgive those responsible.'

He fought for breath, the pains in his chest were crushing and he felt sick. He had always believed he didn't belong anywhere, no relatives, no family, no one who cared and now he had found the only thing he had ever really wanted from the time he was a kid at the orphanage up the road. And at this moment he knew he would never have it.

The picture of the beautiful girl affected him deeply. His mind returned to that night and a young girl with striking eyes at the bar, but Martin had nudged him and told him it was time to go. He had left that duffel bag by the juke box. He hadn't cared and had never given a thought to who she was or the devastation it would cause to her family, his family. What sort of monster was he? He began to feel an emotion taking place which he had never experienced before and tears tumbled from his eyes. In all his life, he could never remember crying but this, this was a tragedy and he had been at the heart of it. He had as good as killed his own sister, a sister who in his cold-hearted, shameful way he had sentenced to death all those years ago.

He had two brothers, too. What he would have given to have bonded with them and enjoyed being part of their lives; recognising the two of them added to his pain. There was never going to be a happy ending to this and as he pulled himself together, he noticed his mother was still speaking. 'Yes, and that is the Casey family you are now part of.'

A stillness and calm suddenly came over him and he wiped away the tears and asked about his father.

'Your father wasn't William, no. That man who fathered you was a bad person and I really don't like thinking about that part of my life, and would rather not say any more.'

'I need to know who he is, it's my right,' he added forcefully.

'It's not a nice story, Connor, and one I have never told anyone, not even my husband William, God rest his soul.'

'But I need to know,' Connor demanded. 'Tell me now. I want to know the whole story, you owe me that much.'

Mary told him her story. When she had finished, he was filled with anger, hatred, and fury. He felt murderous. He managed to get control of himself and rose from the chair. He took his mother in his arms and squeezed her gently as though she was porcelain, a treasure to be handled with care. She, too, was tearful. He hugged her sobbing face to his chest protectively.

Another emotion he realised he had never known before filled his heart. Love! He suddenly felt protective of this woman he had only just met.

'Now, when can we all get together so that I can introduce you to your brothers and you can tell us all about your life?' Mary asked softly.

'I have to go now. Things to sort out but maybe we can all meet when I get back,' he said as he looked deeply into those emerald eyes, his eyes, Maria's eyes.

'Well,' Mary said as she wrote on a pad by the phone, 'this is my telephone number, call me when you get back. I am so happy you found me, Connor. Oh, I never asked you how you found me but tell me all about it tomorrow. You don't know what this means to me. You coming back into my life fills a huge void, my heart is now whole again.'

He didn't reply. He held her once more in his arms. A mother in her son's arms. He gave her a loving kiss on the cheek.

His face was set with a grim determination as he turned and walked away from his mother, knowing he would never see her again.

***

'Billy? It's your mother. I need to see you and Ryan round at my house as quick as you can. I've got some important news which I'm so excited about. How long will you be?'

'Mum, let me try Ryan and if he's round at his office, we will be there in about fifteen minutes.'

'Okay, hurry,' she said, before slamming the phone down in her excitement.

***

'What do you think she wants, Bill?' Ryan asked as Billy swung his car out of the roofing yard and headed towards his mum's house.

'God only knows,' he replied. 'Maybe she's won the lottery or something. Anyway we will find out soon enough and after that, you and I need to have a serious chat.'

They pulled up outside their Mum's house and walked quickly up to the front door, which she had left open. They made their way into the lounge where she was sitting with a huge smile on her face.

'You okay, Mum, what's up?' Billy asked.

After she revealed her news, the two brothers were in shock. Neither knew what to say. They mirrored each other, feigning surprise and happiness, trying to match their mother's mood but falling short.

'So what do you think of that, then? Isn't it wonderful, you have an older brother and you will be meeting him tomorrow. He's away on business today but said he will phone me tomorrow.'

Both brothers felt sick at the news. The idea that he was the same, well, half the same blood as them, was a terrifying thought. After Teddy's revelations and now this, Billy's mind was spinning. He couldn't believe this news. He desperately tried to hold it together for his mum's sake. He had one question for his mother though.

'Mum, you say all this happened when you were fifteen, back in Ireland, but how come you never told us anything about it. What is the story?'

'I've never told anyone the whole story, not even your father, God rest his soul. The shame I have carried my entire life keeping this secret has been a burden, but today I told Connor and now I must tell the two of you, too.'

And so Mary began to tell her two sons what happened all those years ago.

CHAPTER FIFTY-FIVE
Ireland 1945

She liked to walk the track through the woods on her way home from school, especially in winter time when the afternoon sun was low in the sky. She neared the clearing when two local lads suddenly appeared as if from nowhere. They were in a boisterous mood, laughing and pushing and shouting. They walked the narrow trail directly towards Colleen. She was frightened and knew that this would be an unpleasant confrontation.

They were well known around the village for getting into mischief. They were feral and everyone expected nothing but trouble from them. When the drink was on them, they had no respect for anyone or anything and left a trail of destruction whenever they wanted a bit of fun.

'Well, if it isn't the young virgin, Colleen O'Malley,' said the older of the two.

'Shut your dirty mouth, you feckin' gobshite,' she screamed, surprising herself at her language.

'Ah come on, Colleen, let's just have a look at what's under that blouse of yours. I bet they're lovely. Come on now,' said the younger boy.

Colleen felt panic. Menacingly, the bigger one approached her and tried to stroke her face and she pulled her head away, but he quickly grabbed her by the hair. He jerked her head back, demanding, 'Now, Colleen, don't be a spoilsport. We only want a bit of fun.'

'Leave me alone, ye bastards,' she shouted.

One was now standing behind her and she could smell the drink on the pair of them; the one in front of her belched his stinking breath in her face. He pulled her face towards his and said, 'Look, you dirty little bitch, you're going to do as we say or you will get a good battering for your troubles and if ye tell anyone about this, we will be doin' it to yer mammy next.'

He pushed her hard and she fell backwards over the outstretched leg of the boy behind her. The bigger brute was on top of her in a second with his hand up her skirt, pulling at her pants. She struggled against his hand to keep her legs tightly closed but his frustration grew and he punched her hard in the face, yanked her pants off and stuffed them in her mouth.

'Right, let's have a look at what she's got.'

Over his shoulder, she could see the other boy standing behind, watching and smiling and rubbing his hand up and down inside his trousers.

She couldn't scream and she felt herself gagging. She knew she needed to keep calm to come out of this alive. It took a massive effort of mind over matter to blot out what was happening to her body as she lay spread-eagled on the ground.

Her mind escaped her body and floated up to the top of the singular old, gnarled oak tree which had been stripped bare of its leaves. Its grey branches, like the grasping fingers of the undead, reaching up to the heavens seeking life and sustenance. Those branches became her focus and she tried to concentrate her mind up there. At the top of the tree she imagined she could see a robin preening itself. She studied the bird closely, tried to magnify it in her mind, its small beak, its protruding chest, its scarlet marking. She felt if she reached out, she could touch it.

The last she remembered was the twisted grin on his face and his thrusting and the pain, rhythmically, moving hard and fast in and out of her. His urgency grew and she blacked out.

***

She awoke to find her mother sitting next to her bed.

'My God, Colleen,' she cried, 'Thank the Lord you're back with us. What happened to you?'

'Oh, Mammy,' she mumbled, 'They—' but before she could say more her mother interrupted.

'Yes, I know. Thank God those boys were about. They found you in the woods. Said they chased off some travellers who were trying to hurt you. They carried you back here and you've been unconscious since.'

'No, Mammy, it was—'

Her mother cut across her again and said, 'I know, the boys said they hid in the woods, watching what was going on. They had seen you drinking with these travellers as well. Being real friendly. Oh, the smell of drink on you, Colleen. How could you? The embarrassment of it all. The boys are with the garda, making a statement. They said you were drunk. Oh my God, the shame.'

'No, Mammy, it wasn't like that at all!'

Colleen gasped for breath and could smell the whisky on her.

How had this all happened? Maybe it was all a bad dream. She slumped back on her bed and fell into a deep sleep.

***

'Colleen, the doctor's here to check you out now,' her mother said as she entered her bedroom and began to tidy up a little.

The morning sun was bursting through the window and she realised that she must have slept all night, although she wasn't quite sure what day it was or how long she had been asleep.

After a while, the doctor came down the stairs and spoke with Colleen's mother, who was sitting at the kitchen table.

'Mrs O'Malley,' said the doctor, 'it appears she has severe bruising to her face and some swelling to her nose, eye and mouth. However, she did complain about pains in her stomach and after examining her, but only in a cursory fashion, I could establish she has bruising around the top of her thighs near her— erm—'

'Oh, no, Doctor, you don't think she was—'

'I cannot be sure but when she's feeling a little better, she will need to come to the surgery for a check-up. We will do some tests then we can make certain if she really has any long-term damage, so to speak,' before adding, 'I'm very sorry.'

A few days later, at the doctor's surgery, she had the tests, which she didn't understand. Afterwards, she walked home quickly with her mammy, who was hoping she didn't run into any neighbours who might ask any embarrassing questions. She would keep her daughter at home until the results were known.

A few days later, Father O'Brien called round to discuss the way forward, as he put it.

'Caitlin, I believe that you will find the Church very helpful in the circumstances and on your behalf, I have already been in touch with my bishop. The advice I have been given is that

Colleen should go away for a while, at least until the matter is resolved.'

'Oh, Father, I just don't know. She's only a young girl and—'

'Caitlin, people will talk and the shame would be unbearable for you. This way you can tell everyone she has gone off to become a lay sister at the convent and no one will be the wiser.'

Father O'Brien convinced her that in the circumstances, there was really no other way for the matter to be resolved. He would take Colleen tomorrow, before she began to show, and let the nuns deal with the problem. In the end, Father O'Brien and shame had won the argument.

The next morning, her mother wept as she handed her daughter the only coat she owned, helping her to put it on, saying, 'You take it, Colleen, you'll need it more than me.'

Colleen cried as she shuffled slowly down the pathway to Father O'Brien's car, wearing the coat and carrying an old brown suitcase.

The journey in the back of the priest's car was long and she was in tears for most of the drive. Eventually, they drove through a set of big wrought iron gates then along a curved driveway, pulling up outside an extremely old, huge and scary convent. She looked out of the car at the frightening structure towering above her and suddenly felt so scared and alone.

She opened the car door and was met by a nun who immediately whisked her away. She trailed behind as she was led to a large dormitory where there appeared to be at least twenty beds, all with someone asleep in them. The nun pointed to an empty bed and said, 'That one's yours, keep it tidy.' She sat on the bed and cried some more. No one came to her to offer any comfort. She climbed, fully dressed, into bed and immediately fell asleep.

Next morning, when it was still dark, everyone was woken by a noisy handbell shaken vigorously by an old nun. She found an apron and a coarse habit on her bed and like the other girls, got dressed for work. Some of the girls she noticed were heavily pregnant. Others, she learned, were there because their families couldn't afford the dowry that would allow their daughter to become a nun. The next best thing was to become a lay sister; fine if you were prepared to be a skivvy and work like a maid.

The girls there spent their days working in the laundry, washing load after load of bedding and clothes. Others helped in the kitchens, producing the meagre plain meals everyone lived on.

The convent was dark and quiet and eerie, and sharing a dormitory with so many girls was both frightening and embarrassing in equal measure. She hated it all.

The months passed so slowly, until the day came when her pains were so bad she nearly fainted. She remembered the nuns taking her to a white room. She remembered the powerful light blazing into her eyes as she lay on a bed. Two nuns held a sheet up halfway down the bed so that she couldn't see what was happening.

Then Mother Superior appeared and seemed to glide into the room like a ghost, whispered something to one of the nuns and then just as swiftly drifted away.

The harsh pains in her stomach; the incessant aching in her lower back; she thought she was going to be sick. Screaming, grinding her teeth, grimacing and moaning, writhing in pain, she dug her nails into the palms of her hands as the pains intensified. Voices urging her to push down into her bottom and then the sharp squeal of a little baby; her baby.

She didn't get the chance to hold her baby. The last she saw was a bundle of howling blankets being carried away.

'Rest my child, it's all over now,' said a kindly sister who was holding Colleen's hand.

'My baby?' she asked through her tears.

'Shh,' whispered the sister, who checked to see that they were alone. Quietly she said, 'A boy!' She fell into a deep sleep and awoke later that day. She cried for the baby she would never know and for herself.

***

Billy and Ryan were devastated by the story. They felt their mother's pain, they were angry and sad. They stood up in unison and walked over to their mum, both hugging her lovingly. When they sat down, their heads were bowed. Their mother could hardly look at them. Feeling the shame she had carried with her for so long, she nervously twisted the pearls around her neck.

Billy asked the name of the older boy. His mother told him. He sat in silence, imagining tracking him down and killing him for what he had done.

Ryan was next to speak. 'Mum, look, there is no shame attached to you for what happened. You were a young girl who was taken advantage of, and the boys that did it should have faced the consequences and been put away.'

'They had played it so well, though, Ryan. They both stuck to their stories and the person who suffered was me. I tried to tell my mother but she didn't want to talk about it. I had brought shame to the family in her eyes and she let the church deal with the whole sorry matter. I never forgave her for it and the day I walked away from our home, was the last I ever saw of my mother and father.'

'What was Connor's reaction to the story?' Billy asked.

'Ah, the poor lad was knocked sideways by it. He was quiet for a long time and then he seemed to suffer a range of emotions, he was sorry and sad but got control of himself. He said he had business to deal with and that he would be in touch tomorrow.'

The two brothers looked at one another and Billy, for once in his life, was lost for words as the darkness invaded his mind once more.

CHAPTER FIFTY-SIX

The cities of Cork and Birmingham had dominated his life. He was born in one and then whilst still a baby, he was spirited away to the other. He had no say in either of those events. In his mid-teens, he had made the decision to return to his place of birth in his quest for some answers. He didn't find out much but had settled down there and started his first job and, most bizarre of all, had become a callous killer.

A decade later, he left Cork to return to the city he would call home for the greater part of his life and then just a few hours ago, he had left Birmingham to make a final visit to Cork.

His childhood and early life had been blighted, his emotional development was stunted and he had been starved of love. Thus, having never known it he couldn't give it. He never knew the sharing of that emotion, the unspoken rituals that formed loving relationships. A look, a touch, a word, a belonging, all had been denied him. The pain of abandonment he had felt growing up in that home was a critical part of fashioning an angry teenager with nothing to look forward to. He remembered the pain and anguish he had felt as a lad. The desolation of finding out that his parents didn't want him, and the resentment and envy he had felt against anyone who appeared to have a normal upbringing with two parents, a family.

Those feelings of abandonment and low self-esteem made him easy to manipulate and whilst his mind was in turmoil, he had been tempted by deviousness, debauchery and, later, killing. He couldn't prevent how he had turned out. Anyway, it didn't matter now.

Self-loathing was something he had never felt before. What he had done to his own sister now tortured his fevered mind and made him feel sick to his stomach. To see the impact the event had had on her mother, his mother, shamed him. God only knows what he would have done to Billy over that land deal; he knew very well that that would have ended in tears too. The thing was, before he had found his mother he felt that he didn't belong anywhere or care for anyone.

He thought back to his time as a sniper and the cruel way he had dispatched all those men; men with families, wives, children. What about their families and the sadness he had brought to so many? How did it all happen? Worse still, he had planted that bomb. It had killed so many and now it would claim its last two victims.

He had never found any good in himself until now. Tonight, he would accomplish possibly the one good thing he had done in his life. He checked his watch and, in the darkness, could just about make out the time. He knew what the routine would be.

The old man opened the door; the sniper picked up his rifle and through his telescopic sights, he could swear the man was looking directly at him and, for a second, doubted himself.

'A split second's hesitation could get you killed,' he heard the voice repeating in his head. Now was not the time to think. He couldn't stop himself though; he kept seeing the face of his sister in the photograph his mother had showed him. He shook his head, trying to clear the image, but it was impossible.

'Get that shot off and everything will be right,' he murmured to himself.

He brought the rifle in to his shoulder, quickly sighted his target and pulled at the trigger. The bullet hit the wall one inch to the right hand side of his target's head. The miss stunned and amazed him. He couldn't believe it, he never missed. His hands were shaking, his fingers seemed unresponsive. A slight panic set in. That split second of hesitation proved he was human after all, but it was too late for redemption.

He re-sighted and this time slowly inhaled deeply to stop his index finger from fidgeting; exhaling, he slowly let his breath out, gently caressing the trigger. The figure on the old sofa was staring out into the darkness. The bullet smashed through the middle of his forehead. The whisky glass fell to the floor and shattered.

Dropping the rifle next to him as he lay on the ground, he slid his hand across to the Browning HP Automatic pistol. He opened his mouth wide and stuffed the barrel inside. He squeezed the trigger and the bullet made its exit through the back of his skull.

CHAPTER FIFTY-SEVEN

Billy slept badly that night, wrestling with the shocking news his mother had revealed the previous evening. He opened the doors to the café the next morning to be confronted by Dave Jones, who walked in looking very serious.

'Bill, I think we had better sit down, I've got something I need to tell you.'

They sat opposite each other. Dave was not a handsome man, but he had clear blue eyes which he focussed on Billy. He opened a folder, studied it for a few seconds and then looked up.

'Hey, Dave, don't get me worried. What's happened?'

'Well, Billy, last night we were contacted by the garda and were informed that they had found the bodies of two men on a farm outside a village in Cork. It appears to the garda that the two deaths are connected.'

'Okay,' Billy said edgily, 'but what does that have to do with me?'

'Well, nothing directly, other than the fact that one was a businessman who is well known to us both. He had a note in his pocket and it's got a Birmingham phone number on it. They asked if I would check it out.'

'I'm still struggling, Dave.'

'Billy, we've checked the number out and it belongs to your mum.'

Billy was silent for a long while.

'Dave, the man is Connor Flynn, isn't it?'

'Yes,' Dave replied, unable to hide his surprise at Billy's conclusion. 'He apparently shot dead an old man and then killed himself.'

'And that man's name was Michael Doyle, wasn't it?'

Dave was amazed.

'I think you know a bit more than I thought. You had better tell me what you know first.'

For the third time in twenty-four hours, the story of what happened to his mother all those years ago was retold and at its end, Dave puffed out his cheeks and asked Billy a question.

'That's incredible, unbelievable. Your poor mother, just a kid. And how do we tell her what's happened?'

'She needs to know, but the real truth would kill her. She's only just found him after all this time and now he's dead. The fallout is what bothers me. The newspapers and media will have a field day with this story if they connect the dead men to her. Look, Dave, if it's possible we need to keep things a bit private. There are only four people who know the full story: my mum, Ryan, me and now you. We have to keep a cap on it.'

'But the garda will be asking me questions about the note and any connection there might be between the parties.'

'I know that, Dave, and I am going to ask the biggest favour ever of an honest cop and a good friend. You need to come up with a cover story to explain away that note. I know it's a massive ask but if any of this ever got out, it would tip my mum over the edge.'

It was Dave's turn to think long and hard. He stood up, nodded to Billy and left the café.

CHAPTER FIFTY-EIGHT

That afternoon, Dave Jones pulled up outside Mary's house and knocked firmly on the front door. He hoped that the story he had come up with would be enough to convince Mary that her long-lost son had died accidentally in Ireland. He never liked cover-ups, the truth always came out in the end but, for now, he would help his mate and play his part. The news he was about to break to Mary was bad enough but all the other gory details would be kept from her.

Mary opened the door and was taken by surprise when Dave introduced himself and flashed his ID.

She covered her face with her hands.

'What's happened, it's not my family is it?'

'I think you had better let me in and I can explain everything to you.

'Where's your kettle, Mrs Casey? I'll just make you a cup of tea,' he said as he made his way to the kitchen and found the kettle and cups.

Mary sat back in her armchair, alone with her thoughts for a couple of minutes until he came in with her cup of tea.

'I've put two sugars in. Now try and be as calm as possible because I have some bad news for you. We believe that you have recently had contact with a man named Connor Flynn. There was a note found in his jacket pocket with your phone number on it.'

'Oh no, no, not another one, I only saw him yesterday,' she sobbed, 'and we had only just found each other after fifty years apart. He was my son and was taken from me as a baby, you see. What's happened?' she sobbed.

'Details are still a bit sketchy as we are awaiting a full report from the garda, but I am sorry to tell you that he has been involved in a tragic accident in Ireland and I'm afraid that he has died from his injuries. I'm very, very sorry,' he said softly.

After giving her a few moments, he added, 'Once we have the full story we will explain everything to you. Is there someone we can call to sit with you?'

'Yes, my son, Billy, his number's by the phone in the hall.'

Dave made the call to Billy.

In the silence that followed, her mind raced with thoughts of what had happened. An accident, probably a car crash, she thought. What else could He throw at her? She would never forgive Him.

She had been so happy after meeting him yesterday and had been imagining all the conversations they would have, catching up on their lives and getting to know each other properly. It had all been snatched away now. Her misery was complete and she wept uncontrollably.

CHAPTER FIFTY-NINE

A few days later, Dave was back at the café with even more grim news and, once more, they sat opposite each other in the booth. Dave began to reveal what he knew regarding the life and death of Connor Flynn.

'Bill, this latest information is turning this story into quite an epic tale.'

'Nothing was ever simple with that bloke, Dave.'

'Okay. Well, brace yourself because by the end of it you will be amazed.'

Dave related the information that had been given to him by the garda, detailing how Connor had arrived in Cork in the early sixties and got a job working for Doyle.

'This Doyle character was a confirmed IRA member; his own father had been shot dead in a raid in the 'twenties when they were rounding up local IRA men. His brother accidentally blew himself up when his bomb-making went wrong so they all had deep roots in the organisation and after the split in the IRA, he joined the Provisionals.'

He continued, 'Now this is where it gets even more interesting because from about nineteen seventy to nineteen seventy-two, there were a number of shootings carried out by a sniper in the border areas around South Armagh and Belfast which all bore the same MO. So far, at least five can be linked directly to the very same rifle used to kill the old man. Forensic testing is still continuing but they are pretty certain that there will be more victims and remarkably, the only fingerprints on it are those of Connor Flynn. It has been confirmed that the last target in Ireland was a guard from the Maze who was shot dead by a sniper in Crossmaglen. He was shot from the ramparts of a church where a shell casing was found, once again linking it to the same rifle. Then, there was nothing for more than twenty-five years, that is until he nailed Michael Doyle, once again with that rifle. That quiet period was no coincidence, as the sniper was then back in Birmingham, starting his building company.'

'Whoa, Dave, are you telling me that Connor Flynn was a sniper?'

'It certainly looks that way. We could never connect him to the Birmingham Brigade at the time but it's possible the Provos set him up in the building business to provide funds for the organisation. It was difficult to unravel exactly what he was up to but he had become pretty wealthy and in recent years, our intelligence has been that he was involved in buying cocaine, large amounts too. When cut and sold on the streets in Dublin and Belfast, it became a very lucrative business for the Provos. The net was slowly closing in on him and we nearly had him when we received a tip-off that he was going to Ascot to do a very big deal, bigger than the ten grand he told us he lost in the Queensway Heist anyway. We were closing in on him and others connected to a very large drug dealing syndicate. We believe that there was a quarter of a million pounds involved but some clever buggers got there before us and messed up our plans to pull him and the kingpin, Mr Big, at Ascot.'

'Yeah, I remember reading about that heist. It was very cunning, them Villa bastards would do anything for a few bob,' Billy joked nervously.

'Well, there were a number of names in the frame for that one, even Protestant gangs from Belfast. We passed our files to the RUC some time ago to see if they can get any further leads as we have hit a brick wall this end.'

Billy was relieved to hear that.

'So he was a cold-blooded killer then, Dave? It's unbelievable to think that he was in the midst of us all and he had murdered so many people.'

'Yes, Bill, I'm afraid villains lurk in the most unexpected places. So, armed with the information you gave me regarding your mum, and knowing that she had revealed the whole story to Connor as to who his father was, it then appears he went back to kill him.'

'But why kill himself too?' Billy asked.

'Well, we could certainly say he was of unsound mind when he did it. Let's face it, the first fifteen years of his life were spent in an orphanage which probably didn't help. Sometimes, some of those kids come out of those places with terrible hang-ups. We've seen it all too often in this job. Add to that, a serious personality disorder which manifested itself in the cold-blooded murders of troops and police, and you have a ticking time bomb.'

'But, Dave, he had a lot to live for and plenty of money too. No, something must have pushed him over the edge.'

'Well, I have a theory and it's this. I listened very intently when you revealed your mum's story, how she had told Flynn about her rape which apparently made him very angry. She also told me that she was startled when she showed him the photographs of the family, especially the one of Maria. She remembered his agitated reaction when she told him that she held the IRA responsible for murdering her daughter. She said he was close to tears. My presumption is this: he was involved on some level that night and by implication, with planting the bomb that killed your sister. Indeed, his own sister. So the visit to your mum was a cataclysmic revelation on many levels. Having found his mother, he also learned who his father was which must have been an even bigger shock; then the whole thing begins to unravel and he can't cope. He implodes. Imagine it. Not only was Mick Doyle, his adopted, trusted father figure, the man who had defiled his mother but he was also responsible for recruiting him and turning him into a killer. Then the topper was: Doyle was his real father. I think that's enough to send him over the top; something snaps and—'

'Well, I'm just glad he saved us the problem of sorting him out, to be honest, because the way I felt about him when I heard—'

Billy managed to stop himself from finishing the sentence. Now was not the time and this was not the person to reveal what Teddy had told him some weeks earlier.

They both paused for thought.

'So where do we go from here, Billy? Obviously I will need to speak to your mum again and tell her how he died. I have informed the garda that the note was of no significance, only an enquiry from a client regarding a possible purchase of a retirement apartment in one of his developments. I think that one has been put to bed.'

Billy thought of his poor mother and how she would mourn that long lost son. As much as he would like Dave to tell her everything so that she would know what a piece of scum he was, he realised that she would never recover from the knowledge that her own son had been responsible for the death of her daughter.

'Dave, I really appreciate you coming to me with all the details but I don't want my mother to know them all. Hopefully, the press won't dig around. After all, to all intents and purposes he was an orphan who grew up in a children's home. She had changed her name years ago and then it changed again when she married my father, so no family connections at all. No, it will be sufficient for her to know that he flipped and killed the man who had violated his mother and then, knowing he had done wrong, shot himself to save her any shame. Make him sound good, Dave, for her sake.'

'Okay, Bill, you're a good son and I know what your mum means to you. I'll do it like that and I know you will be there to help her through.'

CHAPTER SIXTY

The cancer was a particularly virulent type which had invaded her liver and spread to other organs, and was slowly sucking the final vestiges of life out of her. She knew that she didn't have long left and hoped the delivery to His loving arms would come soon. Through the haze of her drug-induced sleep, she had many wondrous dreams and was in the middle of another when she was gently shaken awake.

'Mother, are you awake?'

Slowly opening her eyes and trying to focus, she nodded.

'What is it?' she mumbled.

'He's dead.'

There was no need to explain any further.

They had followed his life from the time he had come back to Birmingham and were aware of his achievements. They had both greedily and secretly enjoyed his success. The news had her searching for some clarity in her fuzzy mind.

'He's dead?' She repeated it once, twice, three times.

She nodded, closed her eyes and immediately, instead of re-entering the crazy, weird hallucinations of her drug-induced state, she was that young woman once more; the memories flooded back, vivid and shocking.

Her journey through life had not been easy. Her mother was a tyrant full of contradictions and a strict Catholic. Mother and daughter attended church regularly and it was natural for her mother to discuss any personal problems with her priest. Often, she would complain about her husband, who she knew sought sexual relief from prostitutes. Then she would grumble on about her daughter, Deidre, who was beginning to become rebellious and hard to handle.

His advice regarding the husband was a bit flaky, 'Trust in God,' etc, but he was less interested in that problem and more interested in offering counselling for the young girl. Like a shark smelling blood, he circled his prey, encouraging the mother to send the girl to him for private sessions in the sacristy.

Initially, the priest gave her some small tasks to perform and over time gained her confidence. It wasn't long before he started to touch her intimately. Then he took her virginity in that dark room, threatening her with eternal damnation if she ever told another soul.

The priest made it obvious to everyone that she was special to him and the mother was grateful to see the change in her daughter, whose goal now appeared to surround becoming a nun.

The young girl knew what the priest did was a sin but her determination to enter His service, plus the priest's promised support, meant she ignored the possible psychological damage it may have caused and concentrated on her future. She did think at one point that she may be replicating her mother's behaviour and obsession with the Catholic religion but whatever, her main goal was to join an order. There she could take classes and enter a novitiate. That sinful priest would not deter her. In fact, she believed he could be of great assistance in achieving her ambition.

When she heard that the bishop was to visit her church, she decided it was time to put her plan in motion. She managed to find a minute or two when the priest was not at the bishop's side and held a whispered conversation with the bishop. Fortunately, the bishop was impressed with the young girl's desire to answer her calling and had encouraging words for her.

The priest had been busy that morning with some members of his congregation and when he turned around he noticed her leaving the bishop's side. He could see her saying, 'Thank you for your help, Your Grace.' She smiled at the bishop as she walked away.

Later, in the sacristy, with a controlled rage in his voice, the priest asked what she had been talking to the bishop about.

'I decided to tell him everything,' she replied.

'What have you done, you stupid girl?' he blustered.

'I told him everything about us,' she teased, knowing she had control and for once he was at a disadvantage. She could see in his eyes the fear of what might happen to him.

'I told him of my ambition to become a nun and how helpful you have been. I also said that you had promised to assist me by contacting the convent and securing me a position.'

'Oh, did you, now?' he replied cagily.

'He was so nice to me; told me to speak with him again whenever I needed help. So, I think you and I have an agreement, don't you? There will be no mention of what you have done to me as long as you keep your promise to help me.'

He realised he had been outsmarted by the bright teenager. He didn't like it one bit but, for her silence, he would do what it took.

Those haunting memories of what happened at the priest's hands, had scarred her young life and she buried her dark secrets deep inside, hoping that time would allow her to come to terms with it all.

At eighteen, she flourished in her chosen calling; it was her vocation. She was given a new name, Cecilia. After two years, she would take her first vows of poverty, chastity and obedience. Another three years in His service was evidence of her authenticity to her calling and ability to live a religious life. Then the final service, where her Rosary crucifix was exchanged for a pewter one, a plain silver wedding ring worn on her right hand, and lying prostrate in the form of a cross on the chapel floor, were the final parts of the ceremony to become a Bride of Christ. She didn't feel pride, as she felt that was sinful, but she was happy to serve Him now for the rest of her life.

So, Sister Cecilia was to continue her good works at the Woodside Children's Home, helping disadvantaged and orphaned children. As one of her duties, she was given the job of trying to tame a wild young boy who caused havoc whenever the mood took him. Rigid discipline was her initial strategy, with regular canings, but the boy seemed to gain strength from the punishment; she began to think that the devil lived inside him. She sometimes thought she wasn't beating the badness out of him, she was beating it further in. Every day seemed to be a battle with the boy and the regime of canings began to take its toll on her, triggering those suppressed dark memories of her youth to surface.

The struggle within herself had laid dormant for many years but she felt an emotional explosion nearing the surface. Feelings she couldn't control began to invade her mind. Dark thoughts of the Sacristy and the priest, and what he did to her. Had she enjoyed it? She had never told her mother about it. Why? She was to blame, she had encouraged him. She knew it was wrong to feel this way. She prayed hard and asked for His help. The tumult within her head was taking its toll.

The abused would become the abuser.

Lately, she felt differently about the boy who was now nearly fifteen, and was big and awkward. Something excited her; a depravity grew and the beatings were becoming more an outlet for her than a punishment for him. She knew she would find it hard to resist taking that next step. The thrilling thought of taking it further with the boy became something she thought about a lot.

One night, he came to her room as ordered; she knew she would be in big trouble if she was caught but the excitement outweighed any consequences.

He knocked softly and she quickly pulled him inside, pinning him against the door.

She was silent for a while and then slapped the cane at his genitals.

'You dirty boy, why are you getting excited?'

She gasped and breathed harder, coming up close to him, leaning her hands on his shoulders for support as though she was about to faint; she brought her face close to his. He could feel her warm breath. She seemed to be losing balance and her legs were shaking. She was powerless to resist the vile, salacious and disgusting thoughts invading her mind. Depraved and excited. Breathless, she fell back on the bed, pulling up her habit and parting her legs, revealing herself momentarily.

He was fascinated to see a woman's body for the first time and could hardly believe what he was looking at.

She knew this would be enough to start with and harshly hissed, 'Okay, that's enough. Go back to your room. I shall let you know when I need to see you again.'

When he had crept back into his bed he thought that the whole experience had been so compelling and imagined all women would be like this. He thought about what he had just seen and a lust for sex was born which would obsess and possess him.

Their secret assignations were regular now and were rarely interrupted, except when one day they had forgotten the time. Sister Angelina had softly tapped on her door to inform her that the evening meal was being served. They both froze at the idea of being caught out. They didn't realise that Angelina had listened at the door many times.

One day in the garden, Angelina took the chance and blurted out what was on her mind.

'I know what you and Connor are doing.'

'Don't be so silly, what do you mean? Your imagination is running away with you.'

'Well I have heard things and words that were evil and I'm sure if the Reverend Mother was to hear that you have a boy in your room she wouldn't be happy, would she?'

Cecilia looked into her young face and asked her what she was going to do with her knowledge.

'Well, I know it's wrong and sinful, what you are doing.'

Cecilia knew she must take control of Angelina and the situation before it got out of hand.

'Angelina, we need to discuss this matter further, so come to my room after Vespers this evening and I will explain all about those feelings and what it means.'

Later that evening the boy tapped lightly on her door as usual, hoping that maybe tonight would be the time she would allow him to complete his education. Her voice, throaty and sensual, whispered, 'Come in.'

He was met by the scene of her dressed only in a thin cotton chemise, through which he could see her triangular badge of womanhood. She lay seductively on the bed as the candle flickered. Outside, a huge storm was erupting with forked lightening filling the sky, closely followed by the booming bang of thunder. The rain was hard and hammered against the windows like a blast of tin tacks fired from a machine gun.

He stood by the bed, watching her. His mouth was dry with anticipation. She pulled him towards her, groaned and gasped. The boy was a pawn in her game and she took control. She guided him, and he was eager to learn. At the conclusion she moaned and rolled on to her back.

'Now get off to bed,' she ordered.

He dressed quickly and left; she closed the door after him and walked over to her hanging closet and drew back the curtain which covered the small hanging area where she hung her few clothes. She offered her hand to Angelina; the young novice was wide-eyed and bewildered at what she had witnessed from the small gap in the curtains behind which she had been hiding. Cecilia guided her over to the bed and asked, 'Did you see all that you wanted, Angelina?'

'It was the most incredibly sensual display anyone could wish to witness,' she replied.

'Did you like it?'

'Ooh, yes.' With those words, Cecilia knew she had a new ally and co-conspirator.

'Don't worry about that, tomorrow you must pray harder than you have ever before and He will forgive your sins, He always does. Remember, only He can judge us. Of course we must never talk of what goes on here to anyone, do you understand?'

She nodded her agreement; as Cecilia gently caressed her hair, she said, 'Now lie down next to me and relax.'

***

Although her mind was a maelstrom of confusion, for a while she had been lucid and the memories had been vivid and clear. Then she coughed a coarse, dry cough, gasping for breath. One last single breath. Her head fell to the side and her lifeless eyes stared into the distance.

Sister Angelina, sitting at her bedside, burst into tears.

Now both were dead, she would keep her promise and tell him the truth.

CHAPTER SIXTY-ONE

He had made his final arrangements, knowing that he would never be returning from Ireland. He had hastily organised everything before he had left. The reading of the last will and testament of Connor Flynn took place at a solicitor's offices in Edgbaston. His mother was sole beneficiary.

Sadly, Mary sat and listened to the solicitor droning on, finding it all too much to bear. The financial details meant nothing to her. The only thing on her mind was the thought that she had lost her son, found him again, only to have him taken away from her in such tragic circumstances. The whole affair had left her feeling wretched.

She politely asked the solicitor if her sons could deal with it all on her behalf and requested that he drew up those papers to give them the legal powers to do so. She didn't want any part in it. She rose from her chair wearily and caressed the hands of her two sons. Looking into their faces, she said, 'You two can deal with all this,' and quietly closed the office door behind her.

In reception, she asked the young girl to get her a taxi and to tell the boys when they came out that she had gone home.

Later, as Mary sat in her armchair going over and over the information she had been given by Dave Jones after his second visit, she had been stunned to learn that he had taken his own life after shooting Michael Doyle dead with a rifle. She blamed herself for revealing the story of her rape which must have affected him deeply, but she still couldn't understand how quickly Connor had found Doyle, then killed him so cold-bloodedly. By telling him the truth, she had sentenced Michael Doyle to death but why did her son have to kill himself?

His body was flown back to Birmingham from Cork. So once again, as in life, he was in death making that round trip between the two cities. But this would now be his final resting place.

Through the whole episode, Billy had been steadfast and reliable and had managed to combine the role of dutiful son and advisor. He had convinced his mother that due to the circumstances in which Connor had died, now was not the time to make any public announcements about her relationship with him. He was hoping the fact that while everyone believed he was an orphan from birth, no one would link the two.

'Mum, the last thing you want now is for the whole world to know the full story of what happened to you in those woods all those years ago; how you gave your baby away. No, that's the last thing you need.'

He knew it sounded harsh and he hated having to play on the shame she still felt but he needed to delicately guide her through the next few weeks and protect her from the truth. A truth too shocking for her to comprehend. He also managed to make her understand that she could not attend his funeral, well, not when there were other people about, but assured her that he and Ryan would take her to say her final goodbye when everyone had gone.

It was a depressing day for Mary as they sat in the car watching the final mourners leave the graveside. Billy was sure that most had come just to make sure he was indeed dead. When he felt comfortable that there was nobody lurking about, he opened the rear door and he and Ryan helped their elderly mother from the car. She looked frail and weak. The events of the last week had taken their toll on her. Her two sons had to support her to the graveside, one on either side, taking her by the arms. Her hair was now heavily streaked with silver but in the late afternoon sunlight, her emerald eyes still shone in her proud and distinguished face.

She stood alone by the grave and scattered a handful of dirt on the casket, her sons waiting a few steps away. She grieved one last time for the son she had never been allowed to know. Tearfully she looked down at the coffin.

'My dear long lost son, I'm so sorry I never got to know you. Words are useless now but there was always an empty space in my heart where you should have been and it will now never be filled. Rest in peace,' she whispered.

The sun disappeared behind a black cloud, signalling the start of a storm. Heavy droplets of rain began to fall as her two boys ushered her back to the car. She sat alone in the back seat, quiet with her own thoughts. Her sons sat in the front, knowing they could never reveal the truth of it all. Never tell her of the misery and heartbreak Connor Flynn had wrought on their family.

As they drove away, they didn't notice the man standing behind a giant oak, watching their every move.

CHAPTER SIXTY-TWO

If the two brothers had thought recent events were emotionally taxing, now meetings with the solicitor had both their heads spinning. The mammoth task of unravelling Connor's business affairs was complex on many levels.

Billy had already thought this one out though, ensuring that all funds were transferred to a number of Swiss bank accounts. That trail would be impossible to follow should any person or organisation wish to track where the money had gone. He had to make sure his mum and family would be safe and secure, and that no one could ever link them to Connor Flynn.

He left Rita to run things back at the café. Ryan relied upon the ever resourceful Margaret to keep things ticking over at Casey Roofing. The pair spent hours assisting the solicitor with dismantling and selling off the building, development and investment companies.

There were many building companies in the city who would very much like to buy Flynn Developments, especially to get their hands on the land-bank the company owned, including the old battery factory at the back of the café. That bought a wry smile to Billy's face. He would now be involved in the sale to Flynn Developments of the Greasy Spoon, Sid's bike shop and Harry's bakery, making it a mouth-watering proposition for the would-be suitors. He would make sure that the three little businesses all benefitted from that particular transaction.

The brothers had concluded most of the details required by the solicitor with regard to the business side of things, but Connor also owned a house in Edgbaston. They arranged to meet at the property before the solicitor placed it for sale with a top class estate agency at Five Ways. Arrangements had been made with a house clearance company to clear the furniture and belongings, and the brothers decided to make a visit to the house out of curiosity.

They pulled into the driveway and Billy said, 'Okay, Ryan, you have a look round downstairs and I'll take upstairs,' as he opened the front door.

'What are we actually looking for then, Bill?' Ryan asked.

'That bloke was never straightforward so let's just have a shuffty and see what turns up.'

Ryan walked into the lounge and noticed the mirror still hanging over the fireplace and wondered why the house clearers hadn't taken it.

'Bill, where are you?'

'Okay, I'm on my way, nothing up here,' he shouted back as he descended the stairs, carrying a nun's habit and wimple in his arms. 'Look at this,' he said. 'What do you think this is all about?'

He threw the outfit on the floor.

'Beats me,' Ryan said. 'Nothing much to report here.'

Billy pointed to the mirror and said, 'What about this?' He walked forward to lift it off the hooks which supported it.

'Well, how about this then? A wall safe. Mm, now that could be very interesting,' he said as he twisted the handle to try to open it, to no avail.

'Okay, all we need now is someone who knows their way around safes and I know just the man, Percy Packer, the Safe Cracker, as we used to call him. Let's give him a call.'

Percy was just finishing a job and was ready to call it a day and head home but Billy sweet-talked him into popping round just to have a look-see.

Percy arrived just before five, a small, studious-looking, thin man with metal-rimmed spectacles, a full beard and noticeably long, piano player's fingers.

'Okay,' said Percy, 'let's have a look at what we've got. A wall safe, is it? Behind this mirror, I suppose.'

He walked across the lounge, lifted up the mirror, turned it round and placed it on the floor, leaning it against the wall so that the back was facing him.

'Right, now this could be a very long job and if it's two hours and I have to get my tools from the van, or two minutes, it's gonna cost you two hundred and fifty pounds.'

'Well, either way, Percy, we need it opened and we prefer to go for the two-minute option, please.'

'Right,' said Percy as he became very serious, placing his head against the safe and pressing his ear to it as though listening to the tumblers. He twisted the combination dial three times and slid the lever across and the door flicked open a fraction.

The brothers were dumbstruck, looking at each other in awe at the skill of the man.

'There you go,' he said. 'One wall safe by Chubb, three number combination, now open and ready for business.'

'You are a magician, Percy,' Billy said in amazement. 'How did you do that?'

'Well, it's a skill that's taken me years to learn and if I told you how I did it, I'd be breaking the safe crackers' code of silence but as I know you so well, I'll let you into a little secret. Most safes are set up with what's called a 'try out combination'. Now most people are too lazy to change it or can't be bothered to go through all the rigmarole, so it's common for them to leave it be. Most try out combinations are industry standard and widely known by locksmiths. This one was changed, though,' he paused, 'and if you pay me my cash in my hand now, I'll tell you how I cracked it.'

He was teasing them, knowing that they would crush the cash into his hand very quickly to learn the answer. Billy handed him the cash which he counted, then folded it neatly into his wallet and started to leave.

'Eh, whoa up, Percy, you haven't told us how you did it.'

'Oh yes, sorry about that, Billy,' he said as though absent-mindedly forgetting. 'Here's the thing. The people who do bother to change the combination tend to get paranoid about forgetting it so they write it down and you wouldn't believe how stupid some of them are. Commonly, they write it on the back of the painting or—' he paused for effect, keeping his audience enthralled, 'in this case, the mirror that's hiding the safe.'

The brothers looked at one another and raced over to the mirror which Percy had helpfully left against the wall. They knelt down and read the three numbers written in small writing in the bottom right-hand corner.

'Percy you crafty bast—' Billy started to say but he was already outside, starting up his van, ready to head for home.

They both stood up and laughed. Billy reached up and swung open the safe door. He reached in and took out four very thick brown paper bags bound with elastic bands, plus a postcard-size manila envelope. He threw the paper bags to Ryan.

'I think we both know what's inside those.'

Ryan opened one and calmly reported, 'Wads of fifties. Must be fifty thousand pounds, probably more, in each. His float for the casino, I suspect.'

Billy nodded.

'Now let's have a look at what's in this envelope.'

He pulled out a black and white photograph which was so aged it was turning sepia.

'It's him, must be at the children's home when he was a lad, sitting on a bench in the garden next to a nun,' said Billy as he passed it to Ryan to have a look.

Ryan looked at the picture and then turned it over.

'Oh, and written on the back it says, 'You will never forget me – C.' What do you make of that then?'

'You know something, Ryan, I'm not even going to hazard a guess because what do you keep in a safe, eh? Valuables. So along with a mountain of cash he keeps this photograph, meaning it's important to him. Then you read something like what she's written on the back and then look over in the corner of the room and see that, too,' he pointed to the nun's outfit, 'and knowing what he was capable of, the mind boggles. A heart as black as pitch,' he added, shaking his head.

CHAPTER SIXTY-THREE

It had taken over eighteen months, but that morning Mary signed the final paperwork and the Flynn Group was no more. Every business asset, personal property and bank account had been sold or closed; they all breathed a sigh of relief.

Billy had already spoken with his mum and she had made it plain that any decisions he made regarding the financial matters, were good enough for her.

They left the solicitor's office and climbed into Billy's car.

'So, Mum, where do we go from here?' Billy asked over his shoulder to his mum in the back seat.

'Son, I never got to know Connor and he seemed to be so successful, it would have been wonderful to have enjoyed it all with him. He was so near to us, a few minutes away for all those years and I didn't realise it. Him dying and leaving me everything is a sort of reward and I don't deserve one. I didn't do anything for him other than to give him life. It all makes me feel so sad. You know, I have signed papers putting you in charge, Billy, and, with Ryan's assistance, I know I can trust you to deal with the whole thing. Look, the pair of you know more about business than I ever will and at my age, I won't need much to see me to the end of my life. I don't want anything to do with it. You two will do what's right, just make sure the ones we care about are all looked after and if you do that, I will be very happy indeed.'

They dropped their mother back at home and sat talking in the car for a while.

'You know when Teddy told you Connor was part of the IRA? How did you feel? Must have been a shock,' Ryan said.

'I was in turmoil for a while and I could hardly keep it together. I always believed we would have some outstanding business to conclude with Mr Connor Flynn, more than we first thought. I can't tell you how much I wanted to kill him and if you hadn't stopped me that day, he would have been dead. Then a couple of days later he saves us the trouble and does it himself.'

'Karma,' said Ryan, 'he couldn't live with himself.'

'Well, you know something, brother, I've been thinking about it all and, yes, there is a sort of karma thing going on and do you want to know something else? Yesterday I went to church. One of those modern ones it was, don't mention it to Mum though, you know how she feels about the whole religion thing now. Anyway, I sat in that church, trying to figure out how me and you come to terms with all this, you know; Maria, Dad and Connor and the money. I mumbled a sort of prayer and asked for a sign to tell me what to do.'

Ryan was in suspense, not believing his brother was saying these words. His mouth was agape and he said impatiently, 'Well, did you see a sign?'

'Yes, Ryan, I saw a sign and do you know what it said?'

'What, Bill, what did it say?' Ryan said, desperate for the answer.

Billy placed a hand on each shoulder and looked into Ryan's expectant face.

'Mate, it was a green sign and it was over the door and it said EXIT.'

'You bastard,' said Ryan as Billy creased up in hysterics, 'I thought you were going to come out with something profound and deep, you twat!'

'But, mate, that's it, that's the part you're not understanding. That was the sign and it's the only sign. If you can get past the Catholic mumbo jumbo and it hasn't got you scared about ending up in eternal damnation, that's all there is. You make an exit. Evil like what robbed us of Maria and then Dad, good that finished Connor and his old man off, and then there's something in between, just like Mum says. We are here, we are living and who knows when we go through the exit door ourselves? We're both getting older, mate. How long have we got? How long has Mum got? We are here and we must look after our families and enjoy the moment. If that money will allow us to do anything then we will do what Mum says and look after our own. I bet if Maria was here she would say, 'Go on, do it!' It's not easy to forget the past and where all this money has come from. I don't like it one bit but we can only concern ourselves with the future now. Let's not let the evil that's been perpetrated on this family screw us up, otherwise evil will have won and I'm not having that. So I've had an idea.'

'What's that?' Ryan asked.

'Well, I have already thought of a few things actually and that involves us in getting away for a good long holiday, out of this country and away from the stress and strain. Three long months away because that's all they allow you on a holiday visa, I've checked. I thought we should find out what all the fuss is about this Australia place, what do you think?'

'Whoa, that's a great idea, wait 'til I tell Jenny. Her mum and dad haven't seen young Donovan yet and he's nearly five, and they haven't even met me, so it will kill two birds with one stone, so to speak. What else?'

'Me and Rita are moving to a new house. We have bought a big five-bedroomed Victorian house with a servant's cottage in the grounds, it's round the corner from you. Me and Rita sealed the deal and paid the deposit last week. There will be enough room in the main house to have Mum living with us and Sean and Suzanne can live in the cottage. We can set up the Casey community in Barnt Green where we can all be close and keep an eye on each other. And with the café sold, I was thinking we could start up a little property business: buying and selling and renting. Well, with Mum's, ours and your flat, we've already got three properties to rent out and we can expand from there.' He smiled that smile and Ryan knew there would be one last thing.

'Okay,' said Ryan, 'and—' he said expectantly.

'Oh, yes, just to start off our little property empire from the land bank of Flynn Developments, a small company called RyBilld Ltd bought three of the most sought-after building plots in Edgbaston at a knock-down price.'

'Who is RyBilld Ltd?' Ryan queried.

'Oh, I believe the main directors' names are Ryan and Billy, are you with me? Jenny and Rita will be co-directors, it's a family company, you know,' he laughed

CHAPTER SIXTY-FOUR

Plans were in motion.

A few weeks before they left for Australia, Billy made a number of phone calls, some to a London number and a few local calls. He wanted to ensure everything was in place and sought confirmation from his solicitor that his instructions regarding a number of money transfers had been carried out.

Jenny was busy planning too. She was happy to be organising the whole trip and had been given carte blanche to take them all on an unforgettable holiday of a lifetime and show off her son, her husband and her country.

So in the run-up to Christmas, as they entered a new century, the travelling party gathered at Birmingham International Airport that evening. Emirates now flew directly to Dubai and then onto Sydney, a route they had recently established, taking advantage of Birmingham's central geographical position and giving relief to the overcrowded London airports.

Jenny had beguiled Ryan not only with her looks and vivacious personality all those years ago, but with the stories of life back in Australia, particularly the sights of Sydney; more especially about a little place up on the Central Coast of New South Wales called Avoca Beach where her parents lived and she had grown up.

She never thought she would get him to make the trip, leaving his business, his golf and his beloved Blues but now, here he was. In fact, here they all were, flying first class and taking up twelve seats.

Besides herself and Ryan, there was Mary, Billy and Rita, Sean and Suzanne, Harry and Gloria, and Sid and Rachel, not forgetting little Donovan.

'Eleven of us, eh,' quipped Billy, 'makes a full team with little Donovan the twelfth man and probably good enough to bring back the Ashes!'

He sat back in his seat and watched the excited chatter and happy faces of the group. He was satisfied that he had carried out his mum's instructions to the letter. He mused, 'Mum said, look after everyone we love, so here we go.' He tilted his seat and stretched out as he lay back in his comfortable first class armchair and let the Airbus A300 take the strain.

After landing at Sydney, Jenny had arranged for minibus taxis to take them directly up to where they would be staying, which would be their base.

Situated about an hour north of Sydney, up the F3, the beautiful little beachside resort has a long sandy beach which stretches to North Avoca, forming one large bay. It has a village atmosphere with small shops selling the bits and pieces like beachwear and food, a baker, cafés, restaurants and even its own little bijoux cinema that belonged in another, more genteel Victorian age.

Contemporary beach houses and apartments surrounded the bowl, looking down over the ocean, and Jenny had encouraged them to enjoy its laid-back, easy-going lifestyle.

Jenny had booked them into three luxurious three-bedroomed apartments across the road from the surf club, with panoramic views of the ocean and beach.

After lugging the suitcases in and making sure everyone was comfortable, the brothers left the others to rest up for a few hours after the exertion of their journey across the world. They decided to take a stroll to the beach to unwind after what seemed like days of travelling.

They stood on the terrace of the surf club, surveying the breath-taking view. Billy quipped, 'Ryan, do you remember our holidays in Bournemouth when we were kids? It was a struggle to find enough space to put down a towel on the beach because there were so many people. Well, look at this, kid. You could put a million towels down and still find room for more.'

'It's bloody amazing, isn't it? The sky is so big too. No wonder Jenny loves it here.'

'Yeah, and she gave this all up for you. She must really love you, mate.'

'I know. I love that woman too. Come on, let's get back.'

Later that evening, Jenny took everyone to meet her parents, Eric and Sheila, and of course, her granddad, Ron, or Pops, as she called him.

The evening air was warm and dry and as the sun began to set, the group descended on Eric and Sheila's house; the pair were so excited to be seeing their daughter again and, for the first time, meeting the man who had meant so much to her that she had given up everything to be with him. But the big bonus for them was they now had a grandson.

Eric had got the Aussie favourite, the 'barbie', fired up and as the group relaxed in the comfortable surroundings amongst the palms and eucalyptus trees, the chardonnay and longnecks flowed. The travellers got to know their hosts better and were regaled with tales of the old days when Ron was a young lad back in Brum.

They were tucking into their steaks and two lovely fresh salads Sheila had prepared, when Sean got to his feet.

'I think this might be a good time to tell you all our good news,' he paused. 'Suzanne's pregnant and the baby is due in September this year.'

Everyone cheered and clapped and wished them the best; Mary was in tears at the thought of being a great-grandmother. Billy was overcome and cuddled them both. 'That's brilliant news and when we get back, I've got a little surprise of my own. There will be a little cottage just for the three of you in the gardens of the new house me and Mum have bought.' He pulled them both towards him and kissed both proudly. The night ended with Pops playing his old ukulele and getting everyone singing along.

Jenny gave them a few more days' relaxing down at the beach before she gathered them all together to begin phase one: sightseeing in Sydney. She had booked them all into the Shangri-la Hotel with its views over the Harbour Bridge and the Opera House, and within easy walking distance of both.

Early the next morning, they sailed the harbour on a yacht in full sail with young Donovan taking the wheel, under supervision from the captain. He steered them under the Harbour Bridge, allowing the group to take in the most amazing views of both the bridge and the Opera House.

Later, from Circular Quay, the group took a ride to Woolloomooloo to enjoy a pie with peas at Harry's Café de Wheels, determined to try out the food at the world famous pie cart. After an afternoon snooze, they had dinner that evening in the slowly revolving restaurant at the top of the Sydney Tower, two hundred and fifty metres above the city with panoramic views of the Harbour City. Jenny managed to fill each day with something new and after ten days they headed back to Avoca for a week of rest and recuperation.

Next, it was a flight to Cairns in Queensland and on to Port Douglas where they explored the Great Barrier Reef, having sailed out on a hovercraft. They landed at a pontoon moored miles out in the middle of the ocean. The younger ones donned flippers, snorkels and face masks to see the beautifully exotic shoals of coloured fish, and the strange and spectacular living organism that is the coral reef. Even Rita joined in this one and was in awe of the underwater world she felt privileged to see.

What Rita didn't expect was the trip they made to the night zoo, armed with a torch and getting up close as she watched the keepers feed the crocodiles. They soared out of the water with their jaws open wide enough to swallow a child, displaying their razor-sharp teeth, causing her to scream in terror. After that experience, she was treated to a display of the world's most deadly snakes which she was grateful to find were confined behind strong glass. The night ended with a barbecue and sing song with Billy dragged out to the front to play the wobble board as everyone joined in with 'Tie me kangaroo down'.

It was back to Sydney and only a couple of weeks before the end of their holiday. Next up, the older ones in the group were treated to a trip on the famous Indian Pacific train that runs from Sydney to Perth via the Blue Mountains, Broken Hill, Adelaide, Kalgoorlie and on into Perth. They dined on the finest food and wines, sleeping in comfortable cabins, and taking in the breath-taking scenery over three days and nights.

The younger ones flew the five hours and met them in Perth for a few days before flying to Darwin. Then down to witness the wondrous sight of the sun setting over Uluru.

On their final flight back to Sydney, Ryan stood up in the aisle of the plane and made a speech.

'On behalf of us all, Jen, I would like to thank you for organising such a magnificent holiday. I believe we have seen most of Australia in our time here and it has been a wondrous tour of your country, and we are grateful and honoured to have been treated so royally.' Donovan was standing at his side and he continued, 'Today is a special day as it's a double celebration: to my beautiful wife, Jennifer, I wish you a happy birthday and as you are the love of my life, it's appropriate that today is also Valentine's Day. So as a special surprise, I would like everyone to sing along with Donovan, who will lead us off.'

The young boy began singing the opening lines of 'Happy Birthday' and not only the group joined in, but the whole plane sang heartily, reducing Jenny to tears.

Their holiday had been a huge success and as their time in Australia came to an end, she was so thrilled and proud when young Donovan at last got up on a surf board at Avoca, bringing back memories of her own childhood on the same beach.

The goodbyes were emotional, especially for Jenny, but it was made easier with Ryan presenting Eric, Sheila and Pops with first class tickets to come over to England in the summer to stay with them.

CHAPTER SIXTY-FIVE

While the Caseys and friends were touring Australia, a number of things were happening back in England.

In Birmingham, it was fortunate that Billy and Rita were on the other side of the world as the greedy bucket of a bulldozer smashed its way through the front door of the Greasy Spoon. Spilling glass, timber and bricks, it demolished a dream they had started all those years ago. The ravenous machine devoured the building, destroying a lifetime of memories as its iron jaws consumed the last meal served at the Greasy Spoon, which was the café itself.

The bike shop and the bakery were next on its menu. Hungry for chaos and destruction, a further swing of its bucket signalled the end of those two close companions from a time when small and personal was important.

In the city centre, an elderly man left his new apartment in the Mail Box building. Billy had told him, 'Teddy, it's yours, rent free until the Grim Reaper calls.'

Teddy was happy with life as he ambled slowly down to the station at Birmingham New Street to catch the express train to London Euston, travelling first class.

Meanwhile, in Central London, a well-refined middle-aged senior sales executive, dressed in a cashmere and silk suit by Ermingildo Zegna, a crisp white silk shirt and tie, wearing the highly polished shoes of an ex-military man, slipped behind the wheel of one of the world's most well-known luxury cars.

CHAPTER SIXTY-SIX

The highly polished black doors and brass nameplates trumpeted wealth and affluence but to the lad from Sparkhill who had been born in a back-to-back, in poverty and paucity, couldn't have cared less; he had had a happy life

He pushed open the door using its large brass knob and immediately sank into a carpet that he thought must have been two inches thick. The whole reception room was decorated with antique furniture and gilt-framed paintings. The silence was palpable, there seemed to be no one about and he thought how easy it would be to turn over a gaffe like this. Suddenly, from behind part of the wooden wall panelling a concealed door opened and an attractive young lady appeared. Slim with blonde hair gathered in a smart pony tail, she seemed to glide across to his side and with a cut-glass accent asked, 'Mr Criglan?'

'Yes, miss,' Teddy replied.

'Follow me, please; Dr Al-Takari is ready to see you.'

Teddy followed the expensive trail of perfume which from his minuscule knowledge of the perfumery business, he surmised was not from his stall in the Bull Ring Market. This one actually smelt nice. He was led into another sumptuous room where a small Middle Eastern-looking gentleman sat behind a big antique desk. Framed certificates adorned the walls, along with photographs of smiling, happy people.

The man waved an open hand, offering Teddy a chair.

Dr Hossain Al-Takari was a renowned surgeon, having specialised throughout his career in prosthetics and orthotics, including the treatment and rehabilitation of wounded soldiers in the Middle East. His knowledge of the subject was vast and he rarely visited his Harley Street consulting rooms, relying on his extremely capable staff to deal with matters in his London office. A few days earlier, a coincidence of timing meant he was on hand to take a call requesting that he personally conduct the consultation with his next client.

He had been intrigued by the telephone call from the man, who was well-mannered and obviously fully aware of the surgeon's standing internationally in the treatment of limb replacement. The caller, surprisingly, had displayed an understanding of prosthetics and furthermore, a knowledge of the surgeon's reputation; obviously he had done his research into the subject. The caller concluded the conversation by requesting that all accounts should be addressed directly to him and would be paid without question. That worried him a little.

'Let me begin, Mr Criglan, by asking how I can help you and maybe answer any questions you may have,' the surgeon said.

'Well,' replied Teddy, 'it's like this. I was born minus a right hand and all my life I have lived with this hook,' he said, holding up the offending article. 'It's not been unhelpful, considering the line of work I've been in since I was a lad, but I think it's high time I retired from my job and settled down. And I would like to become more or less like everyone else, or at least appear that way.' He waved the hook again.

The surgeon replied, 'Okay, there are a number of different ways we can help, from a simple silicone hand where we would match your skin colour, veins, and hair, or the latest electrode and sensor, or—'

Teddy interrupted.

'Sorry for butting in, Doc, the false hand that looks real is just what I was thinking and would suit me fine at this time in my life.'

'Okay, Mr Criglan.' The doctor paused and searching for confirmation of what he had been told by the caller some days earlier, asked, 'May I broach the subject of payment? Private health care does not come cheap and the final tally may reach many thousands of pounds.'

'No worries there, sir,' Teddy smiled, ''cos I'm not paying.'

'I'm sorry?' the surgeon questioned.

'No, no,' explained Teddy. 'You will be paid, but not by me. You see, I have a very good friend whose life, and probably the lives of his family, I saved, so he owed me one and this is his way of paying me back. It was all to do with a grape on one side of the scales and a bunch of bananas on the other, you see. Anyway, you won't understand that, but let me reassure you that the man who has set all this up is beyond doubt one of the most reliable and trustworthy people I have ever had the good fortune to meet, and all your accounts will be settled on the dot.'

The doctor was happy to hear the confirmation he required and replied, 'You are lucky to have such a benefactor and I am pleased we have got the matter out of the way. I apologise for any embarrassment I may have caused you by being so gauche.'

'Well, I'm not sure what gauche means, Doc, but your apology is accepted,' Teddy laughed.

While Teddy was discussing the details of his replacement hand, Nigel Kirkpatrick, a senior sales executive who sold luxury Rolls Royce cars from a showroom in Berkley Square, London, was driving north up the M1 towards Birmingham.

Nigel, a former officer in 2 Para, the Second Battalion Parachute Regiment, had been educated at Eton and after going up to Oxford to gain his degree in law, ignored the opportunity to enter the family stockbroking business and went straight to Sandhurst. He gained his commission and served his country with honour in the Falklands War, being amongst the first to land at San Carlos Water, taking part in the Battle of Goose Green.

On leaving the army and still against family advice, a good friend had mentioned there was an opening as a luxury car sales executive, a complete switch in tempo and very appealing because of that. He arranged an interview with one of the directors of the company which he attended wearing one of his Savile Row suits, a Turnbull and Asser shirt and his regimental tie.

After recounting his life story to date, he was offered the position without further ado and had been at the company for more than seventeen years. He enjoyed the challenges the job presented and blissfully, due to his background, easily managed to establish common ground with the majority of his rich clientele.

This morning, he was delivering a brand new Rolls Royce Silver Seraph in Fountain Blue, the colour adding a further touch of class to this expensive tribute to British car engineering, which was hand made in Crewe although they were now powered by a BMW 5.4 litre, V12, five-speed automatic engine.

As the car purred along at just less than one hundred miles per hour, he sat comfortably behind the wheel surrounded by the lavish and luxurious interior, finished in magnolia Connolly leather upholstery, piped in French Navy with matching carpets and a glossy burl walnut veneer dashboard trim.

It swept past the more mundane vehicles on the motorway and Nigel was aware that, as usual, the Rolls was getting its fair share of admiring looks, confirming the fact that this new model was undeniably a head turner.

As he sped along, he thought of the many clients he had dealt with over the years in his job selling these luxury cars. He had sold to pop stars and the nouveau riche, lords and ladies, millionaires and billionaires, but this client was unusual in his own way.

The buyer had not visited the showrooms to look at the car and all business had taken place over the phone, with payments made by bank transfer from a Swiss bank account. Not unusual in itself as many of his sales were made, sight unseen, to the rich and famous, who couldn't afford to take the time out of their busy schedule to pop into the showrooms. The purchaser sounded like a Brummie but very personable all the same, thought Nigel. When discussing the details of the sale, Nigel was instructed to call his client Billy, who paid the full list price of one hundred and fifty-five thousand, one hundred and seventy-five pounds. This figure was rounded up to one hundred and sixty thousand pounds to include delivery to be made by Nigel, in person.

The car was to be delivered to a night club called Divines on the Hagley Road in Birmingham with the keys, log book and registration documents to be handed over, in person, to a man named Lenny Freeman. He was to also deliver a handwritten note which Billy had dictated to Nigel the previous day when he had phoned from overseas to check that everything was in order. He also requested one last favour.

'Nigel, my old mate, I need you to do one last thing for me. It's going to sound silly to you, but I need you to call into a greengrocer's shop and buy a couple of things.'

He couldn't comprehend the subtle meaning of the gifts and with a sigh concluded, 'Mm, now I've got to admit this is all very bizarre, very intriguing. I would like to meet this Billy Casey and hear the whole story.'

He slowed a little to take the exit on to the M42 and looked down at the note which lay on the passenger seat next to the gifts he had purchased, wrapped in two brown paper bags

The two brown paper bags contained a bunch of bananas in each, similar in number and weight, as per his instructions. The note beside them read simply, 'Sorry for any disrespect and I hope this balances the scales – Billy'.

CHAPTER SIXTY-SEVEN
Six months later

The Casey family were at ease with life after the tumultuous events of the last few years. The scars were hidden deep inside but calm had descended over them.

Billy was fully occupied running RyBilld, content with his lot, enjoying his role and only needing occasional help from Ryan, who was still busy with his roofing business.

He still woke early after all those years of opening the café at six and to fill those early hours, Rita's recent present of a little puppy helped to fill the time with an early morning walk. He had called the dog Boo as he was such a surprise; he had never owned a dog before and found the energy and unconditional love of his good-natured pet to be a blessing.

He arrived at the office as usual at eight thirty and opened up, making his way to the back kitchen to boil the kettle for a cup of tea. Suddenly, he became aware that someone had followed him in and was standing behind him in the doorway.

He spun round, his fist clenched ready to strike the first blow.

The man raised his hands, signalling to him that there was no need for violence.

'Well, who the fuck are you then and what are you doing in my office?' he shouted.

The man spoke quietly, 'Recently, I have been made aware of whom my parents were. You wouldn't believe me even if I told you who my mother was, so perhaps we will leave that for another time.'

Billy was getting frustrated and as calmly and forcefully as he could, he said, 'Come on, I'm running short of patience. Tell me why you're here and why you barged into my office and make it quick.'

'Okay, then. My father, well—' he paused a while. 'Well, both of my parents actually passed away within days of one another. I had a visit from someone close to my mother who revealed some stunning information. I didn't go to my mother's funeral but I did attend, albeit from a distance, the funeral of my father. You did, too, you came late when everyone had gone and I wondered why. I followed you when you left and it's taken some time to trace you but at last I have found you, Billy Casey. So now I have a question for you. What exactly is the connection between your family and my father, Connor Flynn?'